D1069379

"Eleanor Hunsinger's N　　　　　　　　rful adaptation of the Scriptural narrative of Prince Jonathan and the future King David. The story is compelling and was unusually difficult for me to put down. Her descriptions of the personalities and locations are vivid and vibrant, making the reader feel part of the action. The hand of God is vitally apparent in both the delightful times and the difficult times. I cannot wait for the other Scripturally based novels she has in preparation to become available."

J. David Scherling, PE, D. Min.
Civil Engineer, Retired
Former Missionary with Wycliffe Bible Translators
Author

"I have known Eleanor Hunsinger since my childhood. Her over twenty years of missionary service in rural Africa has given her perspective on life in a tribal and clan-based culture, as Israel also had in eleventh century BC. Her own call to a life of service to God helps her identify with the faithful Jonathan.

This book blends the author's love of Scripture, history, geography, and culture into an uplifting story of Bible heroes that inspires us to make our commitment of faith and trust in God. You will never again read the Book of 1 Samuel the same.

The daily life of Israel's original first family is pictured in a realistic, easy-to-understand story you will long remember."

Dr. Jim Garlow, Ph.D.
CEO, Well Versed
New York Times Best Selling Author
Author of 21 books

"Eleanor Hunsinger has written a masterful novel of the life of biblical Jonathan. It rivals any other that I have read on the life of this righteous royal person. Once begun, you will not want to put it aside until finished."

Barry L. Ross, Ph.D.
Professor of Old Testament, Retired
Bible Commentary Contributor

"It's an exceptional writer who can take you to a time and place you've never been and make you feel right at home as you walk and talk with the characters for whom it was reality. Eleanor Hunsinger is that kind of storyteller. She'll help you envision ancient landscapes clearly in your mind's eye, introduce you to people whose innermost thoughts and motives you can hear, weave together historical details that make the complexities and motives of biblical heroes and villains come to life. Prepare to become a time traveler as you explore human nature with her and discover the Divine Designer who is arranging, shaping, and revealing His artistry in the unfolding mystery of your own life today, just as He did for the personalities you'll enjoy getting to know in these pages you won't want to quit turning."

Dr. Jerry Pence, D. Min.
Senior Pastor, Brooksville Wesleyan Church
Former General Superintendent, The Wesleyan Church

MARK OF THE COVENANT

THE STORY OF JONATHAN, PRINCE OF ISRAEL

ELEANOR HUNSINGER

ACKNOWLEDGMENTS

I would like to thank Calvary University (formerly Calvary Bible College) and Johnson County Library (KS) for the use of their resources during my research for this book some years ago. I also thank Rev. Richard Lauby for loaning me books from his personal library and Mary Ann Hubbard for her initial editorial assistance. I appreciate my sister, Marian Graham, sharing her home with me during my research and preliminary writing.

I thank Anne Paine Root for her editorial assistance as I prepared the manuscript for publication. I appreciate Dr. Barry Ross, former Old Testament professor, reviewing the text for accuracy. I am grateful for Dave and Delores Scherling, Wilma Wissbroecker, and Elsie Myers for their proofreading and advice. I am very thankful for Larry Goodwin's kind assistance in solving my computer problems. I appreciate Dan Mottayaw's technical assistance in preparation for publication. Thanks to everyone who had a part in helping this book come into existence.

Lastly, I thank God for using one of Romans 8:28's "in all things" (Covid-19 pandemic and lockdown) to revive my dream for this novel. Only with His wonderful help throughout the writing process are you reading it today.

DEDICATION

To my brother, Dennis Hunsinger
and to the memory of
my late father, Mr. Albert Hunsinger
my late stepfather, Rev. Paul Davidson
and my late brother-in-law, Rev. John Betters
and
To all Christian men who have blessed my life.

CONTENTS

1

LOST DONKEYS

Alone, Jonathan watched twilight fade behind the distant Carmel Mountain Range. Night settled over the Plain of Jezreel. Behind him the protective northern shoulder of Mount Gilboa loomed into the blue-black darkness. The subdued voices of the army camp seemed to pause a moment, and Jonathan caught the faint gurgle of water rushing from the nearby mountain spring. Around their campfires, trained Israelite soldiers and inexperienced village volunteers huddled in small groups discussing the enemy, comparing weapons, trying to hide their fear. The odor of cooked lentils and baked unleavened bread wafted through the camp, mingling with the haze of campfire smoke that hung over the valley.

In a tent behind him, Jonathan's two brothers had retired for the night, worn out from the nearly four days' march from Gibeah. He remained seated on the ground, waiting.

Where was Father? Jonathan glanced around again, still perplexed that King Saul had not appeared for supper. *So unlike him.* Before going to sleep he must talk to the king about any final instructions. He shifted his weight, seeking a more comfortable position on the clumps of grass.

The vast Philistine army spread out across the valley five miles away. Below the western slope of the Hill of Moreh the commanders were, no doubt, reviewing last-minute preparations for tomorrow's assault. Armed with iron swords and spears, protected by metal breastplates and shields, and equipped with swift horse-drawn chariots, they would sleep tonight with confidence.

The Philistines. Jonathan raised his eyes to the dark heavens. He thanked God this was not his first encounter with the powerful enemy. One by one, he recalled battles during the past twenty-six years in which the Lord Jehovah helped Israel face—and defeat—the coastal warriors. All Jonathan ever wanted to do with his life was keep God's Chosen People free from the pagan Philistines. An evening breeze had come up, clearing away some of the smoke, and he took a deep breath. Was that desire perhaps a call from God, after all—like the boy Samuel's?

The unbidden idea startled, but intrigued, him. Snatches of an early childhood conversation teased at his thoughts. He closed his eyes as he tried to coax from his memory details of a long-ago day back in Gibeah. A day that changed his family forever—the day his father went searching for the lost donkeys.

"Please let me go with you, Father." Four-year-old Jonathan's hand clutched Saul's broad shoulder as he shook it excitedly. "Pleeeeease."

From his seat on the courtyard ground, Saul looked steadily into the pleading gaze of his son's dark eyes, a look that always melted his determination. No man could be prouder of his son. The farmer lowered his head to hide his weakening resolve.

"I'm a big boy now," Jonathan said. "I can help you find the donkeys. I promise."

"Who would protect your mother and Baby Malki-Shua if you leave?" Saul said in a serious tone. In dawn's increasing light, he glanced across to their corner bedroom. A baby's sudden, persistent cry came from the doorway, emphasizing his question. "I thought you were my little soldier."

"BIG soldier," the boy said without a trace of self-consciousness, thrusting the stick in his right hand out like a spear.

Jonathan had never actually seen a soldier, Saul knew, but the older boys in their street had and he mimicked their actions.

Saul tousled his son's wavy black hair, then slipped his arm around his waist. "You are my firstborn, Jonathan. There will be plenty of time in the future for you to help me find things. Today I need you to stay home."

"Oh." The boy moaned, his arm going limp, the make-believe spear hitting the ground with a thump.

Saul finished tying the sandal thong around his ankle. "But if you would like a ride to the town entrance, I'm sure that would be all right."

"Thanks." Jonathan jumped up and down, then threw his arms around Saul's massive shoulders. "You are the best father of all."

Grandfather Kish owned one of the better homes in Gibeah, a small town situated in the central mountains of the Land of Israel. Unlike the one-room structures of many craftsmen and peasant farmers, rooms lined Kish's central courtyard. The bedrooms and family room were on the street side, with the entryway to the front gate passing between Grandfather's bedroom and the kitchen storeroom. Across the courtyard from the entryway, a staircase between the kitchen and the grain storeroom led to the rooftop.

Hearing the gate open, Jonathan and Saul looked up to see Kish coming down the passageway leading a donkey. Gatam, a family servant, emerged from the kitchen carrying two blanket rolls and two sacks of provisions.

"Ready to go?" the patriarch said when he reached his son.

"Yes, if everything is prepared." Saul got to his feet.

"I hope it doesn't take long to find the donkeys, but I'm sending a couple days' worth of supplies, just in case."

"I can't imagine them straying that far. They only broke out last night. We should be home by nightfall."

"Well, they didn't tell anyone which direction they were taking." Kish smiled up at his son. "I'm just glad the two older ones didn't bolt with the rest."

After tying the supplies on the pack animal, Gatam reentered the kitchen to fill a goatskin waterbag from a jug near the door. The three generations of the family started toward the front gate. Jonathan, remembering the promised ride, grabbed one of his father's fingers and held on tightly, skipping along to keep up with Saul's long strides.

Saul paused and looked over at Jahra, a house servant, who stood near the kitchen holding the bundle of firewood he had just collected. Saul motioned towards the gate with a jerk of his head. The servant deposited the wood and joined them. Coming from the kitchen, Gatam swung the waterbag over his shoulder and picked up the donkey's lead rope.

Grandmother Jedidah followed Gatam out of the kitchen, brushing flour from her hands and flecks of cracked wheat from her faded brown tunic. She hurried to the passageway to see them off. "Travel well," she called to her only son. "The Lord be with you."

"The Lord bless you," Saul responded before stepping out into the street.

Saul paused to look down at his son. "It seems I nearly forgot your ride." He smiled down at Jonathan, then swung him up to his broad shoulders.

Jonathan hoisted his knee-length tunic up around his thighs and adjusted his father's headdress, which he had knocked askew, before clutching his father's hands. Smiling and laughing, Jonathan turned to give his grandmother a cheery wave as they moved on down the street.

Saul stood nearly a foot taller than anyone else in his family—than anyone else in his clan or tribe, Grandfather always claimed. From Jonathan's vantage point high above the pedestrians in the dusty lane, he felt like the most important person in the world, confident of his father's solid frame beneath him.

"Gera, Pharez," Jonathan called to two boys standing near a doorway. "See me." The boys paused to watch the procession advancing toward them. "I wish my father was that tall," Jonathan heard Gera say as they passed in single file.

The ride through the small town ended all too soon for the young boy. As Saul swung him down, Jonathan protested loudly. "Just a little farther. Please."

"I promised a ride to the town entrance," Saul said. "A man keeps his promise."

"All right." Deflated but undefeated, Jonathan said, "But next time promise longer." He threw his arms around his father's thick, muscular leg and gave a quick squeeze. "Hurry back."

"And take care of everyone while I'm gone." Saul stooped to hug his son. "Goodbye, Big Soldier." After embracing his father, Saul straightened his headdress and started down the hillside path, Gatam and the donkey following.

Grandfather Kish reached down to grasp Jonathan's hand, and they watched the travelers go. "I guess it's time to go back," he said after a few minutes, holding Jonathan's hand out toward Jahra.

"Can't we go check the wheat first?" Jonathan hoped to prolong the special outing. He had never been down to the fields, but after the high ride on his father's shoulders he felt grown-up.

"I suppose." Grandfather never admitted his intended destination. "But if I send Jahra home without you, just remember, I can't carry you like your father does. If you get tired, don't start whining."

"I won't."

Jahra turned to go, and the two took the path through the olive grove to the valley below. Like all towns and villages in the Promised Land, Gibeah sat on the hillside, surrounded by vineyards, gardens, and olive groves. Valleys and lower slopes were reserved for planting fields of grain.

The silvery-green leaves of the olive trees lay motionless in the morning stillness, suspended on branches above thick, gnarled trunks. Sunshine filtering through the leaves cast a patchwork of light down the smooth ash-colored bark and across the grove floor. Jonathan laughed as he pointed to one tree, whose misshapen trunk reminded him of a game he played with Gera and Pharez, twisting in all kinds of crazy positions.

They paused as the edge of the grove to survey the golden valley. "What is that brown thing?" Jonathan pointed to a large object in the distance near a small tree.

"That, my boy, is a stone formation. We call it Ezel. It serves as a boundary between fields."

"It must be huge. Maybe someday I can go out and climb it."

They started on. The field lay farther away than Jonathan anticipated, and his little legs were tired when they reached their destination, but he said nothing. He watched Grandfather run his hand through the standing grain. "Is it going to be a good harvest?"

"It appears to be—if the locusts don't invade before we get it cut."

Jonathan's head shot up as he searched his grandfather's face for traces of worry. Seeing none, he decided the threat wasn't very likely. Grandfather walked down the edge of the field as he looked out across the wheat. Stopping beyond an oak tree, he reached out and ran his index and middle fingers up a stalk, holding the grain in his hand as he studied it a moment. "Looks like we have some tares to pull out."

Jonathan rose on tiptoes and peered at the grain. "Are they bad? Can't you just leave them?"

"No, darnel can be poisonous. We can't let them mix with harvested wheat. It would make us sick."

"Who planted it?"

"No one," Grandfather said, shaking his head. "The seed blows in the air sometimes. Or fell off when we harvested last year. It could have been carried by birds."

"How do you know it isn't wheat?"

Grandfather brought down a second stalk to compare the two. "The kernels are smaller, see." Jonathan nodded. "Because the wheat kernels are heavier, wheat bows down when it is ripe. Tares stand, making them easy to spot—and remove."

"I hope Father finds the donkeys soon," Jonathan said, fingering the yellow grain. "Before the locusts get the harvest."

"I do too. Let's go home now and see what Grandmother has for breakfast."

Turning, they started back toward town. "Is that the high place up there?" Jonathan pointed to the top of the cone-shaped hill, where a little square stood silhouetted against the blue sky near a spreading tamarisk tree.

"Yes. That is the altar where we worship the One True God."

"The God who divided the Red Sea for Moses?"

"Yes." Grandfather smiled down at him. "You remember my stories very well." He placed his hand on the boy's shoulder. "What other story do you remember?"

"Gideon's army defeating the Midianites with lamps and trumpets." Jonathan stretched out his arm. " 'A sword for the Lord and Gideon,' " he shouted the famous quote, lowering his voice as deeply as possible.

They crossed the valley and started up the path. Jonathan spotted a building at the west end of the hilltop. The short gray-white limestone tower stood out against the brown and faded green of summer's wilting grass. "Who lives up there?"

"That's a Philistine lookout."

The startled boy dashed behind his grandfather and pressed

against his right side, peering out from behind the folds of his protective cloak. "What are they looking for? Do they want to fight the Israelites?"

"We hope not." Kish put his arm around the boy. "So far, they just watch the highways and keep an eye on Gibeah."

Jonathan avoided looking at the Philistine tower as they walked up the slope to the olive grove. Once there, he flopped down in the shade to rest. "I know I can't have a ride on your shoulders," he said a few minutes later, recalling the earlier warning. "How about just on your back?" The pleading look of his brown eyes worked to softened Grandfather's resistance. "After all, I am the only grand-child you can give a ride to," he concluded with a smile. "Malki-Shua is just a baby."

"Yes, and you both will grow up all too fast."

"When I grow up, I'm going to become a soldier and fight the Philistines," the four-year-old said, regaining some of his bravado. Grandfather frowned down at him before squatting. Jonathan, laughing, threw his arms around Kish's neck, ready for the ride.

"Don't grow up too soon," Kish said as he stood up. "Just enjoy playing for a while yet."

That evening when Mother knelt to unroll Jonathan's sleeping mat, he touched her shoulder. "Can we pray for Father?" He knew Grandfather sometimes prayed about things.

"Sure." She put her arm around him. "Would you like to say the prayer?"

Jonathan stood beside her and raised his hands, palms up, as he looked toward the ceiling. Grandfather said God was up above in heaven. "Lord God of Israel," he began, remembering how Grand-father started his prayers, "please help Father find the lost donkeys. And don't let the Philistines come down and hurt us. Keep the locusts from eating the wheat. Grandmother needs it for making bread. Take care of Mother and Baby Malki-Shua, Grandfather and Grandmother, and me." He paused. "Oh, and Pharez and Gera, too. Thank you."

He smiled up at his mother. "God is our friend, isn't He?"

"Yes. We are His chosen People."

Jonathan curled up on his mat and relaxed. The God of Israel would watch over them all.

Leaving Kish and Jonathan at the town entrance, in the early morning sunshine Saul and Gatam made their way down the gradual incline to the valley road below Gibeah. Although the latter rains were over and the weather had turned very warm, Saul spotted a few remaining crimson and white anemones scattered along the hillside. Purple thistles, however, reminded him that not all color held the promise of true beauty. Oxen and cattle grazed on the stubble of the newly harvested barley fields below.

"What a time to lose the donkeys." Saul glanced over at the field of standing wheat. "Just when we need them most."

"Wheat harvest is still a week away," Gatam said. "We should be back in plenty of time to haul sheaves to the threshing floor."

"I hope you're right."

When they reached the road junction, they paused to look both ways. "Do you want to go north or south?" Gatam said.

Saul sighed. "Neither, actually."

Since Saul's young cousins, Abner and Nadab, had failed to properly fasten the gate of the animal pen the night before, Gatam made no comment. A servant never criticized his master's family to their face.

Saul shielded his eyes as he scanned the horizon and distant hills. "North, I guess."

The rocky peaks of the watershed rose to the east as they followed the dirt highway. Inquiring from anyone they met about the missing donkeys, the two men covered several miles before stopping to eat a breakfast of bread and raisins.

They pressed on, exploring the valleys and skirting the hills. The *wadis*, or stream beds, still held water from the latter rains of spring. The cool liquid felt good on their tired dusty feet as they waded through in their sandals.

Occasionally one of them climbed the side of a scrub-covered hill, his eyes searching the countryside, but to no avail. The terebinth trees were once again in leaf. The men sometimes found a spot of shade beneath one for a brief rest.

The rugged plateau of the territories of Judah and Benjamin ran from Hebron north for thirty-five miles to Bethel. A religious center eight miles north of Gibeah, Bethel set on a low ridge between two small valleys. The Prophet Samuel visited Bethel on his biannual tour, holding court and delivering messages from God. Saul attended some of these events. The town, known by the Canaanites as Luz, played a vital part in Hebrew history. Abraham had built an altar on a hill east of it. There Jacob experienced a vision from God with a ladder reaching to heaven.

Bethel's crossroads location always fascinated Saul. One road ran north to Shechem, he had been told, another up to Gophna and west to the Great Sea, and a third east through a mountain pass down to the Jordan River. As a boy, Saul dreamed of one day taking all three. A few years before he had trekked down to the river. Today, he would go north.

By early afternoon their zigzag journey brought the travelers to the road below Bethel. Knowing the town would not shelter the missing donkeys, they filled their waterbag at a small stream gushing from the foot of a cliff before searching the valley and moving on.

Beyond Bethel the tableland dropped off, and they saw more open valleys. The broken countryside gave way to hills covered with olive groves and vineyards, villages perched above them like crowns. The road descended through a steep, narrow stream bed to a lovely valley.

The donkey's sudden bray startled a flock of swifts. They rose in the sky, a black cloud of flapping wings against the clear background. Their *si-si-si* shriek broke the afternoon stillness, unnerving the animal, and it balked until they disappeared.

Still not seeing the lost donkeys, the men passed through a gorge with cliffs jutting out above. In the next valley fertile fields of wheat stirred in the breeze. A road to the northeast led to the rounded hill that held the ruins of the sacred town of Shiloh. Saul thought of the city's glorious past and the priest Eli's tragic death. *Israel's sad history.*

Glancing at the sinking sun, they hurried on the last two miles to Lebonah, hoping to find lodging for the night. Two girls were drawing water from the village well, and one volunteered to refill Saul's goatskin from her waterpot. He thanked her for her kindness and asked directions to the local inn.

Between two shuttered shops in the little marketplace, the men found the simple structure—the village's gift of hospitality to travelers. Saul pushed the gate open. Gatam led the donkey in and tethered it to a pole.

"Here I thought I'd be sleeping in my own bed tonight," Saul said. With a sigh, he sank onto a pile of straw in a corner of the open-faced enclosure.

A few minutes later the gate swung open, and a middle-aged man entered. He had no donkey or baggage; his clothes were worn, but clean. "The Lord bless you," he greeted them.

"The Lord be gracious to you," the travelers said.

"Please don't spend the night here." The villager stepped closer. "I am Amal son of Jakim. My wife has supper prepared and we have a sturdy rooftop. We repacked it just last week. Come home with me, my brothers."

Relieved, the two followed the man up the narrow, winding street to a small stone house identical to all the others. The typical one-room dwelling was divided between the lower level and an upper platform several feet higher. Smell of smoke from the cooking pit permeated the house. Saul suppressed a cough. Amal led their donkey in after them, and tied it to a pole that supported a roof beam.

The welcome aroma of cooking lentils and leeks greeted the visitors. As Saul glanced down at the cooking pot in the shallow fire pit, he realized how hungry the long trip had made him. He thanked God he would enjoy more than bread and dried fruit for supper.

After washing their hands, the three climbed the short stairs to the platform to await the meal. Saul sat down cross-legged on the table mat, rolls of sleeping mats stacked against the far wall behind him. He recognized the young girl dishing up the lentils as the one who filled his waterbag. Thank God for the hospitality of Israelites, to whom a traveler was always a brother.

The wife brought up the bowl of lentils and a basket of flat-bread. The men paused as the host spoke the Israelite meal bless-ing. "Blessed are You, Jehovah our God, King of the world, who brings forth bread from the earth."

They began tearing off pieces of bread and dipping them in the common bowl to scoop out bites of lentil stew. As the men ate, Saul told about life in Gibeah, in answer to his host's questions. He ended with a report of the missing donkeys. Down by the fire pit, the women ate in silence.

Later the travelers followed Amal up the outside staircase to the flat roof, which was surrounded by a parapet—a short protec-tive wall commanded by the Law of Moses. No one wanted to pay the ultimate price of bloodguilt for someone's fatal fall.

Roofs in Israel were slightly slanted to allow rain run-off. They provided valuable space for dry season daily living, especially to one-room houses. A partial sack of grain and two clay jugs sat in a corner of Amal's rooftop. He and his guests sat down near the back parapet and relaxed in silence, enjoying the refreshing breeze.

Conversation resumed with discussion of difficulties the Israelites faced from the dominating Philistines. At bedtime the wife brought up sleeping mats and the visitors' blanket rolls and spread the mats out along the opposite wall. Saul and Gatam soon retired for the night. One couldn't miss the lingering smell of fresh clay as they stretched out on the mats, but, having walked many miles, it didn't take long to fall asleep.

Early the next morning Saul and Gatam left Lebonah and headed north through the hills. Saul stopped to admire one deep east-west valley; the hillside villages reminded him of home and family.

As a son and only child, Saul felt the responsibility of maintaining the family line and inheritance. It was his duty alone to preserve the House of Kish in the clan of Matri. Already having two sons helped relieve some of the pressure.

His father had trained him well for the work involved throughout the agricultural year. Kish was beginning to slow down. With Jonathan and the baby now, Saul would soon be teaching them what he knew. The generations moved on.

Saul prayed he would be as good a father as Kish. Being one of God's Chosen People had great privileges. The Philistines would like nothing better than to destroy them and the Land. The thought weighed on him as they skirted the steep hill on the far side of the valley.

Coming around the hillside, Saul stopped, speechless. The Plain of Shechem spread out before them, mile after mile, a patchwork of barley stubble and unharvested golden wheat fields. "Amazing," Saul exclaimed after a few minutes.

To the east, low dark hills rose like a giant shield above the plain. To the west, twin peaks guarded the far end. "Must be Mount Gerizim and Mount Ebal," Saul said.

Gatam nodded. "I think you're right."

Even more majestic, snow-capped Mount Hermon dominated

the northern skyline. Saul knew the mountain's melting snow kept the Jordan River flowing year-round. Now that "the days of sun" were here, cool mountain air helped form the dew of Hermon, so vital to maturing crops. His farmer's eyes drank in the beauty of the scene before he tore himself away to move on.

Following the eastern range a few miles, they came across boys herding sheep. Saul walked over to question them and find out their location.

"This is the district of Shaalim," one teenager said. "We haven't heard of any stray donkeys, but if you want to discover where they are, go up to the village and ask the sorceress." He jerked his thumb toward the hillside houses behind him. "She can tell you anything you want to know."

"A sorceress!" Saul leaned back, struck by the blow of unwanted information. "In Israel?"

"You don't have one in your village?"

"No, we do not—and I pray we never do."

The boy looked puzzled. "I'm sorry we can't help you, then. Peace be with you, and I hope you find your animals."

"I can't believe it," Saul said when he reached Gatam. "They wanted me to consult a witch." He kicked a clod of dirt, sending it bouncing down the road and shattering in a dozen pieces. "After our tribes renounced their idols at Mizpah a few years ago, how could anyone consider seeking help from evil spirits?" He stomped on one of the fragments as he passed it. "The Law specifically commands us not to practice divination or sorcery." Anger flashed from his eyes; dutiful Gatam kept quiet.

Reaching the main road, Saul turned a complete circle, his gaze sweeping the area, then he stroked his bearded cheek. "I don't think the donkeys have come this far north. Let's head back. We can scout the valleys to the west as we return."

Gatam followed with the pack animal as they retraced their steps.

Seeing no villages at sunset, the two men decided to camp in a small recess at the base of a hill. Gatam gathered sticks and fallen branches from the hillside and stacked them nearby. After making a bed of handfuls of dry grass, he removed a flintstone and short scraping knife from a provisions sack. Soon, sparks flew, ignited the grass. Gatam gradually added pieces of the kindling. A glowing fire provided the best protection from a lion or bear that might stray up from the thickets of the Jordan River banks or down from a forest in the hills.

"This is the district of Zuph," Gatam said to Saul as they ate their bread, dried figs, and raisins. "I grew up in a village not too many miles from here."

After Gatam added more wood to the fire, he rolled up in his blanket and soon fell asleep. Saul sat thinking of the sorceress in Shaalim and of Israel's spiritual condition. The Tabernacle in Shiloh had been destroyed by the Philistines before he was born, but when he reached his teen years the tribal leaders began listening to the Prophet Samuel's message of repentance. Edging closer to the fire, Saul stared into the flames as he recalled that wonderful day at Mizpah when Israel renounced her idols.

Saul stood next to Father Kish on the edge of the crowd in Gibeah, glad for once for his extra height. Samuel, traveling through the Land delivering the word of the Lord, made a rare visit to their town. People milled around Saul in the afternoon heat, but he concentrated on the prophet's message.

"If you're returning to the Lord with all your hearts," Samuel's voice rang out, "purify yourselves of the foreign gods and Ashtoreth. Commit yourselves to the Lord. Serve him alone, and He will deliver you from the hand of the Philistines."

Samuel paused to look around. "How can God's Chosen People expect His help when they worship the very gods their heathen enemy worships?"

The truth convicted the men of Gibeah. Young Saul joined the people surging up the hill to the high place, where the altar to Baal and the image of Ashtoreth stood. Demolishing them, they promised to serve the One True God alone.

Samuel's message struck a chord with the other tribes he visited, and they also destroyed their idols. Samuel called them to meet at Mizpah, where he would intercede with the Lord on their behalf.

Mizpah, "the Lookout," sat on a high hill west of Gibeah, near Gibeon. Kish and his brother Ner made the short trip, accompanied by their teenage sons, Saul and Tarea. Since the whole congregation of Israel rarely met, Saul felt excited to be part of the assembly. Samuel led the worship as men drew water from the well and poured it out before the Lord, a sign of pouring out their hearts in surrender and repentance. Then they fasted and confessed their sins.

Saul had never attended anything like it.

Not everyone, however, was thrilled by the convocation. The Philistines, Israel's overlords, heard of this illegal meeting from their scouts. They swept up from the coastal plain to quell what they considered a rebellion.

"Please," the unarmed Hebrew men, frantic with fear, begged Samuel, "don't stop praying for us. Ask God to deliver us from our enemies."

Samuel took a lamb and offered it for a burnt offering to the Lord. Men on the edge of the crowd watched the approaching army in the distance. Samuel sent a fervent petition up to the Lord Most High.

God answered.

Sudden claps of thunder shook the earth. The startled Philistines were overcome by panic and chaos. The Israelites witnessed God's miracle and rushed to pursue the fleeing army, picking up weapons the confused soldiers dropped. The Israelites killed many as they chased them down to below Beth Car. Saul had never fought in a battle. His heart pounded with excitement as he rushed after the pagan enemy.

It did even now, just thinking about it. He reached out to push a stick farther into the embers of the campfire.

When the impromptu militia congregated again following the victory, Samuel had located a large stone. He set it up between Mizpah and Shen for a memorial and named it Ebenezer--"stone of help." The Israelites proceeded to recapture the towns the Philistines had taken from them.

Since then, the Philistines had reestablished lookouts in the Land and sometimes harassed individuals out in the countryside, but they had not troubled the Children of Israel in battle again. Even the Amorites withdrew from their alliance with the Philistines. Israel had peace.

Samuel truly was a man of God. Saul looked up from the campfire to the star-filled heavens. He struggled to keep his eyes open. And Israelites were God's People.

Saul removed his cloak and folded it for a pillow. After spreading out his goats-hair blanket, he placed his headdress on a provisions bag and added his girdle-belt to the collection. Yawning, he lay down, pulled the blanket up over his tunic, and soon drifted off to sleep.

The twitter of birds in a nearby oak tree roused Saul early. He noticed Gatam's blanket lying in a neat square near their food bags. A sliver of pinkish-orange sun already shown above the rounded hills in the east. Saul always tried to beat the sun in rising, and he jumped up to fold his blanket, damp with dew. Taking a drink from the nearly empty waterbag, he looked around for the servant. Gatam called a greeting from the hillside as he descended.

Saul returned the greeting and took the last piece of bread

from the bag. Tearing it in half, he handed a piece to Gatam. "I think we might as well head home," he said before taking a bite. "I'm sure by now Father has stopped thinking about the donkeys and is worrying about us."

"From up there," Gatam said, inclining his head toward the hill, "I could see Ramathaim Zuphim not far away. A man of God lives there. He is highly respected, and, unlike the sorceress, his prophecies come true. Let's go see him. Perhaps he can tell us which way to take."

"I thought we'd be home that first night, so I didn't fill my money bag. We've just eaten the last piece of bread." Saul brushed a crumb from his beard. "If we went, what would we give him?" It would be very impolite to seek help from an important man without presenting a gift.

Gatam fished in his girdle-belt and pulled out a small money bag. "I have a quarter of a shekel of silver, if that helps." He extracted the small piece of metal and held it out in his palm. "I'll give it to the *seer* so he will tell us what direction to go."

"Good." Saul smiled with renewed hope. "Let's be on our way."

2

SAMUEL

Samuel's earliest memory was of Mother Hannah telling him how special he was—to her and to God. Every evening, with the sunset fading above the western foothills, she called him in from playing with his half-brothers and -sisters. After supper she rolled out his reed sleeping mat, then she and Father Elkanah pulled him close, told him a story, and prayed with him before tucking his blanket around his shoulders and kissing him goodnight.

He couldn't remember some specifics of those long-ago stories, but he never forgot their truths. God loved Father and Mother enough to give them a special little boy named Samuel.

Elkanah also taught his son about their family heritage. They were members of the tribe of Levi, selected by God as the priestly tribe of Israel. They belonged to the clan of Levi's son Kohath. A very important fact, Father insisted. "Your lineage is your birth record. Knowing your family line is the only way you can claim you are a descendent of Abraham and one of the Children of Israel."

They lived in the territory of Ephraim, Elkanah explained, because the Levites were only assigned towns in the Promised

Land, not a territorial inheritance like other tribes. Samuel heard people call their area the Land of Zuph. He was proud his great, great, great grandfather's name was Zuph. God had given Samuel a very special family.

When Samuel grew old enough, his parents took him to the Tabernacle at Shiloh to live with the high priest Eli. That fulfilled a promise his mother had made to God before his birth, she said, so was very important. She had also made a Nazarite vow, promising his hair would never be cut with a razor. Just like the judge Samson. Samuel smiled at the thought.

Tears came to Samuel's eyes as he watched his parents leave that day, but he knew they still loved him. Eli took his hand and led him to his new home.

Every year Samuel's mother attended the Feast of Tabernacles, bringing a new linen robe she made for him. She always seemed to know his size. Sometimes, watching children of Shiloh walking down the street beside their parents, he would squeeze his eyes shut and try to remember his home back in Ramathaim Zuphim.

Samuel missed his parents very much, but he never forgot the message of their stories. Better yet, Eli knew the same stories. Many nights the young boy would scoot up close to the old man and ask him to tell him about Abraham or Jacob, Joseph or Moses, Joshua or Gideon. He never tired of listening. And listening meant someone being with him, talking to him. He was not alone.

Shiloh sat on a rounded hill, seventeen miles east of Ramath-aim. The hill stood lower than those surrounding it and deep ravines on two sides made Samuel think God carved the hill and set it apart especially for His holy house. Beyond the ravines the hill country of Ephraim rose around them in rugged splendor. Samuel hoped when he was older that he could explore those hills, maybe even find his old home.

The Tabernacle rested on a leveled area on the top of the hill, first erected there by the great leader Joshua. Although it had been moved to other locations, Eli told him, it was always brought back to Shiloh. Now that the Israelites' wilderness wanderings were over and the tribes had settled in the Promised Land, the priests had made the sacred tent a more permanent structure.

Samuel loved his little room near Eli. Each night he carefully spread out his robe so it would not be wrinkled the next day. He did not miss having a lot of playmates, because Eli taught him so many fascinating lessons about his new home. Occasionally the high priest took Samuel to play with his grandchildren.

Samuel prided himself on delivering Eli's messages accurately to the various priests, especially to Mahli, whose bushy eyebrows reminded him of Father Elkanah. Samuel began with simple messages like, "God's servant Eli is calling you." As he grew older the sentences became longer, but he rehearsed them as he searched for the recipient. One rule he always obeyed: No running in the Tabernacle.

Eli made plain to Samuel from the beginning that he should never enter the inner court, reserved for priests on duty. Even the Holy of Holies was off limits to all but the high priest, and to him only once a year.

Samuel envied Eli being able to see it all. Maybe someday he, too, could be a high priest. He knew that was God's special calling, so he would have to wait and see. Hophni and Phinehas would come first, he was sure. They were older and were Eli's sons. Then the grandsons would probably be next. Still, God saw his heart and how much he loved helping people become free from their sins.

A large enclosed outer courtyard for worshipers surrounded the inner sanctuary of the Tabernacle, which was divided into the Holy Place and the Holy of Holies. Eli described the holy areas and their furnishings in such detail Samuel could picture them in his mind.

The furnishings of the Holy Place consisted of three things: an incense altar made of acacia wood covered with gold, the gold-plated table of the presence-bread—or showbread, and the golden lampstand. Eli drew lines in the dirt to help him understand where each was placed behind the curtain.

The Ark of the Covenant stood alone in the Holy of Holies. Eli stretched out his arms to demonstrate its size, four feet long and two-and-a half feet square. The box contained three historical objects given to the Israelites by God: the two stone tablets of the Law, a pot of manna, and the rod of the high priest Aaron. The Lord caused the rod to bud one time, Eli explained, to show Aaron's God-given authority over the people. The Ark was plated inside and out with gold. A lid, known as the "mercy seat," covered it. On top, golden cherubim, one at each end, spread their wings. Samuel could only imagine the beauty.

During certain sacred duties, the high priest wore a special ephod, made of costly materials worked with gold, scarlet, and purple. It covered the breast down to the hips and was held in place with two shoulder-bands and belted at the waist. An attached colorful, bejeweled breastpiece held the Urim and Thummim—the stones for revealing God's direction to His people. Seeing Eli dressed in the ephod reminded Samuel how special the high priest was. Samuel felt honored to be his helper.

Outside, in front of the Holy Place, stood the Altar of Burnt Offerings. On it the priests offered animal and grain sacrifices brought by worshippers for repentance, thanksgiving, and petition. The priests also offered daily sacrifices morning and evening. Watching the slaying of the animals, Samuel felt sympathy for them, especially the little lambs. Their *baa, baa* tugged at his heart. Sin must be an awful thing if the helpless lambs had to give their lives so people's sins could be forgiven.

Besides male priests—sons of the original high priest Aaron, Levites served in the Tabernacle. That included his family, Kohathites, descendants of Jacob's son Levi.

Women assistants performed household duties, washed the large curtains that enclosed the area, and kept the courtyard clean.

Adjoining the outer court were rooms the high priest had built for himself and priests on duty. Samuel occupied one.

"Your father will be here next week," Eli said one night following prayers. A big smile lit up Samuel's face. He loved the times his father came to serve in the Tabernacle, although one week was never long enough to suit Samuel. His small room always had space for Elkanah's sleeping mat.

Back in his room, Samuel took off his robe. Would there be a new baby to announce? After Samuel's parents brought him to Eli, God had blessed Mother with other children. Last count, two. No new one was brought to the Feast last year, so maybe he had another brother or sister by now. He lay awake thinking of more questions and of all the things he wanted to tell his father about life in Shiloh.

Elkanah arrived the day before his duties started, greeted by Samuel's big hug. Father answered his questions. Yes, there was a new sister, Adah, born two moons ago. Samuel felt sad to hear their old neighbor, Widow Leah, had died. There were three new lambs this spring. His brother Zophai lost a front tooth last week.

Elkanah fulfilled his week of duties. The morning he left for home he went to the marketplace for things on his shopping list, taking Samuel along. They strolled the street, greeting merchants and looking in shops. At Shimea's bakery Father bought a little honey cake for each of them. Samuel licked his fingers to not waste any of the honey that oozed from the nut-filled pastry.

"It's our secret," Father whispered. "Don't tell the others."

Back at the Tabernacle, Elkanah added his purchases to his carrying bag. The time had passed quickly; the goodbyes always came too soon.

"You are your mother's firstborn," Elkanah reminded Samuel, placing his hand on the boy's head, "dedicated to God before your birth. Remember to be a good boy and obey Eli."

The farewell sounded like a benediction, and Samuel never tired of hearing the words repeated each time. "I will," he said, giving his father a parting hug. Tears stung Samuel's eyes as Elkanah picked up his sleeping mat and bag to leave. Still, Samuel delighted in being Eli's helper, because Eli was God's servant.

"I think you are old enough to begin studying with a teacher," Eli informed Samuel one evening after prayers. Samuel had never considered that he might be able to read like Eli. Moses had been well-educated while growing up in Pharaoh's court in Egypt, Eli said. Moses taught Aaron and Joshua to read and write, and they taught others, passing on their knowledge to the next generation of leaders.

Samuel began the long, slow process of learning to read the Law and write Hebrew. At times Phinehas brought his son Ahitub to study with Samuel. They were about the same age, and their struggle to read the Hebrew letters and words cemented their friendship. Some afternoons while one of the women attendants washed Samuel's special robe, the two ventured down to the marketplace. Samuel always felt half-dressed in just his tunic, but that is all the other boys ever wore. Unlike them, his dark hair hung down to his shoulders, but that did not bother him. He kept his mother's promise to God.

Away from the restrictions of the worship center, the boys laughed and talked freely as they explored the shops. What progress had the carpenter made on his latest yoke? Did the leather worker have new sandals on display? They paused to watch a waterpot emerge from the potter's hands and rotating wheel, or a piece of cloth lengthen on the weaver's loom as he passed the shuttle back and forth through the taut hanging threads. A whiff of baking bread drew them to their favorite shop.

"How're the Tabernacle boys?" Shimea would call from his doorway, seeing them approach. "Come in, come in." The tantalizing smell would pull them inside as the baker bustled around to find each boy a little round loaf of bread. "No charge. No charge," Shimea would say, shaking his upraised hand. "I'm thankful you came along to help me get rid of my leftover dough."

Munching the still-warm bread as he sauntered down the street, Samuel would marvel that Shimea ended up with leftover dough every time they happened by.

As the boys grew older, they explored the ravines and hills around Shiloh. Sometimes they went down to the road below town to watch travelers pass by. Too young to serve as priest, Ahitub didn't come to the Tabernacle often for the sacrifices.

The years passed, and one day a startled Samuel realized how much things were changing. It did not seem quite right. Eli's hair had grown white; he walked with a stick for support. Sometimes he stumbled over things in plain sight.

Eli let his sons Hophni and Phinehas carry out more and more of the sacrifices. Early on, Samuel had asked the two to tell him stories like their father did. They didn't seem interested in speaking about God's powerful help to the Children of Israel. More often now, Samuel overheard people complaining that the two were selfish and greedy with the sacrificed meat. How disappointing.

One evening Samuel noticed Hophni touching one of the women helpers in the Tabernacle like Father used to touch Mother back in Ramathaim. He gasped when they disappeared alone into a side room. Since Hophni had a wife at home, Samuel knew that was not right. He wanted to go in and tell Hophni to stop, but he was afraid to speak against the important priest.

He blushed with shame, and he ran to his room. Throwing himself down on his sleeping mat, he wept. This was God's holy house. How dare they! Somehow even his little room seemed dirty from the sin he just witnessed.

A few days later Samuel came around a corner in time to hear Eli scolding his sons. "If you do not repent, God will judge you," the high priest said. "You are to be an example of how God's people are to live, not a pagan."

Samuel held his breath and backed away, praying he had not been noticed. The stern speech did not seem to change the sons' behavior, however. After that Samuel tried harder to obey Eli, hoping to make up for the bad priests.

One morning while Samuel read in his halting voice a passage from the Law to the patient Eli, a visitor appeared in Shiloh. He came straight to the Tabernacle and announced he had a message from the Lord. Eli stopped everything to listen.

The prophet began by recalling Israel's deliverance from Egypt and God choosing the tribe of Levi for the priesthood. He accused Eli of scorning God's sacrifice and offerings by indulging his sons and their evil ways. Because of this, God would cut short Eli's strength and family line. "This is God's warning to you," the prophet said, lifting his hand in the air. "Because your family does not obey the Lord, our God, your two sons will die. The rest of your family will die either now or later in the prime of life." Eli winced, but did not interrupt.

Samuel's eyes grew wide, his mouth agape. He had never heard a prophecy before, but he knew God's words came true. Look at Moses at the Burning Bush, or the angel that visited Gideon.

"The Tabernacle will be destroyed," the messenger said in conclusion, "and God will raise up a faithful priest who will follow what is in His heart and mind."

Samuel stood a moment, numbed by the horrid news. Then a surge of fright swept through him, propelling him out the court-yard entrance. He did not stop running until he reached the northern ravine. He sank to the ground, panting, as he tried to control his shaking. What could he do to stop this terrible thing from happening? If they all died, what would happen to him?

In the months following, Samuel became so busy running errands for Eli during the Feast and daily sacrifices that he almost forgot the prophet. One night after listening to Eli's bedtime story and prayers, he slipped under his blanket and fell asleep in the comforting glow of the olive oil lamp.

"Samuel." The voice woke him.

Who called? He jumped up and ran to Eli's room. The high priest never summoned him at night; he must need help. The sleeping Eli woke upon hearing Samuel.

"No, I didn't call you," Eli said, rubbing his eyes. "Go back to bed."

This happened three times, unnerving the confused boy. The third time Samuel came, the old man paused, as if thinking. "Samuel." He cleared his throat. "The next time the Voice calls you say, 'Speak Lord, your servant is listening to whatever you have to say.'"

This time the boy returned to bed relieved, and lay waiting, too excited to sleep. What did the Lord want from him?

"Samuel."

He sat straight up. "Speak, Lord, your servant is listening to what you have to say." Later he regretted his eager reply.

God assured him with stern words that He would fulfill the terrible prophecy of the recent visitor—not a message Samuel wanted to hear. The Voice stopped. What a relief.

Samuel slid under his blanket and pulled it over his head. His stomach tightened and the sweetish smell of the burning lamp almost made him sick. He tossed and turned a long time before drifting off to sleep.

At daybreak Eli insisted on hearing God's message. Samuel hesitated until Eli coaxed it from him. Poor Eli.

The boy continued to help the priest. Knowing the old man would soon be gone, he asked many questions.

~

As years passed, Samuel applied himself harder to his studies. He knew he would also, in time, teach others so tried to learn all he could while he still had a chance.

He studied history with a certain sadness. The Children of Israel cherished their great heritage. Under the leadership of Moses and Aaron, the Lord delivered them from slavery in Egypt. The Israelites were prone to idolatry and independence, however, and often reverted to ungodly ways. In judgment for rebellion against His directions, God condemned them to wander in the wilderness for forty years—until the generation of adult rebels died off.

Moses died, and Joshua led the Twelve Tribes across the Jordan River into the Promised Land. After conquering the new Land and dividing it among the tribes, Joshua died, leaving them without a strong leader. Would this happen when Eli and his sons died?

Soon the Israelites began adopting the pagan practices of the Canaanites they had partially displaced. Hilltops were favorite places of worship. Israelites failed to destroy the idols of Baal and the poles of Asherah, the mother goddess, that crowned the heights overlooking the larger towns. Some began worshipping the idols rather than the One True God; others mixed their worship together. Losing their moral conscience, sacred prostitution and child sacrifices did not seem so horrible anymore. Samuel shuddered at the thought.

At times God allowed enemy tribes to invade and oppress the Israelites. Only then would they turn back to Him in desperation. In His mercy, God would raise up a person, a "judge," to lead them against the oppressor. Eli had Samuel memorize the list of Israel's judges and learn their stories. As Samuel listened, he could see the cycle repeat over and over—sin, repent and obey; sin, repent and obey. Israelites did not learn very well, did they? Priests at the Tabernacle seem to be the only leaders that endured.

Studying history, Samuel prayed God would help him be a righteous leader of His people if that time ever came. He began speaking to the worshipers traveling to Shiloh, sharing his burden for Israel's sin, calling on them to repent. Only then would God deliver them from their foreign oppressors, he said, conviction in his voice.

From as far away as Dan in the extreme north to Beersheba in the far south, pilgrims who came to celebrate the annual sacred feasts listened to Samuel and went home impressed by the young man's spiritual qualities and leadership. As people grew more and more disenchanted with Hophni and Phinehas, they turned to Eli's assistant.

And then it happened—the worst day in Samuel's life.

Who formulated the plan Samuel never knew. One autumn following the Feast of Tabernacles a crowd of men organized themselves into an army to overthrow the Philistines and gain independence. Without national repentance or consulting God, they attacked the enemy encamped at Aphek. The Philistines over-powered the Israelites, killed four thousand, and sent survivors fleeing back to their camp at Ebenezer.

"What went wrong that the Lord brought defeat on us today?" the soldiers asked each other, shaking their heads in dismay.

"God's presence is not with us," one man said. They all agreed.

"Let's bring the Ark of the Covenant from Shiloh," someone shouted, stepping forward. "Joshua had priests carry the Ark in front when our forefathers crossed the Jordan. God performed a miracle and the waters parted." A group quickly surrounded the speaker. "The Philistines carry images of their gods into battle with them. If we bring the Ark to the battlefield," he said, "God's presence will be with us and save us from our enemies."

A delegation hurried off to Shiloh, where they found Hophni and Phinehas finishing the evening sacrifice. They outlined their plan. The two priests agreed. They did not bother to consult the elderly Eli.

Borne by priests, early the next morning the Ark appeared in Ebenezer. The disheartened Israelites shouted for joy at sight of the sacred box which none of them had ever seen. "Victory is ours!"

The Philistines heard the uproar and sent spies to find the cause. The report alarmed them. "A god has come into the Israelite camp," they said. "We're in big trouble. This has never happened before." They held their heads in grief and wailed, "Woe be on us!"

"Who will deliver us from these gods?" a leader said. "They are the same gods that struck down the Egyptians with all kinds of plagues." He raised his spear in the air. "Be strong, fellow Philistines. Be men, or you'll become their servants, as they have been ours. Now let's go fight!" The rallying cry brought the army to attention. They poured out of camp, rushing to Ebenezer.

The clash quickly escalated, the fighting fierce, the odds over-whelming. Even with the presence of the Ark, the battle turned into a rout for the out-armed Israelites. Thirty thousand were killed; the rest deserted in all directions. Hophni and Phinehas lay lifeless on the corpse-strewn battlefield. Most tragically, the Philistines captured the Ark of the Covenant.

When Eli came out for the morning sacrifice, he was horrified to learn the Ark had been removed from the Tabernacle without his permission—or God's direction. He let out a keening wail and started for the entrance.

"Where are you going?" Samuel called.

"Down to the road." Eli hobbled on, the tip of his cane moving back and forth to clear the way. Samuel grabbed Eli's four-legged stool and hurried after him.

They did not stop until they reached the town entrance. Ahitub and several priests were congregated out on the road with ordinary citizens, scanning the valley for sign of a messenger.

The high priest, overweight, feeble, and blind at ninety-eight, sat wringing his hands as he waited for news from the battlefield. "The Ark. The Ark," he said between sobs.

Too soon, a Benjamite rushed from the fray to Shiloh. Samuel saw him coming, his clothes torn and dust covering his head. It could only signify one thing—disaster. A wail rose from the crowd gathered down the road.

Eli heard the commotion and sent for the runner. Trying to catch his breath, the runner delivered the news, one statement at a time. The high priest moaned in a loud voice at news of the defeat. Hearing of the death of his sons, he let out a piercing cry. "And the Ark has been captured," the messenger said, concluding his sad report.

The aged Eli gasped at this last information, clutched his chest, and swayed precariously. Before Samuel or Ahitub could reach his side, Eli toppled backwards from the stool. Samuel and others heard his neck crack and watched in shock as the high priest took one final breath.

Death wails filled the air.

Eli was dead, the priests killed, the Ark gone. What else could go wrong? Samuel brushed at his tears. He took a long, last look at the face of the man he had grown to love as a father, then stooped to cover Eli's face with a corner of the priestly mantle. As Samuel stood up, he caught sounds in the distance of the approaching army.

The victorious Philistines celebrated their triumph. They now had proof their god Dagon was more powerful than the Israelite god. They had captured his gold-plated box. Emboldened, they pursued the battle across the hills and valleys to Shiloh.

Sensing impending danger and realizing he could do nothing for his dead foster-father and mentor, Samuel ran to the deserted Tabernacle. He prayed for God's wisdom and protection as he grabbed two empty sacks from the storeroom. He pushed the precious scrolls of Moses and Joshua into one sack. The high priest's ephod hung from a wall peg in the Holy Place. He shoved it into another sack and added a few other sacred objects.

At the last minute, he dashed to his room, half-apologizing to the dead Eli for breaking the rule against running. He grabbed a clean tunic, found a loaf of last week's showbread, and wrapped it in the cloth. Swinging a sack over each shoulder, he fled across the northern ravine to the hills of Ephraim.

Only as he sat concealed in the cover of a hilltop woods did Samuel realize what he had just done—enter the forbidden Holy Place and peer into the empty Holy of Holies. Yet, God had not struck him dead.

The sun had begun to set when a shout drew his attention back to Shiloh, announcing the Philistines' arrival to plunder, slaughter, and destroy. He clapped his hands over his ears to block the noise.

Later, he tried eating bread but, without a drink of water, choked on the dry piece. With no blanket, for the first time he slept in his special robe. Life would never be the same. He drew the two sacks under his arms and prayed for God's protection over the sacred bundles. In the darkness, he jumped at unfamiliar forest sounds; it took hours to fall asleep.

An acrid smell woke Samuel at dawn. He crept through the trees to the hilltop and peered from behind a large oak to watch dark smoke billow from the center of town. "The Tabernacle," he cried out. Tears coursed down his cheeks.

The visiting prophet's warnings had come true.

Under cover of deepening afternoon shadows, Samuel escaped

to Ramathaim Zuphim. Elkanah and Hannah welcomed him with joy, but news of the destruction filled them with grief.

Over the months, Samuel got to know his three brothers and two sisters, whom he had only met when they came to the annual feasts. Elkanah hired a bricklayer to add an upper room on the east end of the rooftop. Samuel and Zophai moved into the new room and became good friends.

Samuel celebrated Eve's wedding with the family at Zeradah. He never participated in such festivities in Shiloh and, although they would miss their oldest sister, he rejoiced with her and Joash. He only regretted having so little time to become acquainted before she moved away.

Mingled with his joy, a heaviness weighed on Samuel as he mourned for willful Israel, who tried to gain God's deliverance without fulfilling God's requirements. News of the slaughter of priests who did not escape the carnage filtered across the hills of Ephraim to Ramathaim. Samuel envisioned faces of those he knew and wondered if they had survived, especially Mahli.

The Philistines soon found their famous booty to be a mixed blessing. The Israelite god became unhappy in their land and caused serious problems. They placed the Ark in the temple of Dagon in Ashdod beside the idol. Dagon, however, kept toppling over on his face. The people refused to keep the destructive box any longer and sent it to another town. Problems arose wherever it went, so they finally sent it back to Israel.

Judeans out harvesting wheat near Beth Shemesh looked up one day to see the Ark coming up the road on an unaccompanied cattle-drawn cart. Someone ran to call local Levites, who offloaded it onto a large rock located in the field where it stopped. The townspeople celebrated by chopping up the cart for a sacrificial fire while the priests prepared the cows for a burnt offering to God in praise for the Ark's safe return.

When some of the curious men raised the "mercy seat" lid and looked inside the Ark, God struck them down; seventy died for their sin. Afraid, the people of Beth Shemesh sent word to the people of Kiriath-jearim, asking them to come take possession of the Ark. They transported it to the home of Abinadab and consecrated his son Eleazar to guard it. For nearly a century it remained with the Household of Abinadab.

Back home in Ramathaim after years of absence, Samuel wandered aimlessly around town. No high priest, no Tabernacle to serve in, no worshipers to hear him preach. A gradual understanding came to him that this loss was a God-given opportunity for his true ministry. By taking the Ark into battle, the Israelites had revealed their spiritual barrenness. To them God dwelt in a box at the Tabernacle, not in their hearts and daily lives. God allowed them to lose the symbol of His presence in order to gain His true Presence. Only repentance from sin, not rebuilding the Tabernacle, would bring a national recovery.

In prayer Samuel sought God's will for his life. If no Tabernacle remained to which the people could come, he decided, he must take the worship to them. Ramathaim meant "twin heights," but the town was often called Ramah, "the height," since it occupied just one of the peaks. On the adjacent one, later known as Naioth, Samuel raised an altar to God at the high place and called the people to worship.

Gathering as many men as would listen, he began teaching them the word of God and how to read the scrolls and write. These students formed the nucleus for a school of the prophets and constructed a building to house their classes. During the dry season Samuel led them across the countryside, preaching and prophesying.

Samuel also repeated to his students Eli's stories that once filled his lonely evenings. The thrill of the greatness of a Mighty God remained as fresh as at the original telling, the students just as eager.

"You need to write these down," a young prophet said to him one day when he finished sharing the life of Gideon—one of the prophet's favorite Judges.

It occurred to Samuel that, in Eli's ninety-eight years, the old priest knew much information on the judges first-hand, or from those who did. Now Eli was gone, as were Hophni and Phinehas. Who else knew these accounts? Who else would remember them once Samuel died?

Encouraged, the next day Samuel drew a new scroll from the storage chest in his upper room. After mixing soot and resin in a shallow cup, he added, drop by drop, olive oil and water until satisfied with the consistency of his ink.

First, Samuel jotted down the list of Israel's Judges, thankful the wise Eli had insisted he memorize it. He began by writing about the death of Joshua. As the lines on the scroll multiplied, so did Samuel's insight. "Another generation grew up, but they neither knew God nor all He had done for Israel," he penned. If one generation forgot, God's Chosen People would be doomed.

Samuel resolved to never let that happen, to never stop reminding the Israelites. At that moment he knew his life's calling. The natural human spirit was one of rebellion. Samuel recalled Moses' description of the serpent in the Garden of Eden. Every living soul had been affected by Adam's sin. Only constant obedience to God would change that nature. Only remembering would keep them from sin.

Samuel established a circuit, twice a year making rounds to Bethel, Gilgal, and Mizpah before returning to Ramah. In each town he held court, taught about God, and led worship. He often repeated stories Eli had taught him, applying the truth to present-day life.

Sometimes upon returning from his latest tour, God inspired Samuel to add the story of the next Judge. When he finished the list with the final Judge, Samson, he added the story of Micah and the Danites. Space remained, but no further inspiration came from God. He placed the scroll back in the chest and waited.

Whether he added another story or not, God had already given him the ending—words which predicted spiritual disaster: "Everyone did what he decided was right in his own mind." The phrase haunted him.

One winter Elkanah developed a cough, which deepened over the weeks and sapped his strength. In spite of Samuel's prayers and those of the family and student prophets, one night the frail Elkanah died in his sleep. Samuel postponed his circuit tour for the funeral and to be with his mother. The days of mourning ended, but Samuel felt no urge to resume his travels.

Zophai had married four years before, so Samuel and his two younger brothers moved down to the lower floor to be with their mother. After supper Samuel usually retreated to the rooftop, his haven after difficult days.

"Samuel," Hannah called one evening after the dishes were cleared and the table mat rolled up.

"I'm up here," Samuel called back. "Shall I come down?"

"No."

He heard the two boys, Gershom and Uriel, talking as they came out the door and headed up the street to visit Adah and her new baby.

Samuel continued to think about his lesson for the prophets the following day. A few minutes later, he looked up to see his mother's head rising above the staircase. He rushed over to help her. "Mother, should you be climbing the stairs by yourself?"

"I'm not that old."

"I could have come down."

"I had to come up. I need to talk to you in private." She linked her arm around his elbow. "Before I die."

Samuel guided her across the rooftop to his favorite spot for relaxing. "Now, what is on your mind?" he said after they were seated side by side.

Hannah sat for a moment, hands clasped, the right thumb moving back and forth over the left. "Samuel, I . . . I hope you never held it against me for taking you to live with Eli."

"Of course not, Mother. You fulfilled your vow to God."

"It wasn't easy," Hannah said.

"Obedience usually isn't."

"I wasn't abandoning you." Her hands lay in her lap, motionless. "After you were born, I never went back to the Tabernacle until you were old enough to be left with Eli. My love for you ran so deep. I guess I was afraid if I took you each year and brought you back, when the time came for you to remain behind, I might break my promise. I couldn't risk that."

Samuel had never thought much about what it cost his mother to fulfill her vow. She had sacrificed more than he. He reached out and clasped her left hand, resting them on the rooftop between them.

"When I gave you back to God, I gave all I had," Hannah said. "He had removed my humiliation of being barren. What more could I ask?" She hesitated. A baby's cry down the street reminded her of those days, encouraging her to continue. "Every year at the Feast, Eli would pray for Father and me that God in His kindness would bless us with children to take your place. God gave us five more."

Samuel raised his eyes toward heaven. "Praise be to the Lord God."

"None could replace my firstborn, however." She squeezed his hand. "Coming home from the Feast each year, I had to surrender you once again to God. I began immediately to make your new robe for the next visit. Every stitch I took I did with love." She brushed a tear from her eye.

"My inspiration was Jochebed," Hannah said. "Think of a mother placing her little baby in a basket and hiding it in the bulrushes in the river, never knowing if he would survive, never knowing if she would see her little son again. God gave her baby back for a few years, then she took him to the princess at the palace, as promised. It often comforted me to know Jochebed went through the same situation as I."

Hannah paused. Samuel did not speak.

"Jochebed may never have seen Moses again. By the time God spoke to him at the Burning Bush, he was eighty. He never got to tell her about that experience. That might have made all her sacrifice worthwhile."

"I've never told you about the night God spoke to me, have I?"

Hannah shook her head. Samuel began the story of God's four calls in the night, finishing with the prophecy against Eli's household.

"Moses had his Burning Bush; you had your Voice in the Tabernacle." Hannah took a deep breath. "Watching you grow, from Eli's little helper, to his assistant, to his replacement thrilled my mother-heart. I am amazed that God included me in His plan."

Samuel reached over to cradle her hand between both of his, and they sat in silence.

"Neither have I told you," Samuel said, "how much I looked forward to the family's annual visit to the Feast and the times Father served in the Tabernacle."

"He told me about your special honey cake treats," Hannah said, smiling up at her son. "He never told the other children."

"Before Father left for home, he always placed his hand on my head and said, 'You are your mother's firstborn, dedicated to God before your birth. Remember to be a good boy and obey Eli.' Each time it was like a benediction."

"He probably sacrificed more than I. You were his son too, but I'm the one who promised you to the Lord. He let me obey my vow."

Minutes passed. "We grieved for the loss of the Tabernacle and Eli," Hannah said. "But after twenty years God gave you back to care for us in our old age."

Samuel put his arm around his mother and pulled her close. They sat in the stillness, letting tears flow.

"Thanks for opening your heart to me," Samuel said.

"Where would Israel be today if Moses and you hadn't been born?" Hannah asked.

"And where would Israel be if our mothers hadn't been willing to place God's will above their own?"

Doors along the street began closing for the night. Reluctant to break the sacred moments, they continued sitting together.

"We're home, Mother," Gershom called as the boys returned.

Stars began twinkling overhead. Finally, Samuel helped his mother to her feet. He offered a prayer of thanksgiving, kissed her cheek, then accompanied her down the stairs.

Longing for a family of his own, Samuel pleaded with God for a devout wife who would support his ministry. When a student introduced Samuel to his sister, Keturah, the prophet heard God's whisper of approval. They married shortly before Hannah passed away.

In a few short years the house filled with happy young voices and cries of infants. Samuel looked forward to the thrill of having his sons, firstborn Joel and his brother Abijah, join him in worship. His heart rose in adoration. "From generation to generation, You are God."

One morning Joel watched his father unroll a new scroll, roll it back up, and tuck it under his arm. "What are you going to write about this time?" the boy said. Samuel had told the children the stories from his scroll of the Judges, as well as from those by Moses and Joshua.

"I'm going to tell about how God has helped me since I was a little boy."

"Since you helped Eli in the Tabernacle?"

"Since before I was born."

"Oh." Satisfied, Joel ran off to play.

Samuel had felt for some time he should pen his life's story. With both his parents now gone, he wanted to preserve their story as well as his own. He headed up the outside staircase to the vacant guest room, where he could write uninterrupted.

Through it all, Samuel could trace the hand of God. As surely as the Lord led Abraham and Moses, so He had led Samuel. The scroll and quill lay untouched on the table. God was a faithful God, eternal, righteous, and just. Samuel sat bathed in the presence of Jehovah, his heart full of reverence and thanksgiving.

Gratitude for Eli, also. He still missed his old mentor.

Did any of the family of Eli survive the attack on Shiloh? The question occasionally troubled Samuel. No one ever mentioned them. Given the reputation of Hophni and Phinehas and the rousing defeat by the Philistines, perhaps they wanted to live and die unnoticed.

After finishing court in Bethel one day, a man approached Samuel. "Do you remember me? I'm Ahitub, son of Phinehas. And this," he said, putting his hand on the boy's shoulder, "is my first-born, Ahimeleck. We call him Ahijah."

The surprised Samuel threw his arms around the friend of his youth and wept tears of joy. "God be praised. I've thought of your family and prayed for you for many years."

"Thanks for your concern." Ahitub looked down, swallowing hard. "When we heard the sound of the Philistine army getting closer that day, we knew they would be in Shiloh by sunset. We hurriedly buried Grandfather. You remember the family cave-tomb in the southern ravine." He looked up at Samuel, who nodded. "The shock was too much for Mother. She went into labor. Then tragedy struck again. She died in childbirth. We were barely able to bury her and escape to the countryside with baby Ichabod."

"Ichabod." *No glory.*

"Mother named him. The last words she spoke were, 'The glory has departed from Israel.' " Ahitub paused for a deep breath, seeming to relive the painful experience. "We've built a settlement north of here," he said. "The family is doing well. I miss the Tabernacle and Grandfather."

Shared sorrow bonded the friends in silence.

"With Eli gone," Samuel finally said, "my only thought that day was the Tabernacle." He described rushing to the sanctuary to gather the scrolls, ephod, and sacred instruments. "Come back to Ramah with me," Samuel said. "I would like to return them to you. I'm a prophet, not a high priest." He shook his head. "Perhaps God will restore the priesthood of Israel. I've built an altar to God in Ramah and, as a Levite and with no high priest, I offer sacrifices. Other towns also have altars, but many have desecrated them by worshiping Baal."

Ahitub promised to come as soon as possible.

Two weeks later Ahitub walked with Samuel across the ridge from Ramah to Naioth, overjoyed to visit Samuel's ministry. Impressed with the school of the prophets, he insisted Samuel keep the sacred scrolls of Moses and Joshua used in their studies.

Samuel had mentioned restoration of the priesthood. Ahitub had thought a lot about it during the two weeks and quizzed the prophet about the regulations and responsibilities of the office. If God led, he wanted to be prepared.

After three days, Samuel prayed a blessing on his friend, then the two embraced. Ahitub picked up the sack of rescued supplies, and they promised to keep in touch. Watching him go, Samuel felt relieved of responsibility for the holy objects.

In Samuel's travels, people listened to his message. The Land and the People were one. Given by God, chosen by God. As long as the People obeyed God, He would protect the Land. Indifference and disobedience broke that covenant made with Abraham.

God convicted Samuel's audiences of their sin. In repentance, one day they assembled with the prophet at Mizpah. With a fresh boldness, Samuel insisted they put away their idols of Baal and Ashtoreth and serve God alone. The meeting became a great spiritual revival. In a severe thunderstorm, God gave them a tremendous victory over the terrified Philistine army.

The only military expedition Samuel ever led gained a truce that lasted many years. In recent times, however, the Philistines had begun making incursions into Israelite territory, reestablishing lookouts. Samuel feared their success once again signified Israel's spiritual decline.

Sitting alone on the rooftop in Ramah one evening, Samuel listened to the night sounds of the town—the chirping of a cricket from a crack in the brick wall, a father calling his children in from play, the bleating of a hungry lamb, the *who-who-who* of an owl in the tree down the street. The familiar sounds soothed his exhausted spirit after the difficult day listening to people's problems and complaints.

Samuel's hand brushed across the rough texture of the floor, one spot wearing smooth by the nightly gesture. Being a judge in Israel wasn't easy. Being a father was even harder.

Samuel recalled his childhood days serving the high priest in Shiloh. Eli was a godly man, but an indulgent father. The older and more blind he got, the more despicable his sons had become, treating the sacred with contempt. God had judged Eli and his sons.

With the passing of decades, Samuel's energy level decreased. His gait grew slower as he walked the miles of his circuit. He admitted to himself the work had gotten to be more than he could handle. So, he trained his sons Joel and Abijah to serve as judges and sent them to Beersheba in southern Judah to hear area court cases. Now disturbing reports were filtering in about them acting dishonestly, greedily taking bribes to make favorable decisions. How did he fail? Tears filled his eyes. Would the judgment of Eli's family fall on his?

Samuel didn't have long to wait for an answer.

One afternoon a few months later, a man knocked on Samuel's door with a message. "You are wanted at the town entrance."

What now?

For centuries the unoccupied areas just inside town entrances served as public meeting places. Business and social transactions were finalized there, laws enforced, and council sessions held.

Samuel slipped on his sandals and followed the man through the marketplace to the small open square. The size of the large assembly surprised him. Even more when he recognized men from Bethel, Gilgal, Mizpah, and other towns along his regular circuit.

With greetings exchanged, Ardon the Ephraimite, serving as spokesman, introduced the matter of concern. "You are growing old, and your sons aren't righteous like you. Appoint a king to be our leader, like all the other nations have."

Murmurs of agreement filled the air.

A king? Samuel's forehead wrinkled in a frown; his heart sank. He had not known what to expect, but their asking for a king was the last thing that would have come to mind. Did they know what kings of other nations demanded of their people? He stood in stunned silence until the spokesman's polite cough penetrated his jumbled thinking. "I'll have to pray about this." Samuel glanced over the unsmiling faces of men he considered friends.

"Of course," Ardon said. "We will come back tomorrow for a reply."

Samuel watched the men go, then wandered out the town entrance and along the slope to the adjoining hill. He leaned against the stone altar and buried his face in his hands. "Like all the other nations." The galling phrase pounded his mind like a carpenter's mallet.

The One True God had chosen Abraham from the city of moon worshippers, Ur of the Chaldees, and created from him a great nation. The One True God had led his Chosen People from slavery in Egypt to the Promised Land. A king to lead them? Could a man do better than God? Perhaps knowing someone was always in charge would be better than having sporadic judges arise from time to time to unite the fragmented, often contentious, tribes. But to be like other nations—pagan nations? Samuel's shoulders shook with his sobs. What happened to the Israelites' resolve at Mizpah to serve only God?

When other nations went to war, their kings led them in battle. Had the elders' request come because no military leader had recently stepped forward to lead an attack on the menacing Philistines? Without a king, Israel would never have a standing army. Or was it because the judges had relied on the unseen God, but now the Israelites wanted a visible presence they could depend on?

Didn't people realize judges died, but kings ruled from generation to generation? If they thought Eli's sons were immoral and his sons too greedy to judge fairly, what did the people plan to do when a king's wicked son came to the throne—and used their taxes and an army of their sons to enforce his demands and perpetuate his evil reign? They might reject a priest's or a judge's sons, but no one would dare oppose a crown prince.

"Like all the other nations." The mallet pounded on. After all God had done for his Chosen People, why lower themselves to that level? The one thing God did not want them to become was like all the other nations. Yes, God had mentioned a king to Moses; it was recorded in the Law. Having one was not wrong, but their motive was.

Samuel pushed back from the altar and brushed the dust from his cloak. "It's not up to me," he said, looking across at the town that hosted the disturbing delegation of elders. "Only God can give an answer to His people." He raised his eyes to the cloudless heavens. "Show me Your response, Lord."

That night Samuel sat on the rooftop long after the town had gone to bed. "I've tried to lead the people in paths of righteousness." He lifted his heart to God. "But it hasn't been enough. Your people want a king, instead." Looking up at the glimmering stars, Samuel felt a calmness settle over him. Closing his eyes, he opened his heart to God's reply.

"Listen to what the people are saying," the Lord said. "It is not you they are rejecting, but Me. They've been this way since the day I brought them up from Egypt. They forsook Me; now they forsake you. Go ahead and listen to them; just warn them solemnly. Let them know what a reigning king will do to them."

"Thank You for Your faithful leading," the prophet prayed before rising to descend the stairs.

Samuel cautiously opened the door, hoping to prevent the inevitable scrape. Easing himself inside, he made his way up the steps of the platform to the sleeping mat his wife had rolled out for him. He paused to look down at Keturah. The lamplight defined her lined, but relaxed, face and highlighted the silver in her hair. He stood for a moment, listening to her soft, even breathing.

Perhaps if Israel had a king, he too would sleep better. Samuel removed his cloak and hung it on a wall peg. Then again, a king might only add weight to his constant concern for his people.

The sun had already risen over the peaks of Ramathaim when Samuel opened his eyes. Realizing he had overslept, he jumped up and changed his tunic. He placed his headdress over his long graying hair and secured it with a headband as he hurried out the door and down to the town entrance. From the far end of the market street, he could see the elders milling about. His heart bled for the deluded men.

At least he wouldn't be around to see the consequences of their disastrous choice. He held up his hands for silence, determined one last time to try to dissuade them.

He delivered the message from the Lord, warning them that a king would demand their sons as soldiers, craftsmen, and field hands; their daughters as palace servants; their fields and groves as his personal property; a portion of their harvests as taxes; their servants for his workers; their livestock as his own; and themselves as slaves. "When that day arrives," he said, "you will cry for relief from this king you've chosen, but the Lord won't listen to you."

"We don't care," the spokesman replied. "We still want a king. Then we'll be like surrounding nations, with a king to lead and fight our battles. We are already hearing reports of the Ammonites stirring up trouble east of the Jordan. The Philistines are becoming bolder, also. We need a king."

Samuel turned and bowed his head, telling God what the men had said. "Give them what they want," the Lord replied.

The prophet pivoted to face the assembly. "All right. God has heard your request. Everyone go on home. We will wait for Him to reveal His choice."

The men smiled in relief and rose to congratulate each other on their success. "God wants us to be like the other nations, after all," Eliphaz said to his neighbor as they started home to Bethel. "Who do you think He will choose?"

"I've no idea." Meremoth shook his head. "I can't think of anyone in Bethel who would inspire my confidence in battle with the Philistines."

"It is an awesome responsibility, isn't it?"

3

A NEW KING

While Gatam tied the supplies on the donkey, Saul surveyed the area surrounding their camp site. Walking west down the valley, they wound around several hills before catching sight of the twin peaks of Ramathaim Zuphim ahead. Cheerful female voices broke the morning stillness as they approached the hill. A line of girls, waterpots on their shoulders, headed for the spring below town.

"Is the seer home today?" Saul asked the first in line.

"Yes. He's just ahead of you." She lowered the waterpot. "The people are offering a sacrifice. He arrived this morning to officiate. If you hurry you can stop him before he goes up." She stepped off the path to let them pass. "No one starts eating until he arrives to bless the sacrifice and join his invited guests."

They thanked the girls and quickened their steps. *What good timing.* As they neared the town entrance, a man came out. His beard was gray, but his stride sure and steady. He paused as the travelers approached. "The Lord bless you," he greeted them.

"The Lord be with you, also. Would you please give me directions to the seer's house?" Saul asked.

. . .

"I'm the seer," Samuel replied. He looked up at the tall speaker. An unexpected feeling came over him. This was the man God had spoken to him about yesterday. The new king!

Making his circuit visits during the past few weeks, Samuel had viewed the men he judged and led in worship from a new perspective. Which one would the Lord select to lead His People? He started back to Ramah, disappointed he had never sensed God revealing His choice. Then yesterday noon God had spoken so clearly.

Samuel smiled up at Saul. "Go on up to the high place," he said, pointing toward the path along the edge of town. "Today you'll eat with me. In the morning I'll let you go and will tell you all that's in your heart. As for the donkeys you lost three days ago, don't worry, they've been found." The shocked expression on the traveler's face was something to behold. "And to whom is all the desire of Israel turned," Samuel said, "if not to you and your father's family?"

Saul stared at the man. His forehead wrinkled in a frown. Suddenly he recognized the prophet as Samuel. Why hadn't Gatam mentioned the man of God's name? And what did Samuel mean by the strange comment about the desire of Israel and his family? Saul searched his mind for an explanation. Then he recalled the assembly in Gibeah a few weeks ago when Hamul reported on the elders' request to Samuel for a king. Surely the prophet didn't mean he was the choice.

"I . . . I'm a Benjamite," Saul stammered in protest, "from the smallest tribe of Israel. My clan is the least important of the tribe of Benjamin. Why say such a thing to me?"

"Come." The prophet turned toward the path. "Please go on up," he said, motioning with his hand for them to lead the way.

Gatam tied the donkey's rope to a nearby tree, and he and Saul preceded Samuel along the route up the hill. Gaining the summit, they saw a throng of people milling around the high place, talking to each other as they waited for the feast to be served. Smoke curled up from the fire pits on the north side of the hill. The smell of cooking meat stimulated Saul's appetite.

Samuel pressed through the crowd, and Saul caught a glimpse of the altar. Stained with fresh blood, it stood in front of a building a hundred feet away. "Welcome to the school of the prophets," Samuel said, leading him and Gatam inside the stone structure.

A large low table ran the length of the room. Two dozen men sat on the floor around it. The head place remained unoccupied, and the prophet led his guests to the place of honor. Saul looked around, puzzled, then took his seat. Almost as if he were expected, it seemed.

A few others joined them before Samuel stood to bless the feast with prayer. Then he went outside to bless the remaining people. Saul overheard him tell the cook, "Bring the piece of meat I gave you to prepare for my special guest." Saul became more curious. How did Samuel know he was coming?

The cook followed Samuel inside, carrying a leg portion on a platter, which he placed in front of Saul. The farmer from Gibeah studied the choice serving, aware of its meaning. Samuel leaned over to him. "Eat up. I reserved this piece especially for you when I first invited guests."

"This is delicious, and I was famished," Saul said later, "but I'll never be able to finish all this."

"Just eat what you want."

Samuel stood up to begin the celebration by introducing one of the students. Feasts were times for learning, as well as worship and eating. Samuel and other students took their turns, recalling God's dealings with Israel during her long history or leading in praise to God and in prayer.

The sun had long passed its zenith when the crowd began to scatter. Samuel brought his guests back to town. Gatam set off to find lodging for the donkey. Samuel invited Saul to the rooftop to rest, then led him to his favorite place to sit. Ever the religious leader, the prophet soon began pouring out his concern for Israel's spiritual lethargy and sin.

Saul listened, fascinated. Samuel was as straightforward and intense with one person as with a crowd. Saul scooted closer to not miss a single word.

Samuel spoke of his longing to see God's mighty power revealed on behalf of a repentant nation. "My work," he said, "is to inform all the tribes of God's Laws and urge them to obey the injunction, 'Listen carefully, O Israel: The Lord our God is one Lord: And you must love the Lord your God with all your heart, all your soul, and all your strength.'"

Righteous Israelites quoted the creed from Moses' Book of the Law every day; coming from this godly man infused it with a breath from heaven. Saul placed his hand over his heart as he sensed God's nearness.

Afternoon shadows shrouded the town. "Israel will never again be great until her leaders are totally obedient to God," Samuel said in conclusion.

Saul remained silent during the prophet's monologue, half envying the opportunities enjoyed by the students in the school on the hill. This lesson was more nourishing than the piece of meat he had consumed at the feast.

Samuel rose to go. "I know you're tired from your miles of trekking through the countryside." He walked over and opened the door to the upper room. "I'll send your servant up with a lamp. Enjoy your rest. I'll awaken you early. I know you're anxious to be on your way."

Saul's gaze followed Samuel across the rooftop. Not a word about "to whom is all the desire of Israel turned." He chuckled at his erroneous conclusion. And he had been afraid Samuel meant he was to be king. At least that worry wouldn't keep him awake tonight. He breathed a sigh of relief.

Saul awoke hours later to the *tur-r-r, tur-r-r* of turtledoves roosting on the parapet outside his door. From the little window high in the wall, he could see the night sky beginning to lighten. Time to get up, unfortunately. He tossed aside his blanket, yawned, and shook Gatam. "A short night, but we must get an early start."

Saul picked up the olive oil lamp and pulled the door open. A breeze set the flame dancing, and he cupped his hand around the wick. Gatam rolled up the blankets and tossed them over his shoulder.

"If you're ready, come on down and I'll send you away with a blessing," Samuel called up to the men as they reached the stairs. While the servant went to the stable to retrieve the donkey, Saul refilled the waterbag. Samuel handed him one of their provision bags, replenished with food.

"I'll see you to the road," Samuel said when Gatam arrived. He accompanied them out the door.

Framed by the high windows in houses along the vacant street, the soft glow of lamplight was the only sign of life in the sleepy town. By the time they reached the town entrance the sky was turning light blue-gray and the skyline held a faint pinkish tint. A rooster's crow broke the stillness.

A watchman greeted them in the marketplace. As they stepped outside the town entrance, Samuel turned to Saul. "Please tell the servant to go on ahead. Stay here a few minutes. I want to give you a message from God."

Gatam walked on, allowing the donkey to munch the grass as they went. Samuel led the way along the edge of town for about fifty feet before reaching into the girdle-belt beneath his cloak to withdraw a small horn flask. "Please kneel," he said to the tall farmer. Removing the stopper, he poured olive oil on Saul's head and kissed him—a sign of homage and allegiance.

Saul's heart pounded. Samuel's unexpected action bewildered him. *The prophet has just anointed him for some purpose. For what? King? Me?*

Samuel helped Saul to his feet. He felt his legs shake.

In his thirty years, Saul had never once considered Israel having a king, let alone being that king. As far as he knew, God always sent leaders to His people—Moses in Egypt, Joshua crossing the Jordan, judges who rose up in time of need. Only recently had he heard murmurings. Samuel was getting old, Saul had to admit, and his sons certainly were not like their father.

"Hasn't the Lord anointed you leader over His Chosen People?" Samuel said, interrupting Saul's troubled thoughts. Without further discussion, Samuel began prophesying. "When you leave here, near Rachel's tomb, at Zelzah on the border of Benjamin you will meet two men. They'll tell you, 'The donkeys you're looking for have been found. Now your father isn't concerned about them, but about you. "What shall I do without my son?" he keeps asking.'"

Saul listened, transfixed.

Near the great tree of Tabor, Samuel went on to predict, Saul would meet three men going up to worship at Bethel. One would be carrying three young goats, another three loaves of bread, and a third a skin of wine. They would greet him and offer him two of the loaves, which he should accept. From there, Saul would go on to Gibeah, where he would meet a procession of prophets coming down from the high place. They would be playing musical instruments and prophesying as they came. The Spirit of the Lord would come on Saul, and he too would prophesy as God changed him into a different person.

"Once these signs are fulfilled, do whatever your hand finds to do. God is with you," Samuel said. "Moses, in his fifth division of the Book of the Law, commanded that when we go to battle the priest should come and encourage the army with words from the Lord." Samuel placed his hand on Saul's shoulder. "You are now the Commander of Israel. When the time comes for you to fight, call your men and go down to Gilgal. Let me know, and I will come and sacrifice burnt offerings and fellowship offerings for you."

"You travel all over the countryside," Saul said. "How will I know where to find you?"

"Someone always knows where I am." Samuel smiled at him. "The Land isn't that big. You won't have to wait more than seven days before I arrive to tell you what to do."

Saul stood silent. He had never received a personal prophecy before and hardly knew what to say. The anointing filled him with confusion and a feeling of inadequacy. The prophecies were so specific. That reassured him a little. If they happened, he would believe the prophet; if not, maybe the old man was getting senile.

Samuel prayed a blessing on the future king and embraced him and Saul turned to go. Down the hill he saw Gatam beside the spring, letting the donkey slake its thirst before the journey home.

With long strides Saul started down the path. Suddenly an unfamiliar feeling washed over him, an outpouring of confidence and strength. He no longer needed the confirmation of the prophecies. A sense of awe filled him as the sun crested the hills of Zuph. He was anointed by God. He had been chosen to lead His people. "Help me, Jehovah, to be faithful," he prayed.

As Saul approached, Gatam looked up and stared at his master. Saul ignored his confused expression. He could not reveal the secret to Gatam—or anyone. If true, it was too overwhelming; if not, it was too ludicrous. But it was true, Saul's heart insisted. God had confirmed it by His Spirit.

From the town entrance, Samuel watched the two men go. "Benjamin—the smallest tribe of Israel," he repeated Saul's objection when they met yesterday. The statement brought to mind one of Eli's lessons from long ago. That, in turn, reminded him of the scroll of the Judges he had completed over a couple decades ago— with space to spare. Suddenly, he sensed a revelation from God. The Lord Himself had reserved that blank spot! Samuel must finish the scroll with the sad story of how the Benjamites had become so few. Overwhelmed by a divine presence, he lifted his head and praised God.

Glancing again at the receding travelers, Samuel softly said, "I'll see you in Mizpah." He turned with a smile. "But first, breakfast."

A hundred questions swirled through Saul's mind as he walked the miles home. How would this turn of events affect his parents? Ahinoam and the children? the people of Gibeah? Would he have to move? There was no large city to serve as a capital. Who would look after the farming after Kish passed away? Would the people really accept him as their leader? What exactly did a king do, anyway?

The trip home went as Samuel foretold. As Saul approached the turn-off to Gibeah, he contemplated how much life had changed. He had stood at that junction three days ago, regretting the need for the unplanned search. God certainly had strange ways of accomplishing things.

In the valley below town, Saul saw Kish's brother checking his wheat field. "So, you're finally home," his uncle said. "Where've you been the past few days?"

Saul gave a brief rundown of their search for the missing donkeys and mentioned his visit with Samuel. Ner asked what Samuel told him, so Saul relayed the assurance the donkeys had been found. He omitted mention of the kingdom discussion and the anointing.

Climbing the slope to Gibeah, Saul saw a procession coming down the path from the altar on the high place. Flutes, tambourines, lyre, and harp accompanied the men as they praised God with joyful worship and prophesying. Handing Gatam the two loaves of bread, Saul sent him on up to the house with the donkey while he went to meet the singing procession. Suddenly the Spirit of God came on Saul, and he joined in.

"What in the world's happened to Saul?" confused onlookers asked each other. "Has he become a prophet?"

After the men filed by, Saul walked on up to the high place. He knelt before the altar in adoration and thanksgiving to God. Every one of Samuel's prophecies had come true. Surely the kingdom awaited.

Gatam's advance arrival alerted Jonathan to his father's return. He waited at the gate until he saw Saul coming up the street and ran to meet him. "I protected Mother and Baby Malki-Shua from the Philistines," he said with pride. Saul scooped him up in his arms. "And we found the donkeys without you."

Saul kissed his son. "I found something greater than donkeys," he whispered, letting a hint of his secret slip out.

"What?" Jonathan drew back and searched his father's face for a clue.

"I can't tell you just yet, but someday soon I will. But don't tell anyone. It's a secret from God."

"Like God talking to Abraham?"

"Sort of."

"Then you're very special."

"And you are my special son." Saul hugged him close. "What have you been doing while I've been gone? Have you started harvesting wheat?" Saul walked into the courtyard and put Jonathan down to greet his family. Standing on the sideline, the boy studied his father's face. What was his secret from God?

With the barley and wheat safely stored in bags and clay jars in the granary rooms, Kish and Saul relaxed a few days before tending the grape vines in their patch of vineyard. One afternoon on their way home they noticed people congregated near the town entrance. In the center of the crowd stood a stranger. "The Prophet Samuel commands all Israelite men to meet at Mizpah the third day after the New Moon," he announced.

"I wonder what he's planning to do," Kish said, looking up at his son. Keeping his eyes on the messenger, Saul shrugged. "I guess we will soon find out," the older man decided.

"Maybe he'll anoint the new king," the farmer standing next to Kish said. "Perhaps God has finally spoken."

Early on the fourth day of the month the men of Gibeah set off for nearby Mizpah, their animated conversations full of curious speculation and expectation. Saul kept quiet, but his relatives did not seem to notice. He volunteered to lead the donkey carrying the family's blankets and food supply, happy to devote his attention to something that demanded no answer, something that would not scrutinize his reaction to their comments and wild guesses.

By the time they approached Mizpah a crowd had already gathered. Those from a distance had arrived the afternoon before. "I'll take the donkey to the camp site and join you later," Saul said. His cousin Tarea volunteered to go along. Saul said he could manage.

Saul turned off the road to the area where pack animals were tied. Nearby, haphazard collections of camping provisions and bundles of firewood were deposited next to gray-black circles from last night's cooking fires. He stood motionless, watching others arrive, deposit their loads, and tether their animals before rushing off to the meeting.

A nudge from the donkey reminded Saul of his chore. Hand firmly on the lead rope, he picked his way through the cluttered scene to the oak tree at the far side. He found a spot for the bags and donkey, but he could not force himself to join the men from Gibeah. He slumped against the tree trunk, his mind in a whirl, his heart racing, overwhelmed by sudden reality.

A vast throng ranged over the hillside—men from populous

Judah, leaders of Ephraim, farmers from Gilead beyond Jordan, priests of Levi, elders from Naphtali. Who was he to lead them? Saul slid farther down the tree trunk. These were men who united to rout the Philistines here at Mizpah fifteen years ago. Their ancestors, he knew, also decimated his own tribe of Benjamin a few centuries before. Grandfather Abiel once told him the terrible story.

Homosexuals in Gibeah had tried to rape a traveling Levite but, failing to get hold of him, they contented themselves by abusing his concubine until she died. The distraught Levite divided her body into twelve pieces and sent one to each tribe, reporting what had happened. Outraged Israelites met at Mizpah and demanded the Benjamites surrender the villains. When they refused, the Israelites fought them, burned Gibeah and other towns, and killed 25,000 men. The tribe only survived because six hundred men escaped, one of them Saul's ancestor.

And that wasn't the only intertribal battle Israel ever fought.

Saul watched as Samuel exited the town gate, then buried his face in his hands. Panic gripped him. "Oh Lord, how am I—a nobody—to gain respect from the important tribes and unite them into a kingdom?" he prayed aloud.

Unaware of Saul's absence, Kish and Ner stood with the other Benjamites, waiting for Samuel to appear. The sun stood high in the sky when they saw the gray-haired prophet make his way out of town to the assembly. The crowd hushed as he stepped onto a rock ledge and raised his hands for silence.

"This is the word of the Lord to Israel," Samuel said in a loud voice. " 'I brought Israel out of slavery in Egypt. I rescued you from the power of Egypt and all the kingdoms that opposed you.' But you've rejected your God, who in His kindness saves you from calamities and distress. You've said, 'We insist you set a king over us.' " He paused before announcing, "Now we will begin the process. Present yourselves before the Lord, tribe by tribe and clan by clan."

Samuel called for an elder of each tribe to come in front of the congregation. After praying, he selected the man from Benjamin. Calling representatives of each Benjamite clan, he chose Matri's. As the head of each family came forward, he placed his hand on Kish's arm. "Where's your son? Has he arrived?"

The farmer's shoulders jerked as he suddenly realized the implication. Saul, a king? Surely not! He glanced over at the collection of Gibeathites. Saul was not among them. "I haven't seen him since we separated back down the road," he replied. "I don't know where he is."

The prophet paused a moment to pray for guidance, then turned to one of his student prophets. "He's over at the campground, hiding with the baggage. You remember the guest of honor at the feast in Ramathaim? Go find him."

The buzz of thousands of voices arose from the waiting men. "What kind of man is this new king? Does anyone know?" "Why a Benjamite, instead of a Judean?" "Does he know anything about leading an army?"

When the student returned with Saul in tow, the men strained to catch a glimpse of their new king. "Tallest man I've ever laid eyes on." "Very handsome." "He certainly looks stately." "I'm impressed." "That's the guest at Samuel's feast a few weeks ago, isn't it?"

Samuel extended his hand down to help Saul up to the rock platform. Saul looked out over the congregation. A few striped cloaks dotted the throng of various shades of solid brown. Thousands of curious faces stared up at him as the crowd grew quiet.

"See the man chosen by God," the prophet said. "There isn't another like him among all the people of Israel."

"God save the king!" Shouts filled the air and echoed down the valley. "Life and health to our king!"

Samuel managed to get the people quiet again and explain the regulations of the office of king. He wrote them down on a parchment scroll to later deposit for safe keeping. He dismissed the people, who murmured in surprise at the unexpected shortness of the meeting. Samuel stood, watching them collect their belongings and start for home. He sighed and brushed a tear from the corner of his eye. "God, help this choice to not be the disaster I fear it will be."

As the crowd broke up, young men pushed forward to congratulate the new king and pledge their loyalty, anxious to find favor with him and to defend the infant kingdom. Their words filled thirty-year-old Saul with courage. He smiled for the first time that day.

Others felt differently. "How can this young fellow deliver Israel?" he heard a man grumble, disappointed the little tribe of Benjamin had been honored above his larger one.

"He isn't getting any gifts from me," an old man responded.

"He'll have to earn my respect," another said.

"Prove you're qualified before I offer support," a well-dressed merchant challenged as Saul walked past.

Saul ignored the derogatory comments. If God had chosen him king, God would have to convince the kingdom. He certainly did not intend to pick a fight with his subjects the very first day.

Kish and the other men of Gibeah retrieved their donkeys and followed the band of men who surrounded Saul. They were pleased one of their own had been chosen.

Saul knew some wondered, Why him?

4

THE GIBEONITE DECEIT

Lying on his stomach in the enclosed courtyard, Jonathan methodically lined up a row of small stones parallel to the kitchen wall—the army of Israel. He began distributing a second row, the Philistines, when the sound of voices in the street caught his attention. *Father.*

Jonathan jumped up, dropped the handful of stones, and ran to the gateway to welcome Saul home. Maybe the meeting at Mizpah today had something to do with Father's secret. If not, he hoped Father would tell him soon.

The gate swung open, and Grandfather Kish walked in, followed by his brother Ner. The men brushed by the boy as they hurried down the passageway and around the corner. Jonathan peeked out the gate, but he saw no one coming. His shoulders sagged. His father had not come. He stomped his foot. "I'll never find out the secret," he said, shoving the gate shut.

Jonathan ran back to the courtyard, now edged by afternoon shadows. Grandfather stood outside the sitting room door with Grandmother and Mother. A big smile wreathed Ner's face. Kish talked rapidly, punctuating his speech with excited hand gestures.

Grandmother suddenly twirled around in a dance of joy, waving her arms above her head as she praised God. Mother Ahinoam stood beside her, Baby Malki-Shua on her hip, her face expressionless.

"What happened?" Jonathan pressed against his mother's side. "When is Father coming home?" Ahinoam put her hand on the top of her son's head without replying, her eyes still on her father-in-law.

Grandfather broke off his announcement to lean down and grasp Jonathan's shoulders. "Your father, my boy, is the new king of Israel. You are a prince."

"A what?"

"The son of a king. God has honored the tribe of Benjamin with great honor. Israel's first king is from the House of Kish. Blessed be Jehovah."

Still celebrating, Grandmother took Jonathan's hands and swung him around in a circle. The four-year-old laughed, the lively movement more exciting than the idea of being a prince.

A few minutes later the gate burst open. Saul strode in, accompanied by a group of young men. Jedidah ran to greet him with kisses and hugs as tears of happiness ran down her cheeks.

"My son, the king," she repeated over and over. "My son, the king."

Kish welcomed the visitors and invited them to rest after their long walk. Jedidah rushed over to the kitchen to organize the servants to prepare a meal for the guests.

Startled by the noisy crowd, Malki-Shua began crying, and his mother retired to their bedroom. Jonathan watched the strangers from the safety of the doorway but, feeling shy, he followed her inside.

"Is it great to be a king?" Jonathan said.

Ahinoam sat down on a reed mat and began nursing the baby. "I suppose so." She sighed. "But a king must lead his people in battle. The Philistines are more powerful than the Israelites. Look what happened to Hophni and Phinehas."

Jonathan did not know who Hophni and Phinehas were, but he remembered the Philistine lookout he spotted a few weeks before. In the lamplight he saw a tear roll down her cheek. "Don't worry, Mother, I'll protect you from the Philistines." He patted her shoulder. "I won't let them hurt Father either."

"Oh, Jonathan, I hope not. I don't want you going to battle either."

"But God helped Gideon defeat the Midianites, didn't He?"

She brushed away the tear. "God is Israel's only protection. We must trust Him."

"Father can be God's king, and I'll be God's prince."

Jonathan sat down beside his mother, and she put her arm around him. Men's voices in the courtyard rose and fell as new arrivals joined the celebration.

"Everything will be all right," Mother finally said. "Let's unroll the sleeping mats and prepare for bed."

The visitors stayed for several weeks. Almost daily, someone stopped in with a gift for the new king. Jonathan watched as Jahra cooked pots and pots of lentil stew. Grandmother finally resorted to buying bread from Pilha's shop to feed all the guests.

Some mornings the visitors went hunting in the nearby hills, bringing back a deer or gazelle. If not so fortunate, partridges or doves had to do. Jonathan always looked forward to the meal those evenings, even if he had to eat in the family room with the women.

The heat of summer eased, and the people of Gibeah started harvesting grapes, then olives. The visitors helped Kish and Jonathan before leaving in groups of two and three, deciding to go home to their work also. Dark rain clouds gathered in the west. The servants pulled the yokes and plows out of the corner storeroom in preparation for planting time.

One evening when Saul sat alone in the courtyard, Jonathan sidled up to him. "Father, was being king the secret you found when you went looking for the donkeys?"

Saul smiled and pulled his son down beside him. "It was. Now God has made it known to everyone."

"When are you going to battle?"

"Not until God tells me." Saul hugged his firstborn. "We're God's Chosen People, but we learned from the battle at Aphek to only fight when God is with us."

Jonathan didn't want to admit he worried about the Philistines. Asking Grandfather, he had learned the sad fate of Hophni and Phinehas. He felt relieved when everyone got busy with the farm work and seemed to forget about the kingdom.

Months passed, and life went on as usual. Men came to consult Saul, but they did not stay. The latter rains came to an end and harvest began. Grape and olive harvest followed. The days of sun eventually gave way to the days of rain. Kish and Saul planted another crop.

One evening Grandfather invited Jonathan and Malki-Shua to sleep in his room, and they ran to ask permission from their father. Jonathan loved sleeping with his grandparents.

The sun shone and the other blankets were empty when Jonathan awoke. Jumping up, he straightened his tunic, and he ran outside to find Grandmother. He saw his father first.

"Come see your new brother," Saul called to him from the doorway of the family bedroom. Father went inside and returned with a bundle in his arms, which he lowered until Jonathan saw the face of a tiny baby. Wrapped as snug as a cocoon, the baby's arms and legs were bound by strips of cloth and they crossed his forehead and under his chin. "This is your new brother, Ish-Bosheth. You can call him Ishvi, if you want."

"Where'd he come from?"

"From God."

"Why is he wrapped up like that?"

"So that his arms and legs will grow straight."

"Is he a prince too? Like Malki-Shua and me?" Jonathan reached out to touch his soft cheek.

"You are all princes, but you have the special honor. You are my firstborn. Someday you will be king."

"When?"

"After I die."

Jonathan clutched his father's cloak. "I don't want you to die."

"Oh, it will be a long time from now—when I am very old, older than Grandfather, after you become a father and have a son of your own."

Jonathan couldn't imagine being that old. He quickly forgot the threat of death as he went to find Malki-Shua to show him their new brother.

Grandfather Ahimaaz and Grandmother Milcah came from Mizpah the next day to see the new grandbaby. Soon, more relatives arrived, crowding the courtyard. Jonathan felt like a stranger in his own home.

When Ishvi was a week old, the family males gathered in the family sitting room for the ceremony of circumcision. Neighbor men came to join the celebration. Children were excluded, so Jonathan went to play with Pharez and Gera. Following the festive meal, the visitors left. Sorry to see his Mizpah grandparents go, Jonathan was relieved things were back to normal.

"Jonathan, more and more you have Grandfather Ahimaaz's eyes," Mother said the next morning. He wasn't sure what that meant, but he determined when they came again, he would pay attention.

The two boys slept in their grandparent's room for another month, then moved back to the family bedroom next door. Mother kept busy with the new baby. Jonathan decided to take responsibility for Malki-Shua. He tried to teach the three-year-old how to play new games. He became very protective when they went outside the gate to join the neighbor boys in the street. Jonathan's friends did not seem to know he was a prince, so he decided not to tell them.

~

Shivering in the crisp evening air, Jonathan pulled his cloak closer and buried his arms in its folds. Malki-Shua had already gone to sleep, and, despite the cold, Jonathan hoped Mother didn't call him soon. He loved to sit with the men of the family, feeling grown up as he listened to adult talk.

Jonathan stared into the courtyard fire, captivated by the tongues of orange and blue flame that danced up and down. Like soldiers in battle. He let his imagination run. One flame leaped up, then died down and another took its place. The end of a stick protruded from the fire and he pushed it forward with his big toe, causing the tongues to blaze higher. What was it like to fight to save God's People from their enemies? He looked across the fiery battlefield to where Grandfather Kish and Father sat. They were preoccupied in conversation, their faces highlighted in the orange glow.

"Did you send a messenger to Gibeon?" the older man asked, turning to his son.

"They promised to come as soon as they finish harvesting wheat. I don't think they were very happy, but what choice do they have? I'm the king, and they are the servants of Israel."

The two men continued discussing the proposed addition to the house. The Gibeonites would build three upper rooms, giving Saul's family private quarters. The courtyard and three vacant lower rooms would be used for conducting kingdom business and entertaining guests.

The tongues of fire grew shorter. Now they were servants,

working hard every day instead of leaping high in victory. But tomorrow they would just be ashes. Jonathan was glad he was not a servant.

"Why are the Gibeonites our servants?" Jonathan said during a lull in the conversation. Boys should remain silent during an adult discussion, but his natural curiosity often got the best of him when no visitors were present to frown at his poor manners.

"The Gibeonites, my child, must pay for their deceit," Grandfather responded. "Israel must never forget their story."

At the word "story," the six-year-old jumped up and came around to sit beside the older man. Nothing could be better on a cool evening than listening to one of Grandfather's great stories of God. Jonathan still remembered the one about God calling Abraham to leave the far-away place called Ur to go to a Land God would give him. And all Israelites could repeat the account of Moses leading the Children of Israel through the Red Sea. His favorite, however, featured Joseph in Egypt, a man who stayed true to God when everyone did him wrong.

Jonathan snuggled next to Grandfather and felt a large warm arm slip around him. He looked up into the man's eyes, aglow with the reflection of the fire, and waited for Kish to begin.

"Long ago, during the days of Joshua, God told the Children of Israel to drive out all the nations from the Land He promised to give them."

"Why did they have to do that?"

"The Canaanites, Hittites, Amorites, and others are very wicked people." Grandfather explained they worshiped idols instead of the One True God, giving glory to lifeless stones for the wonderful care God provided. Worse yet, some offered their children as sacrifices on their altars. Men and women did wicked things together, calling it worship.

"One day shortly after the Children of Israel entered Canaan a group of men came to the Israelite camp down in Gilgal to talk to Joshua. They looked very bedraggled and tired. The sacks for their supplies were worn out, the wineskins cracked and mended, their sandals worn and patched. Their bread supply looked moldy and dry."

"They must've traveled a long way to see Joshua," Jonathan said.

"So it seemed." Grandfather nodded. "And so they told Joshua. 'We want to form a league with you,' they said. 'But maybe you live nearby,' Joshua replied, being a little suspicious. He remembered God had commanded the Israelites to drive out all the heathen tribes. 'We're your servants,' the men said. 'We come from far away. We heard how God helped you in Egypt and protected you when the kings east of the Jordan attacked you. When we left home our bread came warm from the oven. Now it's dry and moldy. Our wineskins were new; now they're cracked. Our clothes and sandals have worn out during our long journey.'"

The Israelites believed them and failed to inquire from God. They made a covenant with the men, promising to protect each other's lives, liberty, and property. Three days later they found out the men were Hivites from nearby Gibeon—men who should have been driven from the Land. But the Israelites were bound by the covenant they had made, unable to punish the Gibeonites.

"They lied," Jonathan said.

"Yes." Clearing his throat, Grandfather continued. "Joshua asked why they deceived him. 'Because we were afraid,' they said. Joshua told them they were under a curse. Now they would truly be Israel's servants, cutting wood and carrying water for the community and for the Tabernacle."

"Were they sorry?" Jonathan asked.

"No." Grandfather shook his head. "When the Amorites heard of the covenant, they were angry with the Gibeonites for getting special protection. The Amorites decided to attack them. The Gibeonites sent word to Joshua, 'Come save your servants.' So, our soldiers went to rescue them. God performed a miracle. He sent large hailstones against the enemy and made the day longer so they could finish the battle. To this day, the Gibeonites have been our servants."

Grandfather grew quiet. Somewhere in the hills beyond town a jackal howled. Jonathan stared into the glowing coals, where only now and then a wisp of flame stirred. Not only had the "soldiers" died out, even the "servants" seemed to have gone to sleep.

"Let Joshua's mistake be a lesson to you," Saul admonished his young son. "Never make a covenant with the enemy."

No one spoke for a moment.

"Jonathan, time for bed," Ahinoam called from the doorway, her dark form outlined by the lamplight in the bedroom.

"Thanks for the story. I'll always remember your lesson," Jonathan promised. Giving Grandfather, then Father, a quick hug, he ran off to bed.

~

Gatam stooped to deposit his armload of sickles on the ground beside Kish. The farmer sat in a patch of early morning sunlight in the middle of the courtyard, counting his coins. The clink of metal-against-metal alerted Jonathan and Malki-Shua, and they ran over to investigate.

"I think we need to buy a new sickle or two," the servant said. "Some are wearing pretty thin."

"I noticed them last wheat harvest. I don't know whether the Philistines will be more generous with their tool sales this year, or not."

Saul walked over from the storeroom to add two plowshares to the pile of implements. "If we don't keep trying, we may end up with nothing," he said.

"One, two, three." Kish touched each wooden handle as he began counting the sickles. "Four, five, six, seven, eight. Those are two-thirds of a shekel each. Three axes at a third of a shekel each. The two plowshares are also two-thirds apiece."

"And the mattock." Jonathan struggled to lift the heavy pick head. "How much is it?"

"Also, two-thirds." Kish reached out to relieve the six-year-old of his burden. "So how much does that make, Saul?"

"Over eight shekels. Did Pagiel bring the goads?"

"Not yet." Kish glanced over the inventory. "That leaves the knives."

Jahra came out of the kitchen with the cooking knives wrapped in a piece of old cloth. He handed them to Gatam, who shoved the tools into saddle bags. Pagiel soon appeared with the goad tips and two donkeys. When Gatam finished packing the bags, he tied them on the donkeys, along with camping gear.

Kish stood up and handed him the moneybag. "Here are twelve shekels for sharpening and twenty to buy a new sickle or two, if you can get them. Hurry home. Harvest will be ready in a week or two."

Gatam and Pagiel disappeared out the gate, and the other servants returned to their duties. Saul went into their bedroom and Malki-Shua ran after him.

"Why do they have to go to Philistia to sharpen the tools?" Jonathan said to his grandfather. "Can't we just sharpen them ourselves? Why ask help from the enemy?"

"I wish we could." Kish placed his hand on the boy's shoulder. "Unfortunately, Israelites don't know iron-working—and the Philistines intend to keep it that way. They're afraid if we learn how to make sickles, we will also learn how to make spears and swords."

Jonathan's eyes brightened. "Then we could drive them out of the Land."

"Their point exactly." Kish sighed. "So, every year we pay good money to keep ourselves powerless."

"Where did the Philistines learn to make iron?"

"Long ago and far away. Remember how Moses led the Children of Israel out of Egypt?" Jonathan nodded. "Well, the

Philistines also came from another land, called Caphtor—some island of the sea. Before that they lived in a northern country where people knew how to make iron."

Jonathan reached up and grasped Kish's hand, looking up at him. "Don't worry, Grandfather. If God could lead His People out of slavery, someday He'll help us learn to make tools and sharpen our own iron. Then we can have swords and spears to fight the enemy."

"I pray it will be so." Kish smiled down at his optimistic grandson. Oh, for the hope of a child.

Gatam and Pagiel followed the road north to Gibeon. Turning west, they descended the pass of the Upper and Lower Beth-Horons through the central mountain range to the foothills, or Shephelah. The Valley of Aijalon, a broad fertile plain, was one of the easier passages up to the central mountains—too easy to repel the Philistines. The Israelites called it Valley of Smiths, or *Ge-haha-rashim*, since it led to the metalsmiths.

The western entrance to the valley turned slightly northward. The town of Gezer sat above it on a ridge, high and isolated. Originally a Canaanite royal city and later conquered by the Egyptians, the Philistines now occupied the fortified town.

Since the road from Gibeon ran mainly downhill, the servants arrived before sunset. Following the path up the hillside, they passed through the city gate and crossed the marketplace. They turned into a narrow, shadowed lane. Gatam shuddered as he looked up at the thick city walls looming above them.

"I feel like a prisoner," he whispered to Pagiel.

They went straight to the shop of the smith they had previously patronized. They bargained with him over the price and left the tools for his sons to sharpen. Since they had once more given him their trade, the smith reluctantly agreed to sell them two new sickles.

The men found lodging in an inn where they had stayed before and tethered their pack animals for the night. They spent the next day browsing through the marketplace and wandering the streets. During their stroll up one street they came across a cave, above which stood a slightly curved row of standing stones, or *masseboth*.

"Is this the place where they worship their gods?" Pagiel said, shielding his eyes as he gazed up at the five-to-ten-feet-high objects.

"Maybe it's a memorial to the kings of Gezer?" Gatam replied. Wishing to remain inconspicuous, they didn't ask anyone.

Late that afternoon they returned to the shop to pick up their tools. Loading the donkeys at daybreak, they started the twenty-mile climb to Gibeah, glad to safely end their foray into Philistine territory.

5

SAVING JABESH GILEAD

Wiping the sweat from his brow, Alemeth looked across the field of barley stubble to the remainder of his unharvested patch of wheat. The stalks waved lazily in the afternoon breeze. "God has blessed us with a good crop," he said to his sons, Ulam and Rosh. "We should eat well this year."

Ulam wound a cord around the neck of a grain bag and tied it tightly.

"Let's load some sacks and take them into town before nightfall," the farmer said.

He grabbed a bulging bag and slung it up to the right side of a donkey while Rosh lifted a second one on the left. Ulam secured them to the animal with a rope and they loaded a second donkey. Ulam patted the first animal's rump and it set off at a slow gait.

"If you hurry, we can make another trip today," Alemeth called to the young men as they moved up the path. He wished they owned more donkeys, but as a poor farmer he had learned to work with what he had. Getting his grain home from the threshing floor would take several trips.

Alemeth brushed the chaff from his face as his vision focused on Jabesh Gilead. The center of town sat on a knoll two miles east of the Jordan River. Houses spilled down its gentle incline to the edge of the plain, where they refused to yield to the encroaching fields. Behind the town to the east, slopes rose steeply to the broken plateau of northern Gilead. Between the town and the plateau stood an isolated hill, its lower western side a sheer wall of rock ribs. Above the rocks the hillside gave way to a broad level shelf that encircled the hill. On the inner side of this recessed area, the stone walls of a fortification encompassed the flat hilltop.

Immediately south of the knoll and hill, the River Jabesh, a perennial stream, emerged from a gorge in the plateau and flowed down a shallow streambed across the valley plain. The upper city dominated the countryside. From its heights Alemeth had seen the pagan city of Beth-shan in the Valley of Jezreel to the northwest. Behind Beth-shan loomed the rounded top of Mount Tabor. As Alemeth began tying the mouth of another bag of wheat, he thanked God for the safe city in which he could raise his family.

Another farmer and his three sons arrived at the communal threshing floor with a load of sheaves. Alemeth greeted them before stretching out on a pile of straw to rest, glad he had already finished the job. "Here comes a caravan," he heard one of the boys say a short time later. He sat up to watch the column of men and pack donkeys coming up the valley.

"Merchants," the younger son commented before throwing another pitchfork of sheaves onto the stone floor.

Alemeth rose to take a closer look. "Looks to me like families. There are children with them." He frowned. Caravaners did not travel with their families. He paced back and forth beside a heap of straw. Something seemed wrong.

When the procession arrived a few minutes later, Alemeth learned the awful truth. Nahash, king of the Ammonites, had attacked their village to the east. They had set out for Jabesh, the capital of Gilead, to escape. The weary travelers plodded on to the city. Alemeth, growing more alarmed, did not resume his rest.

Watching Ulam and Rosh's rapid pace as they returned, Alemeth knew they had met the caravan and heard the bad news. The sons made another trip to the city before sunset halted movement. As they sat around a campfire that evening with the other farmer's family, guarding their harvest, a sense of foreboding filled Alemeth. How far west did Nahash intend to come? How soon would he reach Jabesh?

The men took turns at night watch and were relieved to see the sun crest the horizon. A few minutes later a trumpet blast from the fort alerted the citizens below of trouble. Messengers came to report the guards on the wall had seen a column of smoke rising above the plateau. Ulam and Rosh, like other farmers in the valley, hurried to transport more grain. Alemeth prayed for protection of his crop.

By noon more refugees were streaming in with reports of the awful atrocities Nahash's army had committed against those who resisted his forces. Carrying a handful of supplies, that night the residents of the lower city trooped to the fort to sleep. Before dawn they awoke to another sound of the warning trumpet.

Alemeth and his sons hurried to the fortress gate, following their neighbor Jether, a town elder and merchant. "I pray God gives you wisdom," the farmer said to the merchant, glad he wasn't responsible for decisions regarding safety.

At the fortress gate, they learned that during the night the Ammonites had surrounded their city. The harvest lay in enemy hands.

Dismayed, Alemeth tried to concentrate as he stood at the edge of the town meeting, struggling to hear the elders' discussion. As he worked his way closer to the elders, his thoughts kept going back to the past. Ammonite revenge. They would not go easy on the Israelites.

Many years before, the Ammonites had attacked the Israelites living in Gilead, then crossed the Jordan to invade the territories of Judah, Benjamin, and Ephraim. For eighteen years they ruled the area they conquered. The Israelites finally acknowledged their sins and destroyed the Baals and Ashtoreths they had been worshiping. God, in His mercy, forgave them and came to their assistance.

Having been rejected by his half-brothers and clansmen, a Gileadite named Jephthah had fled into exile in the land of Tob, where he collected a band of followers. The Israelites called for Jephthah to return and lead their army against the Ammonites. With God's help, they not only reclaimed their lost territory but captured twenty additional towns. Jephthah led Israel for six years and the Israelites had enjoyed relative safety since. Now Nahash came seeking redress of his people's loss.

Thrown into confusion, the people of Jabesh Gilead looked on as the elders huddled to consider their options. "What choice do we have?" Onam said. "Without our harvest, we can't survive."

"And Nahash has already captured other towns in Gilead," Jether added. "We can't expect help from them."

"Did you hear what he does to women and children if towns resist?" Joash said, wringing his hands.

Jether felt sympathy for the father of three beautiful adolescent daughters.

Hezron held up his hand for silence. "Let's make a treaty with Nahash. If he preserves our harvest and our lives, we will serve him. What else can we do?"

Agonizing over the decision, the men finally agreed. They announced the decision to the crowd, then sent a delegation out to meet the king. The suggestion of a treaty of submission seemed to suit Nahash. After all, an annual tribute from them would add to his wealth. Destroying the city, he would gain nothing. He made clear, however, that he planned to set the terms of submission.

"I will make a treaty with you, but only on one condition— that

I gouge out the right eye of every one of you, bringing disgrace on all Israel."

The men of Jabesh were speechless at the brash king's demand. They huddled together in a desperate conference. "To lose our right eyes is to kill us," Onam said, his voice hushed.

Everyone nodded, knowing that in battle a soldier held his shield in his left hand to protect his head and body. Peering from behind it with his right eye, he would wield his weapon with his right hand. To gouge out a man's right eye meant to leave him unable to use his shield, completely exposed and defenseless.

"What can we do?" Jether asked, his mind frantically searching for a glimmer of hope.

"Let's ask for seven days reprieve," Hezron said. "We can send messengers throughout Israel, asking for help. If no one comes to our aid, we will have to surrender."

When Nahash heard the offer, he smirked.

He thinks no Israelite from across the Jordan will come over here to defend our people, Jether realized. He knows they can't even muster enough soldiers to dislodge a Philistine lookout from their own hillside. Jether felt gnawing in the pit of his stomach.

Nahash smiled as he threw out his chest. "I accept your terms. I'll see you in seven days. Be sure to bring the keys to the fortress gates when you come."

As the dispirited elders trudged up the hill, Nahash's coarse laugh followed them.

That afternoon a band of young men left the safety of Jabesh to cross the Jordan and spread out across the Land. Jether prayed as he watched them go. The tribes had not cooperated in a planned attack on an enemy since the days of Eli, many decades ago. Was there hope for them now?

Saul looked at the western sky and smiled. Another day's end meant he could go home to a nice meal and his sleeping mat. He guided the donkey, its back-cradle piled high with bundles of wheat, to a spot beside the threshing floor and dumped the stalks. Behind him he could hear his father instruct the servants to unload the other donkeys as they came in and bring them home, leaving Gatam, Pagiel, and Ocran to guard the harvest during the night.

After Saul disconnected the yoke of oxen from the threshing pole, he and Kish started back to town with the team. Saul had just unyoked the oxen in the animal shelter when a piercing wail split the air. The men looked at each other with concern as the town seemed to erupt.

"What's wrong now?" Kish said. "Sounds like everyone is weeping."

"I suppose old Hodiah died. He's been sick a long time."

"That's not a death wail. Something worse. Let's hurry."

Saul carefully fastened the gate, not about to let the oxen or donkeys escape again at this busy time of year. Once inside the town, they met Ner and their neighbor Hamul.

"What's going on?" Kish said.

"Terrible news from Jabesh Gilead." Ner informed his brother and nephew of Nahash's attack.

"Gouge out their eyes! How can he disgrace the Israelites like that?" Saul's face flushed as his scowl deepened. "Where are those messengers? I want to talk to them."

A crowd gathered as the two messengers who had come to Gibeah repeated their story. A surge of holy rage filled the king. "The Ammonites can't get away with this," he said in a loud voice. "We will fight for you."

"We have very few men here in Gibeah," his uncle reminded him.

"Not men of Gibeah—or even men of Benjamin. No, every man in Israel." Saul spoke above the deafening wails. "Men, follow me to the animal shelter."

78

The younger men jogged to keep up with Saul's long strides; the older followed behind. At the pen the king pulled a short knife from the sheath fastened to his girdle belt. He stabbed the neck of one of the oxen, then a second. Dividing the animals into pieces, he distributed the meat to the Gibeathites as he mentally formulated his announcement. He thought of the men who earlier rejected him as king. Deciding to eliminate any excuse for noncooperation, he added the name of the respected Samuel to his decree.

"Take these pieces to the towns throughout Israel with this message: This is what will happen to the oxen of anyone who does not join Saul and Samuel in battle." Saul looked around to make sure they understood. "Tell the men to meet in Bezek in three days."

The Gibeathites divided the list of the twelve tribes and hurried off to inform them. The king sent his cousin Abner to Ramathaim with a special message to Samuel, asking him to join the men and officiate at a sacrifice before they started into battle. Kish offered the two messengers a place to stay for the night.

"Jabesh Gilead is the home of our ancestress," Kish said later as they shared lentil stew and bread. He told the story of the Levite and his concubine. Six-hundred men had survived the ensuing battle, and four hundred were given wives from Jabesh Gilead.

Saul listened again to the sad account he had heard in childhood. Now he had a chance to help them. His first military act as king—helping his own. He smiled across the bowl at the two Gileadites.

As Saul crossed the Plain of Shechem the second day, he recalled the morning he first saw it, the day preceding his anointing as king. Now he must lead God's Chosen People—and he had God's full backing. He sensed the Spirit of the Lord upon him as they took the road northeast from Shechem.

Saul paused in the road to shake a pebble from his sandal. He should have anticipated Nahash's attack. This was always the active time of year in their part of the world.

With the end of the rainy season, merchant caravans began moving up and down the great trade routes, their camels loaded with spices, silks, silver and gold. Farmers sharpened their sickles, preparing for harvest. Kings organized their armies and polished their weapons, ready to reclaim territory they lost in battle a few years before, or to expand their borders as a buffer against an enemy. Other rulers were content to raid the threshing floors of neighboring kingdoms, stealing the harvest to keep the people poor and undernourished—and powerless to create trouble. This time Nahash would not succeed, Saul vowed. He clenched his teeth in determination. God would fight for them.

Bezek lay on the high road from Shechem to Beth-shan, at the edge of the hills overlooking the Jordan River south of Mount Gilboa. Fourteen miles west of Jabesh Gilead, it sat along a *wadi*, with easy access to the river. Saul and his retinue were glad to reach the village by sunset.

The next day Samuel arrived, as well as 300,000 men from Israel and 30,000 men from populous Judah. Hearing the message from Saul, they had dropped everything and headed to Bezek, filled with the awe of God's fearful power.

The king surveyed the rag-tag band of men that milled about the field. They held an assortment of weapons. Some carried short bronze daggers. A few had managed to obtain rectangular leather-covered shields. Saul noticed an occasional bronze-headed spear, remnants of the Philistines' defeat at Mizpah nearly two decades before. Some farmers carried wooden clubs. Most of the men, however, relied on the bows and arrows they used in hunting. The quivers of the more fortunate ones held metal-tipped arrows.

"God is our defense," Samuel reminded the king as the two walked among the men, "but we still need to formulate a plan and organize the troops."

"Today we will consecrate ourselves for battle," Saul said. "Tomorrow morning you will offer the sacrifice, then we will divide the men and begin our march."

Following sunrise and the sacrifice by Samuel, Saul called the two messengers from Jabesh Gilead to his tent. "Go on home. Tell your leaders, 'By the time the sun is hot tomorrow, you'll be delivered from Nahash.' "

The men thanked the king for coming to their rescue and hurried off with the encouraging news. Saul spent the morning dividing the men into groups of fifties and hundreds, then appointing captains over each. At noon he sent them pouring down the gradual gradient of the *wadi* road through the hills.

Reaching the last hill, Saul and two scouts climbed it to get a good view of the rift through which the Jordan River flowed to the Dead Sea. At the southern end of the Sea of Kinnereth a broad, well-cultivated sunken valley, the *Ghor*, dropped off a few miles downstream to form a lower terrace, the *Zor*.

Saul recalled the night around the fire eight years before when he and his cousins hatched a plan to explore the Jordan River and its banks. He smiled, remembering his mother's protests. "You'll get killed by a lion, or drown, or fall and break a leg. Something bad is bound to happen in that God-forsaken jungle."

Kish overruled, and the boys left with blankets and packs of supplies tied on a donkey's back. When they came home unharmed, even Jedidah listened to their fascinating tale of the trip. *What a memory.* Saul watched the soldiers march down the *wadi*. If Mother believed that trip to be dangerous, she should see him now.

Saul glanced down at the serpentine river. Farther south, the ragged banks of the *Zor*, or Thicket, were a flood plain of jungle. Willow, poplar, and twisted tamarisk trees vied for a spot with the undergrowth of oleander, cane, shoulder-high thistles, tangled bushes, and creeping vines. Saul rubbed the spot where thistles once grabbed his arm. The stinging persisted long after he extracted all the spines he could find. The *Zor* served as a haven for wild animals, which he never mentioned in his mother's presence, and the young men had kept their bows and slings handy.

Except in spring flood stage, the river stretched about one hundred feet wide and three to ten feet deep. There were more fords below the hills of Ephraim than the Wilderness of Judah farther south, Saul remembered. The current of the northern section also flowed slower than in the south. As Saul made his way down the slope to rejoin the troops, he thanked God for the gathering site at Bezek and the ideal location for the river crossing.

The men reached the *Ghor* by late afternoon and advanced across it in the gathering shadows. Fording the river, their weapons held above their heads, they climbed the eastern bank and waited for the cover of darkness. Saul called his captains together and laid out his strategy for a three-pronged attack. The messengers had described Nahash's camp between the town and river, so the Israelites decided to advance from the north, west, and south during the fourth watch of the night. Scouts were back by midnight to confirm the earlier information.

The two messengers from Jabesh Gilead had reached home by mid-afternoon and slipped into the fort to report to their elders.

"Praise be to God for hearing our cry," Jether said as the townsmen listened to the good news. "Now we must inform Nahash."

Hezron glared at him, incredulous. "Inform the enemy of Saul's attack?"

"Certainly. We must tell him tomorrow we will surrender to him and he can do what he wishes with us."

"But—"

"You have no desire to surrender to a dead king?" Jether said with a chuckle.

"You're right," Onam said. A broad smile spread across his face. "With our 'good news,' Nahash will sleep well. A relaxed army is a defeated one."

During the last watch of the night, the men of Jabesh Gilead quietly assembled near the fortress gate with what weapons they could find, ready to pour down the hillside to assist the advancing army.

In the Israelite camp, Samuel offered a prayer, and Saul's men crept across the valley with only the stars for light. The soft barley stubble muffled their advance. As the sky began to lighten and the stars fade from view, Saul's younger cousin Abner blew a trumpet. The men charged the sleeping camp.

The startled Ammonites jumped from their blankets in panic and, seeing the massive Israelite army, ran for their lives, many forgetting their spears and daggers. Israelites grabbed the abandoned weapons and gave chase.

The beleaguered men of Jabesh Gilead swarmed out the gate to join them. Soon the dead and dying were strewn over the plain as Saul and his men pursued the invaders in all directions. The Ammonites became so scattered no two were left together to defend themselves. The boastful Nahash suffered a great defeat.

The Israelite army encamped late that afternoon outside Jabesh Gilead, where they joined the townspeople in celebrating God's miraculous victory. Walking through the troops with Samuel, Saul thanked them for their bravery and cooperation. In the din of flutes and lyres, songs and chants, he noticed several young men of Gibeah talking to their elders.

He walked up in time to hear Libni exclaim, "Where're the men who grumbled back in Mizpah, asking, 'Shall Saul rule over us?' Bring them out and let's put them to death."

Saul grasped Libni's shoulder so firmly he flinched. "This isn't a day to put to death the Israelites whom God has rescued," the king said. "Let's celebrate, not seek revenge."

Samuel stepped from behind the king. "Praise the Lord for your forgiveness and wisdom, Saul. God's People must be united, not split apart by jealousy and bickering. God has confirmed to all Israel through this victory that you are His choice for king." He turned to Hamul and Ner. "This would be a good time to reaffirm the kingship, wouldn't it? Why don't we go down to Gilgal tomorrow for another ceremony?"

Gilgal held special meaning for the Israelites. It served as the first camping site of the Children of Israel after they crossed the Jordan River on dry ground. The memorial pillar Joshua set up remained standing. Constructed from twelve stones taken from the dry riverbed, it stood not only as a witness to God's power to divide the water but also to forty years of miracles that brought them to the Promised Land. At Gilgal the Israelites celebrated their first Passover in their new Land. They also renewed the rite of circumcision, the symbol of God's everlasting covenant with Israel.

Samuel had a special reverence for the Gilgal camp that sat northeast of Jericho, six miles west of the river. He recalled its great history every time he made his circuit stop there.

Now it would hold new meaning.

Rising early before the weary soldiers stirred, Samuel stole out of camp and walked toward the river. With Saul's two-fold success in uniting the Israelites and defeating the Ammonites, the prophet realized his responsibility as judge over the people had ended. He would always be the spiritual leader, praying for the people and teaching them the way of God, but, in spite of his misgivings, the time had come to promote the kingdom. He must leave the outcome with the Eternal God. As he walked, he prayed until peace filled his heart.

The men were up when the prophet returned to camp, and the group soon started south. They could feel the decrease in elevation as the river valley dropped from the outlet of the Sea of Kinnereth to the inlet to the Dead Sea. The summer heat followed them on their thirty-seven-mile journey through the *Ghor*. Arriving the second evening, Samuel informed the people of Gilgal of the meeting the next day. They immediately began making preparations.

The following morning Samuel presided over the sacrifice of the fellowship offering and the celebration. As the afternoon sun began its descent, he climbed to the raised area near the altar and held up his hands. Conversations ceased. He took a deep breath before beginning the most difficult speech of his life.

"I've listened to everything you requested and have set a king over you," he reminded them. "Now you have a king to lead you. As for me, you can see I'm old and gray-headed. My sons are here with us," he added, recalling the reasons they had given for demanding a king.

He had wept many nights over his sons' disappointing behavior. He longed for assurance the accusations against them were never applied to his own character.

"I've been your leader from the time I was young," he said. "I stand before you, giving you an opportunity to testify against me in the presence of the Lord and the king He has anointed. Have I taken anyone's ox? or donkey?" He surveyed the massive audience and paused to let them speak. Several men shook their heads, but no one stepped forward. "Whom have I cheated? or oppressed?" he asked. "Have I accepted a bribe from anyone to make me close my eyes to justice? If I've done any of these, I'll make it right."

Throughout the questioning several had murmured their confidence in Samuel's innocence.

Standing near the front, Eliphaz of Bethel assured Samuel in a loud, clear voice. "You haven't cheated or oppressed anyone. Nor have you taken anything from our hands."

"The Lord is witness against you," Samuel said, "and also his anointed is witness, that you've not found anything in my hand which isn't mine."

"The Lord is witness," the men chorused.

A sense of relief washed over the prophet. His reputation stood, because he had behaved circumspectly his entire life.

Ever the teacher, the reassured Samuel felt God prompting him to take advantage of this one more opportunity. He began a brief lesson in Hebrew history, going back to their deliverance from slavery in Egypt—the foundation to becoming God's Chosen People. He went on to recall their disobedience, and the enemy attacks that followed. When the Children of Israel repented, however, God came to their rescue. When Nahash began moving against the people of Gilead, the prophet reminded them, they wanted a king. Now they had one.

"If you fear the Lord, serve and obey Him, and do not rebel against His commands, and follow your God, very good! But if you choose not to obey the Lord, but instead rebel against His commands, His hand will be against you, just as it was against your forefathers."

The men stirred in the afternoon heat, mindful of their past failings. Samuel raised his eyes to the cloudless sky. To show God's power, he declared, although it was only the time of wheat harvest, he would call on God to send thunder and rain—four months early. By this they would realize their wrong in demanding a king.

The people stood in awe as they watched the sky darken. Their faces registered terror when the unseasonable rain descended. "Pray to the Lord for us so we won't die," they begged. "We were wrong in asking for a king rather than depending on the One True God."

"Don't be afraid," Samuel said, his voice calm. "Even though you've done this, don't turn away from serving the Lord with all your hearts. Don't turn to useless idols that can't rescue you. He chose you for His very own. For the sake of His great name, God will not reject His People."

Samuel placed his hand over his heart. "I promise not to sin against the Lord by failing to pray for you. I will continue to teach you the way that is righteous. You must choose to serve Him faithfully with all your hearts, and always remember what great things He has done for you. But if you persist in doing evil, you and the king you wanted will be destroyed."

Pronouncing a blessing, Samuel dismissed the Congregation of Israel. As he watched the men go, the day seemed a strange benediction. Nearly twenty years before he had gathered the people at Mizpah to commit their lives to God. Peels of thunder had frightened the Philistines, who fled, the Israelites chasing them and winning a great and long-lasting victory. Today, instead, the Israelites trembled at the thunder. Was this a foreshadowing of things to come? Would the king they insisted on having today someday face defeat at the hands of the very army from whom God once delivered them?

As the setting sun painted the hills across the river with hues of pink and mauve, Samuel bowed his head. "Lord, help me to be faithful, whatever others do. Guide me to those whose hearts are eager to serve You. Make my ministry fruitful until the day I die."

While the other tribesmen took the nearest roads back to their homes, early the next morning the men of Benjamin and Ephraim followed the *Wadi* Suweinit, the Valley of the Little Thorn Tree, from Gilgal through the gorge of Michmash to the central mountain range. Saul rejoiced in their victory over Nahash, and he thought of Joshua and his men following the same streambed up to Bethel more than three hundred years before. Now he had the task Joshua left unfinished. There were still pagan nations left unconquered in the Land. Would he finally succeed? He looked over at the prophet Samuel, gray-haired but sure footed on the gravel road. With God's help, and Samuel's, he would do his best.

Twelve miles up the pass the men of Michmash and Geba dropped out, and a little later the men of Bethel turned up the northern road. Samuel went with them on his way to Ramathaim.

Catching sight of the height of Gibeah rising above the intervening hills to the south, Saul's heart quickened with thoughts of home. His family awaited him—and so did the wheat harvest. And inquisitive Jonathan. Saul smiled.

Hearing cheers in the street outside, before he reached the gate Jonathan knew the warriors had returned victorious. He dashed over to open the gate, then waited impatiently for his father's arrival. Ner, Tarea, Abner, and Saul came up the street, talking and laughing. Jonathan feared his father wouldn't notice him, but he was wrong. Saul reached down and, lifting him up, carried him into the courtyard, where Kish and the women stood waiting.

That evening, when they were finally alone, Jonathan begged his father to tell him about the battle. "God helped you, just like He did Gideon," the boy said, his eyes wide with wonder, as Saul concluded.

"Our God is the God of Abraham, Isaac, and Jacob," the king reminded him. "We are His Chosen People."

"And I choose Him, like He chose us." Jonathan felt a warm sensation, like a burst of sunshine, spread through him. "I want to be His prince when I grow up."

"You will be, my son." Saul hugged him close. "His prince and my Big soldier. I'm counting on your help with the kingdom."

6

LORDS OF THE PHILISTINES

Achish had never seen his father so upset.

"Nahash is defeated," Maoch declared, his voice rising. "Did you hear? Defeated at the hands of Saul, king of Israel." The lord of Gath stopped pacing and whirled around to glare at the four other Philistine lords. "What have our mountain lookouts been doing?" he demanded. "Juggling pomegranates and playing knucklebones? We not only didn't know Israel had a king, the lookout at Gibeah hadn't a clue the king lived right under their noses. Now what do we do?"

The lord of Ekron averted his eyes from Maoch's probing gaze. His nephew had recently been stationed at Gibeah. No one spoke for a moment, the tension palpable.

"Perhaps we should confer with our allies to the north," the lord of Ashdod, host of the conference, suggested in a calmer voice. "We must cooperate to defeat Israel. After all, the Ammonites weren't our only hope. We Sea People have always stuck together."

Standing near the wall, Achish saw the lords of Ashkelon and

Gaza nod in agreement. His father's face relaxed a bit. Yes, the Sea People. They might be scattered now, but they were all blessed by their gods. Achish smiled.

The lord of Ashdod walked over and, placing his hand on Maoch's shoulder, drew him back toward the others. The movement eased the pressure, and the rulers began their discussion.

Unused to listening in on stressful war councils, Achish suddenly felt the need of fresh air. He slipped out into the open courtyard, spied a staircase, and climbed to the roof. The young prince slowly turned, surveying the ancient town. Beyond the housetops of Ashdod, he could see sand dunes to the west. Behind them lay the Great Sea—the Philistines' former water route to success. Closing his eyes, he inhaled the sea breeze as he recalled his people's proud heritage.

Gath sat on the edge of the limestone foothills that served as a buffer zone between Philistia and the Israelite hill country of Judah. The lofty fortress guarded the entrance to the Valley of Elah. As the sun went down and the watchman closed the town gates for the night, Grandfather Abimelech used to gather Achish and his cousins around him in the courtyard and tell them stories of the Sea People.

Long ago, the family patriarch had said, brave men and their families migrated from a faraway place called the Aegean region to Anatolia and the Great Sea islands of Caphtor and Cyprus. Still listening with one ear, Achish looked up at the streaks of sunset in the western sky and dreamed of boarding a merchant ship in the port of Ashkelon. His goal—the islands of the sea.

Achish never tired of listening to his grandfather's endless stories. He told how the enterprising Sea People loaded ships full of merchandise and established trade with the powerful nations of Syria and Egypt. Pride welled up in Achish's chest when he learned his ancestors soon became strong enough to invade the two kingdoms. Abimelech so vividly described the two-hundred-year-old sea battles with the Egyptians that the boys were sure he had participated in them. The Philistines had always been great warriors. Pharaoh Ramses III repelled their advance against Egypt, but he eventually conscripted their heroic soldiers into his army and allowed their families to occupy the coastal area he controlled along the eastern end of the Great Sea.

Ramses assigned the Philistine division of the Sea People the territory just above Egypt, west of the Negev and south of the city of Gaza. The Anakim, giant cousins of the Canaanites, ruled Gaza and the cities north of it. "The Pharaoh probably thought the giants would overpower us," Grandfather had said with a chuckle. "We certainly proved him wrong. More and more Philistines arrived, and we finally gained enough military strength to become the ruling class in the five Canaanite city-kingdoms." When they had gained control, the Philistine lords had formed a league, creating a strong central authority.

When Achish and his boyhood friends tired of their games, they used to make the rounds of Gath's craftsmen, watching them work. To the prince, the most fascinating were the metalsmiths. As they forged long broad-swords and triangular daggers from red hot iron, the prince realized why the Philistines were so powerful. Even in the new land they were able to use the Aegean technology of iron-smelting they brought with them from Caphtor—knowledge none of the Hebrews or other nearby nations possessed.

One evening Achish had asked his grandfather why the Israelites caused them so much trouble. Abimelech said the invading Israelites had tried to conquer the coastal portion of Canaan, which they claimed their god gave them. They failed. This encouraged the Philistines, who later felt squeezed in their small territory. When they saw the Hebrews were weak, they began pushing beyond the foothills into Judah. They were able to capture Gerar, Jabneel, and Sharuhen. Over the years, control of the cities along the edge of the Shephelah seesawed back and forth between the Philistines and the Israelites. Gath also lay along the edge, and the young prince very well knew the danger.

Thoughts of danger reminded Achish why he had come to Ashdod. Walking over to the western parapet, he sat down on the rooftop and let the breeze play over his face as he contemplated the Philistines' present situation. Downstairs, his father and the other lords were reevaluating their strategy for achieving their long-held dream of conquering Israel. They had mentioned cooperation with other Sea People as their best hope.

Achish's acquaintances did not include any of the Tjekker, who had settled north of Philistia between Joppa and Tyre. Nor had he met the Sea People who pushed into the Valley of Jezreel, taking over Beth-shan. But he did know that by working together the three groups had been able to gain control of the trade routes from Damascus and Gilead to Egypt.

Achish could understand the Hebrews' unhappiness. Besides loss of revenue from the merchant caravans, the Sea People threatened to separate their tribes north of the Valley of Jezreel from those to the south. Maoch had secretly discussed with his son the Philistines' plans to someday launch an attack through the Valley of Aijalon, pressing up past Beth Horon, Gibeon, and Michmash down to the Jordan River. This would separate the Israelites' central tribes from those of Simeon and Judah in the south.

With the loss of Nahash, their ally east of the Jordan, the Philistines could no longer count on a simple strategy of encircling Israel, dividing it, and strangling it to death. News of Israel's defeat of the Ammonites at Jabesh Gilead had, indeed, complicated their plan, but Achish remained encouraged. He recalled Grandfather's many tales of triumph, such as when their soldiers captured the troublesome Israelite strongman, Samson, and bound him.

Their gods were more powerful than the Israelites' invisible god. The prince turned to reverently admire the lovely temple of Dagon, which stood on the high place of Ashdod. The Philistine patriarchs had brought their religion with them from Caphtor, but no one could remember it now. Once in Canaan, they adapted theirs to the local gods Dagon, Ashtoreth, and Baal-Zebub. Achish knew central worship at the temple had helped unite and strengthen the confederacy. Dagon was a mighty god. To the Canaanites, their gods' power existed only in their territories, but the Philistines' gods had power beyond their borders. In any war, the nation whose god proved strongest and most willing to help won.

Abimelech's favorite story highlighted the day he helped capture the sacred box of the Israelites' god and destroy their flimsy temple in Shiloh. The box proved a problem for the Philistines, and they sent it home with a gift of appeasement. Their military victory at Aphek had, however, already assured them the Israelite god did not have greater power than Dagon. The recent news from Gilead did sound disturbing, but Achish knew the Philistines had no intention of letting the new Israelite king create a strong nation. Not with Dagon on their side.

Taking one last look at the temple, the prince descended the steps two at a time. He entered the meeting room in time to hear the lords summarize their new strategy.

If refusing to sell the Israelites iron weapons did not prevent them from winning battles, the rulers determined, they must at least disarm the enemy of any swords, spears, and daggers they captured during the battle in Gilead. From now on, whenever Philistine patrols stationed at lookouts throughout the central mountain range met Israelites, they would confiscate any metal weapons they carried. They would also search unwalled villages and towns. The Israelites must be stopped!

Maoch and Achish left for home the next morning full of hope. Defeating the Israelites might take a little longer than originally planned, but the powerful Philistines would prevail. Dagon would fight for them. Achish felt a surge of confidence as they started across the plain.

It also helped to know they had a family of loyal giants living right in Gath. The previous week, Achish had measured himself, back-to-back, against Goliath. The ten-year-old stood as tall as he.

7

HARVEST TIME

With wheat harvest finished, two dozen Gibeonites arrived in Gibeah to begin constructing the addition to Kish's house. The second story rooms were to be added to the long side of the courtyard, opposite the front gate. The men first made sun-dried bricks in the valley below town, then brought them to the courtyard. From the safety of their bedroom doorway, Jonathan and Malki-Shua watched the workers carry loads of bricks up the staircase. When others began mixing water and marly clay into mortar, they crept closer for a better look.

The Gibeonite men carried waterpots from the village spring, a task usually reserved for women or kitchen servants. One morning Jonathan witnessed a pot splash over the side, drenching a man's shoulder and back. No wonder they didn't want to come work on the house. But that was part of their punishment for deceiving Joshua, Jonathan thought, recalling Grandfather's bedtime story beside the courtyard fire.

When the days of sun grew hot, Jonathan felt sorry for the men. Slowly the walls rose above the parapet. Woodcutters brought ceiling poles and eventually the roof completed the new rooms.

Grape harvest took Jonathan's mind off the construction for a few weeks. By the month of Elul at the end of summer the Gibeonites announced they were finished constructing the new addition. The young prince trooped upstairs behind his father and Grandfather Kish to inspect his new home.

The addition had a door at the entrance to the family living room. A passageway down the courtyard side passed through the open middle room to the family bedroom, which also had a door.

Walking through the empty rooms, the pungent smell of plaster still strong, Jonathan decided he liked the new arrangement. None of his playmates lived on a second story, so he had something to tell them about. Following Father down the stairs, Jonathan heard him say, "I think we should call Samuel to dedicate our new home. He could come celebrate the Feast of Tabernacles with us here in Gibeah."

The annual fall Feast of Tabernacles, or Feast of Ingathering, celebrated God's goodness to His Chosen People. Thanksgiving for an abundant harvest came from grateful hearts.

"It would be an honor to have the prophet as our guest," Kish said. "The whole town would turn out to celebrate. In fact, we could invite the people of Mizpah, Gibeon, Michmash, and Geba. It would be like the old days when the Tabernacle stood in Shiloh."

As time for the celebration drew near, Jonathan and Malki-Shua watched Gatam and Pagiel build the festival shelters in the courtyard, staking out the four corners by driving poles into the ground. Ocran and Laban brought armloads of branches and vines from the hillsides, which they wove into roofing mats.

Jonathan went to observe Pharez's father and brothers make a simple A-frame for their rooftop. They had no courtyard. Gera's family also planned to celebrate on their roof.

Grandfather's prediction turned out to be correct. By the time Samuel arrived, the citizens of Gibeah were prepared. Pilgrims from other towns had come early to build shelters in the valley below town.

Grandfather explained the week-long festival to Jonathan. The Feast of Tabernacles commemorated the Children of Israel's journey from Egypt to the Promised Land, when they lived in tents and temporary booths for forty years. According to God's instruction to Moses, men, women, and children were to carry palm fronds, fruit, leafy branches and poplars. During the ceremony they were to wave them before the Lord as they rejoiced for the year's good harvest.

Grandfather Ahimaaz and Grandmother Milcah arrived from Mizpah the day before the feast began, along with uncles, aunts, and cousins. Jonathan and his brothers ran to greet them and receive their hugs and kisses. They didn't see these relatives often and, when asked, delighted in demonstrating their many games and activities.

Mother occasionally told Jonathan he had Grandfather Ahimaaz's eyes. He wasn't sure what that meant. After they arrived, he studied the older man's face carefully. The only thing he noticed was when Grandfather's mouth smiled his eyes seemed to sparkle in agreement.

The first day of the Feast, the fifteenth of the seventh month, Samuel called a sacred assembly. With work forbidden that day, everyone went to the hilltop for the sacrifices. Jonathan ran out into the street in search of Gera and Pharez, the leafy branch his father had given him hoisted as high as he could reach. The boys chattered excitedly as they waited for their families.

By the time Kish and Ahimaaz's families reached the hilltop, the crowd had grown dense. Saul lifted his three sons up, one at a time, to catch a glimpse of Samuel and the sacrifice. When the prophet finished, he exhorted the people to obey God. Jonathan could not hear much being said, but it did not matter. He knew he pleased God by waving his branch as high as he could. When individuals began bringing sin offerings and thank offerings to present to the Lord, Ahinoam took her sons home.

That night Jonathan and his family slept in one of the courtyard shelters, looking up through the leafy roof at the stars and full moon overhead. The next morning Jonathan, Pharez, and Gera met in the street to compare experiences. The morning sacrifices continued, even though work could be performed until the twenty-second, the great closing day of the Feast. Jonathan did not go up the hill again.

The morning of the twenty-third Kish took his thank offering to the altar, accompanied by male family members. Afterward Samuel came to ask God's blessing on the new addition. Jonathan listened closely to the prophet's prayer. He had never seen Samuel before that week, and he was fascinated by his long graying hair and beard.

Jonathan looked up at Samuel with reverential awe. This was the man who spoke for God, and he was praying for their house. They had the most special house in town. After enjoying the celebration meal, the Mizpah relatives left for home.

As night settled over Gibeah, Jonathan lay on his mat staring up at the new rafters. Today Samuel had blessed this very room; tonight, the great prophet slept in the family's old room downstairs. In the quietness, the six-year-old sensed God's presence very near. Recalling his own past sins, he promised God he would be a better boy, obeying Father every time, coming when Mother first called, sharing with Malki-Shua, and looking after Baby Ishvi without complaining. He closed his eyes tightly. What would it be like to be a prophet of God? Being a prince would have to do, he decided, as he drifted off to sleep.

Jonathan awoke one morning six months later to the sound of voices calling back and forth across the courtyard. *Barley harvest.*

He scrambled up from his sleeping mat. Grandfather had promised he could help this year. He ran down to the courtyard, still gray with early morning shadows.

Father and the servants were already walking toward the gate. Pagiel carried a handful of sickles. Gatam, Ocran, and two hired field-hands followed, carrying back cradles for the donkeys. Prepared for a hot day in the field, each had a waterbag slung over his shoulder.

Jonathan ran to his grandfather. "Are we ready to go?"

Kish stopped and looked down at the seven-year-old. "I thought my little sleepyhead would miss this," he teased. "Does your mother know you are going with us?"

"I'll go tell her," Jonathan called over his shoulder as he darted to the kitchen. Back in a flash, he caught hold of Grandfather's large, rough hand. "Let's go."

By the time they reached the animal pen, Gatam, Ocran, and the field-hands had harnessed four donkeys and tied the wooden cradles to their backs. The crew set off.

Other farmers and their sons were on their way to work, and the men greeted each other as they made their way to the valley. The sun rose over the hills to the east, bathing the barley fields in a rich gold. Kish and Jonathan stopped at the threshing floor to wait. The other men headed for the family's parcel of land.

Pagiel distributed the sickles to the other servants, and they spread out across the field. Saul grasped the wooden handle of a sickle as he ran his fingers along the crescent-shaped shaft and studied the edge. Satisfied the Philistine metalsmith had done a good job sharpening it, he grabbed a handful of stalks and brought the blade down against them, slicing through the dry stems. Transferring the loose cuttings to his left arm, he grabbed another handful. When his bundle seemed thick enough, he tied it with a few strands of straw and stood it upright in the stubble. After the tenth bundle, he walked back to where Gatam stood with the donkeys.

The harvesters worked their way south. Sheaves soon dotted the cleared area. Saul and Gatam and two others came behind with the donkeys, stacking the bundles into the back cradles. After tying the loads with ropes, they started toward the community threshing floor.

As they brought the first load up the hill, Saul saw Jonathan jump up and down, then run to meet him. The men unloaded the sheaves onto the spot of ground Kish had chosen for their harvest pile.

Jonathan rejoiced when Father arrived with another load, and they stopped for breakfast. Out in the country, under the bright sun, covered with flecks of chaff, the smell of straw and animal flesh permeating the air, the boy declared it to be the best breakfast he had ever eaten.

"It's great to be a farmer." He tossed a few raisins into his mouth. "We're helping God care for His crop."

The two adults exchanged smiles. "God wouldn't have much of a crop if it weren't for our hard work," Saul said, before taking a bite of bread.

Jonathan looked up at the Philistine lookout occupying the far end of the hill. "We don't have to trust in pagan idols to make our crops grow, do we?"

"The One True God blesses His creation and those who obey Him," Kish said.

"It's too bad the Philistines don't know that." The boy absently moved strands of loose straw back and forth with his bare feet. "They'd stop bothering the Israelites if they did."

No one spoke as the men pondered the idea. Finally, Saul rose to go.

Grandmother Jedidah appeared at noon with additional food

and water. The weary Jonathan followed her home and needed no coaxing to join Malki-Shua for a nap. That evening they returned to the floor, along with Jahra, carrying fresh bread and a vegetable and goat stew. The men gathered around and devoured the delicious meal.

Jonathan soon tired of the daily trips to the field and contented himself with playing with Malki-Shua and teaching Ishvi to walk.

A few mornings later, Jonathan jumped up from his sleeping mat, not about to miss the last day of harvest. Today threshing began. As he ran out the family room door, he saw Gatam disappear down the entryway, a roll of grain bags on his shoulder. Grandfather came out of his bedroom, and they called goodbye to Grandmother on their way out the gate.

By the time they reach the animal shelter, two of the servants had the team of oxen yoked. Since Saul had sacrificed the other pair the previous year to call the men of Israel to battle against the Ammonites, the one team would have to do all the treading again this harvest.

Kish and Jonathan led the team of oxen to the threshing floor.

The thirty-foot-diameter floor had been hewn from the rocky hillside, the stones plastered in spots with clay to make it smooth. A vertical pole stood in the center with a second pole stretching out horizontally from it. Kish fastened it to the oxen's yoke as the animals stood patiently waiting.

The two servants scooped pitchforks of sheaves from Kish's harvest stack onto the hard threshing floor and spread them out. The oxen began circling, their hooves breaking the straw and loosening the heads of grain as they made their endless journey, round and round.

Jonathan followed Kish and the team, shouting words of encouragement and occasionally tapping the animals with a short stick. Soon Saul and Gatam brought more bundles from the field.

Growing tired, Jonathan frequently took brief rests on the short wall that protected the floor. After a while Kish halted the animals and the servants swept the grain and straw to the side. They added more sheaves. Kish picked up his stick and tapped the oxen, who stood munching the stalks in front of them. The crunching sound of straw being trampled sounded again as the threshing resumed.

By late afternoon, Saul and the servants brought in the final load of barley sheaves, rejoicing the harvest was safe from locust, wildfires, or unattended hungry livestock.

That evening the western breeze came up. When the men had finished eating, they swept the pile of straw and grain to the east side of the floor. Gatam and Pagiel grabbed the thick wooden five-pronged winnowing forks and began tossing the mixture into the air. As the straw blew away across the wall, the heavier loose grain and smaller chaff fell to the floor. With the straw eliminated, other men scooped up the grain and chaff mixture in winnowing shovels and tossed it until only the grain remained on the floor. Saul and Ocran swept it into a heap at the edge of the circle.

After several minutes, Kish and Saul returned to town with Grandmother and Jonathan, leaving behind four of the servants to finish winnowing that days' threshing and to guard the harvest.

The next morning when the men returned to their threshing, Uncle Ner's wife and two daughters joined Grandmother at the pile of grain. With large sieves, the women began the task of sifting yesterday's harvest to remove the unwanted particles—small stones, pieces of clay from the floor, straw, and dirt. They occasionally tossed the grain into the air and blew away the chaff that swirled up. Then they picked out the grains of darnel, now black instead of yellow.

When finally satisfied only barley remained, they dumped it into a grain bag. At the end of the day, it would be taken to the house. After harvest, what remained unsold would be stored in large clay jars in a windowless room.

Jonathan didn't go back to watch the threshing, or the sifting. He decided he would wait until he grew up before trying to be a farmer.

Wheat harvesttime a month later didn't hold much interest for him.

Fruit harvest rounded out the agricultural year—grapes, then figs, ending with olives. People claimed grape harvest to be their favorite—not the work, but the festive atmosphere.

One summer afternoon the gate opened, and Saul came down the passageway, followed by Gatam leading a donkey. The deep baskets tied to both its sides were heaped with grapes. The men carried them to the rooftop and dumped them on the drying mats Grandmother had laid out. Jonathan scurried up to watch. When the men were gone, Grandmother came up to spread the plump purple grapes out to dry. Jonathan knelt to help her. A few days later the men brought another load.

Jonathan went upstairs every afternoon to check the progress as the grapes shriveled into raisins. Sometimes he helped Grandmother turn them or watched as she sprinkled them with oil to keep them soft. When they were just right, she pressed some into raisin cakes; the rest she stored loose in clay containers.

As harvest progressed, Jonathan heard the sound of voices and rattle of clay jugs one morning. He ran down in time to see Grandmother on her way to the winepress, following a cartload of empty vessels. Jonathan begged to go along.

In the vineyard Kish and Ner's young relatives took turns in the winepress treading out the juice from their load of grapes. Singing, clapping, and shouts of encouragement accompanied the boisterous treading as onlookers joined the celebration. Jonathan skipped along the edge of the group, dancing and clapping. Good natured ribbing rewarded anyone who slid or stumbled in the slippery juice and skins.

Jonathan wriggled his way through the onlookers to watch the juice flow out the hole in the press floor as Saul and Abner took turns pulling full jugs away and replacing them with empty ones. When finished, Saul guided the loaded cart back to the house. The servants carried the jugs into the kitchen storeroom. Grandmother gave Jonathan a sample of the purple juice.

He smacked his lips. "Thanks for the treat."

The family enjoyed the fresh juice for several days. Mother also boiled the juice until it became a thick syrup, called *dibs,* for use in cooking or baking sweet treats. After the remaining juice aged forty days, Grandmother and Mother would make it into sweet wine for drinks. Wine served also as a disinfectant to clean wounds or sores.

After their grapes were cared for, Ahinoam took the boys to the winepress to watch the treading one morning. The experienced Jonathan grabbed Malki-Shua's hand and pulled him through the crowd to the winepress. Malki-Shua clapped and jumped up and down, deliberately falling down from time to time as he mimicked the boys in the press. Other children laughed at his antics.

Another treader fell and a howl of delight filled the air. The sudden noise frightened Ishvi, who began crying. Ahinoam put his hands together and clapped them as she swayed back and forth. Soon the baby's cries turned to giggles.

"I'm going to be a vine dresser when I grow up," Malki-Shua announced when they started down the path to town.

"You'll get awful hungry if you don't plant any barley and wheat," Jonathan said.

"You'll get hungrier than me if all you do is fight the Philistines," the four-year-old countered.

"Now, boys, don't argue." Ahinoam shifted Ishvi to her right hip. "You'll probably end up doing all three." *Unfortunately,* she feared.

Fig harvest a few weeks later went much like grape harvest. The women dried the fruit and pressed them into cakes.

Olives came last, the final harvest of the year. Everyone knew which trees in the communal grove belonged to whom. Grandmother and Mother spread a large cloth under one of their trees, and the men took turns beating the loaded branches to loosen the olives. Watching, Jonathan recalled the morning Grandfather had taken him to the wheat field when Father went searching for the lost donkeys.

When the men paused to rest, the women scooped up the fallen olives and collected baskets full to take home and preserve in salt water. Later, they made a fine breakfast with bread.

The men took the remainder to the olive press, where they poured them into the large hollowed-out stone saucer. The men took turns pushing the pole attached to an upright stone wheel around the circle to crush the olives to extract the oil. They brought the filled jugs home to the kitchen storeroom.

Everyone appreciated the valuable liquid. Women used it in cooking, medicine, and making soap, to fill lamps, and to rub on the skin and hair. An abundant olive harvest insured lamplight through every night of the year. Pity the families who slept in the dark, their oil supply shrinking and them too poor to buy more.

The Feast of Tabernacles at the close of harvest season celebrated God's goodness to His Chosen People. Jonathan recalled the various crops he had helped bring home that year. His family was really blessed to have a God Who cared about them.

8

SAMUEL'S VISIT

Jonathan peered over the top of the parapet. The courtyard below appeared empty. Cocking his ear, he listened for several moments. No one stirred, not even the servants. He squeezed the ball in his right hand. No guests today. It was safe to go down. Father gave strict orders about the children remaining upstairs when he had official guests or business. Disobeying once had taught Jonathan the seriousness of the offense.

"Come," the nine-year-old called across the rooftop to his brothers, who were building the walls of a miniature house with sticks. "No one's in the courtyard. Let's go play ball."

The three scampered down the steps into the rectangle of afternoon sunshine and began tossing the ball back and forth. Grandmother Jedidah had made the ball for them, padding the wood center with sheep's wool and sewing it into a casing made of strips of cowhide. With the days' work completed, the boys often enjoyed many hours playing catch or in other activities they dreamed up.

The game progressed quietly, a dull thud and groan marking the occasionally missed ball, a low laugh proclaiming triumph in a difficult catch. When Jonathan grew tired of the repetitive motion and slow pace of the game, he had a bright idea.

Drawing back his right arm, he slung the ball at Malki-Shua, half-way down the courtyard. Jonathan's eyes, however, were on three-year-old Ishvi, so the ball caught his oldest brother unprepared as it whizzed by. Jonathan laughed at his success in throwing Malki-Shua off guard.

"You were good, Jonathan," Ishvi called to his hero as he clapped his hands. "You tricked him."

"Not fair," Malki-Shua shouted over his shoulder. By the way he ran to retrieve the ball from the kitchen corner, Jonathan could guess his plot of revenge. "Now it's my turn."

Malki-Shua turned to sling the ball at Jonathan but, instead, his mouth fell open and his arm dropped to his side. He backed up against the kitchen wall and stared past his brothers. Ishvi's gaze followed his, and he ran to stand beside Malki-Shua. Both boys lowered their heads.

"What's wrong?" Jonathan said, puzzled by the halt in the game. He turned to see what they were staring at, and his heart skipped a beat. There, twenty feet behind him, stood the prophet Samuel. Jonathan's head dropped and his cheeks burned as he hurried to join his brothers.

Jonathan heard the prophet walking across the courtyard to them, and he felt his throat tighten. All too soon he saw the worn sandals stop a few feet in front of him. He waited for the scolding. When Samuel did not speak, he swallowed the lump in his throat and stammered out an apology.

"I . . . I'm sorry we disturbed your rest, sir. We aren't allowed in the courtyard when Father has guests, but we didn't know you were here. We were just having—"

"Fun," the man of God said. Jonathan nodded without looking up, then he felt an arm slip around his shoulders. "It is true, I had been resting," Samuel admitted. "But when I heard you boys playing so happily, I recalled my own childhood. I thought, 'Perhaps these boys would like to hear a story about a boy and how God called him for a special job.' "

Jonathan's head shot up and his eyes widened with delight. "Really?"

"We love stories," Malki-Shua said.

"So, where shall we sit?" The prophet looked around the enclosed courtyard.

"I'll bring you a cushion," Jonathan volunteered.

"There's a sitting mat." Samuel pointed to the opposite corner. "Let's use it." The gray-bearded man led the way to the mat, where he sat down, cross-legged. The boys gathered around him. He cleared his throat as he surveyed their faces.

"Many years ago," Samuel began, "a man named Elkanah lived in the hill country of Ephraim. He had two wives who made him very happy. Peninnah had many children. Elkanah loved them very much and taught them the way of God. The other wife, Hannah, had no children. She felt sad as she watched Peninnah and her children do things together. 'Why hasn't God blessed me with children?' she wondered."

Jonathan nodded, thinking of Grandfather Kish, who once told him of the days when he had no children. He had prayed and God gave him a son, whom he named Saul; *Shaul* meant "the asked for." But Jonathan called him Father. He smiled as he returned his attention to the story.

"Every year Elkanah took his family to Shiloh to celebrate the Feast of Tabernacles," Samuel continued. "When he sacrificed his animal in worship to God, he divided his portion of the meat among his wives and children and himself. But he always gave Hannah a double portion, because he loved her and knew how sad she felt being childless."

As Samuel had watched the three silent princes pressed against the wall minutes before, the phrase, "Like a row of pigeons perched on a parapet," flashed through his mind. Now as they sat gathered around him in a semi-circle, their eyes riveted on him, their mouths slightly open, they reminded him of baby birds waiting in the nest for another morsel of food. He smiled at the descriptive comparisons.

"It wasn't enough for Peninnah to have all the children, however," Samuel said. "Because she grew jealous that Elkanah loved Hannah, she taunted her. Hannah would get upset and start weeping, then she couldn't even eat." Samuel saw Jonathan frown in sympathy and immediately felt a special bond with the young prince. "Elkanah felt sorry for his wife. 'Hannah, why are you crying?' he would ask. 'Why don't you eat with us? Am I not better to you than ten sons?'"

"One time after they finished eating in Shiloh, Hannah went to the Tabernacle to pray. Tears ran down her cheeks as she poured out her heart. She made a promise to God, 'O Lord Almighty, if you will only consider your servant's distress and remember me, and give me a son, then I'll give him to the Lord for all his life. I promise no razor will ever be used on his head.'"

"As she prayed, her lips moved but no words came out. The old priest, Eli, noticed her and thought she had become intoxicated. He scolded her, but she explained she had been praying, pouring out her grief." Samuel paused a moment, thinking of her pain. "Eli replied, 'Go in peace, and may the God of Israel grant your request.' Hannah left with a happy heart. She could eat and smile again. The next day she joined the family in worship."

Jahra came through the gate carrying a load of firewood. Ishvi turned to watch him, but Jonathan didn't seem to notice; he sat absorbed in the story.

"When the family got home, God answered Hannah's prayers." Samuel saw Jonathan smile with relief. "A year later she held her own baby boy in her arms, watching Elkanah and Peninnah leave for Shiloh. Hannah decided she wouldn't go back until her son became old enough to be left with Eli, as she had promised God.

"When that time arrived, she made the boy a beautiful linen robe to wear at the Tabernacle and took him to Eli, along with a special sacrifice. Hannah told Eli, 'As surely as you live, my lord, I am the woman who stood here a few years ago praying to Jehovah. I prayed for this child, and God granted my request. So today I give him to the Lord. For the rest of his life, he will be given to the Lord.'

"The boy stayed with Eli and helped him in the Tabernacle. Every year his mother visited him, bringing a new robe she made just for him. The boy served happily in God's House, knowing he represented God's special answer to prayer."

Jonathan scooted closer, and Samuel smiled at him. The nine-year-old listened so intently the prophet found it difficult to keep from focusing his gaze exclusively on the boy.

"One night when the lamp of God still burned in the Tabernacle," Samuel resumed, "the boy went to his room and fell asleep on his mat. When he heard someone call his name, he got up and ran to see what Eli wanted.

" 'I didn't call you,' Eli said. 'Go back to bed.' The boy curled up in his blanket and went back to sleep, but again he heard someone call his name. He ran to Eli, but Eli hadn't called him." The prophet saw Jonathan's foot wiggle and he knew the eldest prince itched to ask who called him. "The boy went back to bed, and it happened a third time.

"This time Eli knew the Speaker's identity. 'Go back to bed,' he told the child. 'If He calls again, answer, "Speak Lord, your servant is listening to what you have to say." ' The boy's heart pounded, and goose bumps rose on his arms as he returned to his little room. He appreciated the burning lamp; he didn't have to wait in the dark. Why is God calling me? he wondered. He lay on his mat, shivering under his blanket as he waited."

The sons of Saul sat spellbound. Would God call again? Samuel knew the question perched on the tip of their tongues, just as the child had wondered that night long ago. "The boy lay a long time, almost afraid to breathe," he continued. "Then he heard the Voice. 'Samuel! Samuel!' The boy replied, 'Speak Lord, your servant is listening to what you have to say.'"

Seated directly in front of Samuel, Jonathan's lips parted, and he gasped. "You were that boy, weren't you?"

"Yes." Samuel said, his voice low. "I am that boy."

"I wish God would call me like that," the eldest prince half-whispered as the story ended.

"Oh, He has," Samuel said.

A furrow creased Jonathan's forehead. "When?"

"Before you were born, God planned your life. He knew your father would become the king and you would be his firstborn son. Someday you will become king also." The prophet reached out and placed his hand on Jonathan's knee, looking straight into his eyes. "God has called you to obey His Laws. He wants you to prepare yourself to be a leader in Israel. You must do right even when it is hard, even when others do wrong. You have a great honor, Jonathan, but also a great responsibility."

Samuel's eyes moved to the face of Malki-Shua. "God calls each of you boys to serve Him, just as He called me to serve at His Tabernacle. You must love the Lord with all your heart, as the Law says." He smiled at little Ishvi and rumpled his dark hair. "But while you're young, enjoy playing ball, tag, leapfrog, or hide and seek. All too soon you will be grown up, with much work to do."

"Thank you for the story," Jonathan said, looking up with admiration at the prophet. "Now we know you were once a boy like us. We'll love God even more, because we know He calls boys to serve Him."

"You are good students. Easy to teach. Maybe I'll tell you another story sometime."

"Please do," the trio chorused.

"Now I must go meet your father." Uncrossing his legs, Samuel rose to his feet. "I promised to offer the evening sacrifice at the high place. Peace be with you."

"And with you, peace." The boys stood up.

"He really is a man of God," Samuel overheard Jonathan say as he started toward the gate. "Someday I hope God speaks to me like He did to Samuel."

The prophet turned around to wave as he stepped into the street. Nice boys. Samuel had arranged to meet Saul in the market-place, and he hastened his pace. Very nice boys.

Saul waited for him by the baker's shop. Samuel inhaled, thinking of Shimea back in Shiloh and his "leftover dough." The two made their way up the hillside to the altar. Saul towered head and shoulders above Samuel. The townspeople were already assembled.

"You have three wonderful sons," the prophet said as they walked the dusty path, "I met them in the courtyard this afternoon."

"I'm sorry if they were bothering you. I've instructed them never to play in the courtyard while we have official guests."

"They didn't really disobey. I rested in my room, and they didn't realize anyone was around. We had a good talk."

"Not much of a conversation, I'd venture. I've tried to teach the boys proper respect for elders and important people." That, both knew, meant keeping silent unless spoken to.

"I'm afraid I rather dominated the conversation," Samuel confessed. "In fact, I told them a story."

"I'm sure they loved that."

"They're attentive listeners." Samuel grew silent as they walked along, then he cleared his throat and turned to the king. "As I came through town, an idea struck me. Perhaps you would like me to assign a young man from the school of the prophets to teach your sons."

Saul stopped and turned to Samuel. "That sounds like a wonderful idea. I'm busy—and not much of a teacher."

"All Israelite boys need to learn the Law and the ways of God, especially the king's sons. They would be good students." Samuel paused, then looked deep into the king's eyes. "Saul, take advantage of that quality while they are willing to learn. I guess I didn't enough. I . . . I somehow failed my sons. I know it; the whole nation knows it." He bit his lower lip to still the trembling. "I don't begrudge God choosing you as king," he finally continued, "but if my sons had been godly men, people would have been content to let them lead. Every day I mourn their wicked ways. The people rejected them for their corruption. Don't let that happen to your sons."

Neither spoke for a moment, then the king placed his large hand on the prophet's shoulder. "I'm sorry."

The understanding and sympathy expressed in those two words touched Samuel.

"I'll do my best to remember your advice," Saul promised. "Sons are a heritage from the Lord."

9

ETHAN

The eastern evening breeze, soft and warm, teased a wisp of hair on Jonathan's forehead. Just right for sitting on the rooftop and visiting. He heard the sound of footsteps on the staircase and slid down the floor to make room for Grandfather Kish next to his father. The rough surface scraped against a callous on his right hand, reminding him of the exhausting days of the recent wheat harvest. Relaxing at home in the evening certainly beat winnowing grain. Each year Father gave him a little more responsibility in the fields. Tonight, his muscles no longer ached, but the callous remained.

After exchanging greetings, the two men discussed village news and plans for the next day. The three boys listened in silence. Then Kish turned his attention to them, asking what they had done that day. When they finished reporting, he placed his hand on his oldest grandson's knee.

"Jonathan, we Benjamites have a long-standing reputation for accuracy with the sling. Years ago, our tribe had seven hundred men alone who were left-handed yet could hit a hair from a distance with sling and stone."

Ishvi's eyes widened. "Can you do that?"

"Not quite." Grandfather laughed a gentle laugh. "But as a boy, I did have a good aim. Father used to send Ner and me out to care for the sheep, so we needed to know how to kill hyenas and jackals, or at least frighten them away. Occasionally lions and bears wandered up from the thickets along the Jordan. We always carried a club, or rod, and our trusty slings."

"When can I learn to use a sling?" Jonathan knew Pharez's oldest brother had been teaching Pharez.

"Well, I began thinking this afternoon; ten is about the age I learned. It's easier to learn when you are young. Your work during harvest shows me you are a responsible boy who would use a sling wisely."

Jonathan's thumb brushed across the callous on his right hand. His hard work had paid off in more ways than one. "Will you teach me tomorrow?" Kish looked at Saul, who nodded his approval. Jonathan wriggled with anticipation. "Maybe Pharez and Gera could come with us."

"Why don't we work alone at first. They can join us later."

Jonathan hid his disappointment that his friends would not be with them. What could he say? Elders ruled.

The next morning Jonathan hurried downstairs before the sun came up. While waiting for Grandfather to come out of his room, he searched the courtyard for stones that might work in a sling. The door finally opened, and a smiling Kish stepped out. Over his left shoulder he carried a waterbag and shoulder bag. In his right hand he held two slings. They made their way out the gate and down the narrow street. As they passed shopkeepers on their way to work, Kish greeted each by name.

The two walked down the hill, through the olive orchard, and on toward the valley. Grandfather stopped several times to pick up a stone and drop it in the bag tied to his girdle-belt.

"Here," he said, holding out a smooth round stone an inch in diameter. "This is the best size and shape. See if you can find more like it."

The boy scoured the ground as they made their way to the edge of the field of stubble. Once there, Grandfather handed him the smaller sling.

"I still remember my excitement the day Father Abiel presented me with my first sling—fifty-six years ago."

Jonathan's eyes automatically shifted to his grandfather's gray beard. He couldn't imagine being a boy so long ago.

Jonathan proudly inspected the weapon, which consisted of a small leather pouch with two cords, each attached to an opposite edge. Grandfather's sling cords were about two feet long, his shorter.

Kish showed Jonathan how to hold the pouch with his left hand and place the stone in it. He pointed to a target—a tall weed, dead from the summer heat, that stood several yards down the valley. Raising the sling above his head, he pulled the cords taut with his right hand and began whirling the sling in a circle above his head.

The swish of leather cutting the air sounded like a swarm of angry bees. With the momentum just right, Grandfather brought the sling around again and released the tension on one of the cords. The stone shot from the pouch with terrific force, hurtling toward the weed. Brown leaves and splinters of stem flew in all directions as it hit its mark.

Jonathan clapped his hands. "May I try next?" he said, encouraged by Kish's success.

"Remember, I've been doing this for nearly sixty years. It takes practice over and over to become skillful."

Jonathan's hand trembled with anticipation as he placed the stone in the pouch. He began slowly whirling the sling, but the stone fell out before he made a complete circle. The second time he whirled it faster and the stone stayed in, but he released the cord prematurely. The stone hit the ground, digging a hole in the dirt before bouncing away. He looked up at Grandfather, thankful he had refused to invite Pharez and Gera. By the end of an hour, however, Jonathan managed to swing the sling and release the cord with a measure of success, although he never hit a specific target.

Grandfather called a halt to the practice and walked over to a nearby rock, where his waterbag and shoulder bag lay in its shade. Washing their hands, the two thanked God for the food, then ate the bread and raisins as they leaned against the cool side of the rock. Recalling breakfast the first morning he helped at the threshing floor three years before, Jonathan decided a new learning experience must stimulate the appetite. Why else did the same food taste so much better when eaten in a new place?

The two spent another hour aiming at weeds, clods, and tree leaves. Jonathan's arms ached when they finally stopped, but he would never admit it to his patient grandfather. Today marked the first step in his long-held dream of fighting the pagan Philistines who harassed his people. The enemy may confiscate all their metal weapons, but they could never steal all the stones and leather in Israel. He smiled with satisfaction. If the Israelites knew how to use slings well, God would do the rest.

~

Jonathan heard the bedroom door scrape the floor and opened his eyes to see his father's tall form standing in the doorway.

"Are you boys about ready to get up? Today I have a surprise for you."

Jonathan, Malki-Shua, and Ishvi hopped up from their sleeping mats. "What is it?" they simultaneously asked. The two younger ones each grabbed one of Saul's large hands.

"It's a new toy," Ishvi guessed.

"Much more important than a toy. And something that will last much longer."

"Something for a prince?" Jonathan said.

"Something I wish all Israel had. Remember last year when Samuel told you a story?" Jonathan nodded as he smiled at the memory of the Voice of God calling a young boy in the night. "The prophet thought you might like your very own teacher to tell you stories of how God helps His Chosen People."

"Stories about Abraham and Moses?" Malki-Shua said.

"And Joseph?" Jonathan hoped the teacher knew about his favorite patriarch.

"Those and many more." Saul stepped farther into the room. "Today your teacher has arrived. He is one of Samuel's friends from the school of the prophets. His name is Ethan, and he wants to meet you."

Jonathan looked at his wrinkled tunic and attempted to smooth the worst creases. "Maybe we should put on clean clothes first. We don't want him to think we're messy students."

"Sounds like an excellent idea." Father opened a chest and pulled out three fresh tunics while the boys peeled off the rumpled ones they had slept in. When they were dressed, he stepped back to inspect them. "Now you look like princes, for sure."

"We aren't princes because of our clothes," Jonathan corrected him, "but because we're sons of the king."

"But it helps to have on clean clothes," Ishvi said in a serious tone.

"Let's go. Your first day of lessons is going to be a very special day."

Jonathan stopped in surprise when he saw a slim young man step out of their old family bedroom and walk to the middle of the courtyard. A short black beard wreathed his friendly smile. Jonathan had expected a gray-haired man like Samuel. He was going to like this teacher. But he looked so young. Could he possibly know even as many stories as Father?

Ethan led the boys to the sitting mat in the comer, the same corner where Samuel had told them about God's call. The teacher asked each boy his favorite story, then told it in more detail than Jonathan had ever heard. He smiled. Ethan was a good storyteller. Samuel chose the best just for them. They were going to learn a lot.

Watching Ethan talk, Jonathan admired his beard, not yet grown long like older men's. Jonathan rubbed his smooth cheek, anticipating the day he could grow a beard—sign of a true Israelite. This fulfillment of the Law of Moses, Grandfather said, separated Israelites from Philistines and other pagans. Trimming the beard at the sides of the head, a feature of some idolatrous cults, was forbidden.

The next morning Jonathan woke at dawn, anxious for another day of lessons. Although still tired, he knew he wouldn't go back to sleep. Not when Ethan had so many things to teach him.

An hour later the teacher began the lesson with a question. "What makes the Israelites different from all other people?"

"Circumcision," Jonathan replied with confidence.

"Not necessarily," Ethan responded in a slow voice. "The Edomites are descendants of Jacob's brother Esau. They practice circumcision. So do the Moabites and Ammonites, descendants of Abraham's nephew Lot."

"Because God delivered us from slavery in Egypt?" Malki-Shua ventured to answer.

"That celebrated a special deliverance, but it's not the main reason."

"Tell us." Jonathan shook his raised hand, anxious to learn the correct response.

" 'I am the Lord your God, who brought you out of the Land of Egypt, out of the place of your slavery. You must have no other gods before me,' " Ethan quoted.

"That's the first of the Ten Commandments God gave Moses," Jonathan said.

"You are exactly right. The Israelites are the only people who alone worship the One True God."

Then Ethan began telling the story of Creation. The boys, sitting cross-legged on the mat, edged closer as they listened.

The following morning Ethan returned to the story of Israel. "While our forefathers lived in Egypt, they learned many things from the people there. Some were good, some bad. Because the Egyptians didn't know the One True God, they worshiped other gods: Re, the sun god; Geb, the earth god; Hapi, the god of the Nile-flood; Amun, the god of hidden life-power in nature. Osiris, they believe, was slain by his brother and became king of the underworld, so they hope he will help them with life after death. Certain animals are treated as sacred to certain gods, so they view them as representatives of the gods. They sometimes group the gods into families."

"Do we have to learn the names of all these gods?" Jonathan said.

"No, I don't expect you to memorize them, but I want you to know that other nations do not worship the One True God. When you realize our forefathers lived among these pagans for four hundred years in Egypt, it is all the more amazing that they kept their faith in the One and Only God of Abraham.

"When Joshua led the Children of Israel into Canaan, they also met people with different gods, gods that represent the powers of nature. That is why God told us to drive out all the others, so the pagans would not lead our people astray. Who is the main Canaanite god?"

"Baal." The easy question pleased Jonathan.

"Baal is the weather-god. They say he controls the rain, mist, and dew. He defeated Mot, the god of death, so every year he causes the rains to return and bring the earth back to life, producing crops. His wife is Ashtoreth, goddess of fertility, love, and war. His father El is the creator-god, but he's not considered very important these days. El's wife is Asherah, the mother goddess and goddess of the sea. Dagon is the god of grain, Shamash of the sun, and Reshef of war and the underworld."

Ethan smiled at Jonathan. "And you don't have to memorize these names either, although it would be good for you to know what our enemies believe. These gods and goddesses are evil, bloodthirsty, immoral, and don't really care about people. They just do what they feel like doing."

"Like Israelites do sometimes?" Jonathan said.

"I'm afraid so. But the Canaanites say the gods can be kind and generous if they worship them correctly. So, the heathen build temples for them and make sacrifices—sometimes even sacrificing their own children. Priests and temple prostitutes sleep together like man and wife, hoping to convince the gods to do the same, thus making the earth fertile. The Canaanites want gods they can see, so they make idols to represent them and Asherah poles of wood for the goddess."

"No wonder God isn't happy with the other nations," Jonathan said. "Their gods are just the opposite of Him."

Ethan nodded. "God is holy and righteous. He wants us to live righteous lives and worship Him in purity. He created everything for His glory. The Egyptians irrigate from the River Nile, so they worship the god of the Nile. Canaanites depend on rain, so they worship Baal. But we know it is our God who cares for the world all year long and controls the rains. He told Moses, 'The land you're taking possession of is a land of hills and valleys that soak up rain from heaven. It's a land the Lord cares for; the eyes of your God are continually on it throughout the whole year.' How do you think God feels when people worship Baal?"

"Sad," Malki-Shua answered.

"It's like if Mother made me a new tunic and rather than thanking her, I thanked Pharez's mother for it," Jonathan said.

Ethan nodded. "Or if you had a pretend friend and thanked

him instead of God. Baal doesn't really exist, yet he receives the praise and glory meant for God. That is why the Lord commanded, 'Never make for yourself an idol that looks like anything in heaven above, on the earth, or in the waters underneath. Never bow down to worship them; for I am your Lord, a jealous God. I punish the children for the sin of the fathers to the fourth generation of those who hate me, but show love to multitudes who love me and obey my commandments.' "

In the days that followed, Ethan presented the rest of the Ten Commandments and God's reasons for giving them. The next week he pulled a scroll from a bag. "This is God's Law." He unrolled the left stick, exposing the parchment.

Jonathan had never seen writing before and looked at the markings, fascinated that Ethan could read them as words.

"May we learn to read it?" Malki-Shua said.

"It will take a long time. So first you will memorize it. If you only read it, when you have no scroll, you will have nothing. If you learn it in your mind and hide it in your heart, you can carry it with you even when you don't have a scroll. But most of all, remember, these are not just words to read, but a life to live. Knowing words is useless if you don't obey them."

The explanation made sense to Jonathan, and he sat up straighter as he waited for the first line to memorize. Fortunately, Ethan began with one he already knew, " 'Listen carefully, O Israel: The Lord our God is one Lord: And you must love the Lord your God with all your heart, all your soul, and all your strength.' "

Over the months Malki-Shua found memorization easy and enjoyed quoting the day's passage, winning extra praise from Ethan and Father. Jonathan struggled at times and rejoiced when he finally conquered a few sentences. Both, however, rose each morning at Father's first call, eager for another day of lessons.

Sabbath, the seventh day of the week, was a quiet day in Gibeah. It began the evening before. Work ceased, cooking was done before sunset, waterpots were filled in advance, children's play was restricted. People kept the day of rest as commanded by the Law.

With Ethan as part of the family, Sabbaths took on new meaning for the House of Kish. The men and boys gathered in the corner of the courtyard that morning to listen to Ethan read from the scroll and explain the words so even the boys could understand. Grandfather prayed to God, authority in his voice.

Then Ethan closed with the benediction God had given to Aaron through Moses,

"The Lord bless you, and keep you secure:
The Lord make his smile shine upon you, and be gracious to you:
The Lord look with favor upon you and fill you with peace."

The women watched silently from the periphery. Everyone treasured these hallowed moments.

10

PLANTING SEASON

Jonathan's finger slowly traced the words across the scroll as he pronounced each one. He paused to study the next, more difficult word, frowning as he rubbed his eyebrow with the side of his hand. Beside him on the mat, Ethan listened, happy with the boy's progress over the past two years. Ishvi's short attention span and inability to memorize long passages limited his learning, but Ethan had noticed improvement in his youngest pupil over the past few months. Malki-Shua had proven to be as good a student as his older brother. The teacher divided the second hour of the morning lessons, giving separate attention to the older two, correcting any misunderstanding of the Law, and answering their individual questions.

With his finger at the end of the sentence, Jonathan looked up at Ethan and smiled. "Teacher, God really does care about His People. He must have given Samuel the idea to send you to Gibeah. You make the study of the Law so interesting that I can understand it. When you came two years ago, I didn't know boys could learn to read." His finger tapped the scroll. "Now I'm reading God's Word for myself. Thanks for being our teacher."

A rush of tears filled Ethan's eyes. "I know God sent me here. I've never been happier."

That afternoon when Jonathan returned from running an errand for his grandfather near the marketplace, he noticed Ethan talking to his father in the courtyard. When the teacher walked away, he limped slightly. Had he been sitting cross-legged too long, and his foot gone to sleep? Jonathan forgot the matter as he handed Grandfather the tool he had borrowed from Tilon.

When grape and olive harvest ended, Samuel arrived again for the Feast of Tabernacles. The town hummed with excitement as people gathered to participate in the week-long celebration. The prophet spent many hours visiting with Saul, discussing matters of the kingdom, Jonathan supposed. Samuel also spent time alone with Ethan.

Following the rule of the courtyard, the boys were relegated to the rooftop most afternoons, but Samuel called them down one day for a special class. He seemed pleased with their answers about God and the Law and complimented them on their learning. Jonathan decided the minutes with the prophet more than made up for the long hours confined to the rooftop.

Then Samuel left and life returned to the daily routine.

After completing morning classes and doing any necessary chores, if no farm work had been assigned, the princes were free in the afternoons. Now that Jonathan had turned twelve, he loved to explore the valley around Gibeah with Pharez and Gera. Since they could use the sling in self-defense, their parents let them roam about as long as they kept the town in sight.

Jonathan especially loved to go down to Ezel, the rock formation that served as the boundary line for Grandfather's property. Climbing it and looking down on the fields below, he felt a sense of freedom he never had on the ground. One afternoon while harvesting wheat, he and his father had paused to rest beneath the nearby terebinth tree, smelling its distinctive odor as they leaned against the trunk. Soon Jonathan left his father to explore the huge rock and made an important discovery.

On the back side of the formation, a cleft formed a hidden hollow space that was big enough to conceal two or three seated men. Goose bumps had risen on his arms as he pressed himself against the cold stone, pretending to be evading the Philistines. His own secret cave. He would never tell anyone.

But he had. After much consideration, he swore Pharez and Gera to secrecy, then led them down to the special hideout, where the boys squeezed themselves into the niche. Sharing secrets with friends sealed a friendship.

Jonathan's second favorite activity had to be using his sling. At the end of the dry season the boys gathered with their slings at the almond trees above the olive grove, where they used small stones to dislodge the nuts. Most of the dry hulls had split open and curled out, exposing the light brown shells. Often the boys missed their target, getting only a shower of leaves for their effort, but the practice greatly improved the accuracy of their aim. If they did succeed, the stones shattered the wrinkled, leathery hulls and the nuts dropped to the ground.

When several town boys were at the trees, they made a contest of slinging, each collecting his nuts in a pile and counting them to determine the winner. Jonathan loved it when he had the most. In the end, each scooped up his winnings to take home to his mother to use in cooking.

One afternoon Jonathan returned home to find his father standing on the rooftop, studying the sky. He looked up at the grayish-white clouds gathering in the west. "Are they rain clouds?"

"I think so." The king looked down and smiled. "Are you ready to learn to plant barley?"

"You mean this year I can help broadcast?"

"Anyone who can knock down almonds with a sling stone should be able to throw a few seeds into a furrow."

Father put his large muscular arm around his son's shoulders, and Jonathan sensed his teasing. "What did you shoot at when you were young?"

"Almonds." Saul chuckled. "But Tarea always beat me."

That night the first early rain fell, gently soaking into the hard, parched ground. The showers continued, and a week later the soil was moist. One morning Kish brought out the two plows, and Saul and Pagiel hoisted them to their shoulders. Gatam had already gone to the animal shelter to yoke the teams of oxen. Ocran led a donkey through the front gate and loaded a bag of barley on its back. The men left to begin plowing, and the boys settled down to listen to Ethan's lesson.

After class, Kish called Jonathan. The two headed for the valley. When they arrived, the plowmen were far down the field. Jonathan left his grandfather standing in the shade of an oak tree as he ran to watch. The smell of freshly turned earth filled the air, and he inhaled deeply as he hurried down a furrow.

Reaching Saul, the boy followed, the soft wet soil oozing up between his toes. Years before, Grandfather had made the plow, two wooden beams joined together like a sideways T. The long front piece was to be fastened to the oxen's yoke; the plowman held the shorter vertical piece.

Father leaned forward, his full weight on the handle at the top as he pushed the pointed iron plowshare into the ground. In his left hand, he carried a goad, a heavy rod with a sharp metal tip that could be used to knock off clods of mud that stuck to the plowshare. From time to time, he also used it to prod the slow team.

When they got back to where Kish waited, he handed Jonathan a leather bag of seed grain. The boy slipped the strap over his shoulder, letting the bag hang at his side as Grandfather's did. The two moved to the edge of the field. Jonathan watched the older man reach into his bag and, with a broad sweep of the hand, scatter the grain across the furrows. He took a handful and followed the example, but he knew his cast did not scatter so evenly.

Jonathan glanced back to see Ocran had taken over Gatam's plow farther down the field. Father handed his to Pagiel, who sank the plowshare back into the first furrow to cover the grain.

By noon Jonathan had grown tired, so following lunch he and Grandfather continued resting a short time after the others returned to work. When broadcasting the newly broken ground was finished, the sun had begun to drop toward the western hills. Gatam brought the second team up to help Saul cover the exposed grain so birds would not steal it at sunrise.

Jonathan breathed a sigh of relief when they started back to Gibeah. While happy to be included in men's work, he looked forward to bed and two hours of lessons the next morning before he needed to return to the field.

With planting completed, Kish and Saul scanned the skies, praying for the winter rains to soon begin. Without them, drought would spell disaster for the Land. When the regular showers set in, everyone breathed easier and rejoiced that the God of Israel had blessed His People.

On rainy days, Ethan held class in his room. When the sun shone, he sat with his students in a patch of sunlight, glad for the warmth that drove away the morning chill. One day as Saul sat in the courtyard whittling arrow shafts, he listened to the nearby class session.

" 'Do not seek help from any medium or spiritists. They will pollute you. I am the Lord your God,' " Ethan read from the scroll.

"What is a medium or spiritist?" nine-year-old Malki-Shua said.

"One who consults evil spirits for people. Here is a commandment that is even more plain." Ethan picked up a second scroll and unrolled it. " 'When you arrive in the land the Lord your God is giving you, do not do or follow the hated customs of those nations. Never sacrifice your son or daughter in the fire. Never practice divining or sorcery, interpret signs of evil, participate in witchcraft, cast spells on anyone, or become a medium or spiritist or consult the dead. These things are detestable to the Lord, and so is anyone who does them. God will drive out from before you those nations who do them. You must be pure and blameless before the Lord.' "

Saul saw Jonathan squint up at his teacher. "Do we have that kind of people in the Land? I've never heard of any."

"I've never met one, but I've heard of some."

So had Saul. He recalled the day, eight years before, when he and Gatam searched for the lost donkeys in the district of Shaalim. He had been horrified when the shepherd boys innocently suggested he consult the town sorceress. Yes, they did live in the Land. God said because of them He would drive out the heathen nations, yet Israel had let them exist among the people. No wonder the Philistines dominate Israel. They did not obey God.

Saul could not shake the subject from his mind. That evening he called Ethan aside and questioned him about the commandment.

"God does tell us what to do with witches and sorceresses," Ethan told him. "The Law says, 'A man or woman living among you who is a medium or spiritist must be put to death by stoning. It will be their own fault their blood was shed.' "

The next morning Saul sent messengers to call leaders from the twelve tribes of Israel to meet in Gibeah after the New Moon. When they arrived, he issued an edict that all mediums and spiritists were to be destroyed or driven from the Land.

"Spare none," he ordered. "I don't want to rule a defiled people.

Only God can bring deliverance from the Philistines. As long as I am king, we will follow the way of the Lord."

The men fanned out across their territories to carry out the decree, and Saul felt relieved he had obeyed one more command of God.

11

FAMILY LOSS

Loud sobs, punctuated by screams, brought the women of Gibeah
rushing to their doors to watch two men carry eight-year-old Ishvi
up the street to Kish's house, trailed by three friends with tear-
streaked cheeks. Over the past two years Ishvi had grown more
independent of his brothers. He and his friends had been climbing
the short trunk and low spreading gnarled branches of the
sycamore fig tree behind Mahlon's house when the prince slipped
and fell. He felt his right ankle snap, stealing his breath away as
searing pain shot up his leg. The men had heard the boys' frantic
shouts and hurried to the rescue.

As the sad procession neared the front gate, Ishvi's sobs dimin-
ished to sniffles. He would soon be home, where Mother and
Grandmother Jedidah would hold him close and soothe the
suffering.

Jahra took one look at him and hurried out the gate. Soon
Grandfather, Father, and Jonathan arrived home from the field to
comfort him. Father collected items to make a splint. Padding the
leg with soft sheep's wool, Saul placed two narrow boards along

the sides and bound them with strips of cloth as Ishvi watched. The leg still throbbed, but the splint helped.

Over the next few weeks Ishvi enjoyed the family's attention. He slept downstairs in his grandparent's bedroom, and Father carried him out to the courtyard each morning. Ethan allowed him to join in classes when he felt up to it. Friends came to visit him, taking his mind off the pain. They shared quiet games together— rolling round stones through bowed-branch loops stuck in the ground, tossing pebbles into a cracked jug several feet away, and trying to stump each other with riddles.

After two months, Father removed the splint and Ishvi walked stiffly up and down the courtyard, testing his healed leg. He was slow at climbing the stairs at first, but Father had decided the boys were old enough to occupy the middle bedroom, so he was anxious to check it out.

Harvesting finished and the men had time once again to sit on the rooftop and enjoy the evening breeze. One night after the others were in bed, Jonathan slipped back out to where Saul sat alone in the moonlight.

"What's troubling you, Father?" the teenager said.

"Why do you think something is troubling me?"

Jonathan could detect the evasiveness in his father's voice, but he refused to be deterred. "At first I thought you were quiet because of Ishvi's leg. Now the splint is off, yet you still look worried and frown a lot. It's got to be something else."

"Unfortunately, it is several things." Saul sighed. "Including Ishvi." Jonathan waited for an explanation. "Your brother's ankle is too stiff. He can walk, but I don't expect him to ever be able to run."

"Does he need to run?"

"The captain over troops must run or be slaughtered. Ishvi will never be able to serve in Israel's army."

"Perhaps he can take care of the fields and other business instead." Jonathan's eyes automatically turned to the south, where Grandfather's fields lay shrouded in the moonlight.

"That's what he'll have to do." Saul paused, then took a deep breath. "I'm also concerned about your mother."

"Is she sick?"

"She is expecting another baby."

"You don't want more children?" Jonathan asked, puzzled. Every Israelite man wanted a large family. Children were like arrows in a quiver—the more you possessed, the better the family's protection. Saul was an only child, but Grandfather and Grandmother never hid the fact they had always longed for others.

"I want more children," Saul said, "but not if it harms your mother. Ishvi is eight. Most women would have a couple more children by now." Jonathan nodded. "You don't know it, but she recently lost two babies before their time. Now I'm concerned she'll lose the third."

Jonathan expressed surprise at the news. No wonder his mother had those long sick spells when Grandmother cared for her downstairs and wouldn't allow the children in her room.

"I also worry about Grandfather. His ankles swell at times and he gets short of breath just walking up the hill from the fields."

"He's seventy now. I guess he's getting old." Jonathan thought of the dear man who had been the family's strength so many years. "I hope he doesn't die," he whispered.

"Me, too." They heard a door open in the courtyard below and paused until it closed again. "Then there's Ethan."

Jonathan looked up in surprise. "What's wrong with him?"

"Surely you notice his limp is getting worse. The joints of his hands swell. It's strange. Like an old man, or something." He let out a long breath. "The next time Samuel visits, I don't know what he will decide."

"You mean Ethan might leave?" Jonathan felt like someone just punched him in the stomach. They still needed the teacher.

"Perhaps. We can't keep him here if he would be better off somewhere else."

"Where?"

"Ethan comes from a village near Jericho, down by the Jordan River where the winters are warm and dry compared to these chilly, damp mountains."

Jonathan drummed his fingers on the floor as he considered life without his mother, teacher, and grandfather. The evening breeze sent a dry leaf skittering across the rooftop. It symbolized the end of life. He sniffed, trying to hold back the tears. So many problems. No wonder Father looked worried.

Gazing up at the stars that filled the sky, each a tiny point of light against the dark heavens, Jonathan recalled one of Ethan's first lessons. God created the stars. He created man. God looked after those who trust Him. Jonathan turned to Saul. "Father, if God could part the Red Sea for Moses, surely He can care for our family."

"He can. One way He has cared for me is by giving me a son who understands things far beyond his years. You are becoming a man, Jonathan." Saul reached out and put his arm around Jonathan's shoulders. "You will be a real asset to the kingdom, and I am proud to be your father. The Lord bless you, my son." Saul's embrace tightened, then he arose and went to his room.

Jonathan sat rubbing his eyebrow with the tip of his index finger as he pondered the troublesome news. Finally, committing the future to God, he also headed for bed.

Saul's concerns eased when Ahinoam gave birth six months later to her first daughter, whom they named Merab. The beautiful healthy baby had a strong pair of lungs, which she used to inform everybody of her occasional colic. As she outgrew the stomach pains, she developed a ready smile, made all the more vivid by her bright brown eyes. Ishvi adored her, cooing at her and wriggling her toes until she laughed. Later he helped her learn to sit up, then taught her to clap and, eventually, to walk. Observing the two together, Saul felt less sorrow for the son who would never join his army.

Sorrow of another kind came just as the new barley crop finished ripening. The swelling in Kish's legs grew suddenly worse. He could only breathe when propped against the wall. After Jonathan's lessons each morning, he hurried in to sit quietly beside his grandfather. It seemed a comfort to both, and the king appreciated his son's concern. Watching his father's chest heave up and down, Saul felt helpless. Nothing could be done but pray.

Saul divided his attention between barley harvesting and his father. Early one morning when Saul went to check on his father, he realized the end was near. He took his time climbing the stairs, dreading having to waken the boys and inform them.

The princes were somber as Saul brought them into their grandparents' room, where Grandmother Jedidah and their mother kept vigil. Beginning with Jonathan, Saul led each son over to the old man. Kish placed his pale limp hand on the boys' heads and struggled to voice a prayer of blessing on them.

Tears welled up in Jonathan's eyes as he embraced the dying man who had taught him so much about life and God.

"Remember . . . the Law . . . and all the stories." Kish's raspy voice faltered as he weakly hugged his eldest grandson. "Especially the one . . . about Joseph . . . . He's your favorite."

"I'll always think of you when I do," Jonathan promised. "God be with you, Grandfather."

He tore himself away from the man he loved and sat down between his mother and grandmother. Ahinoam put her arm around her firstborn and, leaning his head on her shoulder, he let the tears flow.

When Ishvi had received his blessing, Saul ushered the boys out into the courtyard. Without a word, Jonathan headed for the corner and Ethan. Lessons were cancelled that day, but as the boys cried and Ethan occasionally said a few words, they found solace in each other's presence.

Suddenly, just before noon a death wail pierced the air, causing them to jump. No one in the corner moved as the gate flew open. They watched the people of Gibeah pour through to join the mourning.

The screams frightened Merab and she began crying. Hamul's wife carried her out and handed her to Malki-Shua. He tried to hush her as Ishvi stroked her black hair.

"Wavy like yours, Jonathan," Ishvi said, smiling at his brother.

The wails continued to upset the baby and Malki-Shua took her upstairs. Ishvi followed.

Ethan stayed beside Jonathan as they silently waited for Ner and his sons to go to Zelah, the ancestral village, to open the family cave-tomb. Women gathered in the bedroom to prepare the body. Just before the procession formed for the march to the hillside grave, Ethan laid his hand on the young prince's shoulder.

"Years ago, when you were too little or too tired to walk, Grandfather Kish carried you. Today you feel too full of sorrow to walk. Today the love of God and your friends will carry you."

"Thanks." Jonathan brushed tears from his cheeks. Ethan understood suffering. He understood him.

The two rose to join the men behind the bier. The procession made its way down the winding street. When it came even with Gera's house, he and Pharez stepped into line beside Ethan and Jonathan. The mournful notes of flutes filled the narrow lane and floated up over the housetops. Jonathan swallowed hard. A flute was the voice of the heart when it was too sad to speak.

When the procession came to the edge of town, women began tossing dust into the air as a sign of grief. The wails grew louder as the mourners walked down the hill and across the valley to Zelah, a half-mile away. Up ahead Jonathan saw the gaping hole in the hillside. What would life be like without Grandfather?

Following the burial, the clan gathered in Kish's courtyard. Grandfather Ahimaaz, Grandmother Milcah, and the relatives from Mizpah arrived the next day for the weeklong funeral. The immediate family fulfilled the customary thirty days of mourning.

Evenings had grown quiet during Grandfather's illness, but they had still known he lay just inside the bedroom door. Now he was gone. Ethan's classes helped to fill the emptiness. Still, when no one was around Jonathan often sat in a shady corner of the rooftop parapet and grieved.

Why did life have to end? Especially a good life? Death came as the result of sin in the Garden of Eden, Ethan had taught them. If only Adam could do it over again, and this time make the right choice! That was why, Ethan said, it was important to do everything right the first time. Jonathan thought back over Grandfather's lessons, too. He might be gone, but Jonathan would never forget him.

At the close of the thirty days, Saul took charge of the harvesters as they hurried to gather in the wheat harvest. Soon after, Samuel appeared for an unexpected visit.

Following a long discussion with the king one afternoon, the prophet decided to take Ethan home to his village near Jericho. The sober-faced Jonathan only nibbled at his food during supper. Later, rolling and tossing on his mat, he wadded his tunic together and muffled his sobs so he wouldn't disturb his sleeping brothers. He lay awake so long he overslept the next morning.

Feeling someone shake his shoulder, Jonathan opened his eyes to see his father squatting beside him. Then he remembered. Today Ethan was leaving. Bounding up, he hurried out the door and down the stairs. His brothers and teacher were waiting in the courtyard. Ethan led the boys to the corner for one last prayer together.

Jonathan tried to be brave as he stood in the doorway of Ethan's room watching Samuel pack the precious scrolls Jonathan had learned to love. He thanked God he had spent the long hours memorizing so much. Ethan gave each boy a hug, then Gatam helped him mount Samuel's donkey.

"Goodbye, Ethan," Jonathan said just before the two prophets started down the street. "We'll always remember what you taught us about God."

Tears spilled down the boys' cheeks as they stood at the gate and waved to their teacher. Over the past five years, the young man had become part of the family. His leaving felt like another death.

One hundred miles southeast of Gibeah, in the Land of Edom, Doeg sat relaxed in the afternoon sunshine, growing drowsier by the minute. The family's little flock of sheep spread out before him, enjoying a rest before heading back to the fold. A sudden commotion jarred Doeg fully awake and brought him to his feet. The old ewe was in labor. He picked his way through the flock, also on their feet by now. In the seconds it took to reach the laboring mother, a scrawny lamb flopped out on the grass. Doeg knelt to clear its face with the hem of his cloak, then began stroking its chest. Only a faint sound escaped its lips.

When the birthing process was completed, Doeg let the mother rest as long as possible. "We're in big trouble," he said aloud, wrapping the baby in his cloak. From time to time, Doeg tried to help the weak newborn suckle. The sun began to lower in the west when he coaxed the ewe to walk. Setting a slow pace, Doeg led the flock home. He carried the lamb close to his chest, stroking the soft bundle. Without thinking, he began quietly singing a song his mother sang as she rocked back and forth, a sick child cradled in her arms.

Doeg's father met them at the shelter. He took one look at the pitiful creature. "It's too frail," Mahalalel said, slowly shaking his head. "Won't make it."

"But Father, can't we give it a chance?"

"You're wasting your time." He turned to count the sheep as they entered. "And the bleating will keep us awake all night."

"I promise to take it out to the fold if it wants to suckle." Doeg did not want to admit the bleating could barely be heard. His father for sure would not agree.

"All right. But only three days at the most." Mahalalel closed the gate and walked toward the house.

His son followed, thankful they lived on the village edge, next to the fold. Not that any of the twenty houses stood far from it. Doeg smiled at his triumph. Baal had answered his petition.

After washing up, he donned a clean cloak and joined the family for supper on a mat spread out on the platform. Then Doeg took the lamb out for one more attempt to feed. He chose to sleep on the lower level close to the door. Before crawling under his blanket, he unwrapped the little image of Baal his father had bought on a shopping trip to Sela. He prayed again for his fragile charge.

The lamb's bleating wakened Doeg near dawn. He eased out the door with his well-wrapped bundle. As he neared the fold, cries erupted throughout the village. Doeg paused, perplexed. Had old Esau died? That didn't seem a plausible explanation. A death wail would come from just one house and spread as neighbors were aroused by the sad news.

The sound of running reached him as cries turned to screams. *A raid.* Fear gripped the fourteen-year-old, and he hugged the lamb closer as he ran past the fold into the darkness. He tripped over a stone, nearly dropping his precious pet. After some time, the screams grew fainter, then stopped. Doeg sank to the ground beneath a tree, panting as tears slid off his cheeks.

It took forever for dawn to lighten the sky.

Doeg waited until mid-morning to return home, fearful of what he would find, certain of what he would not—another live human. He approached the village with caution, the silence eerie. He slipped past the fold, now empty. Not even the mother ewe left to nurse her lamb. Mahalalel's house stood wide open, the door dangling by one hinge. Doeg called his mother's name and waited. Sobs choked him as he called again. He peered inside. A few small broken household items lay scattered on the floor. Everything else had disappeared—including his family. Rushing to the corner, he frantically searched for the image of Baal. Only the cloth remained.

Doeg hurried to the neighbor's, finding the story the same. It did not take long to inspect the few houses. In the last one, he found old Esau curled on the floor, moaning in pain. Matted blood covered a gash on his head. His forearm lay bent in a strange position. The teenager tried to help the old man, but Esau insisted he flee in case the marauders returned.

"I think they were Moabites," Esau said between convulsive gasps. "My sons and their families are now slaves . . . . Everything we own is gone . . . . It's hopeless." His words came slower. "May the gods bring vengeance on these blood-thirsty villains."

Behind the door, Doeg found an overlooked jug and cup. He poured a little water and held it to the dying man's lips. Esau thanked him and repeated his warning. Doeg stooped to pick up the lamb. Saying goodbye, he fled out the door.

Footprints and a trail of barley from a leaking sack led east from the ravished village. He chose the road west.

When Doeg reached his early morning hiding place, he stopped to rest. Only then did he realize the lamb had stopped breathing. A sob caught in his throat. But for the frail animal, he too would be a slave. He buried his face in the lamb's wooly coat and wept. Then, surrendering the bundle to the elements and wild animals, he laid the dead lamb—and his dead dreams—beneath the tree.

Occasionally begging food, Doeg traveled for two days before he felt safe enough to stop at a village. A man named Zeri offered him a job shepherding his small flock. The old couple had little, but they promised to pay him when they sheared sheep in the spring. The wife's cooking would be better than the hunger pangs gnawing his stomach, so Doeg agreed to the terms. Seeing their image of Baal brought a sense of serenity. As soon as he earned enough money, he would buy his own idol.

Alone with the sheep day after day, Doeg's thoughts often turned to his future. With no family to negotiate a marriage, he was doomed to live a bachelor's life. He knew no job but sheep herding. He had seen shopkeepers and tradesmen in Sela the few times he had traveled there with his father. With no relative to teach him a trade, however, he was doomed to live a shepherd's life. Only the gods could rescue him.

The rainy season forced the flock to stay in or near the pen. When the rains drew to a close, Doeg led the sheep out to pasture. After weeks in the muddy fold, their coats were a sorry sight. Doeg was encouraged when, with the sheep's renewed activity, the matted clumps gradually worked out of the fleece.

Barley harvest, then sheep shearing. Then payday.

One evening as Doeg led the sheep home, he met a neighbor.

"Bad news. Invaders raided Beten yesterday."

Not again! Visions of the previous year's assault flooded the young shepherd's mind. That night he had lost his family, and his future. He had nothing more to lose—but his freedom. And his wages. He stooped to tug at the last remaining clump in the ram's wool. Sheep shearing was scheduled for the following week. Could he chance it?

"Aren't you feeling well?" Zeri said at the close of a quiet supper.

"I'm all right." The teenager got up and went outside.

By the time the couple rolled out their sleeping mat, Doeg had made up his mind. When he was sure they had fallen asleep, he slipped out the door. Wrapped in his spare tunic he carried their image of Baal.

12

ARCHERY

Since the night Saul sat on the rooftop over one-and-a-half years before and shared his family concerns with Jonathan, Saul had been anxious to teach his firstborn use of the bow and arrow. Perhaps his anticipation went back to the morning he and Gatam set out in search of the lost donkeys, the morning the four-year-old declared himself a BIG soldier. For a king, commander of his nation's army, having a trusted son as second in command was ideal, if not absolutely necessary. They were both responsible for the kingdom, and if the kingdom did not survive, neither would they.

Saul spent long hours carefully whittling two strips of wood, overlapping them, and binding them together with animal tendons and cord to form the body of the bow he wanted to present as a gift to his son. The youth should learn archery on a simple bow first, but this one would give him greater range as he became more skilled.

When satisfied with the wooden body, Saul inserted the string into a small slit in one end. Then, standing the bow on end, he braced his knee against the center, pulled the top down, and inserted the other end of the string into its slit. He raised the bow and pulled back on the string several times to test the tension. Adjusting the string's length twice, he finally bound the ends with additional tendon and set it aside to cure. A few days later he took it down to the valley for a trial practice.

Jonathan would be surprised with his gift, Saul thought as he watched an arrow fly through the air toward a broken branch hanging from a tree. The boy was so mature for his age. The branch snapped loose as the arrow hit it.

That evening after supper, in front of the family Saul ceremoniously presented the new weapon to his firstborn. Jonathan's eyes lit up as he accepted the gift and reverently caressed the wood with his index finger.

"I wish I was old enough to have a bow," Malki-Shua said, reaching out to gingerly touch it.

"You will be in a few years," Father said. "Be patient, son."

Jonathan couldn't wait for sunrise. "May we try it out tomorrow?"

"We can begin bow practice tomorrow, but we will start with a simple bow. Using this one takes more skill. When you're ready for it, you will know you have achieved an important goal." He smiled at Jonathan. "If you're as good with the bow as the sling, the Philistine army better run for cover."

"Oh, Father," Malki-Shua protested. "One man can't defeat the Philistines."

"One man and God could, if that was the Lord's will," Jonathan said.

The next morning Saul and Jonathan went down to the edge of the field, where Saul had tied a bundle of straw to a tree trunk and had daubed it with ashes to form a circle for the target. The king carried two simple bows in his hand. Suspended from his shoulder, a quiver, a long leather cylinder, held two dozen arrows.

Reaching the oak tree, he handed Jonathan a bow and withdrew from the quiver a piece of soft leather.

"The snap of the string can really sting if you aren't used to it," Saul said, tying the armguard to Jonathan's left forearm.

Saul drew a line in the dirt with the toe of his sandal, then stepped up to it. He showed Jonathan the proper stance for shooting and how to pull back on the string and bend the wooden body forward. Placing the end of an arrow against the string, Saul brought its long slender body down beside his bow and shot.

Jonathan cheered when the projectile hit the center of the circle. In two quick steps he reached the toe mark, beaming with confidence. Compared to learning slinging, this should be easy. He grinned at his father, pulled back on the string, and let the arrow fly. They watched it disappear into the tree branches. Jonathan groaned.

"Aim a little lower," Saul said.

Jonathan rubbed his arm. He could see what his father meant by the snap of the string. His second attempt sailed by the tree, two feet to the left. He stood, shocked, his mouth agape. How could his shot have gone so wild? This was tougher than it looked. He grabbed another arrow and tried again. *Even worse.* He stared at the offending circle as he scratched his right eyebrow with his thumbnail.

"It's alright," Saul said. "It took me several attempts to hit my first target."

Jonathan slowly shuffled down the edge of the field to search for his wayward arrows. He returned, determined to try again. Overcompensating his aim, his shot went wide on the right side. His cheeks burned with embarrassment. At least Malki-shua wasn't there to see what a terrible job he was doing. He tried a fifth time with the same results, hopes of a future in archery disappearing with the vanishing arrow.

Jonathan slowly trudged out to retrieve the arrows, each step getting slower. After picking them up, he stood looking down the field. Maybe he should just keep going. Why bother to go back and fail again? Tears of frustration stung his eyes. Father would be so disappointed he spent all that time making the bow for him.

"Try to relax," Saul said when he returned. "You are too tense. It makes you jerk at the last minute."

Jonathan's sixth shot showed no improvement. He glanced across the field to Ezel, wishing he could go there and hide instead of returning home, defeated, to face his family. He lowered the bow and turned his back on the target. "It's no use. I'm no good." His shoulders sagged. "I quit." He tossed he bow on the ground.

"Is that what Joseph did when his brothers mistreated him?" Saul said.

Ouch! Why bring up his favorite Israelite now? "No." Jonathan hung his head.

"You'll never hit a moving Philistine in battle if you don't learn to hit a fixed target first."

Jonathan jerked his head up. Mention of the enemy sent a burst of determination through him. He snatched up the bow and he whirled around. Grim-faced, he concentrated on his seventh attempt, which hit the tree above the straw. The next landed on the edge of the ash circle. He reached for yet another arrow.

Once he got the knack of it, Jonathan never missed the target. As he continued practicing, his shot grew more accurate, and he grew more excited. "This is fun." He smiled at his father. "Thanks for making me keep trying."

"Always remember, the House of Kish aren't quitters."

Preparing for bed that night, Jonathan massaged his aching muscles. But they weren't what kept him awake. Long after the others were asleep, he gazed up at the ceiling, where shadows cast by the flickering lamplight swayed back and forth. One by one, he relived the good shots of the morning. Pharez and Gera should be learning this also. If they were to defend Israel, all young men needed to be skilled with bow and arrow. An idea struck him, and he lay awake another hour mulling it over. In spite of the short night, he arose early the next morning.

"Father," Jonathan said as the two descended the staircase to the courtyard, "wouldn't it be a good idea if all the boys of Gibeah sixteen and older had archery training. If we're to become Israel's army, you need to make sure all of us know how to use the bow well."

The king stopped on the bottom step. "That sounds like a wise plan. Let me think about it."

Jonathan was already thinking war strategy. Saul smiled as he walked out the gate. Someday his son would make a great commander for Israel.

Later in the morning the king approached Jonathan. "I like your idea about archery training. We could even do it in other towns. Cousin Abner is an excellent marksman. He could help us. Most able-bodied adult Israelites know how to use the bow, but even they would profit from more training. From our sessions we could select from each village the best men for a standing army."

That afternoon Saul visited Pilha and the other shopkeepers in the marketplace, inviting their sons to meet the first day of the week in the town square with any bows the family owned.

As the sun rose over Gibeah three days later, Saul and Abner walked ahead of the procession to the valley. The voices of excited young men filled the air as they made their way to a spot where the hillside had broken away, leaving a perpendicular wall of earth. Along the hillside, the men had placed upright boards with bundles of straw bound to each. Ash circles marked the targets. In his hand the king held several types of bows. His cousin carried a long wooden case on his shoulder.

Saul assigned Jonathan responsibility for the full quiver, feathers blossoming from its top like a spring bouquet.

Saul welcomed the men to the training session and had them be seated. "This weapon may one day save your life." He held up a bow. "Learn how to use it, its capabilities and limitations, and its proper care. The Philistines confiscate our swords and spears and, because we don't know iron smelting, we can't replace them. But everyone can make and keep a bow."

"Very true," the youths agreed, nodding and smiling at each other.

"First, let's review the various parts of a bow so we all know the same information." Saul held a simple bow aloft. "The wood is called the body. The body has a back." He tapped the outer side with his finger. "The inner side is called the belly. Since you hold a bow at the center, that part is called the grip and the parts of the wood extending out from it are the arms. This, of course, is the string." He pulled back on the string and let it snap.

"There are various kinds of bows, named for the type of their construction. We will begin training with the simple convex bow." The king held one up and explained its construction from a piece of wood bent in an arc. "The compound bow, however, takes a little extra work to make. It is made from two or more strips of wood overlapped and glued or bound together with animal tendons or cord." He held up an example. Jonathan recognized it as the kind Father had presented to him last week.

"The composite bow is hardest to make," Saul said. "The back is made of pieces of wood, sometimes from various kinds of trees, and bands of sinew. The belly is reinforced under each arm with pieces of animal horn, preferably from a wild goat. The inner curve of the horn is placed facing the wood. The whole bow is bound with glue and animal tendons and sinew." Saul passed around the simple and compound bows for the young men to inspect.

"Bows are not only made of different materials, but also have different shapes," Saul said. "Our ancestors thought the simple arc bow to be best, believing the farther apart the hand on the grip and the one on the string, the better. Later, people discovered if the distance between the two was reduced, yet the distance between the string and the peak of the bow arms increased, the tension and firing range were both improved. They began making the double-span, or double-convex, bow, which sort of has the shape of an upper lip."

Abner stepped forward with a double-span bow and pretended to shoot an arrow.

"The action of the bow comes from pulling back on the string, which brings the ends of the wood closer together, thus putting it under tension," Saul explained. "When you release the string the wood springs back to its original position. The string snaps back, which sends the arrow flying. A bigger bow is more pliable and has greater range, but in battle it is often cumbersome.

"The best bow, of course, is the double-span composite bow, which can shoot an arrow over a thousand feet. Powerful armies maintain workshops to manufacture bows. We make our own, however, and most are compound bows. That's not all bad, since composite bows are very vulnerable to changes in the weather and must be kept in special cases to protect them. Using them also requires special and strenuous training. Abner owns a composite bow, and he will show it to you."

The king turned to his cousin, who opened the wooden case and removed the special weapon. He demonstrated its firing range, and the young men were mesmerized as they watched the arrow fly out of sight. A cheer went up from the audience. Abner handed the bow to Pharez, who treated it with deep respect.

Saul pulled several arrows from the quiver slung over Jonathan's shoulder. "The arrow, of course, is the real weapon. The shaft, or body, is made of wood or, better yet, reed since it is more pliant and easier to shape. To fly properly, it must be long, hard, straight, thin, and lightweight. You will learn to make your own according to your preference. The tail is made of feathers, which help the arrow to fly straight and smoothly. I find eagle or vulture feathers work best, but those of the kite or sea fowl will also work." He held up various arrows as he mentioned the different types of feathers.

"The arrowhead is the most important part of the arrow, since it does the damage. For use in battle, it needs to be hard--made of flint, bone, or metal, such as bronze." Saul withdrew several leaf- and triangular-shaped arrowheads from a bag tied to his girdle- belt and handed them to one of the youths to pass around. "You will see they are thick in the middle. This keeps them from splin- tering the shaft on impact. They also need a central spine or rib if they are to penetrate the joints in coats of mail.

"Each of you will need to experiment with your hold on the arrow to determine what hand position works best to gain the most effective release. As we practice, Abner and I will help you. I hope you brought an arm protector. If not, borrow your friend's. We don't want needless injuries." His gaze swept across the crowd of eager faces, and he smiled. "Now, shall we get started?"

The young men scrambled up from their seats on the ground and gathered their bows and quivers. As the others walked toward the practice range, one of them handed Abner's composite bow to Jonathan. The prince had never seen it before, let alone held it. The bow looked so graceful, almost decorative, with its ends curving away from the string and bending outward. Pulling back on the string, he felt the extra tension of the powerful weapon. He carried it over and carefully placed it in the wooden case. Someday he would make himself a double-span composite bow and master its use, he determined, lowering the lid.

13

AN ARMY FOR ISRAEL

Crouched behind a boulder, seventeen-year-old Jonathan craned his neck as his eyes searched the brown surface of the hillside for a telltale spot of black and white that might give away the position of the rock partridge. The earlier *cok-cok--cokrr* challenge had betrayed its presence. Suddenly detecting the young hunters, it now determined to conceal itself from them—and their cooking pot. The grayish bird had distinctively barred flanks and white cheeks, which were bordered with a broad black line, but the variegated color of the rocky hillside camouflaged it completely.

The prince turned to Pharez and shook his head. By his friend's heavy breathing, Jonathan sensed Pharez' was impatient to move on. Maybe they should give up. Mother could cook something else for supper. He transferred the bow to his right hand.

A new sound caught Jonathan's attention and he raised his hand to signal caution. Turning to a thin gap between the boulder and the hillside, he put his eye to it and waited to see what was coming down the road.

The sound of the heavy tread of feet surprised him. The

approaching voices grew louder, and he held his breath. Who was it?

The first person passed before the crack, not fifteen feet away from the boys. Others followed, four abreast. A big lump rose in Jonathan's throat, and his stomach twisted in a knot as he viewed the profile of the men against the blue sky. Clean shaven faces, straight noses that merged with straight foreheads, erect posture, identical uniforms. *Philistines!*

As the line filed by, the prince got his first close look at the battle attire of Israel's worst enemy. Over their shirts they wore metal breastplates. Below them wide belts held short, paneled kilts that came to a point in front and were decorated with tassels. He could not see the Philistines' feet, but by their firm tread he knew they wore sturdy shoes or sandals.

The headdress looked most intriguing. An ornamental headband encircled a leather cap, which hung down in back to form a neck guard. From the headband a row of slightly curved strips stood up to form a plumed diadem. Were they feathers, or horsehair? Jonathan watched them sway slightly with the body's movement. Maybe they were just leather strips. Or even reeds, he speculated before realizing that, in his fascination, he no longer held his breath. He studied the next man's diadem more closely. Could it be a hairdo? Undecided, he turned his attention to the row of small knobs and zigzag pattern that decorated the headbands. Then his gaze moved down to the soldiers' bodies.

Unlike the rectangular Canaanite shields, these men carried smaller round ones, which were embossed with small metal studs. From each soldier's left side dangled a long, sheathed sword. Jonathan unconsciously formed a grip with his hand as he imagined the feel of the hilt. If only Israelite soldiers were so well armed. Then he reminded himself exactly whom he watched— pagan Philistines. Israelites were God's Chosen People. He fought for them with weapons no man could shape or make.

The last row of soldiers passed, and Jonathan started to relax when he realized one man had stopped. So did Jonathan's heart. The Philistine stooped down and extracted a stone from his sandal, then hurried on. Jonathan let his breath out and turned to Pharez, who crouched behind him, peering over his shoulder.

"Like a flock of hoopoes marching down the road," Jonathan's friend whispered when they could no longer hear footsteps.

"A what?"

"Hoopoes. You know, birds."

Jonathan chuckled at the idea of comparing the proud Philistines to the unclean bird, but when he thought about it, the similarity was striking. The pinkish brown bird had bold bars of black and white on its wings, and its prominent, black-tipped crest stood erect when it walked—just like a Philistine's plumed headdress.

To relieve the tension of the close encounter, Jonathan pursed his lips and gave the distinctive hoopoe call, *poo-poo-poo*. When the boys heard a bird answer from a hillside tree, they leaned back and smothered their snickers in their cupped hands.

Jonathan crawled around the boulder and looked down the road. Seeing the line of soldiers in the distance, he stood up. He heard an arrow zing through the air and glanced back to see Pharez running up the hillside to retrieve a rock partridge. A few minutes later they started home. The afternoon wasn't wasted after all. At least Pharez's family would enjoy meat in their lentil stew tonight.

Abner stood behind the line of ten young men, observing their stance and hold on their weapons as they drew their bows and shot at the targets. As the archery training sessions continued across the Land, Saul had become more and more impressed with his younger cousin's military skill. Satisfied he had found the best, the king appointed Abner commander of Israel's army.

A few feet behind the archers, Saul and six elders of Bethlehem watched the practice. "That second fellow is good," the king said to the man on his right. "Whose son is he?"

"He's the firstborn of Jesse."

"Oh, really?" The king turned to the prominent farmer. "You must be very proud of him. How old is he?"

"Seventeen."

"The same age as my firstborn. In a few years he will make a great soldier. I hope you have many other sons."

"Seven others, including the twins and the baby."

"The perfect number, plus one," the king complimented him. "I trust I find many men as fruitful as you in our tour of the kingdom."

The farmer beamed with pride.

They watched a new group of archers step up to the firing line. Abner counted to five, and they shot.

"Our plan to train an army is going well," Saul told the elders. "Last dry season we covered the towns in Benjamin, Ephraim, and Manasseh. If we make selections in Judah and Simeon this year, next year we can move north to the tribes beyond the Plain of Jezreel and east to those beyond Jordan. Then I think we will be prepared to form a select army of Israel's best marksmen. It is better to be prepared for war than to depend on a hastily called militia like we did at Jabesh Gilead."

"But Jabesh Gilead was one amazing battle," Jesse said. He smiled as he shook his head back and forth. "Seeing God fight for Israel at dawn's first light that morning reminded me of Moses marching through the Red Sea and Joshua around Jericho."

"Think how much more God could use an army that is organized and trained."

"Well, you can count on Eliab's service in three or four years," Jesse said. "Then Abinadab and Shammah—clear down to Baby David. One thing you can depend on from Jesse of Bethlehem is loyalty to God and Israel."

Saul turned to the others. "I appreciate that, and what all of you are doing. You had faith to choose me as your king to lead an army to defeat our enemies. With God's help the kingdom will become so strong the Land will at last enjoy peace and prosperity."

At the end of the third dry season of training, Saul felt it was time to organize his army. Following the Law of Moses, which spoke of young men twenty and older who were able to fight in battle, he called that group to meet in Gibeah to join in the celebration of the Feast of Tabernacles.

As the vast crowd assembled for the last great day of the Feast, the prophet Samuel blessed the people and the new soldiers. From those gathered, Saul chose 3,000 bowmen and slingers for Israel's first standing army.

"Go home and plant the new crop," the king instructed the recruits the final morning of selection. "Make plans with your families. Arrange with the elders of your clans to supply food for their soldiers. Then, when the rains end, return to Gibeah with your weapons, tents, and food. In the meantime, keep practicing."

Those not chosen groaned in disappointment, but Saul encouraged them all to keep training for the day of all-out war, when every able-bodied man would be called up.

That evening as Samuel and Saul rested on the rooftop, the old prophet looked up at the king. "Remember what I have always told you. When you are ready to fight the Philistines, gather your forces at Gilgal and call me. I will come to offer the sacrifice and pray the Levitical blessing on the soldiers."

"I appreciate that. All Israel has deep respect for you. Your word is directly from God and your blessing will inspire even the faintest of heart. I don't know what I would have done throughout the years without your wise advice regarding the kingdom."

The sound of rain falling on the flat roof overhead had a soothing effect on Jonathan as he opened his eyes and looked up at the small window high in the wall. It was still night, but he did not close them again. He was thankful the boys had their own room. He enjoyed the privacy—and did not miss his father's snoring. Rain on, he silently encouraged the weather, yawning as he stretched.

To the farmers of Gibeah, the latter rains were the crowning blessing on the barley crop ripening in the fields below town. This year, to Jonathan the latter rains signaled a complete change in his life. When they ceased falling in a few days, he would become a commander in the army of Israel. He felt a flutter in his stomach. Was it apprehension or excitement—or both? He was only nineteen. Would he be able to handle such heavy responsibility?

Abraham had been seventy-five years old when God called him to leave his homeland for an unknown Promised Land. Moses was eighty when the Lord spoke to him from the burning bush in the desert. "Who am I, that I should go to Pharaoh and bring the Israelites out of Egypt?" he had asked God. Jonathan guessed no one ever felt adequate in their own strength, whether they were nineteen or eighty. God had told Moses that day, "I'll be with you." That was really all they needed. The prince rolled over and closed his eyes. If they felt confident in themselves, they wouldn't depend on God.

The gentle rain lulled him back to sleep. The next thing he knew, morning had dawned. Tiptoeing out of the bedroom, he let himself out the front door, hoping not to waken Malki-Shua and Ishvi. Since the younger ones usually needed a little shaking to roust them from sleep, he knew the precaution was unnecessary.

Closing the door, Jonathan walked over to the parapet. A thin band of light outlined the horizon above the eastern hills—the breaking of dawn, "the eyelids of the morning." The air hung still and quiet. He closed his eyes and inhaled deeply, drinking in the peacefulness as he thanked God for the promise of His presence. A moment later he jumped when a hand touched his shoulder. Opening his eyes, he saw his father standing beside him.

"Come," Saul whispered. "I've something to show you."

The two descended the staircase to the courtyard, still shrouded in deep shadows. Entering the kitchen, the king scooped up a coal from the dying embers in the fire pit and dropped it into a clay cup. They crossed the courtyard to their old family room in the corner. Saul handed the cup to Jonathan and removed from his girdle-belt a key, with which he unlocked the door. Until then, Jonathan had not realized the door had a lock.

The prince had not been in the room since the morning, five years before, when Ethan left Gibeah. A sense of sorrow washed over him as he thought of his beloved teacher, whose condition, Samuel reported, continued to grow worse.

Saul pushed the door open, they stepped in, then he quickly closed it behind them. Retrieving a lamp from the niche in the wall, the king held the coal to its wick. The linen strip caught fire and the flame blazed up, casting a pale light over the room.

In the corner Jonathan saw Ethan's rolled sleeping mat still propped against the wall, along with the one Samuel used when he visited. The short table sat on one side of the room exactly where it used to, the bundle of scrolls missing. Next to the table stood a chest the prince had never seen. Saul knelt in front of it and, with a second key, unlocked the wooden box. After lifting the lid, he pulled back a woolen cover. Jonathan inhaled sharply.

In the dim lamplight, the prince gazed at a double-edged sword. Unlike the *khopesh*, the Egyptian sickle-shaped sword used for striking, this one had a long stabbing blade with a thick center that tapered down to thin edges and a sharp point. It was made of iron. One of the Philistines' guarded treasures!

"Where did you get this?"

Saul lifted the weapon and stood up. "For you," he said, handing it to his son.

Momentarily speechless, Jonathan hesitated to touch the

forbidden sword. "How did you get it without the Philistines knowing?"

Ignoring the question, the king stooped to uncover a second sword. He lifted it out and the father and son stood, facing each other, as they admired the weapons.

"Let's just say God provided them," Saul finally said. "It is better you don't know where they came from, then no one can force you to reveal their source." Jonathan touched the blade's shaft.

"Son," Saul said, "you are now a commander of Israel. I am depending on you, and so is God. With these swords you and I will bring deliverance to Israel. Samuel prayed a blessing on these when he came for the Feast. I have dedicated them to the establishment of the kingdom."

They heard someone moving about in the courtyard. Saul turned to replace his sword, then Jonathan handed the second one to him. The teenager paused just before they opened the door.

"Thank you, Father. I'll keep our secret until God's time to reveal it."

"It won't be long. Our soldiers will be arriving any day now. The Lord be with them."

"And with us."

14

OFFICER TRAINING

After surveying the territory surrounding Gibeah, King Saul decided the area between Bethel and Michmash, six miles to the northeast, to be the best location for his army camp. As the 3,000 young soldiers arrived, he sent them there to set up their tents under Abner's direction.

When Saul arrived with Jonathan the following week, he divided the men into units of ten, sections of fifty, and companies of two hundred. He appointed a captain over each company, then called the fifteen leaders to meet, along with Abner and Jonathan, under the oak tree near Saul's tent for a council session to plan war strategy.

As Jonathan waited for the group to assemble, he rubbed his upper arm. Firm muscle. Years of sinking the plough into rain-moistened ground, pitching sheaves on the threshing floor, lifting bags of harvested grain onto donkeys' backs, and carrying loaded baskets of grapes and olives to the presses had produced more than just food for the family. The security of Israel depended on strong bodies, coupled with God's divine protection. He thanked God he had both.

Glancing around at the men who sat beside him, all at least ten years older than himself, Jonathan's heart beat faster. "Oh, God," he prayed silently, "give me strength and wisdom to be the leader my troops need." He knew how to use the bow and had practiced with the sword. He recognized, however, that nothing could substitute for battle experience; he had none. Samuel had been right. Being a crown prince had privileges, but also huge responsibilities. He held lives in his hands. Wrong decisions, like that of Adam in the Garden of Eden, had grave consequences.

Saul strode across the grass to the commanders, his steps decisive, his massive shoulders squared, his jaw firm. With contagious confidence, he welcomed his new assistants. He began the meeting without hesitation. "Today Israel becomes a true kingdom. We have a standing army to be proud of and one that surrounding nations will fear. You are prepared to defend Israel with your lives. Today the reign of Saul truly begins."

A cheer went up from the chosen leaders.

"This morning we will discuss war strategy," the king said. "The main goal of any battle is to injure and disable the enemy without sustaining serious injury ourselves. Israel has a great history, and we can learn much about successful warfare by reviewing it. As you think over the stories you heard as boys or in recent teaching from Samuel, what victories do you recall?"

The group sat thinking. Beriah, from the tribe of Asher, broke the silence. "Gideon gained a great triumph with only trumpets and torches as weapons."

"Yes. What a mighty victory," Saul agreed. "However, we can't expect God to use that method every time. Joshua certainly did not expect to march around every city and see the walls fall down. What other factors in Gideon's success could benefit our army?"

Carmi, a Reubenite, mentioned the element of surprise, since the attack came in the dead of night. "It created panic. The Midianites couldn't identify each other in the dark, so they killed their own men. They couldn't organize into units or ranks in time to stand against Israel."

"That is the plan you used at Jabesh Gilead," Simeon from Beersheba said. Saul nodded.

"The Israelites used the three-division approach," Zimran from Bethel added. "Uncle Meremoth says you also used that method at Jabesh Gilead."

Saul's face remained stoic, but Jonathan could tell that his father was pleased at the mention of his one military success.

"Are there any other factors we have forgotten?" the king asked.

"The Lord chose to use only three hundred in the attack, so Israel would know the power of God brought the victory," Dedan from Hebron said.

"But, following the attack, Gideon called for others to assist in the pursuit," Saul reminded them. "How does that apply to us today?"

"We have an army of 3,000, but if we are invaded, we would call all Israel to join us," Carmi said.

"The three hundred had a well-coordinated plan of action," Sheba of Gibeon added. "If they had blown their trumpets one at a time the Midianites would have been alerted and the element of surprise lost."

"A good point. Let's think of another battle."

Beker the Benjamite raised his hand. "At Ai Joshua's troops drew the men away from the city by retreating before them. Those lying in ambush behind the city rose up and burned it before the men could return to defend it."

"That is not only a method of war, but also a caution to us about leaving our cities vulnerable," Jonathan said. He had grown impressed with the men's knowledge of Israelite history. His father had chosen leaders who cared about God's People.

"A good observation," the king said. "Can someone think of another battle?"

Kedar of Judah mentioned Bethel, where the men of Manasseh

captured a citizen outside the locked gates and offered him and his family life and safety in exchange for information about the secret passage into the city.

"Our patrols should remember that case when they seek information about the enemy," Abner said.

Adam, a shepherd from near Megiddo, briefly reviewed the story of Abimelech, the son of Gideon's concubine. Abimelech killed his seventy brothers and set himself up as king in Shechem. When the people turned against him, he laid siege to the city. Drawing the people beyond the city walls to fight, he ambushed them, then entered the city and destroyed it. When some sought sanctuary in the tower of Shechem, the citadel, he gathered firewood at its base and set the tower on fire.

"Later, Abimelech failed to remember one important point in warfare," Saul said when Adam finished telling the story. "What did he forget?"

"Never go too close to a city wall," Zimran answered. "When Abimelech besieged Thebez and captured it, the people also took refuge in the citadel. As Abimelech tried to storm it, a woman in the tower threw an upper millstone down and cracked his skull."

"Always remember Zimran's point," Saul warned, looking at the fifteen captains. "No one wants to be killed in such a manner. And what could be more humiliating than to be killed by a woman?" Several low chuckles could be heard.

"Speaking of women, what about the defeat of Sisera," Abner said. "What can we learn from Deborah and Barak's battle with Sisera?"

Jonathan recalled the prophetess' message from the Lord to Barak. "The first thing would be that when God orders a battle, He will ensure the victory."

Saul nodded at his son. "That is a point we must not forget. What else?"

"Sisera had nine hundred chariots," Obal from Ramah said. "But Deborah and Barak drew his forces down to the Plain of

Jezreel. When God sent a downpour, the chariots became mired in the swampy area near the River Kishon. Israel defeated them."

"Sisera hid in a woman's tent," Caleb of Jezreel added. "Jael killed him in his sleep, using a hammer and tent peg. That should teach us not to go into places where we don't belong, and not to trust someone whose loyalty may be in doubt."

"These are all excellent points," Saul said as he concluded the morning session. "We have covered a lot. In summary, we have mentioned methods such as night attacks, the element of surprise, ambush, siege, fire, dividing the army into three units, enlisting all men in battle, and choosing the best site for battle."

After the captains reviewed their observations, Saul commended them and dismissed the group. "Tomorrow we will discuss more war strategy and armament preparations."

The following day the company leaders arrived with eager step, friendly greetings, and a spirit of unity. Jonathan took his seat on the grass beside Carmi.

Saul opened the session by reviewing the prior discussion, then progressed to a new topic. "The Edomites and Moabites have started making border raids again to the south and beyond Jordan. But we know our biggest, most aggressive enemy is the Philistines. Who has seen a Philistine soldier up close?"

Some from the Shephelah had seen a patrol from a distance, but only Jonathan could give a clear description, recalling his surreptitious observation from behind the boulder two years before. In spite of his youth, the men listened with rapt attention as he recounted his experience.

"What sort of bows do they carry?" Zimran asked when the prince finished. He had been one of Saul and Abner's prize students when they introduced archery during their earlier visit to Bethel.

"Surprisingly, they didn't carry any."

"My brother observed that as a teenager," Abner said. "When he helped pursue the Philistines who tried to attack Israel during their meeting at Mizpah, he saw many corpses after the battle. Not many had bows."

"That tells us a lot about their war strategy," Saul said. "What means of offense and defense do they mostly use?"

The men enumerated swords, spears, shields, helmets, breast-plates, and chariots, all for the conduct of short- and medium-range combat.

"By stunning the enemy with a lightening charge, then following up with a swift attack launched from chariots, they believe they can finish us off in hand-to-hand combat." Saul went on to describe what he had learned about Philistine methods of war. Their chariots, driven by two horses, had six-spoked wheels, not the heavier solid-wood wheels of Israelite wagons. They carried a crew of three. The infantry that followed carried round shields, wore breastplates and plumed helmets, and carried two spears and a straight sword. They marched in unison in groups of four. "From what we know about the Philistines, what can we do to better withstand their attacks?" Saul asked.

"The Philistines deprive us of sword and spear," Beker replied, "but by forcing us to rely on bow and sling, we develop skill in long-range weapons. We can kill or injure many before they reach striking distance with their spears and swords."

"Since we don't own chariots, we become more agile on foot," Caleb said. "We should force the battle into the hills and moun-tains, thus making their chariots useless to them."

"God gave Abraham the hill country for good reason," Saul responded. "Any other ideas?"

"We must aim our arrows at parts not covered by helmet and breastplate," Adam said. "And we need good arrowheads to pierce between the joints in their armor."

"If they band together in units of four, we also need to stick together in hand-to-hand fighting," Beriah observed. "Otherwise, they will cut us down, one by one, like a sickle in a barley field. If we use units of four, our backs will never be exposed."

"Good point." Saul smiled at the young man from Asher.

Jonathan nodded in agreement. "If we only carry slings and bows, we will be slaughtered when the Philistines get close," he said. "We may not own swords and spears, but we could carry battle axes and maces for those encounters."

Abner turned to the captains. "How many brought axes or maces?" A few hands went up.

"Will we be wearing breastplates?" Obal asked. "I brought one my father owns."

"It would be good if we all had them," Saul said. "Each captain should survey his men. Count their weapons, shields, and breastplates. We can make what is lacking."

The following day Saul reviewed with the officers the reasons for exemption from military service according to the Law of Moses—betrothal; first year of marriage; ownership of a new, but undedicated, house or of a new vineyard from which the first crop had not been harvested; and fear.

"Fear is as great a threat in combat as the enemy's sword," the king said. "On the battlefield, cowardice can spread like a plague, paralyzing an entire army."

Recalling the lump in his throat and knot in his stomach the afternoon he crouched in the rocky hideout with Pharez and watched the Philistine patrol pass, Jonathan knew his father to be right. He couldn't have moved had his life depended on it.

Saul went on to review physical and spiritual preparations for war. He emphasized eating well, exercising daily, and getting plenty of sleep the night before battle. Jonathan felt proud of his father's wisdom and concern for the soldiers' welfare.

"As God's People, we must obey His Law if we want His help in victory," the king reminded the leaders. He quoted the Law regarding avoiding impurity and abstaining from sexual relations before battle.

"Moses commanded the priest to offer the sacrifice and pronounce a blessing on the men as they set out to face the enemy. When I became king, the prophet Samuel promised me he would come to Gilgal and do this for Israel's army. He renewed that promise at the recent Feast of Tabernacles."

Hearing Samuel's plan relieved Jonathan's anxiety. He respected the prophet more than any other man. Samuel being with them would be like having the presence of God in their midst.

At the conclusion of the strategy sessions, the three commanders helped the captains organize their companies. Throughout the dry season the troops practiced with their weapons. Besides marching, exercising, and running, they also scaled the city walls of Bethel with ladders and climbed cliffs.

Before the early rains fell, the king divided the army. He stationed Abner and one thousand men near Bethel. Jonathan and a second thousand moved to Gibeah. He kept the remainder with him at Michmash. Then he sent them home, one-third at a time, to collect animal hides and more food rations.

Jonathan gave thanks to God that his father left him at home. He loved Malki-Shua but, with Grandfather no longer with them, Jonathan could not see the tall slender teenager being man of the house.

Shorter than Saul, Jonathan had his sturdy build. Malki-Shua had his father's face. Square face, firm jaw. Give him a full beard and more flesh on his frame and he would be an earlier version of his father.

Jonathan wasn't sure whom—or what—he looked like. When he was young Mother always said he had Grandfather Ahimaaz's eyes. He was never sure what that meant. Sometimes Jonathan wished he could step outside his body to view himself. He chuckled at the impossible wish.

Another reason Jonathan was happy to be in Gibeah was concern for his mother. Early in the summer he realized she would soon deliver another child. Recalling her two previous miscarriages, he prayed for her safety and that of the unborn baby.

After dividing the troops, Saul came home from Michmash. A few weeks later four-year-old Merab welcomed a new sister, Michal.

Jonathan held the little bundle, wrapped like a cocoon, and studied her face. She looked more beautiful than Merab had been as a newborn. The defenseless, innocent infant tugged at his soldier-heart. He saw her as a precious gift from God; to the Philistines, she meant nothing—or less. He shuddered, recalling reports of their atrocities to females. He bent down and whispered, "You're a very special princess. God has given you to us, and I promise to protect you with my life." Later as he sat in his headquarters room off the courtyard, he heard her cry. What might he have to go through to carry out that promise?

Besides dividing the army, the king also formed defense units within each thousand, according to the soldiers' abilities. In battle, shield bearers would try to defend the advance warriors, since the bowmen and slingers used both hands when firing. Those carrying javelins, maces, and battle axes would have to form the rear guard for short-range fighting. They could carry their own shields.

A few men, while home, had been able to locate javelins, and Saul incorporated them into their drills. Javelins, similar to large arrows, were made of wood or reeds and fitted with metal tips. They were hurled by hand and javelin throwers carried their supplies in quivers. The loop javelin had a cord at one end, which could be wound around the javelin and the loop held by the finger until thrown. As the javelin hurtled through the air, the unwinding cord would cause it to spin, giving it a steadier flight.

Unlike javelins, the larger, heavier spears were used as thrusting weapons in hand-to-hand fighting. Since the Philistines had confiscated Israel's swords and spears, only Saul and Jonathan now owned them.

On sunny days Jonathan took small hunting parties to the woods near Gibeah. These adventures not only honed archery skills, but also provided meat for the soldiers. When the winter rains began falling, the men billeted in the upper rooms of various homes in the three towns or nearby villages and began making leather breastplates. They also carved shields from wood and overlaid them with leather. Since the Israelites did not have metal breastplates, as the Philistines did, they made the longer rectangular shields to provide maximum body protection.

Men also scoured the hills for round-, egg-, and saucer-shaped stones to use as mace heads. Then they carved wooden clubs for handles. The short handles were widest at the end where they were gripped, thus preventing them from flying out of the warriors' hands when they swung them. They were tapered toward the head. Some made curved handles. The head of a mace had a socket base, which the handle fit into. The men bored the holes before binding the heads and handles together with strips of leather. Heavy, blunt, and made for striking a blow, the mace had somewhat limited use if the enemy wore helmets.

While home, a few men had also been able to locate battle axes. These were of similar size and make as the maces, but the lighter head and the sharp blade could cut or pierce like a sword. Keeping the head of the ax from flying off posed a major concern in its construction. To use against an army wearing armor, Jonathan knew the blade must pierce deeply. Different shapes would work better in different situations. Unfortunately, the scarcity of metal limited the number available to the Israelites.

After Jonathan completed his shield and breastplate, he cut a piece of hide into two tapered strips and sewed them together as a sheath for his still-hidden sword. Then he fashioned a belt and an attaching strap for carrying it.

～

The morning dawned damp and chilly. Jonathan shivered as he walked down the hillside. He paused to admire the almond trees, harbingers of spring, which seemed to have reached full bloom overnight. The pale pink blossoms that covered the trees looked white from a distance, reminding him of childhood days when he had compared them to the snowy-haired men who hobbled around the marketplace. He smiled at the memory and started to go, when he noticed a group of men coming down the valley road a half-mile away.

Returning home, he looked up later to see his father and a dozen men from the Michmash camp enter the gateway. Saul went upstairs to visit his family, then spent an hour conferring with Jonathan. When they finished, the king called in a young soldier and introduced him.

"Abner first spotted Joel during our training session in Dothan four years ago. Even though Joel is still only nineteen, Abner sent for him to come when the soldiers returned with their supplies. Abner has worked with him for several weeks and recommends him as an excellent fighter, faithful in obeying orders and zealous for Israel. Jonathan, I'm assigning Joel to you as your armor-bearer."

"Really?" the prince said, surprised at the unexpected appointment. He smiled at the young man, one year younger than himself, and reached out to shake his hand. The youth's eyes shone with excitement as he extended his.

"From this day forward my life is bound with yours," Joel declared in an oath of loyalty. "May God be with you as a leader in Israel."

15

DECLARATION OF WAR

When the latter rains ended, Saul sent the soldiers home for more supplies. Upon their return, he began full scale weapons practice again. Jonathan knew the Philistines had closely watched the small army in training. Not surprisingly, they moved their lookout from Gibeah to the hill of Geba, a few miles to the north and directly opposite Michmash.

Michmash sat on the north side of the *wadi* Suweinit, part of the strategic road from the coastal plain to the Jordan River. By positioning themselves between the two divisions, Jonathan figured, the Philistines planned both to monitor Israelite action and protect the passage from enemy control.

The Israelites had been a loosely organized group of tribes, whom the Philistines kept disarmed, rendering them incapable of a successful attack. In contrast, the Philistines had thousands of chariots and charioteers, a huge army, and a tight monopoly on weapons production. By the number of additional Philistine troops Jonathan saw moving across the plain below Gibeon, he knew they took the mobilization of the Israelite army seriously.

Farmers soon moved into the fields to harvest barley. With the troops all back in camp, Jonathan felt the need to consult his father. His men faithfully practiced archery and slinging each day, ran long distances to increase stamina, and ate moderately. But an army was meant for fighting, not for practice sessions. Wars were fought during the dry season, now well under way. Jonathan sent a message requesting a planning meeting, which the king scheduled after the New Moon, two weeks later.

As the old moon waned, the young impatient troops caught Jonathan's excitement. Watching the thin sliver of moon rise in the sky one evening, Jonathan's heart beat a little faster. Tomorrow he would leave for Michmash.

Standing on the rooftop of his home, he looked up at the dark blue heavens and poured out his heart to the Lord. "God, help us defeat our enemies and drive them from the Land, as You commanded Joshua so many years ago. You promised this Land to Abraham and his seed, who would be as numerous as the stars in the sky. Give Father wisdom to know when and how to make the first move." Slipping under his blanket a few minutes later, he thanked God for His faithfulness to His Chosen People.

The next morning Jonathan awoke before dawn. Appointing Beker, his most trusted captain, to be in charge during his absence, the prince called the other four captains and sixteen soldiers as an escort. He and Joel led the way down the hillside. The sunshine warmed them as they headed north past fields of barley stubble and waving wheat. The rains had been good, the harvest abundant.

The men stopped an hour later for a brief rest and drink of water before making the last short lap of their journey. Coming around the side of a hill a few minutes later, the soldiers were surprised to see a Philistine patrol twenty feet in front of them.

"Halt!" the pagan captain ordered.

Jonathan's men wore ordinary clothes and, with bows and quivers slung over their shoulders, one might have taken them for hunters—except for Joel. The armor-bearer carried Jonathan's rectangular shield and the sheathed sword strapped to his belt.

"Hand over your sword," the captain demanded. "How did you manage to obtain such a weapon?"

Jonathan's heart sank. He had never even used his sword in battle. How could he surrender it? He shouldn't have brought it, but it was too late. With a sigh, he stretched out his hand. Joel reluctantly pulled the precious iron weapon from the sheath. Jonathan grasped the hilt and looked at the captain, glancing briefly at the plumed headdress that had fascinated him so much a few years before. Suddenly a surge of power filled the prince. Divine power.

"I got it from the Lord God of Israel, who fights for His People," he said as he moved forward to meet the captain.

When Jonathan stepped within arm's reach, he lunged at the officer. The captain, caught off guard, did not have his shield raised to protect his upper chest and head. Before he knew what happened, the sword sliced through his neck. He slumped to the ground. Israelites had never resisted search and seizure, and the stunned patrol hesitated a moment—long enough for the Israelites to draw their bows and fire.

The Philistines instinctively drew their swords, but the Israelites were beyond reach. Arrows found their mark before swords did. The rear ranks of the patrol broke and ran toward Geba, zigzagging through the *wadi* to avoid flying arrows. The Israelites gave chase. They saw only one survivor reach the safety of the lookout.

Jonathan and his men hurried to Michmash. As they climbed the steep hillside to camp, the prince realized the enormity of what had transpired. What would Father think? They were coming to plan strategy. Now the whole situation had changed.

The first sound of death wails carried across the gorge from Geba as Jonathan's men reached the edge of the Israelite camp.

Companies of soldiers stopped what they were doing to stand in front of their tents and gaze across at the lookout. Passing them, Jonathan went straight to Saul's tent. The king's eyes narrowed, and his face became grim as he listened to Jonathan describe the encounter. Whether in self-defense or by deliberate provocation, the attack had the same results—dead Philistines. That meant war!

The king knew his 3,000 men would never stand a chance against the tens of thousands of well-armed Philistines that were sure to pour up the Way of Beth-Horon to Geba. He tried to suppress feelings of panic. He must rally all Israel immediately. He called for messengers. They soon scattered out across the kingdom to blow the trumpet and announce Saul's call to arms: "Let all Hebrews hear. Meet in Gilgal to fight for Israel." A runner set out for Ramathaim Zuphim to notify Samuel.

Saul sent Jonathan and his men back to Gibeah. The prince selected forty bodyguards to defend Saul's family and keep an eye on his hometown. The remainder of his troops he sent to join up with Saul's army. Abner's troops arrived that afternoon.

The next morning Saul marshaled the 3,000 and headed down to Gilgal to form the nucleus of the volunteer army. As an afterthought, he sent Abner to Gibeah in case young Jonathan needed help. They would meet back in Michmash the following week.

Saul's troops reached Gilgal by sunset. With his headquarters tent erected, he planted his spear in front. The next afternoon a few men arrived and began practicing for battle. The king knew more would come in a day or two as word spread. He and his fifteen captains tried to train the recruits as they arrived. But over the following days, men arrived by tens and twenties, not by hundreds and thousands as they had when defending Jabesh Gilead.

What was wrong? Saul stood watching the soldiers march in formation. Was it easier to fight on distant soil than your home territory? Maybe the power of the Philistines terrifies them. Or was it because at Jabesh Gilead they fought to defend their brothers under assault? This time Jonathan had initiated the attack.

Once, when the king walked through the camp, he overheard a young man quote the message as announced to his village: "Saul has attacked the outpost of Geba. Now Israel is a stench to the Philistines."

The king choked back an angry retort as he ducked behind a tent. He could not afford to upset those who had actually showed up to fight.

It did not help the men's spirits when new arrivals described seeing the Philistines flooding across the pass of Beth-Horon, bringing chariots and cartloads of arms with them. Amassing in the mountains, they now occupied Saul's old camp at Michmash and the plateau stretching north toward Bethel. Terrified Israelites were taking refuge in caves and forests, hiding under brush in pits, and lowering themselves into dry cisterns.

That night three hundred of Saul's men deserted.

Samuel received Saul's message and reminder of his long-standing promise. The prophet sent word back he would arrive by the seventh day. Saul felt heartened to know one man had no intention of running.

The fourth day brought more encouraging news as Saul watched a hundred volunteers from Judah coming up the valley past Jericho. When the captains counted the men the next morning, however, the shocked king learned there were four hundred less than the day before.

Archery practice that morning became a disaster; even the remaining men seemed to have lost confidence. Samuel had not arrived yet, and Saul felt the loneliness of bearing sole responsibility for the kingdom.

The next morning Saul assembled the dwindling army. He learned that over a thousand from his original army had crossed the river after dark to flee to the plateau of Gilead. No new arrivals joined them that day.

As the sun set, the king paced up and down in front of his tent. Where was Samuel? They couldn't start without him, but if he didn't show up soon there would be no one left for him to bless. Tomorrow would be the seventh day. Saul encouraged himself with that thought as he called the remaining soldiers to gather for a meeting. He closed with an announcement.

"Samuel will arrive tomorrow. When he comes, we will march to Michmash and victory."

Saul walked back to his tent. Could the others sense the hollowness in his voice? Jonathan would have given him encouragement, but Jonathan was not there. In a way, he was glad. From overhearing fragments of conversations that broke off when he came around a tent or walked past a cluster of men, he knew some blamed Jonathan's action for this terrible disruption of their peaceful lives.

After supper the king sat alone in front of his tent, staring into the campfire as he absently rolled a stick back and forth between his hands. A conversation he had with Samuel years before came to mind—and with it an overpowering fear.

Eli had permitted his two sons to be greedy and immoral. People lost respect for the priesthood. God had allowed the Tabernacle to be destroyed and all three priests to die. Saul recalled the pathos in Samuel's voice that distant afternoon as the prophet spoke of his own family. Samuel's two sons had become corrupt judges. People rejected their leadership. Samuel lost his influence, and God appointed a king in his place. Saul flung the stick into the fire. Now Jonathan had attacked the enemy. People were terrified and deserting in droves.

Saul stood up and his spine stiffened. Eli and Samuel might lose their positions because of their sons, but he refused to forfeit the kingdom because of his son's hasty action.

Stomping over to his tent, Saul lifted the flap and went in. Removing his cloak and sandals, he lay down on his blanket. Sleep eluded him as he tossed and turned, his thoughts churning. Where was Samuel? Saul promised the men he would arrive tomorrow. If he didn't, what would Saul do?

The next morning Saul felt tired and stiff, as if he had spent the day before harvesting barley. Did he even turn over during the night? He stooped to go through the tent opening. Yawning, he stretched his taut muscles to work the kinks out. His gaze automatically shifted to the hill road, down which Samuel should be coming in a few hours.

He walked over to the makeshift shelter, where the animals designated for sacrifice stood looking up at him. He scratched a sheep behind its ears. "You have an important part in Israel's victory," he told it. "By your life God will save the kingdom."

Turning, Saul saw the men behind him milling around, side-stepping last night's campfire ashes, talking in low voices. He called for the captains to meet at his tent. When only thirteen showed up, he walked over to Dedan.

"Where are Kedar, and Obal?"

Dedan hung his head. "Two men arrived from Mizpah after you went to bed. They described the massive Philistine force at Michmash. The news is not good. I think the captains deserted."

Saul felt his face flush with anger. "Where would Israel be today if our forefathers had deserted Joshua like this?"

"Gideon defeated the Midianites with only three hundred men," Zimran reminded him.

"But Gideon had God's blessing. We don't even have that." Saul turned to look up the hill road again, shielding his eyes. "Where can that Samuel be?"

"It's still early," Adam replied. "Let's form ranks and do maneuvers. The troops feel better when they are active. They get restless sitting around."

"You are right," Saul said. "Call the men."

When the thirteen captains lined up the remaining men, they

counted only eight hundred. After mid-morning breakfast they began archery practice. Saul watched proudly as man after man hit a small target nailed to a pole. They may not have swords and spears, but they could shoot within a hair's breadth. Saul smiled with encouragement.

The sun stood directly overhead when Saul called for a break. After a restless night, he quickly fell asleep, awakening refreshed an hour later. He called for Alvah, his armor-bearer, as he came out of his tent.

"Has Samuel arrived?"

"Not yet."

Glancing up at the sun to estimate the time, Saul paced back and forth. Finally, he exhaled slowly and called his troops together. They would at least be near the altar when the prophet arrived.

Dedan ran up to the king, panting for breath. "Sir, fifty more men absconded during rest period. They don't believe Samuel is really coming. They say he knows Israel has no chance against the mighty Philistines."

"But we have God on our side." Saul's voice rose as he spoke.

"Then where is God's man?" Dedan asked quietly. "He doesn't seem to have faith in the kingdom either."

Mention of the word kingdom was like holding a flame to oil. Saul refused to lose the kingdom because of one man's incompetence. He felt his temper rising. God anointed him king. If Samuel wouldn't support the kingdom, then he would by myself.

He turned to Dedan. "Bring the sacrificial animals to the altar."

A frown creased the captain's forehead. "Before Samuel arrives?"

"Before Samuel arrives."

"Yes, sir." Dedan called for two of his soldiers and hurried to the shelter to bring a sheep and a bull.

Saul pulled the hunting knife from his belt and slaughtered the bull, catching the blood in a bowl and pouring it against the altar as he had seen Samuel do. He cut the carcass in pieces and put them on the firewood, which he had sprinkled with coals from the cooking fire. As the crackling sound of igniting twigs and the first smell of sizzling meat came from the altar, the king heard the men behind him whisper, "There's Samuel."

Half-relieved that the prophet had finally arrived, the king felt angry Samuel had come so late—so late Saul had been forced to offer the sacrifice himself. Saul washed his hands before hurrying up the road to meet the man of God.

"I'm so glad you are finally here." Saul embraced the prophet. "What delayed you?"

As his servant waited in the background, Samuel looked past the king to the smoke rising from the altar. "What are you doing?"

Saul stepped back. He had never heard Samuel speak in anger, but he couldn't mistake the meaning of his question. The king's mouth went dry, and he gulped.

"When I saw the soldiers were deserting me, and you hadn't arrived on time, and the Philistines were amassing their forces at Michmash, I was concerned that their army might come down to Gilgal and attack. I didn't want to fight without the Lord's blessing, so I forced myself to offer the burnt offering."

The prophet stared up at the monarch for a moment, then he seemed to look beyond Saul's eyes into the depths of his soul, causing the king to shift uncomfortably. A look of sadness gradually replaced the prophet's angry gaze.

"You have made a foolish mistake," Samuel said. "You have not obeyed the command given by the Lord your God. If you had, He would have established your kingdom over Israel forever. But now your kingdom won't survive. The Lord has searched for a man after His own heart and designated him to be leader of His people, because you have not kept the Lord's command."

Samuel moved down the road to the troops, the distraught king following. In spite of his harsh words to Saul, the prophet greeted the dispirited soldiers and completed the sacrifice.

After reminding the men of God's help in generations past,

Samuel raised his hands out over the faithful warriors and quoted the blessing from the Law of Moses, "Hear, O Israel, today as you are going into battle against your enemies, do not become faint-hearted or full of fear. Do not tremble or panic when you engage them in battle. The Lord your God is the one who goes with you to fight on your behalf against your enemies. He will give you victory."

Smarting from the rebuke and ominous prophecy, Saul ate little of the supper served to him and Samuel. The tension was palpable, but Samuel's voice reassured Saul as he reminded the king that he had promised years before to advise him in his undertakings against the Philistines.

"Return to the hill country and face the enemy," the prophet said. "Jonathan will be a great help to you. The young man is a credit to your training and to the Lord. God will show you when to attack. Only obey His leading."

Early the next morning Saul said goodbye to Samuel, secretly wishing the prophet would accompany him into battle as he had at Jabesh Gilead many years before. After the debacle with the sacrifice, however, he couldn't be sure Samuel would be there at the right moment. So, he watched as the prophet started up the road to the hill country, then turned to supervise his troops in breaking camp.

Assembly brought more bad news. Of the 3,000 soldiers and new recruits, only six hundred remained, Carmi informed Saul.

The king turned so the captain would not see his anger. He just couldn't win. Samuel had arrived late—then blamed the king for doing his job! Saul had forced himself to offer the sacrifice to guarantee God's help, but it gained him nothing. One hundred fifty more had deserted.

1 6

A PRIEST ARRIVES

In the morning sunshine, Samuel slowly plodded up the dusty *wadi* road, his servant and donkey six paces behind. To the aging prophet the previous day's trip had seemed long—and it had been all downhill. Now he must retrace his steps.

Saul had failed the test.

Tears blurred Samuel's vision. Saul valued his kingdom over obedience to God's Law. He saw the sacrifice as a symbol to unite the people rather than a surrender of sin and self to God. *Poor Israel.* They wanted a strong, robust king to lead them into battle. Samuel turned for one last look at the meager army. God gave them the man they wanted. Now they did not want the man or the battle.

As the prophet walked on, his heart bled for the one person who stood to lose the most—Jonathan. The heir had the vigor of youth and a heart for God. He would never have offered the sacrifice, but would have waited for God, however long it took. He deserved the throne, yet God had said Saul's kingdom would not endure.

How would he face Jonathan? Samuel's heart was torn as he

paused to pray for the crown prince. He must minister to him. He raised his eyes to the clear morning sky. Jonathan was Israel's salvation—spiritually and militarily—until God revealed His new leader. Samuel continued praying as he made his way up to Gibeah.

A surprised Jonathan looked across the courtyard at sunset to see Samuel standing by the gate with his servant and donkey. He hurried to welcome his guest, recalling the day he heard the story of the Voice in the night calling, "Samuel, Samuel." A decade had passed since that day, but Jonathan's memory of it remained as vivid as that morning's conversations.

The prophet seemed somber. Jonathan presumed he had seen the sprawling Philistine encampment at Michmash on his way to Gibeah.

"I've come to offer a sacrifice and bless the soldiers," Samuel said.

"I'm glad you have, but the army is in Gilgal."

"I know. I visited there yesterday. It looks to me, however, like this is a considerable part of it. There are only six hundred men with your father."

"Only six hundred?" Jonathan frowned, baffled by the news. "I thought he issued a call to arms throughout the Land."

"He did. Most have gone into hiding. Others have deserted at Gilgal."

"Poor Father."

"Yes, the poor king."

The next morning Jonathan led his men up the hill to the high place. The worried people of Gibeah stood around in small clusters, strangely silent, their faces bleak. After offering the sacrifice, Samuel blessed the troops and encouraged all to be strong in the Lord. The townspeople had great respect for the beloved prophet, and word of his returning home to Ramathaim did not ease their concern.

"Would the Land be in this fix if Samuel still led us?" Jonathan heard one of the older men ask. "Remember the glory of Mizpah?"

"He's the only man in Israelite history who has led us in defeating the Philistines," another said.

Coming down the hill with Jonathan, Samuel insisted he must leave for home. "The Lord is with you," he whispered in the prince's ear as he embraced him in farewell outside town. "You don't need me. God Almighty is Captain of Israel's army. Trust Him, obey His leading, and He will give the victory."

Watching him go, Jonathan smiled. He wouldn't trade that old gray-haired man for all the soldiers in Philistia with their fancy plumed headdresses. Thank the Lord a little boy named Samuel had answered God's call.

Down in Gilgal, Saul and his men broke camp and trudged up the *wadi* road. King Saul heard exclamations of surprise as his troops marched through the Pass of Michmash and caught a glimpse of the enormous Philistine army fanned out above them to the north. He immediately ordered the men to set up camp east of Geba, across the gorge from their former campground. He hoped the activity would take their minds off the impossible situation.

Saul ordered his headquarters tent erected near a large pomegranate tree that stood on the hill at a place called *Migron*—The Precipice. Outside the tent flap, he planted his spear in the ground. Waiting for the evening meal, one question plagued him. How many more would desert during the night?

The king breathed a sigh of relief the next day to learn everyone was still present. Once again in a good mood, he set off for Gibeah to visit his family and give orders for Abner, Jonathan, and the bodyguards to join them at the new campsite.

Jonathan told his father of Samuel's visit and quoted the

prophet's triumphant words. Saul also recalled the prophet's words to him, but he did not share them with his son. "You have made a foolish mistake," the voice accused him over and over.

One night the reproof hounded him until he thought he would go crazy. These were not the words to encourage a king, he wanted to shout. He turned over on his mat and put his hands over his ears, trying to block out the persistent voice. He needed a man of God to offer advice; instead, he got a prophecy of doom. He swallowed to relieve the sour taste in his mouth.

The next evening Saul sat in front of his tent with Abner, looking at campfires that dotted the opposite hillside. The sight was nearly as depressing as Samuel's reprimand.

"Abner, does anyone know if there are surviving descendants of the old high priest Eli? And, if so, where they might live?" After the destruction of the Tabernacle over fifty years before, the family members had not resumed the services.

"I'm sure someone does. I'll ask around."

Pleased with his idea, Saul slept better that night.

"Good news," the commander announced the following morning. "Several men know Eli's great grandson Ahimeleck, or Ahijah as some call him. Do you want me to send for him?"

"Please do. And tell him to bring the sacred vestments—if they still exist."

When Ahijah arrived the following week, Saul's spirit lifted.

"Thank you for calling me," the priest said. "Yes, Samuel saved the ephod and other sacred objects from destruction when the Philistines burned Shiloh. I've brought them. How may I be of service?"

Samuel again! Saul fumed silently. *Always interfering.* He forced himself to cover his annoyance. "Thanks for coming. I feel the need for a man of God resident in our camp. As a descendent of the high priest, you have a closer connection to God than Samuel."

The king ordered four men to set up a tent for the priest. Seeing the sack of sacred objects, Saul hoped the offended prophet

Samuel had not somehow informed Ahijah of Saul's sacrifice at Gilgal.

Later, when Jonathan came to the king's tent for supper, he noticed his father smiling—something he had not seen since Saul returned from Gilgal.

"God is with us now," the king informed him. "He will show us His will."

"God is always with those whose hearts are committed completely to Him, Father. Faith and obedience are essential to knowing His will."

Saul gave him a strange look, then walked away. Jonathan remembered the bewildering exchange as he prepared for bed. What did he say wrong?

Closing the flap on his tent, he carefully uncovered his sword and ran his fingers down the smooth shaft of the blade. "The Sword of the Lord," he whispered as he rewrapped it. Gideon fought with trumpets and torches. God could use any weapon dedicated to His service. This sword—or ten thousand swords— would not save Israel unless God fought for them. Confident of the Lord's assistance on Israel's behalf, the prince soon fell asleep.

In the next tent Saul relaxed for the first time in two weeks. With God's presence in the camp, perhaps Israel would win after all.

A dirty, disheveled man staggered into the encampment the next day with news a Philistine raiding party had attacked Ophrah, six miles northeast of Michmash, killing men, stealing livestock, and robbing granaries. That afternoon others arrived from the Valley of Zeboim to the southeast with similar news. Most people had fled to the numerous caves that honeycombed the hills of the Judean Wilderness west of the Jordan River. Two days later Saul watched smoke rise on the western skyline. Philistines were wreaking havoc on the area around Beth-Horon.

Something must be done to stop them. The smoke grew darker. Soon there will be nothing left of the Land, nothing left to eat. Once again Saul issued a call to arms and sent out messengers to the tribal territories. With so many men in hiding, in many towns the message went undelivered. Seeing a few new recruits join the army, however, encouraged the faithful soldiers. Saul sent spies to gather information on enemy activities. The Philistines were amassing chariots on the plain below Gibeon, they reported, along with more troops.

Harvest time ended and the summer days grew warmer. Jonathan listened with concern one morning as his father declined to make plans for an immediate attack.

They couldn't wait until the rains began, then expect to fight. Where was the Father who last year strode across the grass to plan battle strategy with the new commanders and captains? The king's steps had been decisive, his shoulders squared, his confidence contagious. What had changed?

What was the point of grinding more flint arrowheads every morning if the ones you have are not being used?

Jonathan headed for a spot on the hill beyond camp, needing to be alone to pray. Time was on the side of the Philistines. No, God was on Israel's side. And God always won.

17

BATTLE OF MICHMASH

The twitter of birds in the pomegranate tree awakened Jonathan before dawn—or was it the frustration of fruitless waiting that nagged him from sunrise to sunset. He couldn't be sure.

The Philistines only grew stronger. Jonathan rolled over and sat up. Every day they sat there, cowered by the Philistine display of might, was another victory for the enemy, a few less bags of grain for them, a few less sheep and cattle. Jonathan rubbed his eyebrow with the side of his index finger, then pushed back the tent flap to peer into the semi-darkness.

Joel stirred in his blanket in front of the tent opening. "Something troubling you?"

In the past few months, the prince had come to appreciate his loyal armor-bearer, thinking of him more like a younger brother than a servant. "Let's go for a walk," Jonathan whispered.

Joel scrambled up, folded his blanket, and stowed it in the tent. They strapped on their breastplates. Jonathan picked up his staff. Joel buckled the sheathed sword to his belt and reached down for the shield. The two young men stole across the hillside, sidestepping sleeping soldiers. To the west sat the town of Geba, outlined against the predawn sky, dark and lifeless. The two men greeted the night sentry in low voices as they passed. Following the top of the hill eastward, they paused to survey the countryside.

Below them ran the *wadi* Suweinit, dry now during the days of sun. The valley began below Bethel and Ai to the north, curving east and dropping in elevation on its way to the Jordan River. Passing first through an undulating plateau, the valley narrowed down-stream into a gorge with vertical precipices. Above the steep slopes on the south, Geba perched on a rocky knoll, its fields lying east of town. Across the chasm to the northeast, and lower down the hillside, the town of Michmash nestled in a saddle of land, its fields spread out behind it.

East of Michmash the hill rose in three rounded humps above a perpendicular crag. Black goats-hair tents of the Philistines covered the hilltop. Beyond it projected a long, sharp tongue of land, an open valley dropping off behind it. In the first rays of sunlight, the cliffs of the natural fortress looked formidable to the prince.

Walking on, Jonathan and Joel reached the southern crag of the narrow pass as the sun rose above the eastern hills. Called *Seneh*, or Thorn-like, by the Israelites, the face of the pointed rock generally lay in the shade, appearing dark and cool from the valley below. The ruddy and tawny tints of the northern cliff were crowned with a layer of white chalky stone, which reflected the daily sunshine, giving it the name *Bozez*—Shining One.

The two men stood in silence, awed by the military advantage of the Philistine camp across the gorge. "How does one attack a place like that?" Joel asked.

"Only with God's power," Jonathan said in a quiet, but firm, voice. Watching the camp, he was puzzled to see so few men out in the open after sunrise. "For such a big camp, they don't seem to be very active."

"Maybe they believe in sleeping in."

"Or maybe they're out on raids."

Jonathan lifted his eyes to the cloudless heavens, contemplating Israel's beleaguered position. Suddenly he was a ten-year-old sitting in a shaded corner of the courtyard of their home in Gibeah, endlessly repeating Scripture, sentence by sentence, after his teacher Ethan. The words of Joshua he memorized one morning flashed through his mind. In a hushed voice he quoted, "The Lord has already driven out before you great and strong nations; to this day no one has been able to resist you. One of you chases a thousand, because the Lord God promises to fight for you."

"What did you say?" The armor-bearer stepped closer.

Jonathan turned to him, a rush of hope filling his heart. "We are God's Chosen People, separated to Him by the Covenant of Circumcision. Our God fights for us. Why do we sit on this hill, cringing before the camp of pagans?" He grabbed Joel's arm. "Come, let's approach the outpost of these uncircumcised men. Maybe the Lord will act in our behalf. If the Lord wants to act, nothing can stop Him from saving, whether He uses many or just a few."

"Do whatever you want." Joel touched the hilt of the sword. "I'm with you completely."

Aware of his inexperience, Jonathan paused a moment to reflect. Was this plan inspired of the Lord, or his wild impulse? He could only go if he had God's blessing. Sensing no warning of caution in his spirit, Jonathan began descending the steep slope.

"Come, then, we'll start across and let the Philistine sentries see us. If they tell us to wait until they come to us, we will know it is God's sign for us to break off the encounter. If they say, 'Come up and join us,' we will climb up, because that will be the signal the Lord has delivered them into our hands."

Conscious that they were being watched, the young men made

their way down the long slippery ledge of Seneh and started up the other side. Within minutes they heard a coarse laugh.

"Look!" a voice shouted above them. "The Hebrews are crawling out of their hiding places." One of the soldiers high on the lookout pointed down at them, and others crowded around him.

"Come on up and we'll teach you how to fight like men," another challenged with good-humored contempt. Loud guffaws echoed across the valley.

"The sign from God," Jonathan called over his shoulder. "Let's go."

Nearing the base of the cliff, the two waited for additional ridicule or stones to be hurled down at them. When silence returned, they concluded that, smug in their impregnable fortress, the Philistines had lost interest in the two adventurers. They crept around to the far side of the lookout and began climbing, trying to prevent a dirt slide that might alert the sentries overhead.

When they reached the face of *Bozez*, sixty feet high, Jonathan surveyed the difficult terrain. They would have to scramble up on all fours. "Abandon the shield," he whispered. "We'll trust God to protect us."

The prince used his staff to assist him. Joel had the more difficult task of working around the awkward weapon. They paused to catch their breath just before they reached the parapet of the lookout, then silently swung themselves over the low wall.

A uniformed soldier sat dozing behind his tent, his head uncovered. By his clean-shaven face, Jonathan identified him as a Philistine. Joel handed the prince the sword. He crept over and cut the man down without a noise. Pulling the sword from the dead soldier's sheath, he handed it to Joel. Jonathan picked up the man's shield and sneaked around the tent. Someone screamed. Startled soldiers whirled around to face their attackers, their plumed headdresses shaking with the sudden movement. Those on the far end of the lookout fled toward camp, shouting a warning as they left behind twenty slain comrades.

In camp, the unsuspecting soldiers were getting started with their daily assignments when they heard the commotion. As Jonathan ran from the lookout, he saw them drop dishes and grab their weapons. The Philistine war cry exploded around him. Jonathan paused as Philistine soldiers launched an attack. No one came near him and Joel. They were confused, Jonathan realized. They didn't know their own soldiers.

Besides Philistine commanders and soldiers, Jonathan had heard that their army included Canaanites living in Philistia and volunteer auxiliaries and slaves from allied or conquered nations —including many Hebrews. Even the prince could recognize for which side the beardless Philistines fought, but since Israelites also wore beards, it was not so easy to identify the loyalty of those men. No wonder they were confused. The invaders must presume the whole Israelite army was mobilized.

Philistines were killing bearded soldiers right and left. The bewildered bearded allies also killed each other with weapons or by hurling them over the cliff to die on the rocks below. Jonathan and Joel joined the attack.

Suddenly the earth shook, increasing the pandemonium.

A sentinel on the hill above Michmash set a bonfire to signal lookouts on distant hills to send reinforcements. Jonathan knew the raiding parties would soon be back to join the fighting.

Across the ravine near Geba, Saul's sentries witnessed the pitched battle, with Philistines scattering before it. After receiving the report, the king ran to the top of the hill above camp.

"What's going on?"

"The Philistines are under assault," Abner said.

"By whom?"

"Israel, I presume."

Saul frowned in consternation. "Assemble the troops and see who's missing."

The captains counted their men. There was no one absent from the ranks.

The king surveyed the remnant of his army. "Where are Jonathan and Joel?"

Abner's gaze followed his. "They're not here. They must be the ones in Michmash."

Saul's scowl deepened as he hesitated. Without his order, the battle had begun. Now he must act. But was this God's plan—or another of Jonathan's impetuous acts? The king turned to Ahijah, the priest. "Bring the ephod."

The priest hurried to his tent and returned dressed in the sacred raiment. He placed his hand in the pocket where the Urim and Thummim stones were stored and waited for Saul to inquire from God.

Across the chasm, the sound of tumult grew louder as the anguished cries of the injured and dying echoed through the morning air. Observing the glint from swords and metal shields flashing in the bright sunshine, Saul touched the priest's shoulder.

"Never mind. God is already fighting for us."

Abner sounded the trumpet and the soldiers lined up by ranks. Saul walked out in front of the six hundred men.

"We are joining the battle," he commanded them. "Seize whatever weapons you find abandoned on the battlefield. It may be a long day, but we must not stop until the enemy is defeated, not even pause to eat. Do you understand?" They nodded. Since Saul had not waited for God to give specific assurance of victory, he decided to add an extra measure to ensure it himself. "Cursed is anyone who eats food before sunset, before I have avenged myself on my enemies!"

"So be it," the captains said, affirming the solemn promise.

"Charge," Saul shouted, and they raced down the hill.

Behind him, Abner blew the trumpet again. As the call to arms resonated across the hills, the king could hear the echoing response of trumpets from hilltops in places like Bethel, Beth-aven, and Geba. Men were spreading the word to towns farther away. An encouraging sign. They must be planning to join the struggle. He prayed that villagers hiding in caves would find courage to join them.

The hills of the plateau beyond Michmash were covered with forests or groves, and the woods took their toll. The Israelites, used to the hills, had no trouble catching the Philistines, familiar only with the coastal plain.

When Abner informed Saul that Israelites who had been part of the Philistine army had switched sides, the king knew his vow was paying off. "Are the captains and soldiers informing all who join us of the ban on eating before sunset?"

"Everyone I've asked knows."

"God of Israel, save me."

Hurrying through the trees, Jonathan and Joel paused to help a wounded soldier. When a Benjamite ran up behind them, the prince ordered him to treat the man's wounds. They moved on.

The interruption had taken Jonathan's mind off the battle and, having left camp before breakfast, he realized how hungry he had become. He looked up to see honey oozing out of a beehive in a hole in a tree. Running over, he poked the end of his staff into it and extracted a piece of honeycomb, quickly devouring it. The sweet liquid revived his energy and he reached for more.

A man ran past the prince, then stopped. "What are you doing? Don't you know the king has put a curse on anyone who eats before sunset?" He quoted the Vow.

Jonathan exhaled sharply in disbelief. "My father has made trouble for Israel," he said. He wiped his fingers on his tunic. "Can't you see how a little honey has renewed my strength? If the soldiers ate some of the plunder today, victory over the enemy would be much greater."

The men ran on, occasionally slipping on the honey that dropped from the trees.

The escaping army moved west, working its way toward home. Passing Beth-aven, they fled to the plain surrounding the hill town of Gibeon. Seeing the distress signal, Philistine soldiers encamped there had begun driving away the herds and flocks they had captured during the raids on the Israelites. Carts of stolen grain lumbered down the road behind them.

Terrified Philistines poured across the six miles to the pass at Upper Beth-Horon, Saul's men in hot pursuit. Philistines in chariots wreaked havoc on the Israelites, but sharpshooters' arrows found their mark and horses fell, capsizing the chariots they pulled. Jonathan and his men dodged obstacles as the road became littered with dead soldiers, abandoned livestock, discarded weapons, and broken-down carts and chariots.

Less than two miles down the rough descent, Lower Beth-Horon sat on a rocky ridge overlooking the Valley of Aijalon. The town of Aijalon stood on a long hill skirting the southern side of the valley. Jonathan knew sight of Aijalon would encourage the Philistines. It not only guarded their way home, the valley also held more of their chariots, and by now the sinking sun ended their exhausting day of defeat. Though nursing their wounds and mourning their losses, they would press on to safety.

Jonathan rejoiced as everyone else did to see the sun descend below the western horizon, heralding the end of the Vow. The famished men of Israel grabbed the nearest cattle, calves, and sheep and slaughtered them on the ground. Others built campfires and, hacking off pieces, began roasting the meat. The surprised prince couldn't believe they did not kill and bleed the animals according to the regulations of the Law of Moses. Behind him he heard a familiar shout.

"Stop! You have sinned. Roll that large stone over here immediately." Several shame-faced soldiers obeyed the king's command. "Now, go out among the men and tell them to bring their animals here to slaughter," Saul told his captains. "Don't sin by eating meat with blood still in it."

The soldiers willingly complied, then devoured their meal with joy. They had won a great victory over the Philistines.

After supper Saul called the men together and, with stones from the surrounding hillsides, built an altar to God—the first time Jonathan had known his father to do so. Ahijah offered the evening sacrifice as the men thanked God for His strength and help.

Watching the smoke ascend from the altar, Saul turned to his son. "I wish we had been able to completely annihilate the enemy."

"I do too."

Jonathan stepped closer to his father. His hand brushed a sticky spot on his tunic where he had wiped honey that morning. Saul shifted his weight from one foot to the other and back again as he fidgeted with the neck of his tunic. By the end of the sacrifice ritual, Jonathan knew his father had made up his mind.

Saul called his captains together. "Let's continue to pursue the Philistines tonight. By morning not one of them will be alive."

"Whatever you wish, we will do, O King," replied the loyal soldiers, now invigorated by the feast of meat.

"First, maybe we should inquire of the Lord," Ahijah suggested. "We didn't have time to wait for His direction back in Geba."

Saul nodded. "That's a wise idea. Bring the Urim and Thummim." After Ahijah put on the ephod, Saul stood before the altar and lifted his hands, palms upward, to heaven. "Shall I continue to chase after the Philistines tonight? Will You deliver them into Israel's hands, Lord Jehovah?"

Ahijah waited a few minutes, then withdrew the two stones. In the light of the altar fire, the priest, king, and prince could see the stones came out one side Urim and one Thummim—meaning no reply. Later Ahijah repeated the test, still no reply. When the third answer remained unchangèd, Jonathan noticed his father's shoulders slump. Something was wrong. God did not answer.

"All captains, please come here and let's find out what sin has been committed today," the king said. "For, as the Lord who rescued Israel lives, even if my son Jonathan is at fault, he must die."

As the prince stood in the shadows, the word "sin" sent a stab of fear through him. Until now he had forgotten about breaking the vow. Suddenly the honey on his tunic seemed like the blood of a murder victim. He did not move as the captains stepped before the disturbed king. Jonathan knew some of them were aware of the honey incident. They waited in silence, their eyes downcast. They had no intention of jeopardizing his safety.

"Stand over there." Saul pointed to the right. "I and Jonathan will stand here."

"Do whatever seems best to you," the captain Caleb said.

With no choice, Jonathan stepped up beside his father. Saul turned to the altar again. "God, give me the correct answer. If it is Jonathan or me, may the lot be Urim; if the men, let it be Thummim." Ahijah withdrew the two flat stones. In the light of the campfire, they read Urim. Saul looked down at his son, his mouth nervously working back and forth. "Cast the lot again," he ordered. "If it is Jonathan, let the answer be Urim, if me, let it be Thummim."

Ahijah withdrew the stones. Once again, the answer came out Urim. "Tell me what wrong you've done," Saul commanded his firstborn. In the firelight Jonathan could see the anguish in his eyes.

Jonathan bowed his head a moment, then lifted his gaze. "I didn't know of the vow, and while we were in the woods, I tasted a little honey with the end of my staff." He knew the seriousness of a vow, but he had neither made it nor had knowledge of it. Still, a father had absolute authority over his family. He exhaled slowly. "Now I must die."

Saul's eyes flashed with anger. He had made the vow and forced his men to agree. Jonathan knew he would not recant. "May God deal with me, however severely, if you do not die for this, Jonathan."

"Wait a minute." Caleb stepped out from the other captains. "Should Jonathan, who brought a great deliverance to Israel, die? Never! As surely as the Lord lives, he shall not even lose a hair from his head, for he fought today with God's help. We will pay the ransom."

Others swarmed around the king to defend the prince. Acknowledging the men's response, Saul gave in to their demand. By the way he exhaled, Jonathan could sense his father's relief at being rescued from his vow. Shaken by the incident, the king called off the night attack. The men wrapped their cloaks around them and bedded down for the night around the campfires.

The even breathing of the tired soldiers, punctuated by the snores of others, surrounded Jonathan as he lay between Saul and Joel, staring up at the stars. In spite of his exhaustion, he couldn't fall asleep. "Cursed is anyone who eats food before sunset, before I have avenged myself on my enemies!" The words of his father haunted him, buzzing through his mind like a pesky fly he couldn't quite catch.

All Father seemed concerned about was his own success. The soldiers' needs didn't count. Saul was horrified by the improper killing of the animals for supper, but not at his own senseless vow. Jonathan groaned inwardly. Was the proper slaughter of an animal more important to his father than men's lives? He turned on his side, away from the snoring king. Was Father angry over the breaking of the vow? Or did he hold Jonathan responsible for not being able to pursue the enemy and win a greater victory for himself?

Jonathan reluctantly allowed himself to believe the rumor he had overheard about Saul offering the sacrifice in Gilgal, unwilling to wait for the tardy Samuel to arrive. If it came down to it, did the kingdom mean more to Father than God did?

Jonathan closed his eyes to the embers of the campfire. He pulled his cloak around his shoulders; the smell of smoke saturated the garment. From a tree on the distant hillside, the *who, who, who* of an owl floated down to him, the mournful echo erasing the thrill of the day's victory. For the first time in his life, Jonathan doubted his father's wisdom and commitment to God.

18

CONSTRUCTING THE FORTRESS

At daybreak Saul organized the battlefield clean-up. He assigned the volunteer warriors the task of counting and burying the dead —Israelite and Philistine alike. Since a decaying body posed a health risk, the Law of Moses commanded that even executed criminals be buried.

Men spread out across the hills in search of caves to use as tombs. Others borrowed shovels and mattocks from villagers to dig mass graves in the ground, hard from lack of rain. Saul didn't envy their difficult task. Some sought low areas in which to pile corpses so they could cover them with heaps of stones.

Saul ordered the soldiers from the standing army to collect abandoned Philistine weapons, and he left Abner to oversee the task. Gathering all the treasured iron swords and spears they could carry, the men started up the Pass and back to Gibeah. Some loaded theirs in abandoned carts and conscripted local farmers to use their oxen to pull them.

At mid-morning Saul, Jonathan, and Ahijah left Aijalon. Overhead, vultures and hawks circled the miles of battlefield. The smell of death permeated the air as the sun rose higher in the sky. Along the Way of Beth-Horon they overtook soldiers laden with weapons and soon passed the most advanced ones.

Below Upper Beth-Horon, the three men came upon a pack of dogs ripping flesh from corpses. Angry at the desecration of the dead, Jonathan ran toward them, shouting and throwing stones. The yelping animals retreated a safe distance to await opportunity to return. Saul applauded his son's action. Like all Israelites, he despised dogs, which lived off the garbage heaps outside towns and on the carcasses of wild animals in the countryside. Incidents like this only reinforced his contempt for the scavengers. The men walked on, but not before Jonathan turned to hurl one last stone at the dogs.

Viewing the morbid scene as they went, Saul recalled Samuel's fatal prediction at Gilgal concerning his kingdom. Whatever Samuel had said to Jonathan about trust and obedience to God, Saul remained convinced the prophet had not mentioned the premature sacrifice or the prophecy of doom. Passing dead Philistines, broken-down chariots, and blood-stained weapons, the young commander seemed to exude a confidence the king wished he had. If only they had pursued the enemy to their city walls, perhaps he could forget Samuel's terrible prediction. He thanked the Lord for the presence of Ahijah, which reminded him God had been in the camp and had given them victory in spite of Samuel.

As they walked by towns and villages, people ran out to cheer the king. "Saul has slain the uncircumcised heathen and caused us to triumph over our enemies," women sang, dancing along the road and shaking their tambourines. "The Sword of the Lord is mightier than the sword of the Philistines."

By the time the three reached Gibeah, the sun had begun setting. Enthusiasm had replaced Saul's darker thoughts. With the Philistine menace eliminated, he could live in Gibeah with his family instead of camping at Geba.

Jedidah hobbled out of her room to greet her hero son; Ahinoam and the children came down the staircase, beaming. Saul introduced them to Ahijah and assigned him Ethan's old room. By Malki-Shua and Ishvi's smiles, Saul could tell they were happy to have a man of God once again in the house.

Later that evening as the king stood in the courtyard surveying the large cache of weapons, he knew what he must do to strengthen and ensure his kingdom. If the swords and spears weren't stored in a protected place, in a few years they might fall back into the hands of the Philistines. As he lay awake listening to Ahinoam, Merab, and Michal's soft breathing, he began planning his new fortress.

The following week Saul consulted Abner, Hamul, and captains from the various tribes, then ordered all builders, brick makers, and stone masons in the Land to report to Gibeah. He also scheduled the twelve tribes to deliver food supplies at regular intervals for the workers and the army, and he imposed a tax to pay for building supplies and salaries. From the recruits, the king appointed Tahath of Shechem to supervise the construction of a fortress and palace on the hilltop.

~

Saul stood on the grassy summit above Gibeah one morning, surrounded by half-buried stones, scene of the darkest day the tribe of Benjamin had faced. That long ago day the earlier fortification had been destroyed following the rape of a traveling Levite's concubine. Absently working the soil free around one stone with the sole of his sandal, he tried to visualize the decimation of his people—the cries of anguish, the slaughter, the horizon filled with columns of smoke from burning towns.

Why hadn't the elders been willing to acknowledge the sin, punish the wicked men, and spare their people? Pride and loyalty, of course. In the loose tribal alliance, it was every tribe for itself. Blood bound stronger than any cord man could invent.

The Benjamites had slowly recovered, but the stronghold had been abandoned. Time and nature covered the rubble with dirt. Now, with a new fortress, Saul hoped to restore Gibeah to its former glory, bind the tribes into a cohesive nation, and secure the kingdom for himself.

The dry season was underway. Saul assigned the soldiers to work alongside the skilled recruits until the rains began. Using a thick pole for a battering ram, they demolished the hated Philistine lookout. Onlookers gathered to clap and cheer as they watched the walls tumble to the ground. Men cleared away the debris and the surface layer of the old ruins.

Tahath laid out the fortress perimeter, one hundred seventy feet by one hundred fifty-five feet, and men began the tiring job of digging the foundation trenches. Saul sent builders to supervise the gathering of field stones. Farmers from the region brought their ox carts to haul the stones to the hilltop. For the final task of the season, the soldiers carried jugs of water to the building site for mixing mortar and replenished the pile of stones near each team of masons.

One morning the following summer, the king and priest stood outside the family's upper level living quarters, looking up at the busy hilltop. The echo of voices and the sound of digging floated down to them.

"Since I'm building a fortress for the king and his army," Saul said, "I think it would be good to reestablish the Tabernacle and priesthood. The king of Israel needs representatives of the God of Israel nearby to advise him. Samuel is old and unable to visit his circuit regularly. The Tabernacle, not a circuit, was God's original plan for worship, anyway."

"That would be wonderful," Ahijah said, surprise and excitement in his voice. "We could study the scroll of the Law, then build it according to the plan God gave to Moses on Mount Sinai. Do you want to build it in front of the fortress?"

"There isn't room. We need a place separate from government business, a place large enough to accommodate worshipers coming for Feasts."

"I'll explore the area and see what is available."

Later that morning the priest, accompanied by Jonathan, climbed the hill and walked toward the altar. For several minutes they stood beneath the tamarisk tree. Springtime had ended; the spikes of pink blossoms had fallen from its feathery branches. The tiny leaves that remained swayed gently in the morning breeze.

Only the noise of the builders behind the two men broke the silence. Scanning the countryside, they saw the high mountain near Gibeon, several miles to the northwest. The hill of Geba lay to the northeast. Three miles to the southeast, the village of Anathoth stood on the end of a low, broad ridge.

"There's a hill west of Anathoth that might be suitable for the Tabernacle," Jonathan said. "It is near the road running from Beersheba to Shechem, so would be accessible to people. It is two or three miles south of here, so would also be near the king."

"Let's go take a look. Now that your father has suggested rebuilding, I'm anxious to begin."

An hour later the two men stood on the summit of the hill of Nob. From it they could see the walled city of the Jebusites on the southern end of Mount Moriah, a mile away. East of the pagan fortification and across the Brook Kidron, the Mount of Olives stood in the sunshine, its slopes a blur of silver-green groves.

"I think you have made a good choice, Jonathan. This hill is very adequate. First, I'll visit Samuel and borrow a scroll of the Law. It may take a little time to collect all the supplies specified for use."

"Father will help you. Once he decides on something, he'll

make sure it happens. He can ask for donations from all the tribes. Then they will feel it is their Tabernacle and will come to worship. Only a few old people like Samuel remember the Tabernacle at Shiloh. Grandfather Kish worshiped there, but he's gone."

"When we're finished, we can call the people and dedicate it at the next Feast," Ahijah said.

"A Tabernacle will be a big help to Father. Lately he is very quiet. At times he seems discouraged—like he has something on his mind. He depends on the ephod and the sacrifices for inspiration and assurance."

"You don't?"

"I appreciate all the evidence of God's presence," the twenty-one-year-old said. "But when I think that Abraham had faith in the One True God centuries before He gave the Law to Moses, or even before He instituted circumcision, I realize God is greater than any ritual or place. Faith in God is what counts."

"The Lord bless you, my son." The priest placed his hand on Jonathan's shoulder. "You sound so much like Samuel. I remember meeting him as a child." Ahijah looked toward Mount Moriah, the hill where Abraham had brought his son Isaac, willing to sacrifice him if that was what it took to obey God. "Saul is honored to have you for his firstborn."

"Frankly, I've learned more about God from Samuel and Ethan than from Father," the prince admitted. "So, you can see how important a man of God is to Israel."

They started back to Gibeah, each lost in thought.

The builders returned to renew their work at the fortress, adding courses of stones on the foundation to raise the high casemate walls, finishing the upper part with bricks. The brick makers formed the bricks in molds and laid them out on the valley floor to dry, trying to keep up with the demand.

The distance between the thick outer wall and thinner inner wall was spanned by a roof, which formed a walkway to serve security purposes. The builders partitioned the ground-level space between the double walls into chambers to form storerooms and arsenals. Under siege the space could be packed with rubble to strengthen the fortification.

At the top of the thick outer wall, the men built a crenelated parapet that encircled the fortress. From a distance, it looked to Jonathan like a row of gaping teeth. Much higher than the parapet surrounding a house rooftop, the projections were tall enough to hide a man. Standing before a gap, or embrasure, one could survey the countryside. If under attack, soldiers could shoot through the gaps, then duck behind the projections to avoid incoming enemy arrows.

At the four corners of the fort, Tahath built broad towers that jutted out beyond the walls. These were essential for defense, since from them soldiers could shoot down at the approaching enemy from all directions. The towers would be especially helpful in guarding the gate.

The gate posed the weakest point of any fortification. Tahath spent long hours designing the entrance to the citadel. He plated the wooden outer and inner doors with bronze, hoping to prevent anyone from setting them on fire with a torch or flaming arrow. Huge bolts and beams strengthened the double doors when closed. Just inside the gate they planned to construct a barracks for armor-bearers and bodyguards.

The gate faced east, and the tamarisk tree stood in front of it, near the altar. Saul decided to spare the tree; it would provide good shade for conducting business if the palace grew too warm and stifling in the hot season.

Saul and his sons visited the building site daily to view the progress and adjust plans. By the end of that dry season the walls were up.

People streaming into the hills of Benjamin for the Feast of Tabernacles passed Gibeah to admire the new fortress. Ahijah, who now went by his original name—Ahimeleck, and his family of priestly descent, had worked hard to finish the Tabernacle in time.

Samuel came for the dedication celebration. Jonathan and his brothers were overjoyed to see the old prophet, but sad to learn of Ethan's deteriorating health. Jonathan expressed his disappointment that Samuel stayed at Nob to be close to the daily ceremonies, instead of with them in Gibeah. Having him for a guest was always a special privilege.

As the people stood watching the smoke ascend from the sacrifices, they thanked God for the abundant harvest and the new place of worship. With the recent defeat of the Philistines in the Battle of Michmash, they at last felt Israel's humiliation at Ebenezer near Aphek and the resulting destruction of Shiloh had been avenged.

After the dedication, Samuel visited the new fortress to dedicate it and the future palace to God's service.

Among the crowd at the Feast, Saul had noticed several stalwart young men, whose strength would be invaluable to his army. The week after the royal family got back to Gibeah, he shared his idea with Abner and Jonathan.

"Why don't we visit the towns and villages and recruit eligible men for another standing army. Three thousand aren't enough to fight a battle. If we travel far from home to fight, obtaining a volunteer militia may not be reliable. Having trained reserves we could call on would be a lot better."

Following the latter rains, just after barley harvest, the king and army commanders began their search.

With the return of the dry season, Tahath initiated construction of the king's palace. On his daily visits, Jonathan watched the workers lay the stone foundation of the building, which would sit against the back fortress wall in the southwest corner, farthest from the vulnerable gate. The courtyard in front stood open for meetings, troop assemblies, and family celebrations. The rooftop would lead onto the fortress wall. One noon when the men stopped for lunch, the prince paced off the length and width of his new home—fifty-six by forty-eight feet.

Over the weeks, the brick walls gradually rose above the foundation. The unpretentious two-story palace was L-shaped. A pillared porch would add a touch of finery. Might the porch be too similar to heathen construction for God's approval? Jonathan decided it would provide shelter from the rain, so he kept quiet.

The lower floor had a throne room, fifteen by twenty-four feet, where Saul could conduct kingdom business. He planned to use the large dining room to host his commanders and other official guests at evening meals. A kitchen and the servants' workrooms would take up the additional space.

Saul designated the upstairs as the family's private quarters. Jonathan and Malki-Shua strolled through the rooms, trying to decide which they wanted for a bedroom, knowing Father would make the final decision. After the family moved to the palace, Kish's old home would be turned into a barracks.

Moving day!

Jonathan hopped up and shook his brothers awake. Rolling his sleeping mat, then folding his blanket, he stacked them by the door, ready for the movers to load. He bounded down the stairs. Servants and soldiers already stood beside oxen-drawn carts that lined the courtyard, waiting to be loaded. Other carts lined the street, the conscripted farmers from nearby towns waiting for a load before beginning their uphill climb.

Saul had already left for the Fortress to oversee the placement of the loads, taking Grandmother Jedidah, Merab, and Michal with him.

Jonathan unlocked the storeroom that held weapons, the spoils of war. He smiled and praised the God of Israel for the victories they represented. Joel brought up the cart and the armor-bearers piled the precious booty in it.

Ishvi came down to supervise the transfer of bags and earthenware vessels of grain from the windowless storeroom. Servants and soldiers began the strenuous lifting.

Ahinoam and Jahra oversaw cleaning out the kitchen and its utensils. Three men came in to lift the heavy lower millstone onto a cart and added the upper millstone. They piled on empty baskets to fill the load. The oxen strained to set the cart in motion. Next came the kitchen storeroom. Baskets of dried fruits and vegetables, jugs of olive oil and wine, and bowls of salt and spices were carefully placed to prevent breakage if the cart hit a rut or jerked forward unexpectedly. Another cart took its place and the loading continued. Empty jugs, cooking pots, and utensils completed the last load.

Malki-Shua called Pagiel and his crew to carry out the few pieces of household furniture, the bedding, and floor cushions. The next carts they filled with the ploughs, farm implements, and gardening tools.

Loaded carts filed down the passageway to the gate and empty ones quickly took their place until the house stood bare, ready for the soldiers to clean and occupy.

Jonathan looked around at the only home he had known—the courtyard spot where he declared himself a BIG soldier; the fire pit the men of the family sat around on cold nights discussing farm business and passing on stories to the next generation; the courtyard corner where Samuel told them of God's call in the night and Ethan taught them to love the God of Israel; the second story addition blessed by Samuel and the rooftop where his elders had surprised him with right-of-passage gifts; the room where

Grandfather died; the family room-turned-guardian-of-secrets where Father had presented him his own sword. So many memories!

Reluctantly Jonathan turned to go. The palace awaited.

By the time Jonathan climbed the hill, Merab and Michal had watched their toys being deposited in their corner of Saul and Ahinoam's room, the largest one in the upstairs family quarters. They ran out to pull Jonathan in to see it.

Saul made the assignments. To the three sons he allocated the room next to their parents. Each son would have his own room after he married. Saul gave Jedidah the room on the other side of the staircase from first floor, next to one reserved for family living and meals. Extra rooms awaited visitors and the boys' brides.

On the ground floor, the wooden throne was the only piece of furniture in the empty courtroom. A spear holder stood next to the right armrest. Out on the battlefield the upright spear had come to signify Saul's kingship. He decided to continue the practice.

Next door to the throne room, the king's table ran the length of a large room. Immediately Saul began hosting evening dinners for his sons and military officers. The king claimed the place of honor at the end of the table on the right side, a spear holder beside it. A bodyguard stood behind him. Abner sat directly across from the king. Malki-Shua was seated next to Saul, then Ish-Bosheth. Jonathan sat beside Abner. Other officers filled the unoccupied places when they were in town.

As the weeks passed, the meals became the highlight of Saul's day. Surveying the dinner spread one evening, he eyed the roast lamb—his favorite, surrounded on platters by parched grain and chickpeas. He licked his lips as he took his reserved seat. Baskets of flatbread, bowls of lentil stew, cheese, and fruit completed the meal. He ate heartily.

There was nothing better than a lively meal with his sons and military leaders. The topics of conversation flowed from one subject to another. Saul looked around with satisfaction. Samuel was, indeed, wrong. This fortress was a sign God had established his kingdom forever.

19

THE MOABITE MENACE

With his family and arsenal protected, King Saul focused his attention on national security. Reports had reached Gibeah that the Moabites, descendants of Abraham's nephew Lot, were plundering villages in the territory of the Reubenites. Saul decided to act.

Following a morning war council, Jonathan made his way to Ezel to think and pray—to him as vital a part of preparation as sharpening a sword or filling a quiver. Being older now, there would probably be no daring lone attack in Moab like he made at Michmash. This enemy, however, remained just as menacing. Dropping to a flat spot on the hard surface, he thought of the stories Ethan had taught him and his brothers as they learned the history of God's Chosen People.

Problems between Israel and Moab began years before the birth of either man, their teacher had said. When Abraham and Lot's herdsmen quarreled over available pastureland, the two men separated. Lot chose the rich, fertile Jordan River area, leaving his uncle the rugged central mountains of Canaan. After the Lord destroyed Sodom and Gomorrah, Lot and his two daughters fled to the mountains, where the girls tricked him. Moab and Ben-ammi were born from these incestuous affairs. Jonathan recalled his disappointment when he first heard of this sin. No wonder Lot's posterity had caused problems for the descendants of Abraham's grandson Jacob, or Israel, ever since.

The border scrimmages of the past decades were only the most recent of the problems. It began the long-ago night of Passover and the Children of Israel's escapes from slavery. During their forty years of wilderness wandering God had been faithful to care for His People. When they came at last to the Land of Moab, the Lord commanded them not to confront their distant kin. They passed north of the *wadi* Arnon, Moab's border. Sihon, king of the Amorites, attacked them. Israel defeated the Amorites and took their territory. Og, king of Bashan, attacked next and also suffered defeat, leaving Israel in control of the land east of Jordan and north of the Arnon.

The neighboring Moabites were terrified at this news. King Balak summoned a diviner named Balaam to pronounce a curse on the Israelites. After the diviner refused the invitation twice, God allowed him to go, but God turned the proposed curse into a blessing on Israel. Jonathan smiled as he thought of God causing Balaam's donkey to speak to the diviner. His smile quickly faded when he recalled that Moab found other ways to conquer them. While the Israelites camped nearby, Moabite women seduced the men to participate in their immoral Baal worship. Then a man brought a Midianite woman into camp. A plague broke out and 24,000 died. The men were executed for leading God's people into this gross sin.

Years later, during the days of the Judges, Eglon king of Moab and his allies, the Ammonites and Amalekites, had attacked Israel. Eglon dominated Israel for eighteen years. Jonathan remembered Ethan demonstrating how the left-handed Ehud had slain the extremely overweight king with his double-edged dagger, thus overthrowing Moab's control. Eighty years of peace followed.

Now trouble had arisen again.

Lifting his eyes to heaven, the prince prayed for the army, scheduled to leave at dawn, and for his father and Abner, who would lead them. Peace and confidence filled his heart as he hurried back to the fortress to prepare his weapons.

From Gibeah, Saul led the troops down the *wadi* Suweinit to Gilgal. Seeing the altar on which he had offered his own sacrifice before the Battle of Michmash, Saul tried to shrug off the feeling of guilt as he recalled Samuel's scathing denunciation that day by concentrating on happier moments.

"We renewed the kingdom here at Gilgal after Israel defeated the Ammonites at Jabesh Gilead," he said to Ahimelech, the priest. "If God gives us victory over the Moabites, we will return to Gilgal to offer a sacrifice of thanksgiving."

The army camped on the plain east of Gilgal. Throughout the evening, reserve soldiers from all over the Land arrived. As the sun rose over the hills of Gilead the next morning, the soldiers finished packing their supplies. Ahimelech offered a sacrifice on behalf of the army and pronounced the Levitical blessing on the troops. Then they moved out to ford the Jordan and head south.

Saul watched his son Malki-Shua marching proudly in formation beside Abner. It brought back memories of Saul's own youthful enthusiasm the afternoon the Israelites attacked the Philistines at Mizpah. A first expedition always brought excitement. He loved his firstborn, but he had developed a special bond with Malki-Shua, who had been born the same year Samuel anointed Saul as king. It didn't hurt that everyone told him how much Malki-Shua looked like him.

The Land of Moab lay east of the Dead Sea from the *wadi* Arnon south to the *wadi* Zered. When the army reached its northern border, the scout leader, Jethro, reported that a half-day's journey east of the Dead Sea the Arnon divided into two branches. Along the northern bank, near the fork, sat the city of Aroer.

Between where they stood and the city, several Israelite villages and towns in fertile valleys were held by the Moabites. Ar, the capital of Moab, lay a half-day's journey south of the *wadi*. The scouts saw little evidence of the enemy being aware of their presence.

Saul mobilized his forces and reclaimed the lowland towns and fields. Then they advanced to the highland. As the king stood between Jonathan and Abner on the rim of the *wadi* canyon, they viewed the deep trench the Arnon had cut through the Moab plateau. The actual valley floor through which the stream flowed appeared to be little more than one hundred feet wide, but the opposite cliff rose two miles away. The canyon looked to be to Israel's advantage.

After three years of military inactivity, Saul praised God for another opportunity to fight for God's Chosen People. Watching Malki-Shua's arrows hit their mark, pride in his young son's skill filled Saul's heart.

By the end of a month Saul's men were able to recapture the towns and villages north of the Arnon and return them to the Reubenites. Confident that the Moabites would stay within their borders for years to come, Saul selected the best of the flocks and herds they had captured from the fleeing enemy and headed home. Along the way people turned out to cheer the successful king and his army.

When the troops reached Gilgal, Ahimeleck offered the captured animals as a sacrifice of thanksgiving to God. To the king, the victories at Michmash and Moab confirmed his right to the kingdom and God's blessing on it. Say what he would, Samuel was wrong.

The morning breeze from the Great Sea began reaching the central mountains by the time Saul and Jonathan climbed the staircase to the fortress roof. Leaning through a parapet gap, they looked at the surrounding valley, enjoying the fine spring day. The fields were a deep green. The clouds in the west promised another afternoon shower. With prospects of a good harvest, Israel's army could contemplate its next course of action. Jonathan watched a section of soldiers come up the path to the fortress gate.

Saul spoke, disrupting his reverie, and he only half-heard his father say, "Son, we need to think about getting you a wife."

Jonathan turned to the king with a frown. "A what?"

"A wife. You're twenty-four already."

"Do you have someone in mind?"

"Do you?"

"No." Jonathan shook his head. "All I've wanted to do since I was a young boy was to serve the Lord by ridding Israel of her enemies." He looked at his father, who leaned against the next projection, and repeated his question. "Do you have someone in mind?"

"Actually, I do." The king stepped closer. "Before the battle of Michmash, Abner billeted in Bethel in the home of Gamaliel, a man of good character whose two sons served in Abner's battalion. Gamaliel has three younger daughters. We could choose one of them."

"That was four years ago," Jonathan protested. "They may already be married."

A slow smile played across the king's face. "They aren't. I had Abner inquire last week."

"Is Gamaliel a Benjamite?"

"That is the best part. She would be from our own tribe."

"Do you plan to give me two years off from military service?"

"Two years? Why?"

"The Law of Moses exempts betrothed men from army service and excuses new grooms for a year. Remember?"

"Oh," Saul said with a sigh. "I'd completely forgotten. I guess we had better wait another year or two. We still need to take care of the Edomites and the king of Zobah."

Thank God. Jonathan slowly let out his breath. He wasn't sure he was ready to take a wife. He needed time to get used to the idea. "Do you have the *mohar* collected?" he said.

"I've had fifty shekels saved for two years. Maybe I should go ahead and speak to Gamaliel about your interest."

"It might be better to wait. The family may get tired of a long delay and want her to marry someone else."

"Jonathan!" Reproof filled Saul's voice. "A man marries his sons and daughters into honorable families to provide stability and security for his own family. Kings marry their daughters to other kings or their sons to insure peace between the two nations. No common man would become impatient waiting for the privilege of having his daughter marry a prince, especially the firstborn."

"You prove my point," Jonathan said with a smile. "You will never be able to marry Merab and Michal to other kings or their sons—they're all pagan. So, to guarantee peace, you and I must establish it with Israel's army. Therefore, I must postpone marriage."

Jonathan could read the king's disappointment on his face, but he could not refute his son's reasoning. Neither spoke for a moment.

"Malki-Shua has his eye on Hamul's granddaughter, Sarah."

Finally, he was revealing the reason for discussing marriage. A sense of relief washed over Jonathan. "It won't offend me if my younger brother marries before I do. He can stay home a couple of years and help Ishvi with the farm work."

"Are you sure?"

"Let Malki-Shua marry. I still have work to do for God."

2 0

DOEG

Troop movement and long journeys were always suspended during the days of rain in the eastern Mediterranean region. No one wanted to become mired in mud, marooned on the far side of a swollen stream, swept away in a narrow *wadi* during a cloudburst, or left chilled to the bone in a waterlogged campsite as winter's temperature dropped after sunset.

With the end of wheat harvest and the return of the dry season, disturbing news arrived from southern Israel. Saul organized his forces and marched through the territories of Judah and Simeon south to the Land of Edom, where the descendants of Esau, Jacob's twin, lived. Edom stretched from the *wadi* Zered, east of the Dead Sea, for one hundred miles south to Ezion-Geber on the Sea of Reeds. The rugged land wasn't fertile, but it did have areas of good cultivation. It also possessed copper mines. The Edomites had decided, however, to make additional gains by raiding Israelite villages west of the Dead Sea.

During the Children of Israel's pilgrimage to the Promised Land, the Edomites had refused to allow them to pass through their territory, coming out with a large army to prevent their trespassing. Since, like the Moabites, God had refused to let Israel attack their distant Edomites cousins, the Israelites had turned another direction. Now Saul felt compelled to stop the plundering.

Reaching Edom, Saul sent out an advance patrol. Dedan later reported to Jonathan about their success. Coming around a hill one afternoon, they saw a shepherd seated on a nearby rock playing a flute, his sheep resting in the shade of two acacia trees. Three men crept closer, and the shepherd looked up to see drawn bows with arrows trained on him. Sensing danger, the startled sheep scattered in all directions. The shepherd jumped up and raised his sling to defend himself, but an arrow whizzed by his head. "Drop your sling or I will aim the next one at your heart," Dedan commanded. The stone clattered to the ground and rolled down the hillside as the shepherd tossed his sling in front of him. The three soldiers led the frightened man back to Saul and Abner. The two commanders were very pleased.

"Tell us where the Edomite raiders are camped and we will spare your life," Abner told the young man.

The Edomite appeared to be about Jonathan's age. The prince studied him as the men talked.

"If you promise to let me live, I'll help you." The captive nervously twisted the hem of his sleeve as he spoke.

"What is your name?" Saul said.

"Doeg son of Mahalalel."

"Doeg, you Edomites have been stealing Israel's livestock and grain for many years. Now you have killed some of our kinsmen. The God of Israel fights for His People. If we find the men who have done this, we will not harm the innocent women and children."

Jonathan saw a pained expression cloud the shepherd's face and knew he visualized specific people at the mention of women and children.

"Now, lead us to their camp," Saul ordered.

Wordlessly, the Edomite turned and started across the rugged terrain.

Doeg turned out to be an excellent guide, locating one raiders' camp after another. Edomites came out to resist the Israelite army and defend their people, but Saul's men prevailed.

"Here, Blackie," a Judean called out one afternoon as his unit approached a flock of sheep. The ram raised its head, then bounded forward to the man. Others recognized their sheep and cattle among the recaptured livestock. A few were able to point out the murderers of their relatives. Justice was swift and thorough.

Six weeks later, Israel broke camp after celebrating their success in driving the Edomites back into their own territory. As Jonathan watched Alvah strap the king's sword sheath onto his belt, he heard a voice behind him. He turned to see Doeg standing a few feet from his father.

"Please, sir, let me return with you," the shepherd-informant said. "If I remain in Edom, I will be slain as a traitor."

Jonathan acknowledged the validity of Doeg's fears. Without hesitation, Saul agreed to let him join the Israelites if he promised to loyally serve the king all the days of his life.

As the soldiers walked north through the territory of Judah, Jonathan felt sympathy for the refugee, whose humble obedience to the king matched that of any Israelite soldier.

Townspeople and villagers rushed out to celebrate the army's victory as it passed by. Saul's men returned home by way of Gilgal, again offering a sacrifice of thanksgiving for God's help.

The royal armor-bearers and bodyguards were assigned quarters in the barracks near the fortress gate, and Abner gave Doeg a space among them.

As the days passed, Jonathan's sympathy for the Edomite cooled. One morning he saw Doeg talking with Joel. When his armor-bearer walked away, Jonathan noticed the Edomite's lip curl in a sneer. Doeg saw the prince observing him and quickly transformed the sneer into a forced smile. On another occasion the prince, passing behind Doeg and another servant, heard contempt in the Edomite's voice.

Several months after the army returned from the war, Joel brought a disturbing report to Jonathan. When he passed Doeg rolling up his sleeping mat and blanket that morning, he saw the Edomite hide something inside it. The armor-bearer walked outside but later, after Doeg accompanied Saul out the fortress gate, returned to the room. Unrolling the mat and blanket, he saw an ugly image of Baal, its sightless, carved eyes staring back at him.

"No wonder he seemed so anxious to accompany a hunting party to the Shephelah," the prince said upon hearing the report. "He probably located a Canaanite there and arranged to buy an idol."

"Where would he get money?"

"That shouldn't be too hard. For a long time, I haven't trusted him with Father's possessions—or anything else."

"You too? I thought maybe it was just my imagination. What can we do about it?"

"Probably nothing but pray. Father seems to genuinely like Doeg and trust him. It isn't easy to change Father's mind."

That winter Jonathan's concern turned to matters more alarming than Doeg.

Jonathan shivered under his woolen blanket as he resisted nature's effort to awaken him. During the night the cold brick walls had snatched the heat from the charcoal brazier, leaving behind gray powdery ashes—a poor incentive to discard a warm blanket. Yesterday's early winter cold snap surprised everyone.

He heard his mother's groans coming from the next room. The sound brought him out of his groggy stupor as a pang of fear struck at his heart.

"Please, God, make her well," Jonathan silently prayed. "For Merab and Michal's sake, if not us men's."

The girls, nine and five, had become so quiet. Did they have a premonition? Moving them to Grandmother Jedidah's room spared them seeing their mother's grimaces of pain but signaled the seriousness of her condition. Saul had been to the Tabernacle at Nob the day before, offering a sacrifice on behalf of his wife. By the sound from the next room, Jonathan knew his mother's discomfort had turned to agony.

Looking at Ishvi, he couldn't help contrasting his little brother's relaxed soft snores with his own gnawing fear. The cold rains bothered Ishvi's stiff ankle, so, after several nights of his fitful dozing, Jonathan didn't begrudge him the right of sleeping in. Malki-Shua wasn't stirring either.

Jonathan shoved back the blanket, reached for his cloak and sandals, and slipped out the bedroom door. He walked down the hall past the room Malki-Shua and Sarah would live in following their coming marriage and down the staircase leading to the first floor. On the way he met Saul coming up from the kitchen, a lamp in one hand and a cup of warm water in the other. Doeg came behind with a brazier of glowing coals.

Anger flashed within Jonathan at sight of the untrustworthy Edomite. That thorn in his side. What was he doing here? Jonathan wanted to ask, but instead he said, "How is Mother?"

"Not good," his father said, shaking his head with concern. The king's uncovered head revealed his disheveled hair. Lamplight etched the lines of worry deeper into his face. His eyes were dull with hopelessness. "I don't know what else to do."

Jonathan had never seen his father look so haggard. The knot in his stomach tightened. "We must keep praying," he said.

The men walked on, and Jonathan headed for the warmth of the kitchen fire. He stood, rubbing his hands together above the flames as he implored God to heal his mother.

A few minutes later the outside door opened, and cold air rushed in ahead of Jahra. The servant deposited a bundle of firewood by the wall, then brushed flakes of snow from his cloak. Jonathan walked over and looked out at the courtyard, covered by a blanket of snow that appeared grayish-white under the leaden sky.

Snowfall, unusual in the central mountains, brought back memories of childhood when he and his brothers had run outside to play in it. Under other circumstances he might have hurried up to waken his sisters so they could enjoy it before it melted; today the heavy sky mirrored his spirit. Would Mother live to attend Malki-Shua's wedding? Jonathan stood, rubbing his eyebrow with the side of his index finger as he pondered the troublesome question.

Stifling his feelings about Doeg, Jonathan went back upstairs. The door to his parents' room stood slightly ajar, and he knocked lightly as he pushed it open. Grandmother Jedidah sat beside Ahinoam, gently rubbing her limp hand. Grandmother Milcah sat on the opposite side, wiping her daughter's brow with a wet cloth. Leaning against the wall, Saul stood with his face buried in his hands. Doeg, thankfully, was nowhere in sight.

One by one, the other members of the family got up. Sitting beside the feverish woman they all loved, they whispered words of encouragement and endearment as the hours crept by. More relatives from Mizpah arrived. People slipped in and out of the room as morning turned to noon.

Ahinoam grew quiet. Jonathan hoped she was resting.

The hope proved short-lived. An hour later, without a word she slipped away. Tears flooded Jonathan's eyes when Grandmother Milcah let out a death wail. The long vigil had ended. The screams of mourners arose throughout the palace, and Jonathan could hear it spread to the people in the town below.

Jonathan watched as they drew the blanket over Ahinoam's face. Grandfather Kish, Ethan, and now Mother. Why must he lose all the people who were so important to him? Tears rolled down his cheeks. He still had Samuel.

The men rose to leave the room so the women could prepare the body for burial. Following his father out the door, Jonathan recalled words the prophet once said? "The Lord is with you. You don't need me." Yes, people come and go, but God was eternal. He never failed. Jonathan felt peace fill his heart.

Abner and his brothers started for Zelah to open the family cave-tomb. Messengers left for Mizpah to inform the rest of Ahinoam's family. The sun had come out mid-morning, melting the snow and driving away the clouds, but for Saul and his children the darkest day of their lives dragged on.

Family, soldiers, and townspeople finally made their way outside Gibeah, death wails mingling with the mournful notes of a dozen flutes as the long procession made its way across the valley to the tomb. The melted snow had dampened the earth; there was no dust to toss in the air to express their grief.

Jonathan gripped the hands of his little sisters as they followed the bier bearing their mother's lifeless body. Looking over his shoulder, he noticed Doeg at his father's side, attentively supporting the weeping king. In spite of his personal grief, the familiar sense of foreboding clutched at Jonathan's heart. Why Doeg?

Michal stumbled, jerking his hand. Jonathan picked her up and held her close as she sobbed against his shoulder.

Winter seemed to last forever in the palace, but Jonathan knew it was not the weather that made it so. Although society placed no such responsibility on a man, he tried to spend extra time with his sisters to ease their grief. On nice days he occasionally joined them in games in the courtyard. A few passers-by looked askance at the strange sight of a man entertaining young girls, but he didn't care. They were his sisters he mentally answered their unspoken question as he smiled at them.

"Would you like to go pick a bouquet of wildflowers for Grandmother?" Jonathan asked one morning. "She is so kind to share her room with you." The girls seldom left the confines of the fortress.

Michal squealed in delight; Merab ran to tell their grandmother of the outing.

"This is fun," Merab said as she skipped down the hillside. She plucked a scarlet anemone to add to her collection, then spotted a blue one. "Can we do it again?"

"Maybe next week. When the days of sun set in, the flowers will all be gone."

Michal started to reach for a pinkish-lavender flower.

"Wait," Jonathan called. "That is a thistle. It will hurt you."

Michal's hand stopped inches from the weed. She smiled at her brother and scampered on to a white narcissus, then a lovely red mountain tulip.

When they had a nice size bouquet, Jonathan tied a long plant stem around the combined collections, and the girls ran ahead to deliver their gift. Walking slowly up the hill, Jonathan vowed to personally take his sisters to watch the grape harvest at the wine press—if no battle demanded his service. After all they had been through, the girls deserved a little excitement once in a while.

Some evenings Jonathan left the king's table early to go up and tell his sisters a bedtime story—one Ethan had told him about Israel's heroes. Eventually Jonathan recruited the baker Pilha's granddaughters, who were their ages, as playmates.

～

The latter rains finally came to an end and the days of sun returned, lifting everyone's spirit. Early one morning before barley harvest began, Saul gathered his family in the throne room for an announcement.

"I am marrying Huldah. She is the widowed daughter of one of Grandfather Kish's cousins. She lives in Ramah of Benjamin and has three children, a son in the army and two daughters who have recently married."

There was no talk of war that dry season. Abner allowed members of the standing army long leaves on a rotating basis. Jonathan spent part of his time helping Ishvi with the harvest. Long days and tiring physical labor left him exhausted. Sleep came more easily. The king also found solace in returning to the hard work of the fields. Before grape harvest, Huldah arrived for the wedding.

Jonathan looked on his stepmother's presence as a godsend. The servants worked better when she took charge of household chores. The family relaxed. The girls smiled again and moved back to their father's room. Michal followed Huldah around constantly, fearing, Jonathan felt sure, she might lose this mother also. He prayed each morning for the sister whom he had promised at birth to protect with his life.

Two months after his father remarried, family and friends gathered for Malki-Shua's wedding. That winter Saul became so cheerful Jonathan grew puzzled. As winter skies dropped cold showers over Gibeah, he realized why. Huldah was expecting a baby. After sixteen years, might his stepmother be a little bit apprehensive about giving birth again? His father's obvious joy quelled Jonathan's concern.

Doeg acted as pleased with the news as Saul, complimenting him on his virility. Overhearing his praise, Jonathan wondered whether the Edomite had prayed to the fertility goddess Ashtoreth for a child to cheer the bereaved king.

Some months later wheat harvest came to a close. One afternoon Jonathan and his brothers were counting bags of wheat as the servants brought them from the threshing floor to the fortress storeroom. Hearing their names called, they looked around to see their father hurrying toward them.

"You have a new brother," he declared, beaming. "Huldah has honored me with another son. I've named him Abinadab."

Jonathan hugged his father in congratulations and the others slapped him on the back in jovial celebration. Servants flocked around to add their praise. Michal jumped up and down with delight when she saw little Abinadab and promptly appointed herself babysitter. From the sideline, Jonathan rejoiced to see her so happy again. A week later, relatives arrived from Ramah to celebrate the birth and the circumcision ceremony.

Since his mother's death, no mention had been made of Jonathan's betrothal. He wondered if his father had forgotten it. Then one warm day the king called his son in to discuss military strategy.

Jonathan realized that his engagement had been postponed by the constraint of national security.

2 1

A BRIDE FOR JONATHAN

To Lamech the snap of a bowstring and whiz of an arrow were sweeter music than any harp could produce. Taking aim, he congratulated himself as he watched the arrow fly with deadly accuracy toward a distant thistle.

"You're good enough to be in King Saul's army," Rapha said as the thistle top splintered into a hundred pieces.

Lamech turned to greet his approaching cousin. "How did you know I'd be out here?"

"Where else would I look for Dan's mighty warrior?" Rapha teased.

"Someone has to defend Dan." Lamech lowered his bow. "The Aramaeans are getting bolder. Yesterday they crossed the Jordan and attacked three of our villages. People who escaped arrived here late last night."

"Really! Has anyone sent word to the king?"

"Six men left at dawn."

No one knew what the king's response might be. Nearly a hundred miles from Gibeah, at times the northern tribes felt that no one cared about their safety. For several years the people of the territories of Dan and Naphtali had complained of missing sheep and cattle, suspecting the Aramaeans of stealing them. Now they had no doubt.

Mount Hermon still cast a morning shadow over the land. Lamech looked up at the towering mountain as he contemplated the danger to his people. The Danites had at one time been neighbors of the Benjamites, King Saul's tribe. A few still remained there. Most had moved north, however, after failing to drive the Amorites from their allotted territory. Settling on the west side of the Jordan River at the foot of the mountain, their northern border also delineated Israel's northern boundary. The territories of Naphtali and Asher lay farther west, but neither tribe had managed to extend their control as far north as Joshua had designated at the time of the Conquest.

Lamech's knowledge of the history of Zobah came from listening to discussions by the Danite elders. The Aramaean kingdom of the Anti-Lebanon Mountains stretched from Hamath to Damascus. When its army grew powerful enough, it spread out to occupy one or both of the cities.

Hamath sat on the River Orontes, an important city on the trade route from Mesopotamia to the islands of the Great Sea and the former Hittite empire of Asia Minor. One hundred and twenty miles south, the oasis Damascus sat on the trade route between Mesopotamia and Egypt. The city lay east of Mount Hermon and was watered by the Abana and Pharpar Rivers that flowed from the mountain. Being rich in silver, Zobah's defense could afford chariots. On occasion Lamech, his brothers, and cousins had watched the camel caravans moving along the river road, bearing the enemy's goods to markets.

The town of Dan lay less than fifty miles southwest of Damascus, and when the kings of Zobah controlled that important ancient city, their army often pressed south to buffer their expanded domain. By allying themselves with the Ammonites and mobilizing their chariots, they became a mighty force. Lamech started back to town with Rapha. How far west did the enemy intend to raid?

"Do you think Saul will come to our rescue, or not?" Rapha said, interrupting his thoughts.

"We can only pray."

~

News of the Aramaean invasion brought an immediate response from Saul. With the Moabites and Edomites contained in the south and his family now cared for, nothing personal delayed his leaving. Completion of wheat harvest in most places left the king free to call up the reserves, organize his army, and begin the march northward. The new groom, Malki-Shua, remained at home.

Joel had been promoted to army captain, and Jonathan shared his enthusiasm for his new status as they marched along. He had arranged for Joel to billet with Pharez' family down in town. The prince missed his always being available but was glad the promotion made Joel eligible to join them each evening at the king's table.

Jonathan had never been north of Bethel. As they walked through the valleys, the richness of the Land fascinated him. They came around a hill and looked on the miles of stubble fields covering the Plain of Shechem. Someday he would be king over all this. The idea of kingship momentarily overwhelmed him, but he knew when the time came God would give the wisdom to rule in righteousness.

Following the ancient road past Dothan and En-gannim, they entered the southern arm of the Plain of Jezreel. To the right, the peaks of Mount Gilboa stretched southeast for several miles. The army took the road west of the Hill of Moreh, avoiding the city of Beth-shan, still under control of a branch of Sea People. Beyond Moreh, the isolated hill of Mount Tabor stood above the plain.

None, however, compared to snow-capped Mount Hermon that loomed on the northern horizon.

The men reached the Sea of Kinnereth on the fourth day. Jonathan couldn't help contrasting it to the Dead Sea they had passed on their expedition against the Moabites three years earlier. That lifeless salt sea was hedged in by the barren mountains of the Judean Wilderness and of Moab, whereas the northern lake lay surrounded by fertile plains. Fishing villages dotted its shore.

Dan lay thirty miles north. After the men obtained additional food supplies in the towns, they forged ahead. The men of Dan welcomed Saul and his soldiers when they arrived, and the women danced out to meet them with tambourines and singing. Their doubts were gone. They had a king who cared.

As the sun set to the west, Jonathan looked up at great Mount Herman to the north, painted gold by the hand of God. No wonder the Aramaeans worshiped Baal Hermon. The mountain seemed to reach to the heavens. Its springs filled the Jordan River and the rivers of Damascus that nourished the land. How tragic that they did not realize the One True God created it all.

The next morning the Israelites awakened to chilly morning air and tents drenched with the dew of Hermon. Joined by the Danites, the soldiers moved swiftly to recapture the stolen live-stock, free the raided villages, and destroy the invaders.

Crossing the Jordan near the river's source at dawn the following morning, the army headed northeast, where it surprised the small Aramaean garrisons stationed at outposts below the mountain. Before the Zobahites could marshal their chariots, Saul's army drove their forces back to Damascus, eliminating the threat of border attacks at least for the present.

Rapha was not the only one impressed with his cousin's archery skill. The first day of battle the youth immediately caught Jonathan's eye, and he included his observation in his report to his father. Following the victory celebration a few weeks later, the Israelite army started home, with Lamech as a new recruit. They traveled by way of Gilgal, where the army acknowledged once again God's help in conquest.

Happy to arrive home safely, Saul found his wife and baby well. A few months later Sarah presented Malki-Shua with a firstborn son, Kish. Not to be outdone by her little sister, Merab claimed him as her special baby. After a week the family males gathered to celebrate the rite of circumcision.

Jonathan had never seen his family happier. Watching the two couples hold their smiling babies, he felt a longing he had never experience before. Would this be the year of his betrothal?

With the arrival of the king's new wife and infant, Doeg spent less time in the palace. One morning he came to the throne room.

"Oh, king," he said, "since I am not needed so much these days in the fortress, would you allow me to join the shepherds caring for the royal flocks and herds? I know that work best and would gladly serve you there."

"You have been a loyal servant all these years," Saul replied. "If that is your desire, I would appreciate having your assistance with the royal livestock."

On learning of Doeg's decision, Jonathan rejoiced to have him out of the fortress.

When the family traveled to Nob to celebrate the Feast of Tabernacles, they all had extra praise for God's graciousness that year.

With the defeat of Israel's northern enemies, Saul's attention turned again to his firstborn. Jonathan would someday rule as king and, after him, Jonathan's firstborn son. Having an heir was imperative in every marriage, more so in a royal one. After consulting Jonathan, Saul and ten bodyguards set off for Bethel.

Gamaliel's oldest daughter Abigail had married and the second one, Leah, had been betrothed, the farmer informed Saul, but he expressed delight that the king would consider Deborah as a prospective bride. The fifteen-year-old had left to gather firewood before the group arrived. The two fathers discussed the matter and began planning the betrothal ceremony before she returned with her bundle of sticks and wood.

Deborah lowered her gaze and blushed when she heard the news, but Saul knew she felt just as pleased as Gamaliel. The honor of becoming the king's daughter-in-law and wife of the hero Jonathan presented a rare privilege no girl would refuse.

When Jonathan heard the news back in Gibeah, he breathed a sigh of relief. He'd been accepted. He trusted Abner's judgment of Gamaliel's family. Even more, he believed God had answered his prayers. Deborah would be a good wife. His love would make her so.

A month later Jonathan joined his father and other relatives for the journey to Bethel. The betrothal was as important as the wedding —and just as binding. It could only be broken by divorce, which Jonathan knew he would never consider. If he died during the interim, Deborah would be considered a widow. He quickly pushed that thought out of his mind.

When the family from Gibeah arrived, Gamaliel's wife, Eve, and their two married daughters were finishing preparations for the feast that would follow the ritual. Gamaliel's neighbor Isaac offered his upper room and rooftop to the guests.

Late the next morning relatives and close friends from Bethel and nearby towns came to celebrate the agreement. With everything ready, the two families met for the formal, but brief, ceremony.

Jonathan's hand shook slightly as he presented the *mohar* to

Gamaliel. The man responded with the official words, "You shall be my son-in-law."

The prince looked deep into Deborah's eyes as he gave her the betrothal *mattan*, or gifts—golden bracelets and an embroidered silk headscarf from Mesopotamia. "With these gifts you are set apart as my bride, according to the Law of Moses," he told her in front of the witnesses. Deborah lowered her eyes, but Jonathan had glimpsed the spark of joy. She looked forward to marrying him. Thank the Lord!

The year of betrothal dragged by. Jonathan tried to keep busy drilling his battalion of soldiers but often found thoughts of marriage crowding in to distract him. How could he bravely face the enemy, he often chided himself, yet grow nervous wondering what kind of a husband he would be?

The day finally came when Jonathan hid behind a projection on the fortress rooftop and watched Gamaliel and his family climb the hill of Gibeah. He quickly spotted Deborah, the only one privileged to ride a donkey. Suddenly Jonathan's legs felt weak. Leaning against the wall for support, he reached up to rub his eyebrow with the back of his hand. Peering again at the little caravan, he inhaled deeply. Was he ready for marriage? He'd better be. Day after tomorrow was the wedding.

In the courtyard below, the voices of Gatam and Pagiel called back and forth as they put the finishing touches on the marriage canopy, or *huppah*. Michal's joyful laughter and Merab's calmer comments floated up as they watched the servants string branches along the top. Occasionally Jonathan could hear Jahra's commands coming from the kitchen, where he scurried about, overseeing the preparations for the big feast and week-long celebration. Everyone seemed to want this wedding to be perfect. Jonathan hoped he would not disappoint them.

Two evenings later, accompanied by Pharez, Gera, his brothers, and army captains, Jonathan made his way down to Hamul's house, where Gamaliel's family was staying. They carried the bridal litter on their shoulders. Having participated in his brother's and friends' weddings, the crown prince knew each part of the celebration. But it sure was different when it was your own.

The journey seemed short to Jonathan as he heard Pharez knock on the front gate. The men, who carried torches topped with oil-soaked rags, lit them. The street instantly glowed with light, illuminating the faces of two hundred townspeople who were gathered behind them, singing, playing tambourines and flutes, and dancing with joy.

Feeling overdressed in his new indigo tunic and cloak, the prince wiped his sweaty palms on the sides of his cloak. The door opened and his heart skipped a beat as he caught sight of Deborah, dressed in white, her dark hair on her shoulders, and her face covered with a veil. Their eyes met and Jonathan forgot his doubts.

Pharez helped the bride into the seat on the litter. Four men lifted the poles and started up the street. The bridesmaids stayed close behind, and Gamaliel's relatives followed them. The torch-lit procession wound its way through Gibeah to the palace, the music growing louder as others joined them.

Soldiers at the gate held up blazing torches as the celebrants poured through. Saul waited for them in the courtyard. The king welcomed his guests, and they found seats on the mats laid out for the occasion. Attendants led the couple to the decorated *huppah*. When those who could find space had crowded into the courtyard, Saul walked over to the canopy.

Saul began the short ceremony as he pronounced a blessing on the couple. Jonathan confirmed the marriage contract with the words, "Deborah is my wife and I am her husband, from today forever."

Gamaliel blessed his daughter with the blessing given their ancestress Rebekah:

*"Our sister, may you be the mother
of thousands upon thousands;
may your children possess
the gates of their enemies."*

The end of the blessing signaled the guests, who began tossing grain in front of the couple, wishing them healthy offspring. Next, they presented their gifts.

When the ceremony concluded, men in new light brown tunics served the feast to the guests, who formed circles and shared from common bowls. Cheerful voices filled the courtyard with praise as the people ate the good food. There was nothing better than a wedding feast, they all agreed.

Following the meal, Deborah and her maids retired to the marriage chamber in the second story to await the groom's arrival. Throughout the evening the guests participated in the music and entertainment. Eventually attendants led Jonathan up to his bride. The moment had arrived.

The bridesmaids left, and Jonathan closed the door behind them. He glanced at the walls. Their very own home. This room would always be the most special part of the palace. Here he and Deborah became man and wife.

Turning, Jonathan saw Deborah standing in the middle of the room, her slim figure silhouetted by the lamplight. He walked over to his bride and, slipping the veil from her face, smiled down at her. Stifling the old misgivings that threatened to resurface, he drew her close and held her in his arms.

"Thank you for marrying me," Jonathan whispered. He felt her tremble slightly and realized she also had fears of the unknown. Love rose in his heart for this young woman who had committed her life to him. "The God of Israel is our God," he said softly. "He brought us together as He did Adam and Eve in the Garden of Eden. The Book of Moses records God's instruction, 'Therefore a man shall leave his father and mother and be joined to his wife, becoming one flesh with her.' "

Tears of joy came to Deborah's eyes as she rested her head against Jonathan's solid shoulder. Her husband loved God deeply. She had nothing to fear from a man of God. Reaching up, she put her arms around his neck, and he kissed her for the first time.

Later, after they shared their love and Jonathan lay asleep beside her, Deborah promised God she would be the best wife possible. Of all the men in Israel, God had given her this strong man, who promised to love and protect her. God had answered her prayers beyond her highest hopes.

22

HANNAH

Jonathan was a married man! He looked down at his sleeping bride. It was still hard to believe. Smiling, he tiptoed out the door and walked over to climb to the fortress rooftop. Surveying the countryside in the morning sunlight, he praised God for his new life. Upon returning, he found Deborah sitting on a bedroom cushion, donning her headscarf. He lowered himself to the adjacent cushion and took her hand.

"Deborah, from the beginning, I want our marriage to be dedicated to God," he said. "Every day I am home we will pray together. I want to share with you all the lessons Ethan taught me—at least, those I can still remember." He chuckled. "I am the crown prince, an army commander. I will fight many battles." He looked deep into her eyes. "We never know the outcome of a battle, but I commit each one to God's protection. If anything happens to me, I want you to be able to teach our children to love and serve God, to be true Israelites, God's Chosen People." He put his arm around her. "God has given you to me—a precious gift. I want to be the man of God you deserve."

"You will be," she assured him. They bowed their heads to pray, spiritually united in this wonderful way they were starting married life.

Although the newlywed had a year's leave from battle, Jonathan continued drilling his soldiers. Was it his imagination, or did they respect him more, now that he was a married man? Perhaps he was the one whose thinking had changed.

The idea resurfaced a week later when he went hunting with a unit of soldiers. Nearing the woods west of Michmash, he recalled his first battle, in which he attacked the Philistines with concern only for God's cause. Now battles would not only be fought for the Lord and Israel, but also for the wife he must protect. Marriage changed one's perspective. Anxious to get back to the palace and his bride, he prayed they would soon spot a deer.

The king's dinner that night featured venison. Sitting across from Ish-Bosheth, Jonathan engaged his brother in a discussion of crops. Jonathan always tried to include Ish-Bosheth in conversation before war stories side-tracked him. From Ish-Bosheth's occasional comments, Jonathan knew his brother felt inferior because his stiff ankle kept him from protecting the kingdom. "Feeding the king is as important as defending him," Jonathan often reminded Ish-Bosheth. "An unfed army is a defeated one."

Jonathan savored the piece of meat wrapped in bread as he looked over at Ish-Bosheth. He tore another piece of flatbread and lifted it towards his brother. "Great bread. Thanks." A smile rewarded his comment.

Days turned into weeks and weeks into months. Jonathan observed how well Deborah fit into the family. She willingly assisted the other women in spinning wool and took her turn weaving on the loom. Pausing in the upstairs hallway one morning, he listened as she joined in a discussion with Huldah and Sarah. From her questions, he caught her eagerness to learn all she could.

As they became more acquainted, Jonathan praised God for Abner's suggestion of his wife. When in the fortress, Jonathan always ate lunch with Deborah and sometimes excused himself from the king's table in the evening to be with her at mealtime.

"Would you like to go help Ish-Bosheth harvest grapes?" Jonathan asked Deborah one late summer morning.

"Yes," she said, turning to him with a smile. "I used to do that in Bethel."

At the vineyard Deborah worked as hard as the others and seemed to enjoy pausing for brief conversations with passing harvesters. As the couple walked home that afternoon, she did not speak. When they reached the junction with the path up to the fortress, Jonathan paused.

"You're awfully quiet. I'm sorry if I tired you out."

"No, it isn't that," she said. She looked up at him, tears glistening in her eyes. "Maybe I shouldn't tell you this." She paused and lowered her gaze. "A couple of years ago Uncle Beriah heard rumors Ishpan son of Salma showed interest in me. I prayed hard Father would not consent to such a marriage."

"Ishpan isn't a good man?"

She looked back up, her lower lip trembling. "He's not serious about God. He's a jokester. The treaders back at the wine press reminded me of him. A real show-off." She shook her head. "Worse yet, one day Leah and I were in the marketplace. He stood in front of his father's leather shop talking to friends and didn't see us as we passed. I heard him mocking Samuel's student prophets who came to preach in Bethel."

"Do you think your father would have made such an arrangement?"

"I don't know. It is a good family. Father and Salma were childhood friends. I'm not sure either really knows Ishpan's thinking." She took a deep breath. "Thank you, Jonathan, for rescuing me from him and for being such a wonderful husband."

"I'm grateful you married me." He smiled down at her. "And I promise I won't make you go back to the vineyard."

"No," she said. "Every time I go will only make me love you more."

"Then let's go every day."

She swatted at his arm. "Don't get carried away."

Disregarding society's prohibition against couples showing affection in public, Jonathan gave his bride a quick hug before they climbed the hill to the fortress.

Jonathan thanked God daily for his new bride. So did Sarah. As Malki-Shua's wife grew large with her second child, her energy level and speed of movement declined. Deborah became Kish's self-appointed nursemaid, discreetly keeping a watchful eye when Merab cared for him. Observing his wife try to keep up with the little boy, Jonathan knew Deborah would make as wonderful a mother as she did a wife.

One night following olive harvest, as he gathered Deborah in his arms, she whispered the words that confirmed his suspicion.

"My husband, I am with child."

Jonathan's heart beat faster as love and excitement welled up in him. *A son.* What greater gift could a woman give her husband? Showering her with kisses and tender words of affection, Jonathan knew this would be a night to remember. Deborah was making him a father.

Two months later, as dark winter clouds filled the sky, Sarah delivered a baby girl. Malki-Shua named her for his mother, Ahinoam. Deborah spent many hours caring for the new baby. Once when Jonathan came upstairs to retrieve his money bag, he caught snatches of conversation between the new mother and the mother-to-be. He could envision Deborah's attentive gaze as she tried to absorb the information about childcare she would soon need.

A week after the first latter rains fell, Gamaliel and Eve arrived from Bethel with their son Javan. Jonathan enjoyed visiting with his male in-laws, showing them the fortress, and taking them to watch the returning soldiers resume their drills. After a few days, Gamaliel and Javan headed home, leaving Eve behind to assist her daughter in the upcoming delivery.

One morning the following week Jonathan awoke tired and worried. Deborah's tossing and turning had kept him awake half the night. Before reporting for duty, he informed Huldah and his mother-in-law.

Abner assigned Jonathan's troops bow practice, so he led them to the valley below town. As he walked up and down the line behind the archers, correcting stances and suggesting tips to improve a grip or aim, the prince tried to concentrate on his men. Deborah, however, remained uppermost in his thoughts and prayers. As noon approached and he heard no news, he decided her time had not arrived.

The sun started its descent toward the western mountains when the men reached the fortress. Joel came over to ask Jonathan a question, and the two were deep in discussion as they passed through the gate. When the prince looked up, he saw Huldah standing by the palace corner. She hesitated a moment, then walked toward him. Before she reached him, Jonathan knew he was the father of a baby girl. Had Deborah delivered a son, the women would have sent a runner with the good news.

Jonathan swallowed his disappointment as he listened to his stepmother say, "You are father of a beautiful, healthy daughter."

Jonathan breathed a sigh of relief when he learned Deborah had come through the ordeal safely. Many women didn't. Fleetingly, he thought of the day the high priest Eli died and the Philistines destroyed the Tabernacle in Shiloh. The shock had sent Phinehas' wife into labor. She delivered baby Ichabod, then she died. Thanking Huldah for helping the midwife, Jonathan hurried upstairs to see his firstborn.

Women in Israel were honored by their families, but they had few legal rights. Jonathan had heard men rejoice that God made them male. A daughter was born to be lost by marriage to another family, even another clan, but a son was part of the family forever.

Jonathan knocked on his bedroom door and Eve opened it. Seeing her son-in-law, she smiled before stepping out, leaving the couple alone. The prince strode over to the corner, where Deborah lay on her mat. He knelt beside her, and she opened her eyes.

"I'm sorry. I know you wanted a son."

"I also wanted you to be safe and healthy," Jonathan said, not denying her comment. "Thanks for all you have been through."

He squeezed her hand before peering at the tiny bundle beside her. The baby, wrapped in swaddling strips, looked like any other baby—but she was his flesh and blood! He lifted her and studied her little face.

"She's beautiful, just like you. Someday she will present us with our first grandchild. What shall we name her?"

"Malki-Shua named his daughter for your mother. Is there someone else you would like to honor?"

Thinking over the names of women that he knew, Jonathan recalled the afternoon Samuel told the three princes the story of his birth and childhood. Since that day, Jonathan had admired the woman Hannah, who prayed so hard for a son, then gave him back to God.

"Hannah," Jonathan said quietly, hoping his daughter also

would love God that much. He kissed her smooth cheek, then laid her down. "She's Baby Hannah."

Hearing footsteps, the prince turned to see Michal pause inside the doorway. He stretched out his hand, wordlessly inviting her in. She pressed close to his side, and he put his arm around her shoulders as they looked at the baby.

"Now I have two special little girls to protect."

"I'm not little," Michal said. "I'm nine years old."

Recalling the day in the old courtyard down the hill when he promised himself that he would always protect Baby Michal, he said, "To me you'll always be my special little sister." Deborah closed her eyes, and Jonathan touched her arm lightly. "Rest, now. I'll be back later."

Rising, he tiptoed from the room with Michal.

A gentle evening breeze blew over the heights of Ramathaim, rustling the leaves of the fig trees beyond the town perimeter. Samuel stroked his white beard, deep in concentration. Twilight disappeared from the western sky, leaving the city in darkness. Twilight—his special time of day. The rooftop—his special place to retreat. Twenty-six years ago, on an early summer evening like this, he had sat on the roof and discussed with Saul prospects for Israel's first kingdom. The following morning, he had anointed the farmer as king.

Samuel had been disappointed when Saul, in a panic to save his kingdom, had usurped the right of the priest by offering the sacrifice at Gilgal. Delivering the divine denunciation had been as hard for Samuel as hearing it had been for Saul.

Over the years the prophet grieved for Israel's monarch. Saul's military successes seemed to prove Samuel's announcement wrong, but he never questioned God's revelations and judgments.

He was the Lord's messenger, not the one responsible for carrying them out.

The prophet prayed daily for Saul and for Jonathan, the prince with great potential and a heart for the Lord. If only God would give the king another opportunity, maybe he would pass the test and God would soften His judgment. Lifting his face and spirit to heaven, Samuel prayed again for Saul and the kingdom, then he sat, bathed in the holy presence of God.

In the dark stillness, a new message came to him, and he realized his prayer had been answered. God was giving Saul the opportunity—the responsibility—to carry out a decree pronounced by Moses four centuries earlier: "Destroy the Amalekites!"

The tribe, descendants of Esau's grandson Amalek, roved the Negev and Sinai Peninsula. The Israelites were well acquainted with their cruelty. Samuel had read in the sacred scroll that, shortly after Moses led the Children of Israel out of slavery in Egypt, the Amalekites made an unprovoked attack on the hundreds of thousands of families camped at Rephidim. God had fought for the nearly defenseless pilgrims, their hastily drawn army led by the commander Joshua. As long as Moses kept his hands raised, Israel prevailed; so, Aaron and Hur had supported Moses's tired arms until they won the victory. Throughout the years Samuel thought of this incident when he prayed for the king, lifting Saul's hands as he led the kingdom.

After that battle at Rephidim, God pronounced judgment on the fierce nomads. "I will completely erase the memory of the Amalekites from the face of the earth." Just before Moses died, he reminded the Israelites of this divine sentence, saying, "Remember how the Amalekites mistreated you when you came out of Egypt. When you were exhausted, they met you and destroyed all who were lagging behind. They had no fear of God in them. When the Lord your God gives you rest from all the enemies in the Land promised to you as an inheritance, you shall wipe out the memory of Amalek from under heaven. Never forget this command!"

A few months after the battle at Rephidim, twelve spies explored Canaan. Ten gave a discouraging report that incited the Israelites to rebel against Moses's leadership. God declared they must wander in the wilderness forty years, one year for each day the spies were in Canaan. Chastened, the men changed their minds and decided to advance into the Promised Land. Moses warned against the rash action, but they persisted in their willfulness. The Amalekites and Canaanites met them in battle and defeated them.

That, however, did not end the Amalekites' encounters with the Hebrews. After Joshua's death, the nomads assisted Eglon king of Moab in his invasion of Israel. Later they joined the Midianites and other eastern tribes in raiding Israel, but God gave Gideon a miraculous victory over them. During the time of the later judges the Amalekites occupied part of the hill country of Ephraim. Now, a century later, the Amalekites were causing problems again, plundering the territories of Simeon and southern Judah and carrying off Israelites.

God knew these desert warriors would never leave Israel alone. Deciding the time had come to fulfill His judgment, the Lord had chosen Saul to carry it out—and Samuel to deliver the military order. The prophet sighed as he contemplated his responsibility. Being a prophet was not always easy. The dark sky reminded him of the night the Voice spoke to him in the Tabernacle. What greater privilege could a person have than for God to call your name?

Standing up, Samuel raised his hands to heaven in prayer. "I will leave for Gibeah tomorrow. Give me strength for the journey and the task."

Jonathan lifted little Hannah in the air and whirled around in the bright sunshine as the wavy-haired one-year-old laughed. He loved to hear her giggle. The prince had been disappointed when Deborah presented him with a daughter rather than the coveted firstborn son, but he knew God, not his wife, had made the decision. He never accused God of making mistakes. Now, he didn't know what he would do without this bundle of happiness.

As Jonathan twirled around again, he saw Joel approaching. He was glad to see the captain, whose first-year-of-marriage leave was now over.

"We have a visitor." The captain motioned toward the fortress gate.

Jonathan lowered the girl and turned to see the prophet Samuel standing by the entrance. Placing Hannah on his hip, he hurried to his beloved friend.

"I see God has blessed you in many ways," Samuel said after they embraced in greeting. His wrinkled, age-veined hand reached out to pat the smooth skin of the toddler's arm. He smiled. "What is her name?"

"Hannah." Jonathan watched the prophet's face for reaction.

"Hannah." The prophet whispered the name and tears glistened in his eyes. "You have honored me more than you could ever know." He touched the girl's chubby cheek with his index finger.

"Long after you are gone," Jonathan said, "I will have a constant reminder of your mother's faith and commitment to God."

Samuel extended his arms. Jonathan deposited his daughter in them, wondering if she would cry at the stranger. Instead, she grabbed a fistful of the snowy beard and smiled, causing the men to laugh.

Jonathan inquired about Samuel's family and Ethan's health. He voiced disappointment that his former teacher's condition had not improved. Hannah lost interest in the beard and began squirming. Samuel placed his right hand on the child's head and prayed a blessing on her, quieting the wriggling toddler.

Returning Hannah to her father, Samuel's face grew solemn. "I have come with a message for the king."

Jonathan nodded, then led the way across the courtyard to the palace. After giving the child to one of the servants, he showed the prophet into the throne room where Saul sat listening to a court case.

23

CONFRONTING THE AMALEKITES

Seated on the plain wooden throne, Saul listened to two men from Kiriath-jearim argue a case over a money dispute. The door opened and one of the king's bodyguards entered.

"The prophet Samuel is here," Keros whispered to the king.

Saul finished the case and rose to greet the old prophet as Jonathan ushered him in. After embracing each other in greeting, the king called for a servant to bring a chair and motioned his guest to be seated. Like his son, Saul inquired about Samuel's family and Ethan's health. Apart from the dedications and a few annual Feasts at Nob, he had rarely seen the prophet during the past decade. In spite of their contentious meeting at Gilgal before the Battle of Michmash, the king respected the old man's connection to God.

With pleasantries out of the way, Samuel told the king he had a message for him from the Lord. Saul smiled, pleased God thought more of his kingdom now that he was successful. Even Samuel had come to acknowledge the fact.

"Please tell me," Saul said.

Jonathan stepped up behind his father to listen.

The prophet stood up and, facing the king, began delivering his announcement. "The Lord chose me to anoint you king over His people; so, listen carefully to this message sent from the Lord. This is what Jehovah says: 'I will now punish the Amalekites for the evil they did to Israel when they waylaid them during the exodus from Egypt. Now go, attack the Amalekites. Totally destroy everything they possess. Do not spare a living thing; put to death men and women, children and infants, cattle and sheep, camels and donkeys. Everything.' "

"We will do it," the king said, feeling a touch of camaraderie of years gone by. Aside from recovering a few villages from the Philistines, his army had not done much fighting the previous three years. He welcomed the assignment.

"Remember, this is a 'ban,' " Samuel emphasized. "Carefully follow the Lord's instructions completely. Destroy everything. Totally. Do you understand?"

"Certainly." The king turned to Jonathan. "Mobilize the army immediately. Summon the men of Israel to meet at Telaim."

The two leaders exchanged farewells, and Jonathan ushered the prophet out. Remaining seated, Saul rejoiced God would give him another opportunity to show leadership. He heard footsteps. Doeg stood in the doorway, and he motioned him in.

"Who was that old man?" the Edomite said.

"The prophet Samuel."

"I hope he made a good prophecy for you."

"Actually, he brought a command from God."

"That old man, who can hardly walk, is telling you what to do?" Doeg's right eyebrow raised in surprise. "You have defeated the Moabites, Edomites, Ammonites, Aramaeans, and Philistines? How many enemies has he defeated?" Saul remained silent. "Do all his prophecies come true?" Doeg asked in a quieter tone.

The question jogged Saul's memory of the confrontation at Gilgal. "I . . . I don't know. Not all of them have yet."

"Do what you want," Doeg said with a shrug. "I would prefer someone younger advising me. What exactly was his message?"

Saul repeated the directive to destroy the Amalekites.

"The Amalekites?" Doeg's face brightened. "Are you going to the Negev?"

"We are leaving as soon as we organize the troops."

Doeg paused a moment, then cleared his throat. "I know I'm only a shepherd now, but I did promise to loyally serve you. I don't know much about fighting a war, but I do know the Negev. If I could be of assistance to you, I would gladly accompany you to battle."

Saul felt like a heavy sack of barley had been lifted from his shoulder. "Oh, Doeg, I hadn't even thought of that, but you would be invaluable to us. Speak to Enoch. Tell him I'm using you as a personal assistant for the next month or two. Israel's victory is much more important than herding sheep or donkeys."

Saul smiled as he watched the shepherd rush out the door. What a find! There was no one like Doeg.

As the army passed Nob, Ahimelech joined them. The way from Bethlehem through Hebron traversed the central mountains and by broad undulations emerged on Beersheba, the City of Wells.

"Are you fighting the Kenites also?" Doeg asked his master the evening they camped near one of the wells.

"Why?"

The Kenites were a tribe of the Midianites, but Saul did not consider them an enemy. Moses had married one of their women.

"Remnants of the Kenites often live among the Amalekites," Doeg said. "If you don't have a quarrel with them, maybe I should go to Amalek and warn them to clear out before you attack."

"That is a good idea. We don't want to go beyond God's

instructions. Take a few soldiers with you and leave first thing in the morning."

Overhearing the conversation, Jonathan was surprised at the Edomite's concern. Maybe he had misjudged Doeg.

Later, Saul and Jonathan stood on a hill near Telaim, looking over their military camp. Two hundred thousand footsoldiers and ten thousand men of Judah had converged on the town in southern Judah. The camp covered the hillsides like a swarm of locusts.

"Gone are the days when our men hid from the enemy in caves and cisterns," Saul said. "They fully trust my leadership now."

"Have you told the men about the 'ban'?" Jonathan asked.

"The captains have."

Jonathan started to say something, but he realized his father's mind had already gone on to other matters—war strategy, he hoped. Jonathan continued to consider the ban.

The Israelites had fought many battles over the centuries, but, other than the initial conquest of Canaan, he could not recall any cases where the enemy had been put under a ban—devoted to destruction. Jericho was the first instance. Achan had failed to obey, taking booty for himself and hiding it under his tent floor. Israel suffered defeat in the next battle. Achan and his family perished for his disregard of God's strict command. From that experience, Jonathan knew no one should question God's order of a ban.

The Negev, a broken semiarid area of Israel, lay south of a line stretching from Gaza on the coast southeast through Beersheba and across to the lower end of the Dead Sea. Jonathan's only experience in the region had been when they fought the Edomites. The Negev's southern limits were in the highlands of the Sinai Peninsula. A main road, the Way of Shur, passed from Egypt through the Negev up to Judah. Copper mines dotted the eastern region of the Negev, so the Amalekites and the Edomites protected their territories.

South of Beersheba lay mountainous ridges of the Wilderness of Zin, running west-southwest from the Dead Sea. The natural barrier repelled invasion. The vegetation appeared meager, even following the rains, and Jonathan knew in a couple of months that would also disappear. The rugged hills eventually rolled out into the desert.

Arriving at a city of Amalek, Saul set up an ambush in a nearby ravine. Ahimelech offered the sacrifice and blessing.

When Doeg came to report the Kenites had vacated the area, the king ordered the assault. The fierce Amalekite warriors resisted, but the larger Israelite army overcame them; some fled. Saul pursued them, conquering tent communities and cities from Havilah west to Shur, just east of Egypt.

The soldiers carried out the ban, destroying all the people. One day during a break in the fighting Doeg came to Saul, four men following him.

"Why are the people destroying all the livestock?" Doeg said. "Especially the well-fed ones? It's senseless destruction. What shepherd wouldn't love to have such animals?"

Saul repeated the orders of the ban.

"I thought after each campaign you sacrificed the best animals at Gilgal as a thank offering to your god," the Edomite responded. The other four nodded. "What will you offer if you kill them all here?"

"A good question." Saul had not thought of that. "All right, I appoint you to select the very best sheep and bulls and to be responsible for their care. Use these four men and choose a few others to help you act as shepherds."

A wild cheer went up from the army encampment just then. The six men turned to see a company of soldiers leading a tall, thickly bearded man in chains toward them.

"Here is King Agag," the captain said, coming up in advance of the other soldiers. "We are not sure what to do with him."

"This is tremendous." Doeg stepped up to Saul's side. "You have never captured the king of a nation before."

The statement was true. In Saul's wars the rulers had either not been involved in the battles or had escaped. Saul walked over to the waiting soldiers.

"Greetings, Oh Great One," the chained nomad king said. Saul's eyes widened in surprise at the man's lack of humility and that he did not beg for his life. "News of your triumphs has spread far and wide," Agag continued speaking. "All nations fear you. Now you will be able to raise your greatest monument, memorializing your defeat of the mighty Amalekite warriors."

Mention of a monument surprised Saul. Unlike many rulers of the region, he had never raised a commemorative stone to his victories. Offering a sacrifice at Gilgal had been his way of celebrating. The idea fascinated Saul. If he did set up a pillar, Agag should be forced to witness the eternal monument to his defeat by the army of the Lord.

"Chain this man to two soldiers and guard him day and night," he ordered the captain. "I hold you responsible for his life."

When Jonathan returned to camp with his division of soldiers, Zimran asked if he had seen Agag. The prince frowned, stunned to learn the heathen ruler had been captured, instead of executed. When he saw the sheep and cattle in a makeshift pen outside camp, disappointment filled his heart. Without asking, he knew they too had been spared. Going to his father's tent, he reported on his division's victory in yet another city, then he asked about Agag and the livestock.

"I know what I am doing," Saul said firmly. "They are devoted to God. A sacrifice at Gilgal is death just as much as slaughter in the Negev."

Disappointed, Jonathan walked away without comment.

Unable to locate more Amalekites, when all the divisions had returned to camp by the end of the following week, the army of Israel started home. Late that afternoon Saul stood in the center of the new bivouac site talking to Abner and Jonathan. Doeg passed by the men who were setting up the royal tent, and Saul called to him. The Edomite hurried over.

"I really appreciate all the help you have been in this campaign," the king said, smiling at the thirty-year-old. "I would like to reward your services. Do you have a request?"

Jonathan felt his body stiffen. He prayed he had misunderstood his father's words.

Doeg lowered his eyes. "I . . . I don't know how to thank you for your consideration. I am only a lowly shepherd. What promotion would there be for a person like that?"

To Jonathan, the Edomite's humility seemed feigned. Surely Father could see through him. Saul paused, and Jonathan held his breath.

"Perhaps to become head shepherd."

Doeg's head shot up and his mouth dropped open. "Oh, sir, that would be an honor far beyond what I deserve."

Saul smiled. "Before these witnesses," he said, gesturing toward Abner and Jonathan, "I appoint you head of all my livestock."

Doeg dropped to his knees in homage and thanked the king profusely. Saul, extending his hand to the servant, helped him to his feet.

Trying to hide his feelings, Jonathan bowed his head. Maybe he was just biased. Doeg did show concern for the Kenites. He had done nothing wrong to Jonathan; still, he was a pagan. The prince hoped his father wouldn't live to regret his decision.

Leaving the king's presence, Doeg could not believe his good fortune.

He thought of the village raid that changed his life, his work as a hired shepherd, and being taken prisoner by the Israelites. His plea to accompany Saul home from Edom had been sincere. He had seen what his tribe did to traitors. Without prospect of a better life, he accepted his fate.

But Baal had blessed him, after all. From the day of his capture six years before, he had carefully ingratiated himself into the king's favor, attentively meeting Saul's personal needs, working faithfully as a humble shepherd, volunteering to guide the army in the Negev, and, by disguised flattery, feeding the king's pride. It had not always been easy, but persistence had paid off. Having lived by his wits for so long, he now hoped to enjoy the reward for his efforts.

Doeg tried to contain his joy as he walked away from the king. Enoch would not be happy he had been promoted above him. Doeg smiled. Oh, well, there were other captives of battle who served as shepherds. Their plight bound them together.

As the army approached Beersheba two days later, multitudes ran out to cheer them. "Saul has slain the Amalekites," they shouted amidst the jingle of tambourines and blaring of rams' horns. "Their fierce warriors will trouble us no more. God and Saul have delivered us forever."

The clamor rose to a high pitch when they saw Agag in chains. Farmers turned to admire the beautiful sheep and sleek cattle that came behind.

Heading north the next morning, Saul ordered the men to make camp that evening near Carmel, seven miles south of Hebron. The twenty-mile journey had been tiring, but the soldiers relaxed as they relived their battle triumphs, sharing stories of close calls and other experiences. Thick flocks of sheep and goats covered the district of Maon, a pastoral region with rolling hills. Carmel, *Gardenland*, lived up to its name.

The following day the army remained encamped. Saul told his sons the soldiers deserved a few extra hours of rest. After watching them wander off to be with their men, the king called his bodyguards and sent them in search of a large stone. By midmorning they located one on a nearby farm. It held no comparison to Ezel, but it would have to do. Viewing it, Saul's spirits rose. An ideal commemorative monument.

The cooperative farmer sent his stone mason to plaster the flattest surface. The king called Malki-Shua to the site. Handing him a knife, Saul dictated the inscription he wanted engraved.

After admiring the majestic memorial, the king ordered Agag to be brought in chains to see it. He listened with satisfaction to the captive's words of praise.

"This is as great as any *stele* I have seen for the Pharaohs in Egypt. You will be remembered for this battle as long as time endures."

Hearing the news, other soldiers came to look. When Saul saw Jonathan coming across the field with Joel, he anticipated his first-born's reaction. He didn't know why Jonathan was so negative the last few days. Saul got more praise from Agag than from his own son. He watched Jonathan's face as he read the inscription.

After a long pause, Jonathan said, "Father, Israelites don't set up stones to honor themselves."

"Joshua did at Shechem."

"That was a stone of witness for the glory of God, not himself."

"Son, I have fought hard to make this kingdom what it is today, a nation feared by all." The words sounded vaguely familiar, and Saul remembered Agag's declaration back in camp. He declared, "I have done it all for you, the next king. Can't you appreciate that I want to insure your future?"

"I do appreciate it, Father, but what about the Law? Moses said, 'Do not make for yourselves idols nor set up a standing image or sacred stone. Neither place a carved stone in your land and bow down before it. I am the Lord your God.'"

"That refers to idols," Saul countered. "Anyway, the monument is raised," he said with finality. "God is honored by it as well as I am. Let's begin our march. We need to reach Hebron today so we can be in Gilgal before the week ends."

Saying no more, Jonathan turned to call his troops.

~

Bethel was silent, too silent. With all able-bodied men gone to battle, the women, disabled, and elderly had retired early. Samuel slipped out of the upper guest room and over to the parapet wall. In the old days when he made his circuit, this home of his long-time friend Isaac had been his haven of peace. Tonight, however, Samuel felt restless.

After delivering his message to the king, the prophet had returned home. As the weeks dragged by and no word from the battlefield reached Ramathaim, he decided to travel to Bethel with his servant to be closer to the palace. Isaac had welcomed him with joy, and the two had spent many hours in spiritual fellowship as they waited. Tonight, Isaac had already gone to bed, leaving him alone to ponder Israel's fate.

Samuel ran his hand across the surface of the brick wall, still warm with summer heat. How was Saul doing? If only a messenger would come with news. He looked into the dark heavens, trying to convince himself all was well. The longer he stood there, the more apprehensive he grew. A falling star shot across the sky, his gaze tracing its path until it disappeared. Samuel's spirit sank with it.

In the moonlit stillness, the voice of the Lord spoke clearly. "I mourn that I have made Saul king. He has turned away from me and has not fulfilled my commands."

No! Please, no. Tears welled up in the prophet's eyes and streamed down his leathery cheeks, dampening his beard. Turning, he walked to the upper room and sank to the floor. Stretching out on his sleeping mat, he sobbed his heart out as he prayed the night through.

The sun had not fully risen when Samuel called his servant to saddle the donkey, and the two set out for Gibeah. Following the *wadi* Suweinit, they were approaching the turn to Geba when they met a band of farmers returning from battle. Everyone talked at once as they told the prophet of the victory, of Saul's monument in Carmel, and his side-trip to Gilgal to offer a sacrifice of thanksgiving. The men went on to their villages. The prophet changed course and he and his servant proceeded down the *wadi* road past Geba and Michmash to Gilgal.

When they reached the valley floor, the servant tethered the donkey. While Samuel rested in the shade of a sycamore fig tree, the servant went to inform King Saul of their arrival.

Growing groggy in the afternoon heat, Samuel leaned back against the tree trunk. He closed his eyes to shut out the glare of the sun's reflection off the hills of Gilead to the east. The pleasant sound of sheep and cattle in the distance reminded him of life in Ramathaim. He had started to doze off when he quickly sat upright. Shading his eyes with his right hand, he peered toward Gilgal, hoping against hope he would not see what he feared. Sure enough, there outside the army camp the animal pen appeared full. Slumping against the tree, he buried his face in his hands.

Several minutes later Samuel, still engrossed in his devastating discovery, sensed someone nearby. He looked up to see the king standing a few yards in front of him, a member of the bodyguard and the servant at a distance. Rising to his feet, Samuel struggled to keep from stiffening as the king gave him a welcome embrace.

"The Lord bless you," Saul said. "I am so glad you came. I have carried out the Lord's commands."

"Then why do I hear bleating of sheep in my ears?" Samuel

asked, looking across the plain to the pen. "Why do I hear lowing of cattle?"

"The soldiers brought them from the Amalekite flocks and herds. They wanted to spare the best to sacrifice to the Lord your God. We totally destroyed the rest."

"Wait a minute," Samuel said, raising both hands in protest. "Listen to what the Lord said to me last night."

"Go ahead and tell me."

Saul's smile baffled the prophet. The king had no idea he had done wrong. Samuel took a deep breath.

"At the beginning you were humble," Samuel said, "and you became the head of the tribes of Israel. The Lord anointed you ruler over Israel. And he sent you on a mission, commanding, 'Go and completely destroy those wicked Amalekites. Make war on them and absolutely wipe them out.' " The prophet made a sweeping motion with his right hand, as if obliterating something. "Why did you not carry out the Lord's order? Why did you pounce on the spoils and do this evil in the eyes of the Lord?"

"But I did obey," Saul objected. "I went on the mission just like God said. I completely destroyed the Amalekites, bringing back only Agag their king. The soldiers took the best animals from the plunder devoted to God so they could sacrifice them to the Lord here at Gilgal."

Samuel had prayed all night, hoping he would not need to deliver the severe message from God. Now he must. No reason remained to withhold it; Saul's own reply condemned himself. Samuel looked up grimly at the king. " Oh, Saul, Saul. All the times you have heard me preach how could you miss the truth of my message?" God's prophetic words flowed from his mouth:

> "Does the Lord delight more in burnt offerings
> and sacrifices than in obeying His voice?
> Obedience is far better than sacrifice,
> and to comply is better than the best fat portion of rams.

Rebellion is like the sin of witchcraft,
and conceit is like the evil of idolatry.
Because you have disdained the word of the Lord,
he has rejected you as Israel's king."

Saul's jaw dropped and his face grew pale. His right hand rose to his chest, trembling, as he stepped forward to address the prophet. At first no words came from his mouth. "I . . . I have sinned," he finally stammered. "I have failed to fully carry out the Lord's command and your instructions. I feared offending the people and so I gave in to them." Tears came to his eyes. "Please, I beg you, forgive my sin and come back with me, so that I may worship the Lord."

The words were full of repentance, but the heart was not. Had Saul truly repented, God might have changed His mind, but Saul showed no godly sorrow for his disobedience, only the distress of being caught.

Samuel shook his head. "I will not go with you. You have rejected the word of the Lord, and the Lord has rejected you as king over His People Israel!"

Samuel turned to start back up the *wadi* road. Saul frantically grabbed his cloak to detain him. As the prophet moved away, the well-worn garment tore beneath Saul's grip. Samuel stopped and looked up at the king.

"Now, the Lord has torn the kingdom of Israel from you and given it to one of your more-deserving neighbors," Samuel said, his voice low and firm. "The Glory of Israel does not lie or change His mind; for He is unlike fickle man."

Samuel saw the terrified look in the king's eyes.

Saul's voice grew desperate. "I have truly sinned. But please honor me in front of the elders of my people and before Israel. Come back with me, so that I may worship the Lord your God."

Samuel realized Saul's anxiety was not about his sin, but about its consequences on his royal power. Saul saw the kingdom slipping away from him. If the soldiers found out Samuel's refusal to enter camp and offer the sacrifice, they would know he had denounced Saul. His kingdom could be lost overnight. Saul feared the loss of the prophet's approval more than the loss of God's.

Samuel stood looking at the king, whose eyes pled for the restoration of honor. Slowly the prophet's righteous anger drained away. He wanted no part in creating anarchy or confusion in Israel. God's judgment would fall on the king, but he would not be the one to bring it about. God, in His own time, would reveal the successor.

Samuel's thoughts turned to Jonathan, the man who would never inherit the throne, and he felt compelled to proceed to the camp. To refuse would not only be a rejection of the king, but also of his son. Samuel couldn't bear to think of the pain that would cause the godly prince.

The men, followed by the bodyguard and the servant leading the donkey, made their way past the animal pen, with its contraband livestock, into camp. A cheer went up when the soldiers saw the beloved, old prophet. Jonathan rushed forward to greet him, and Samuel felt the stalwart prince's body shake as they embraced. He knew his father had transgressed the ban.

Tears filled Samuel's eyes. "God bless you for your faith and obedience," he whispered to Jonathan.

When the prophet had finished offering the sacrifice, he turned to the king. To allow Agag to live would be to approve the violation of God's ban. In the hearing of all, Samuel ordered, "Bring Agag, king of the Amalekites."

Saul sent four men to fetch the prisoner. The enemy ruler approached the assembly with a sure step, a sign of confidence that having survived until now, he was safe from execution. When Agag stopped in front of Saul, the prophet moved between them. His anger rose as he thought of the innocent Israelites who, over the centuries, had died at the hands of the wicked Amalekites. He said to Agag, "Just as your sword has made women childless, so will your mother now be childless."

Jonathan wasn't surprised Samuel turned and motioned for his sword. Jonathan handed the weapon to him. The prophet was forced to do what his father should have done.

Jonathan looked up at Saul, who stood expressionless beside him. Father wouldn't listen to him. Nor would he listen to God. Jonathan's heart longed for the days of childhood when he had heard the wonder in his father's voice as he told stories of God's mighty power. These days the thrill in his voice only came when Saul spoke of the kingdom.

The next morning Samuel and his servant left for home. Saul was no longer the true king of God's Chosen People, the prophet thought as they ascended to the central mountain range. Their tie was broken. Never again would God give him a message for Saul. Samuel blinked back tears. He would always think of what could have been.

Back in Gilgal, the soldiers broke camp and headed to Gibeah. As they made their way up the *wadi* road, Jonathan marched his men faster than the others, anxious to get home to Deborah and Hannah.

24

DAVID

Conversation in the palace dining room swirled around Jonathan as he wrapped a small chunk of meat in a piece of bread and lifted it to his mouth. Seated beside Abner, Jonathan caught snatches of dialogue as Joel consulted Saul's cousin about making his new compound bow. Across the table Malki-Shua discussed the new planting season with Ishvi. Ish-Bosheth, Jonathan corrected himself. After his little brother's marriage, he wanted to be called by his real name.

In the hubbub of a dozen conversations, Jonathan did not participate.

The prince's silence stemmed from concern. Since their return from Gilgal three months before, Saul had been strangely quiet. The evening meal had been the highlight of the king's day, and he never missed a New Moon feast. Now, for the fourth time in two weeks he had been absent. Jonathan recalled his father's muted response to the cheers of the townspeople and villagers as the victorious army marched up the *wadi* Suweinit from Gilgal after defeating the Amalekites. Seeing Saul's listlessness during the days that followed, he had encouraged his father to rest.

"You aren't as young as you were when you defeated Nahash at Jabesh Gilead. Twenty-four years makes a big difference."

"It's not that. I just don't seem to be able to focus on my work."

"Are you in pain?"

"I'm not sick."

Watching his father pick at his food, hardly touching the roasted lamb—his favorite, Jonathan wasn't sure. His concern increased when Huldah mentioned waking at night to see her husband standing below their high bedroom window, staring up into the dark sky.

Over the winter, Saul's moods matched the gray, cloudy days. He snapped at his sons over nothing. When little Abinadab and Kish ran to him for a hug, he brushed them aside.

Old Grandmother Jedidah died during a cold spell as the almond trees reached full bloom. Once again, the family, soldiers, and townspeople followed the bier to the family cave-tomb. Watching his father in mourning, Jonathan could not detect greater sadness than the depressed king already displayed.

When the days of sun returned, Jonathan went to discuss with his father the Philistine problem in the Shephelah. Towns were being raided and a village or two captured. If anything could excite Saul, the prospect of military victory did. Maybe he needed a new campaign. The prince was shocked, however, to see fear in his father's eyes at the mention of battle. What was going on? "The God of Abraham, Isaac, and Jacob fights for Israel," he reminded the king.

Saul scowled at his son, his dark eyebrows knit together. Baffled, Jonathan walked away. God and military expeditions were not topics to bring up right now.

A few days later, Abner and Jonathan gained permission to scout the Shephelah from Gezer to Lachish. When they returned after two weeks, Jonathan could not find Saul anywhere in the fortress.

"He's out with Doeg and his men," Ish-Bosheth reported. "He sits for hours listening to the shepherds play their flutes. When he comes back home, he is cheerful, more like his old self."

Jonathan and Abner exchanged puzzled looks.

"Perhaps we need to find a couple of musicians for the palace," the prince said later. "If people hear their king is acting like a shepherd's helper, they may lose faith in the kingdom's security."

"Good idea. Let's ask around and locate the best flute players available."

The plan paid off. As Saul sat alone, slumped on the throne, his face blank, Jonathan led the two flutists into the room. They sat down in a corner behind him and began to play softly. The plaintive melodies seemed to express his father's melancholy mood. Standing beside them, Jonathon smiled, pleased to see his father relax and nod to the musicians in appreciation.

The flame of the olive oil lamp in the wall niche cast a soft glow around the room and over the blanketed form of Keturah on her sleeping mat up on the platform. Samuel wrapped his cloak around him and drew closer to the remaining coals in the cooking pit in the floor. He was like the saying about the ox during the late winter month of Adar. Standing in the shade at noon and shivering at night. He was getting old, he guessed.

Thoughts of aging brought memories of his long life, and he sat for another hour reminiscing about his fruitful ministry. He considered the founding of the school of the prophets to be his greatest achievement. More and more people were hearing of God and His Law through the men he had trained. As for his role in helping Saul become king, he would let God judge. His work was nearly over. He stirred up the coals with the end of a stick. He only had one more responsibility to fulfill. Two, actually. He did promise himself he would continue to pray for Saul. The other task was one he dreaded.

Gazing into the coals, Samuel recalled the morning he had anointed Saul. It had been a difficult assignment, anointing someone to take his place as leader of God's People. The Israelites, however, had insisted on a king so they could be like other nations. The task itself, carried out secretly after Saul came looking for his father's donkeys, had been easy enough. Anointing Saul's successor, however, carried risk.

To Samuel, Saul's deliberate decision to disobey God regarding the ban revealed a deep spiritual problem. Samuel had warned Saul prior to the Battle of Michmash of the demise of his kingdom. Since then, Saul had devoted all his energy to personally insuring its future. To keep his troops happy and loyal, he willingly did whatever it took, even circumventing the ban. Now the king was reaping the consequences of his disobedience. Bebai's son Kileab, an army captain, returned home during the rainy season. He reported to Samuel that Saul had grown moody, suspicious, and withdrawn.

Samuel leaned toward the fire and bowed his head, praying for the king, as he did every night. He wiped tears from his cheeks, his soul torn in anguish. If the people had been content to wait for God's timing, would Jonathan have been Israel's first king? Would his righteous kingdom have endured for many generations? What might have been was beyond knowing. Still, as Samuel thought of the godly Jonathan, he could not help wondering.

Waiting in the night stillness, Samuel heard God speak. "How long are you going to grieve for Saul, since I have rejected him as Israel's king? Fill your horn with oil and be on your way to Bethlehem. I am sending you to Jesse. I have chosen one of his sons as the next king."

It was not the evening chill that caused Samuel to tremble. How would he go to Bethlehem? He didn't get around much these days. If he went and Saul heard about it, the king would know Samuel was up to something. Saul knew the prophecy. He would kill him.

"Take a heifer with you. Say, 'I have come to offer a sacrifice to the Lord.' Invite Jesse to the sacrifice, and I will reveal your duty. You are to anoint for me the son I point out to you."

Samuel smiled. God had already anticipated his concern. He made his way up to bed. The Lord had spoken; Samuel would trust His divine protection. God had been with him thus far, why should he doubt Him now? Samuel pulled the blanket over his shoulders. If he died at the hand of Saul, it would be because God allowed it. It was far better to die in the will of God than to live outside it.

As the sun peeked above the twin hills of Ramathaim the following morning, the servant placed a blanket over the donkey's back and helped Samuel mount. The two men started south, the servant leading the sacrificial heifer. The journey took more than a day, so they spent the night in a small village beyond Gibeah.

Bethlehem lay nine miles south of the fortress. Bounded on the north, south, and east by a valley, it sat on the brow of a narrow ridge that projected eastward from Judah's central mountain range. As Samuel approached from the north, he admired the surrounding fields of ripening barley, the green vineyards along the terraced hillside, and the ever-present olive groves that marked the presence of a town. Samuel followed the road that wound up the hill, then dismounted.

Before Samuel passed through the town gate, he recognized that market day was in progress. The town square buzzed with the sound of gardeners hawking fresh vegetables, craftsmen advertising their wares, and customers haggling over prices. The baker's shop stirred memories of Shimea in Shiloh; the aroma of baking bread never got old.

Near the gate of Bethlehem, the town elders sat conducting their semi-weekly business, a semi-circle of onlookers pressing in close.

Jesse raised his voice as he struggled to overcome the competing din. "I am not sure who would be best, but—"

The men in the back of the crowd had turned their attention toward the gate, and he paused. A whispered word rippled over the audience and down to the farmer.

"Samuel!"

A hush fell over the whole marketplace. Jesse looked around with curiosity at the other elders. Shaking their heads and shrugging their shoulders, the men drew together to voice their speculations concerning the unannounced visitor.

"Samuel has not been to Bethlehem in years," Jesse said. "I wonder why he is appearing now."

"Maybe he received a message from God and has come to prophesy against our town," Kedemah said.

Havilah frowned. "What have we done wrong?"

"Whatever his reason, we had better go greet him." Jesse stood up. The other men rose and walked over to the prophet. "Do you come to Bethlehem in peace?" Jesse asked.

Flashing a smile, Samuel replied, "Yes, in peace; I have come to sacrifice to the Lord. Consecrate yourselves and join me in the sacrifice."

"We will spread the word immediately," Jesse said. "In the meantime, please be my guest during your stay."

Samuel thanked him for the invitation. As the men dispersed to inform the townspeople, Samuel called his host aside.

"Bring your sons to the sacrifice. God has chosen one of them for special service to Him."

Samuel said no more, so the nonplused Jesse hurried up the dusty street to announce the meeting to his family.

Samuel went up to the altar to prepare for the ceremony. All over town men closed their shops as others came from the fields to clean up and prepare themselves. Waiting in the shade of a nearby tree, Samuel saw Jesse arrive with his sons. The prominent farmer happily introduced his offspring.

"This is Eliab, my firstborn. He serves in Saul's army."

Samuel gazed up at the man in his early thirties, handsome and tall. He could not help comparing him to the young Saul he anointed twenty-seven years before. This man was surely the Lord's anointed. He smiled at God's excellent choice.

God, however, had another standard of measurement. In his spirit, the prophet heard the Lord say, "Do not consider his impressive appearance or his height; he's not the one. The Lord doesn't look at things the way man does. Man looks at the physical appearance, but the Lord looks at the heart."

Samuel felt disappointed, but stretched out his hand to greet the next son. "This is Abinadab, my second-born. He is also in the army."

This must be the one the Lord had chosen. Samuel studied the muscular young soldier. No, he realized, it was not he either. Shammah came next, but God had not selected him. Samuel met two other sons and the twins, but the Spirit did not confirm any of them as God's choice.

"I'm sorry, but the Lord has not chosen any of the young men," the prophet said, perplexed. He stroked his bearded cheek as he looked at the ground. God's message had been so clear, how could he have missed it? Then he looked up quickly. "Are these all of your sons?"

"The youngest one, David, is tending sheep. He is only a teenager."

Samuel smiled with relief. "Send someone to call him. We won't sit down until he gets here."

Jesse dispatched Obed, one of the twins, to replace David, and Samuel began the sacrifice. When the ceremony ended, Jesse took Samuel back to his house to await the time for the feast. Walking through the courtyard gate, the prophet saw a muscular youth standing near the kitchen. The teenager looked as handsome as his brother Eliab. His clear complexion and fine features caused Samuel to pause for a second look.

"Arise and anoint him," the Lord said. "He is the one I have chosen."

Taking the horn of oil from his saddlebag, the prophet called David forward and anointed him as his father and brothers looked on. The youth seemed confused by the honor and blushed self-consciously.

"God bless you, my son," Samuel said. "The Lord wants to use you in His service. Obey whatever He tells you to do."

When a trumpet sounded, the prophet and Jesse's family returned to the town square, looking forward to the delicious feast.

The next morning Samuel left for home. David returned to the flock. As he watched the sheep graze in the lush green grass, he picked up his reed flute and began playing his favorite melody. He liked to make up poems to go with the music, but it was easier to do so when he had his kinnor. With the ten-stringed lyre, he could sing as he played. Since his anointing, his heart had been so full of praise to God he felt he might burst. Today a new song formed in his heart. He laid down the flute and began reciting:

"O Lord our Lord, how exalted is your name throughout the earth!
You have set your glory above the highest heavens."

He repeated the lines until they were firmly fixed in his mind, then he picked up the flute and composed a tune to accompany them. Tomorrow he would bring his kinnor instead.

By the time the summer heat slackened in late Elul, King Saul's smile returned and again he enjoyed supper with the men in the dining room. The flutists returned home to help their fathers with the planting. Jonathan breathed a sigh of relief. With Deborah expecting their second child, he had other things to think about besides cheering up the king.

"Thank you, God, for restoring Father to health," he prayed as he stood with his brothers a few weeks later at the Tabernacle in Nob, celebrating the Feast of Tabernacles.

With the onset of winter rains, Saul's dark moods threatened to return. Doeg came to see his master and, at the close of a long conversation, subtly recalled how excited the king had been after his marriage to Huldah and the birth of Abinadab.

"Maybe what you need is a beautiful young girl who knows how to respond to your lovemaking," the chief shepherd said offhandedly before leaving.

Watching him go, Saul admitted to himself he hadn't enjoyed sexual pleasure for a long time. Maybe he did need a younger woman. That afternoon he called Abner in and made his request.

"Find a young girl to be my concubine. Huldah is too old to produce more children. Why should I waste my manhood on an aging woman?"

Abner hesitated a moment, as if wanting to say something, then turned and left. He set out the next morning to search the kingdom for a maiden for Saul, telling no one in the palace of his mission.

When Abner returned two months later with Rizpah, daughter of Aiah, Saul called his family into the throne room.

Curiosity filled Jonathan when Gatam came to announce the special evening family meeting. Rarely were the women included in a family council. Deborah carried a saucer lamp down the dark staircase, followed by Jonathan with Hannah in his arms. When they arrived, Saul sat on his throne with Abner standing beside him. Behind them, a young girl shrank into the shadows. Was Ezekiel taking a wife? Abner's son was old enough to marry, but this was not the usual procedure for a betrothal announcement.

When everyone had assembled, Saul smiled. "I am taking Rizpah, daughter of Aiah, as my concubine. She is now part of our family."

Abner stepped aside, exposing the girl to the lamplight.

Jonathan's heart sank. He tried to hide his shock as he eyed the teenager. Second wives and concubines were not unheard of in Israel, and pagan kings had scores of them, but somehow Rizpah's presence seemed an insult to the memory of his dead mother. He wondered what his father had paid for her.

Jonathan lowered his gaze and stepped behind Ish-Bosheth to support the distressed Huldah. To him, the announcement did not seem fair to the widow who had brightened the king's life after Ahinoam's death. Jonathan recalled the story Samuel told of Hannah and Peninnah. At least Huldah didn't have Hannah's predicament. She had a son by Saul, plus her own three children.

Rizpah blushed at the attention. Jonathan wondered how she felt being attached for life to a man probably four times her age. Aiah, of course, would be thrilled to have his daughter live with the king, no matter how old he was. The prince hoped his father made better matches for Merab and Michal.

Jonathan followed the others out of the meeting. The sons and their wives mutely returned to their rooms, where they quickly closed their doors to whisper their comments in private. Outside their door, Deborah gave Huldah a hug. Jonathan led his sisters and half-brother to their room and kissed them goodnight. Huldah, no doubt, would cry herself to sleep.

Leaving their door slightly ajar, a few minutes later Jonathan heard the king bring the young girl to Jedidah's old room—to spend the night indulging his desires. Father was looking for his own ways to find happiness, instead of looking to God.

The next morning Saul laughed and joked like a giddy youth. Astonished, Jonathan said nothing.

Two months later the king sat alone in the chilly throne room, staring into space.

With the birth of Rebekah, Jonathan temporarily forgot his father's dark moods. He praised God for Deborah's safe delivery once again. While disappointed the baby was not a son, he trusted God to eventually provide an heir. Hannah loved her little sister. Watching his family one evening, Jonathan realized how much more mature and self-assured Deborah had become. Motherhood suited her well, and he thanked God for the day his father had suggested Gamaliel's daughter. He sat down on a cushion beside Deborah and pulled Hannah onto his lap as he prepared for evening prayers.

Unfortunately, things were not going as well with Saul. Hearing his father lash out at Malki-Shua one morning, Jonathan sent word for the flutists to return to the fortress. As he led them into the corner behind the throne and motioned for them to begin playing, he waited for his father to relax. They had only played a few notes when the king whirled around, his face twisted in rage.

"Get out," he growled, pointing to the door. "Do you think I'm already dead? I don't need to listen to funeral dirges."

Jonathan rushed the players from the room, ashamed of the outburst and perplexed by his father's latest mood. Last year the king loved the music; this year he resented it.

"Maybe harp music would be more soothing," Gatam suggested when he heard the news.

"I don't think I dare suggest it," the prince said. "Father knows I brought the flutists in. Next he will accuse me of wishing him dead."

"Let me talk to him."

Later that morning Gatam entered the throne room. The servant smiled at the king before complimenting him on the new royal robe Huldah had made him. The two talked casually of farm work, then Gatam inquired of the king's health.

Feeling free to be honest with his long-time servant, Saul spoke of his lack of energy and his irritableness. "I don't know why I react like I do," he said. "I don't even recognize myself anymore."

"I think an evil spirit from God is tormenting you," Gatam replied. "Why don't you command your servants to search for someone who can play the harp. When the evil spirit from God comes upon you, he can play a soothing melody and you will feel better."

"All right," Saul said with a sigh, "find someone who can play well and bring him here. Anything is worth a try."

Gatam went directly to the quarters of the armor-bearers, where he asked the young men if any of them knew of an excellent harpist.

"A son of Jesse of Bethlehem plays while he shepherds his flock," Joash said. "He's the best I've ever heard. He is also very brave when predators attack his sheep and can use his sling and rod well. Although he is just a teenager, he expresses himself like a mature man. He is handsome and the Lord is with him. I think Saul would be pleased with his services."

Saul agreed to the arrangement. Gatam and Joash set off for Bethlehem. Delighted to let his youngest son go to the palace, Jesse hurried around, preparing a gift for the king. When the two men and the youth left for Gibeah, David led a donkey loaded with bread, a skin of wine, and a young goat. Tucked in the crook of his left arm, he carried his well-wrapped kinnor. Gatam caught the pride in the shepherd's voice when he looked down at the instrument and said, "I carved it myself out of a block of wood."

Gatam watched with relief as Saul welcomed the young man and listened contentedly to his playing. Observing David gently stroke the sheepgut strings, Gatam thought the boy seemed almost one with the instrument. No wonder he took such pride in it.

"Gatam," Saul said one morning, "that boy is a genius with music. I can't thank you enough for finding him. I am appointing him to be one of my armor-bearers. Send word to Jesse that I wish to retain his services."

From then on, when Saul became depressed David would slip into the room and sit quietly in the corner, cross-legged, strumming his kinnor and humming. The king's spirit would lift, enabling him to carry on his work again.

Over the following two years David spent many months at the palace, the others with his father's sheep. When Rizpah gave birth to a son, Armoni, David received a two-months leave as the elated Saul again celebrated his manhood.

The second spring news arrived that drove self-pity and introspection far from the king's mind. The Philistines were amassing their army in the Valley of Elah.

25

GOLIATH'S CHALLENGE

For four years Jonathan had been trying to get his father to deal more vigorously with the border scrimmages along the Shephelah. But how could he tell Jonathan he was afraid? Saul leaned against a projection on the fortress wall, looking through a gap south across the countryside. How could he admit the Lord was no longer with him?

Reports had arrived that morning from patrols in the foothills telling of the Philistine army moving up the Valley of Elah east of Gath. Now the matter had been taken out of his hands. Saul raked his thick fingers through his graying beard. He couldn't stay there forever.

Saul descended the stairs to the throne room, where his two sons, Abner, and the army captains were waiting for him to convene a war council. Their worried looks mirrored his own feelings, and he tried to hide his alarm as he opened the meeting. With only one real option, the session was brief. Afterward he sent messengers to recall all soldiers on leave and reenlist those who had retired from active service.

The urgency and gravity of the situation caused Jonathan to hurry upstairs to pack a few garments and say goodbye to Deborah and the girls. He gathered them in his arms and prayed for the protection of them all.

Calling his captains, Jonathan organized his soldiers into ranks and joined the other troops who were still in Gibeah as Saul started south. An hour later they passed the Jebusite stronghold of Urusalem. Ahimelech the priest came from Nob to join them. They traveled on toward Bethlehem, where a narrow *wadi* led through the mountains to the West.

After camping overnight, the men completed the last leg of the twenty-mile journey. A patrol met them and guided Saul, his sons, and Abner to a hill overlooking a plain. Jonathan heard his father inhale sharply. No one expected the staggering sight—a massive Philistine army camp extending over the far hills.

The Valley of Elah, or Valley of the Terebinth Tree, ran east from the coastal plain through the foothills for seven miles, then divided. The main *wadi* continued southeast for fifteen miles up to the Hebron area, while the narrower one branched northwest, then northeast along the Shephelah. At the point of separation, an oval plain spread out a mile wide and three miles long.

A plateau formed the southwest side of the plain. The fortified town of Azekah, situated on a prominent triangular mound, controlled the entrance to it. On an isolated hill three miles southeast of Azekah, the scouts reported, the town of Socoh sat on a natural terrace above the valley. Between the two lay Ephes-Dammim, where the Philistines had chosen to camp. Jonathan could understand why. The site secured their escape route to Philistia.

Saul called for his men to set up their tents on the hills opposite Azekah, above the entrance to the narrower *wadi*, hoping to defend the Judean hills—and Gibeah—from invasion. Driving the end of his spear into the ground beneath a terebinth tree to stake out his headquarters, Saul sat down to assess the situation.

Jonathan caught a whiff of the terebinth, a reminder of the tree beside Ezel, a reminder of home. He thought of his precious family and sent up a prayer for them.

Saul cleared his throat, bringing Jonathan back to the present. Standing beside his father, Jonathan focused his attention on the military situation. Both sides had strong positions. The plain, a beautiful amphitheater now covered with barley stubble, provided an ideal battlefield. Scattered terebinth trees grew along the sides of a gully that ran through it. The ridge on which Azekah sat forced the valley to twist northward before heading west toward the sea and, perhaps for that reason, the gully clung close to the foot of the northern hills. Saul's scouts informed him that the ravine appeared about twenty feet wide with vertical banks ten to twelve feet deep. This natural barrier would not be easily crossed during battle.

Over the next two days soldiers streamed in from all over Israel. Each arrival bolstered Saul's confidence. The third day the king called a war council and the commanders decided to draw up their battle lines on the plain below. The following morning the men assembled, fully armed. Ahimelech offered a sacrifice and pronounced the Levitical blessing. Then they waited for the Philistine response.

The unexpected response, however, astonished them. Instead of the Philistine army marching forward in formation, a single soldier walked out across the plain, accompanied only by his shield-bearer. He stopped two hundred feet from the ravine and waved his spear at the Israelites. Alone he might not have looked so impressive, but when Jonathan saw him towering over his shield-bearer, the prince recognized the man as a giant.

"Goliath of Gath," a scout said.

Centuries before, the twelve spies who scouted Canaan for Moses had caught sight of the Nephilim, giant descendants of

Anak. The spies' hearts had melted with fear. Jonathan now understood how they felt. Judging from the size of the armor-bearer, Goliath must be ten feet tall—and dressed in full body armor. The morning sun glistened off his bronze helmet. Unlike the breastplates of the Philistines, Goliath wore a coat of mail. It was probably, like King Saul's, composed of hundreds of small pieces of bronze sewn in rows, like fish scales, to a cloth tunic. The giant's legs were protected by bronze greaves.

Goliath waved the spear again.

"Like a weaver's rod," Jonathan exclaimed to Malki-Shua as they stood in the front line looking at the spear shaft. "No doubt the head is iron."

A guttural roar rang across the plain, causing the men to jump. The eyes of all the Israelites were riveted on the lone giant as he stepped forward two paces and shouted at them.

"Why do you come out and draw up a battle line? Aren't I a Philistine, and you the soldiers of Saul? Select a man and have him come down to fight me. If he's able to kill me, we will become your servants; but if I overcome and kill him, you will become our servants."

No one moved.

A harsh peal of laughter echoed across the ravine. "Today I defy the army of Israel! Give me your best soldier and let us fight each other."

The duel, combat by selected champions, was a concept the Sea People had brought with them from the Aegean region. It had also been used in Canaan occasionally, but the Israelites had never fought a battle by contest. Astounded by the turn of events, Saul's face turned pale as he gathered his officers to confer.

The rank-in-file shook with fright as they waited in silence. None of them, Jonathan knew, intended to volunteer. Stepping forward, he saw the look of terror in his father's eyes. The king's knuckles were white as he gripped his spear.

"What shall we do?" Saul asked, lowering his gaze.

"These are the same Philistines God gave victory over at Michmash," the prince said. "The odds are overwhelming, but the God of Israel still controls the situation. He will fight for us again," he said with conviction.

Saul raised his head and he glared at his firstborn. "No!" he half-shouted. His gaze bore through his son. "You will not fight the giant." Jonathan made no reply. "Promise me you will not do like you did at Michmash and go out on your own."

"If no one goes, we may all be slain or become slaves."

"Promise me," Saul ordered, his voice nearly a growl. The notion of Jonathan being killed terrified him more than the prospect of losing his army. The future of the kingdom lay with the crown prince. Whatever Samuel predicted at Gilgal, Saul refused to concede the loss of his royal position or his dynasty. "Promise me," he demanded again.

"All right, I promise." Jonathan sighed with resignation. "But who will go?"

"We'll just have to wait and see," Saul replied.

Down on the valley floor, Eliab and the other men from Bethlehem breathed more easily when the giant turned and headed back toward his army. Breaking rank, the Israelites huddled together in small groups to discuss the dire threat. For the next three hours they milled around their side of the plain and the tents on the hillsides in a daze. What were they to do? At least no battle occurred that morning. A cold lunch of bread and raisins did little to calm their nerves.

By mid-afternoon they saw the giant striding arrogantly across the plain again. Running down the hillside, they formed ranks and marched toward the ravine. Goliath repeated his morning dare. When Israel did not respond in an hour, he roared one last laugh and returned to camp at Ephes-Dammim.

Every morning and afternoon Goliath strutted across the plain toward the ravine to shout his challenge. The days turned into weeks. The moon waned and the new moon lit the night sky, still no one responded.

~

On extended leave from the fortress, David resumed his job of herding sheep. One morning his hand paused on the strings of the kinnor when he noticed the sheep lift their heads toward Bethlehem. Across the valley a group of men came out the town gate and started down the hill. There must be trouble with the Philistines. David supposed Eliab, Abinadab, and Shammah had been called back to the army.

"I guess you sheep will get to listen to my music a little longer," David said to the flock as he resumed strumming. "King Saul won't be needing me for a while."

That evening Jesse and his two unmarried sons sat around the supper bowl enjoying lentil stew and fresh bread. "Leah's a good cook," the farmer said.

Ozem smiled at David. As the oldest son, Eliab, with his wife Leah and family, lived at the ancestral home. Leah enjoyed cooking, and Jesse enjoyed his food. "A really good cook," Jesse repeated, a comment the boys heard daily.

"Trouble in the west," Jesse said to David when the last piece of bread disappeared. "The Philistines have invaded the Valley of Elah. Your brothers left this morning."

"I wish I could have gone too," Ozem said.

"Oh, no, Ozem." Jesse clutched his son's arm. "Not you."

Since the death of Obed two years before, Jesse had been protective of the remaining twin.

"If the Philistine menace becomes too great, we may all have to go."

"For now, we'll let the three boys represent the house of Jesse," his father said with a decisive tone.

A somber mood blanketed Bethlehem each morning as the farmer and other elders met at the town gate to await news from the battlefield. Weeks passed and they heard nothing. As the new moon grew fuller, Jesse's concern also grew.

David stayed out in the field day and night now, leading his flock to whatever pasture he could find as the dry season deepened, and the grass turned brown and withered. Bringing the flock in for supplies one evening, he joined the men of the family for supper.

"The boys have been gone over a month," Jesse told his sons as they sat in the open courtyard. "We've heard nothing."

"No news is better than bad news," Ozem said, trying to console him.

"True, but that isn't enough."

Jesse got up and went into the kitchen, returning a few minutes later with a small half-filled grain sack. Coming behind him, his wife and Leah each carried a hand basket. He walked straight to David. Placing the sack in front of his son, he took the baskets from the women. Jesse sat down beside his son.

"Tomorrow take this ephah of roasted grain along with these ten loaves of bread to your brothers at their camp. Here are ten rounds of cheeses to give the captain of their unit. See how your brothers are doing, then bring me some reassuring word from them."

"All right, I'll leave at daybreak. Ozem, you'll have to take over as shepherd." David stood up. "I'd better get to bed if I'm to get an early start."

Once in his bedroom, he wrapped a clean tunic around his kinnor and tucked it into a small bag. Perhaps the soldiers would like a little music.

Cool morning air and a dimly lit sky greeted David as he stepped out of the town gate. He carried with him his sling and his shepherd's staff. One never knew when he might encounter a wolf or wild dog.

His mind on the battlefield, David started down the hillside toward the valley road to Elah. He had never seen the army of Israel in action. The prospect filled him with excitement. Over the years his brothers had told of their training and participation in the wars with the Edomites, the Zobahites, and the Amalekites. Eliab had gotten in on the earlier battles in Moab.

David grew impatient as he forced himself to slow down to accommodate the donkey's plodding pace. He longed for the day he would be old enough to join the army. Carrying Saul's shield occasionally in the fortress had been the extent of his military experience. He saw the army camp in the distance. How could killing the enemy be different than killing an attacking bear? In either case you were fighting for your life and for those you loved. And the God of Israel, of course. Visualizing the pet lambs that he protected each day, he smiled. He hoped Ozem was taking good care of Morning Star and Beauty.

That morning the men of Bethlehem joined their company in formation on the hillside above the Valley of Elah. "How long have we been here?" Shammah asked Eliab.

"Forty days. I wish we were back in Bethlehem. I would even be willing to herd sheep in place of this daily indecision and humiliation by the enemy."

"I'm sure David would gladly trade you places," his brother Abinadab said.

Eliab made a face at him. "On second thought, I'll stay here. The last person I want to see is David."

By early afternoon, however, David had completed the twelve-mile trip. As he approached the end of the narrow valley, he saw the open plain ahead, where soldiers were assembling. How would he ever find his brothers? He led the donkey toward the sprawling camp, which hummed with a multitude of voices. The men on the plain began chanting their war cry and those on the hillside joined in. With all the noise, David doubted he would be able to get directions. Then he noticed the edge of camp, where carts stood piled with supplies and smoke from campfires curled around cooking pots. Men went about their duties, unaffected by the chanting.

Turning to the plain, David saw the last Israelites join their ranks. He watched with fascination as the Philistine army started across the open fields. He didn't want to miss the action but knew he'd better deliver the cheeses first. He hurried to the supply camp, handed the donation to the supply master, and tethered his donkey to a loaded cart.

"I'll be back," he called over his shoulder as he ran down the hill.

The Bethlehem unit stood near the back of the line and David found it more quickly than he had hoped. He was not sure how to interpret the look on Abinadab and Shammah's faces. Surprise? Annoyance? Shouting above the din, he started to explain his mission when the war cry broke off abruptly.

"I could use some of Mother's good bread," Shammah said, casting a nervous glance toward the battlefield. "Camp rations leave a lot to be desired."

A voice shouted in the distance. Rising on tiptoes to catch a glimpse of the speaker, David was almost knocked off his feet when the soldiers broke rank and ran towards camp. Wondering who could arouse such fear in the Lord's army, he stood his ground. As the fleeing front row came up to him, the soldiers slowed their retreat. David's eyes focused on a lone man standing near the ravine that separated the two armies.

"Who is that?" he asked a nearby soldier.

"You must be new here," the man replied. "Where're you from?"

"I'm David son of Jesse of Bethlehem. I've come to bring supplies to my brothers."

"I'm Reuben son of Rezin from Bethel. That is the giant Goliath of Gath. He comes out twice a day to defy Israel."

"Doesn't anyone oppose him?"

Two men walking by paused to listen when they heard the newcomer's question. Reuben explained Goliath's challenge to a duel. "No one has the courage to face him alone," he finished the story. "Israel is paralyzed with fear."

"That should not be." David felt his anger rising at the idea of the humiliation of God's People.

"Are you thinking of accepting the challenge?" one of the passersby interjected. His stare made David uncomfortable.

"It's a great opportunity," Reuben said. "The king promises great riches to the man who kills Goliath. The king will also give him his daughter to marry and release his father's family from paying taxes."

David's eyebrows raised in surprise. "That's certainly a generous reward. Are you sure?"

"Yes." Reuben nodded. "Isn't it, Micah?"

The man agreed, then asked Reuben about a mutual acquaintance who remained back in camp, too sick to join the fight.

Surely Reuben was exaggerating. David stepped over to another soldier. "What will be done for the man who kills this Philistine and rids Israel of this disgraceful threat? This uncircumcised Philistine has no right to defy the armies of the living God like this?" He received the same answer.

Reuben tapped David's shoulder. "Come, let's find your brothers again."

He started through the milling army, and David grabbed hold

of his tunic to keep from being separated. The man stopped several times to survey the chaotic crowd before moving on. Once again David posed his question of reward to another soldier.

Eliab expressed surprise on hearing David had arrived in camp. As he listened to Abinadab's news, he recalled the times David had pestered his older brothers with questions when they returned from fighting Israel's battles. The boy always uttered some glib comment about the power of God. He had no idea the effort and courage it took to be a soldier.

The sea of men parted momentarily, and Eliab saw David following Reuben. Then they were swallowed by the crowd. Eliab felt his muscles tense as he recalled the day Jesse introduced his sons to Samuel. At first Eliab had not understood the prophet's interest in the family. When Samuel raised his horn and anointed David—the baby of the family—for God's special service, Eliab's anger flared. Once when he ridiculed David, Leah accused him of resentment. He had swallowed a retort and stalked off. The accusation wasn't worthy of a response.

Now David materialized out of nowhere, trying to interfere in his battle. Eliab could not bring himself to admit his embarrassment that his baby brother found the well-trained army caught in a military stalemate.

Eliab saw Reuben shouldering his way through the soldiers and ducked behind a taller man. By the time they reached Eliab, his anger neared the boiling point. Reuben paused to his left, glancing around. Eliab did not reveal his hiding place, but when he heard the boy's voice, he lost his temper. David had inquired from a soldier about the reward for slaying Goliath!

Feeling someone grab his shoulder, David winced as he turned to see his eldest brother. Eliab's lip curled in a sneer. His grip intensified.

"Why have you shown up here? And who is watching your few sheep in the desert? I know how proud you are and how black your heart is. You just came down to watch the battle."

David blushed as Reuben looked from him to Eliab, then hurried away.

Not even a welcome greeting. David frowned. "Now, what have I done wrong? Aren't I even allowed to speak?"

Eliab did not reply.

For David, the excitement of the journey vanished under his brother's scorching accusation. It took a minute for David to remember his errand. "Father sent supplies to you. I gave the cheeses to the captain of your unit, as he instructed. The donkey is tethered in the supply camp." Eliab brushed past him and headed toward the hillside.

David followed. Why was Eliab angry? Was he still smarting over the fact that Samuel anointed David instead of him? David hadn't asked for the honor.

David's mind returned to the present, still amazed at the reward offered by King Saul. He had nearly reached the supply camp when he heard someone running behind him. "Excuse me, but the king would like to see you," he heard someone say. He walked on without turning around, but a hand clutched his arm.

David looked back to see Micah. "Were you talking to me?"

"The king is calling you."

Puzzled, David's forehead wrinkled, then he shrugged and followed the messenger to a terebinth tree on the hilltop, where the royal tents were pitched.

A few minutes before, Jonathan and Abner had been standing in front of Saul's tent waiting for the king to come out, when Joel rushed up to them.

"I think we might . . . have found a man . . . to challenge Goliath," the captain said between gasps for breath.

Abner stepped over to the captain. "Who?"

"Some youth who just . . . arrived in camp with food supplies. I'm not sure he is even old enough to join the army." He took a deep breath. "Micah overheard him talking to some of the men."

"Has he seen Goliath?" Abner queried. "Up close?"

Joel began breathing more evenly. "From what he said, I don't think the size of the opponent matters. It's his beliefs that counts. The youth told our soldiers, 'This uncircumcised Philistine has no right to defy the armies of the living God like this.' "

Joel looked beyond Abner to Jonathan, who stood a pace behind his father's cousin. As their eyes met, Jonathan recalled the morning they had paused on the projection called *Seneh*, a young prince and his armor-bearer, and looked across the gulch at the Philistine camp at Michmash and the sentinel on *Bozez*. Jonathan could hear again his own declaration, "Come, let's approach the outpost of these uncircumcised men. Maybe the Lord will act in our behalf. If the Lord wants to act, nothing can stop Him from saving, whether He uses many or just a few."

Jonathan smiled. "Go bring the young man."

By the time Joel returned with David and Micah, Saul had emerged from his tent, suited up in full armor. Abner called him aside and gave him Joel's report. The king turned back to the teenager.

"The Lord bless you," he said, recognizing his part-time musician.

David bowed before the monarch. "The Lord be with you, O king."

"I hear you are interested in Israel's predicament with Goliath. After forty days, the situation looks more hopeless than ever."

"It does look bad," David agreed. They could hear the giant's loud taunts in the distance. Looking at the plain, then at the king, David continued, "But no one should lose heart over this Philistine. Your servant will fight him."

"You? You aren't able to fight that giant. You are only a boy. He has been fighting for years."

"Don't equate age with experience, sir. I keep my father's sheep. When a lion or bear came to carry off a sheep, I went after it, struck it with my rod and rescued the sheep from its mouth. When it turned to attack me, I grabbed it by the hair, struck it and killed it. I have killed both lion and bear. This uncircumcised Philistine will be no different from one of them, because he defies the armies of the living God. The Lord delivered me from the paw of the lion and of the bear. He will also deliver me from the hand of this Philistine."

The king wouldn't let Jonathan go fight Goliath, so God sent a youth who felt the same way he did to take his place.

As David waited, the three men conferred near the tent entrance. Abner reminded the king there had been no other volunteer in the forty days they had been in camp. Saul looked at the youth standing by the tree, so full of confidence in the God of Israel.

"All right. What do we have to lose, but David?"

Jonathan realized his father had no intention of meekly submitting to the Philistines, even if the boy didn't survive. Saul walked over to David. "Go ahead and fight Goliath. God bless you."

The king removed his helmet and handed it to Jonathan. Working his body out of the coat of mail, he held it out to David. "At least wear this."

David hesitated, then put it on. Jonathan saw him sag beneath the weight as the hemline fell below his knees. The sleeves came down past his elbows. He moved his arms up and down, surveying the awkward covering.

"Here is my sword."

The king handed David his weapon. The shepherd lowered it

into the sheath fastened to the belt. Pacing stiffly back and forth, like a walking carved image, he shook his head.

"I can't use these," David said. "I've never worn such heavy clothes. Nor have I wielded a sword. If I have any hope of defeating the giant, I must use what I am familiar with."

"Suit yourself." Saul said, "I'm just trying to protect you."

Another shout of laughter reached their ears as David removed the heavy coat. Replacing and adjusting his headdress, he pulled his sling from a pouch tied to his belt and picked up his shepherd's staff. "I guess I'm ready."

"Come," Jonathan said. "I'll show you a pass through the ravine."

"No," Saul protested, alarm in his voice. "Let someone else take him."

Jonathan turned to his father. "I promise I will stay on this side. If we leaders don't act courageously, how can we expect our soldiers to? Besides, if he slays Goliath, we need a commander at the head of the pursuit."

Saul sighed. "All right, go ahead."

The tall, muscular thirty-four-year-old prince contrasted himself with the brawny, agile teenager as they started across the short open stretch to the ravine. He had never felt so alone in his life. He looked down at the youth beside him, wondering what the boy was thinking. As they neared the bank, the giant advanced across the deserted stubble field on the opposite side. "He's spotted us."

Stopping under a terebinth tree, the prince placed his hand on the shepherd's shoulder. "God be with you and give you victory."

David scurried down the narrow path through the eroded embankment to the stream of clear water. White, water-polished stones and pebbles littered the stream bed, and he stooped to pick up five suitable stones. He dropped them in his pouch and waded through the shallow water. Using his staff for assistance, he scrambled up the opposite bank. As his eyes reached the level of the ground, he saw the massive giant several hundred feet away. With the man's long strides, it would not take much time for him to cover the intervening distance. Blocking out the giant's loud taunts by humming a psalm, David broke into a run, then Goliath's sudden bellow temporarily stopped him.

Goliath grew angrier. Watching the strongly built Israelite and the youth advance across the plain, he had presumed the prince to be the participant in the duel and the youth his armor-bearer. When the stripling appeared on the Philistine side of the ravine, he waited for the contestant to follow. Then Goliath realized his mistake. What kind of an insult was this, sending out a fresh-faced child for him to slaughter? Israelite men wear full beards. This was a mere boy, and his only weapon was a stick. There was no victory in a grown man defeating a little boy. Perhaps an extra loud shout would send him rushing back across the gully.

"What am I, a dog, that you come to chase me with sticks?" he yelled. But the boy kept on coming. He wasn't going to give up. Furious, Goliath cursed him by his gods, Dagon and Baal. "Come on, then, if you insist," he called. "I'll give your flesh to the birds of the air and the beasts of the field to devour!"

"You challenge me with weapons—the sword, spear, and javelin," David shouted, "but I come against you in the name of the God of Israel's armies, the Lord Almighty, whom you have defied. This day the Lord will deliver you to me, so I can strike you with a fatal blow and cut off your head." Abandoning his staff, David stepped closer. "Today I will give the dead bodies of the Philistine army to the birds of the air and the wild beasts. Then the whole world will know that there is a powerful God in Israel. All those gathered in this valley will know that it's not by sword or spear that the Lord rescues His People. The battle is the Lord's, and He will deliver all of you into our hands."

Goliath's face twisted in rage as he lumbered forward under the weight of his cumbersome coat of mail. Extracting a stone from his pouch, David placed it in the pocket of his sling and broke into a run. He figured Goliath's armor had its weaknesses at the sleeve joints and between the metal scales, but he did not give them a second thought. The one clear piece of flesh that stood out from the giant's bronze encasement was his face, the most vulnerable spot on the face being the forehead. The shield-bearer walked in front of Goliath to protect him from flying missiles. The man stood so much shorter than Goliath that protection of the head was impossible unless Goliath took his own shield, which, so far, he had not done.

David raised the pouch above his head with his left hand and began whirling the thongs with his right. For a minute the city-bred Philistine did not seem to comprehend David's action. "God of Israel, help my aim to be accurate," the shepherd prayed as he released one of the thongs. Within seconds the giant's roar turned to a loud groan as he fell face forward to the ground.

The shocked shield-bearer turned and fled back to the enemy army as David ran toward the downed foe. Yanking Goliath's sword from its sheath, he raised the weapon with both hands and brought it down with all his might below the neck guard of the bronze helmet. The sharp blade sliced through the thick neck on the first stroke, severing the huge head from the mammoth body. Blood spurted in all directions. David jumped back, but not in time to avoid having his sandals, legs, and tunic showered with a stream of warm red liquid.

The Philistines assembled at the edge of the plain behind Goliath cried out in disbelief when they saw their champion fall. The unthinkable had happened. Not expecting anyone to respond to the challenge, let alone win, many had not even brought their weapons. The festive atmosphere turned to panic as, ignoring their own terms of the contest, they fled west toward Philistia.

From the ravine edge, Jonathan witnessed the whole exchange. "Praise be to the Lord of Israel," he shouted as he plunged down the bank and up the far side, his sword drawn as he headed toward the retreating enemy.

The army of Israel was as surprised as the Philistines. Sudden prospect of victory left them momentarily disoriented, then the army captains shouted the war cry as they led their companies charging across the field. Funneling down the fords of the stream, they came up the other side and broke into a run as they chased the army down the Valley of Elah toward Gath, seven miles to the west.

Watching David and Jonathan leave the shelter of the army and walk out on the plain, Saul had turned to his cousin. "Abner, whose son is this boy, David?"

He had promised to give Merab to the man who defeated Goliath. Would this youth become his son-in-law? If so, he needed to know with whose family he would be making a new alliance.

"I really don't know. Gatam brought him from Bethlehem, but I don't remember who his father is."

"Find out for me."

The king saw the two figures pause under a terebinth tree near the ravine edge. Neither spoke as David's tiny form appeared on the opposite side of the gully. Did he do wrong in letting David go? Saul had already instructed his captains to lead their troops up the narrow valley in a hasty retreat if Goliath killed David.

Suddenly seized by fear, the king wanted to hide his face as the giant drew closer. The speck that marked the hope of Israel moved quickly out to meet him. Saul wished he had that assurance. If only God would answer him again. At least Jonathan had that kind of faith.

When Goliath toppled to the ground, the king grabbed Abner's arm and shook it. "He did it. He did it." The Israelites broke into their war cry and dashed forward. Saul pulled his spear from the ground and waved it above his head. "The God of Israel gives us victory. The kingdom of Saul endures."

26

JEALOUSY

Israelite soldiers surged across the plain, spurred on by the taste of victory. Yells of triumph filled the air. The shocked Philistines watching from the hills fled over the saddle of the ridge to the rear of their camp and down the Shaaraim road toward Gath, one of the five principal cities of Philistia. Those on the plain dashed past Azekah toward the Valley of Elah.

The Israelites caught up with many of the escaping men, who had reneged on their promise to become servants if their champion were defeated. Killing the enemy as they went, Saul's men chased them all the way to Gath. The stronghold sat on a white limestone bluff two hundred feet above the entrance to the valley and faced Ashdod, twelve miles to the west.

The sun sank in the western sky, but the Israelites did not give up until they reached the locked gates. Other Philistines ran north toward Ekron, and three companies chased them until darkness halted their progress.

David, standing guard over his dead foe, watched the army pour across the battlefield and charge the Philistines. Dust and barley chaff stirred by thousands of feet clouded the air as it swirled around him. He covered his face with his sleeve, coughing when the air became too thick to breathe.

When the last soldier had passed, David brushed the fine red grit and golden flecks off his clothes before unstrapping the sword belt from Goliath's waist. He swiped the sword across Goliath's leg to remove the blood, then sheathed the weapon. Picking up the severed head by the helmet strap, he headed back to the ravine. As he started up the hillside, Abner hurried to meet him. The smiling commander led him to Saul's tent beside the terebinth tree.

The king congratulated the teenager, but David insisted the credit belonged to God. "Jehovah fought for us, or we would have been defeated."

"Whose son are you?" Saul asked.

"The son of your servant Jesse of Bethlehem."

"He'll be proud of your courage and great victory. I have promised to reward the man who killed Goliath by exempting his father's family from taxation."

"Father will be pleased with your generous reward, sir, but even more so that the king's enemies have been conquered."

Abner cast a glance at the blood-streaked trophies. "I see you found yourself two trophies."

"A reminder of God's great deliverance." David raised the head to waist level and looked at the face of the once-blasphemous pagan. "God makes the final decision."

Saul thanked the youth again, then dismissed him, noting he deserved a rest after his brave fight.

Wandering through the deserted camp, David located his brothers' tent, where he wrapped his souvenirs in empty grain bags. Too excited for a nap, he headed to the battlefield to await the returning soldiers.

Some arrived back in camp that evening, but others didn't make it until the next day. The lower rim of the sun had dipped below the western horizon when David saw Jonathan and his battalion come across the plain, disappear down the ravine, then emerge on the near side.

As the weary men staggered up to camp, Jonathan spied David. He went to congratulate the young giant-slayer. "You are a real hero."

"Oh, no sir, I'm no hero," the shepherd said, shaking his head. "I only did the job God gave me to do."

Jonathan drew back slightly and frowned. "If you don't consider yourself a hero, who would you call a hero?"

"Joseph," came the immediate reply.

"Joseph? Joseph who?"

"Joseph son of the patriarch Jacob."

The response aroused Jonathan's interest. "Why do you consider him a hero? He never fought any battles."

"Can you imagine becoming a slave because of your brothers' jealousy, then being falsely accused by a wicked woman and spending several years in prison for it?" David said, looking up at the prince without a trace of intimidation. "All his early dreams seemed lost forever. Joseph's battles weren't against military foes, sir. He had to conquer the enemies of resentment, bitterness, injustice, discouragement—even success. Joseph faithfully served God no matter what happened to him. Joseph is a real hero."

"That's always been my favorite story too. I pray I will be as faithful as Joseph."

"The one lesson Joseph's life teaches me is to wait for God to act." The burnt-orange glow of sunset highlighted David's earnest face. "Joseph would have died in prison, if necessary, but he never took matters into his own hands." David brushed hair from his eyes. "Once he became a ruler in Egypt, he didn't hunt down Potiphar and his wife and kill them for their false accusation and his miserable imprisonment. When he had the opportunity to punish his brothers, he refused to take revenge on them. He had already forgiven them. He waited for God to act. That's what makes a hero, submitting your whole life to God."

Jonathan contemplated the many times his father had done the opposite, impatiently offering the sacrifice at Gilgal, impetuously making a vow that nearly cost the prince his life, sparing Agag and the best of the Amalekite flocks, making the kingdom—rather than God's will—his top priority.

"You are a wise young man. I pray I will always remember your lesson."

"I have the same prayer for myself." David smiled at the prince. "It isn't always easy to obey God, even though we are God's Chosen People."

"His people are blessed that you killed Goliath. May the Lord reward you in His own way for your faith and courage."

The two tired men turned and walked up the hill.

The following morning Ahimelech gathered the soldiers and offered a sacrifice of thanksgiving to God for the great victory. Abner gave permission for the men to plunder the abandoned enemy camp. They found enough food supplies to last several weeks, as well as weapons, pieces of silver and gold, and other valuables. Piling the idols of Baal and Dagon they had found into a heap, Ahimelech set it on fire. Shouts of praise to the God of Israel filled the campsite.

Later that afternoon Saul called David to his tent. With Abner, Jonathan, Malki-Shua, and the army captains as witnesses, he appointed the youth captain of his bodyguards. David looked bewildered at the unexpected announcement, but when a cheer went up from the smiling officers, he stepped forward to receive the honor.

Holding the upper hand at last, the king decided to take advantage of the victory at Elah. He and Abner organized the army and over the next few weeks moved through the Shephelah, recapturing towns the Philistines had taken from the tribe of Judah. David served under Jonathan's command. Reports of the young hero's brave leadership and wisdom soon reached the king, who was pleased to know he had made a good decision in promoting the hero.

When the Israelites had regained control of the last piece of their territory, they broke camp and started home. The large army slowly funneled up the valley toward Bethlehem and the road to Gibeah. Villagers ran out to hail the triumphant soldiers and sing the praises of the king. Saul smiled at the jubilation. Victory celebrations invigorated him, because every village and town reminded him Samuel's prophecy had been wrong. Saul's kingdom remained strong, his position of leadership firm.

The king progressed half-way through the first village when the words the excited people were chanting dawned on him. He paused to analyze them.

"Saul has killed his thousands, and David his tens of thousands."

The king tried to control his indignation. What gratitude for all his years of hard work! He whirled around to assess David's reaction. The young hero sauntered along talking with some of the soldiers and did not seem to notice the acclaim.

Reaching the next village a half hour later, Saul paid more attention, alert to each word in the victory chant. Once again, he heard the same refrain. Smiling, he acknowledged the people's praise, but inwardly he raged. They credited David with tens of thousands, but him with only thousands. His right hand clenched into a fist. What more could David ask for but the kingdom? Now Saul not only had to keep an eye on the Philistines, but also on one of his own officers.

The men camped for the night north of Bethlehem. The king

happily granted David permission to make a side trip to his family home to deposit his war trophies and report to his father. Saul hoped he never saw David again.

The army reached Gibeah by mid-morning the following day. Saul, dismayed, heard even the people of Gibeah praising David more than him. He stomped up the hill, outdistancing his sons when they paused to join the cheering. While the troops held a big celebration, the king retreated to his throne room, where he flopped in his chair, mulling over the disturbing chant.

Jonathan insisted that David join the king's table for dinner. "You are now captain of the king's bodyguards. You must join the other officers."

The prince guided David into the spacious room and seated him next to Joel. David remained quiet as conversations began, but he listened politely and ate heartily. Saul did not show up for the meal.

Jonathan had noticed his father's spells of silence as they made their way home, but he considered it a sign of fatigue. Once they were back in Gibeah, he pondered in amazement how quickly Saul's elation turned to depression. If such a great victory only enlivened the king for a couple of days in Gibeah, the coming years were going to be awfully long.

One morning Jonathan observed his father sitting rigid on his throne, staring into space, a scowl frozen on his face. "Is something wrong?" Jonathan asked. "You seem worried."

"Why shouldn't I be worried?" Saul said, his expression unchanged, his gaze unaltered. "Did you hear what those people were chanting on the way home from the battlefield? They turn to David like he's some god. Next thing you know, they'll be crowning him king."

Jonathan frowned, surprised by the reason for the king's

depression. "Father, God appointed you king of Israel. He will appoint all our kings."

"*You* are the next king of Israel," Saul shouted, turning toward his son. "And don't forget it."

"David is just a boy. He was excited to save God's people from the pagan enemy." The moment Jonathan said it, he regretted his choice of words.

"Saved? Saved? What have I been doing all these years, playing tag?"

Jonathan slowly exhaled. "We all have the same goal—to defeat the Philistines. We must be united, no matter who God uses." He turned and walked from the room. He could not comprehend Saul's anger over the victory, nor his reaction to David. How could anyone feel threatened by a cheerful lad who only loved his harp, his nation, and his God?

The following week Malki-Shua had a suggestion. Perhaps David's music could revive the morose monarch. Given the rage Jonathan observed earlier, he discouraged the idea, but his brother seemed undeterred.

Gatam found David talking with the armor-bearers in the quarters near the front gate. The servant brought him to Malki-Shua, who explained the situation and asked him to play the kinnor for the troubled king. David retrieved his harp from his camping gear, and, slipping into a corner behind the throne, he began strumming softly. Jonathan stood with Malki-Shua behind the throne to await their father's response.

The music touched the king. He stood up and began prophesying that God would bless his kingdom and prosper it. Jerking his spear from its stand, he waved it about as he spoke. A smile lit up his face, and Jonathan breathed easier. His father's condition was rapidly improving.

Saul's smile did not signal happiness, however, but one of self-congratulation at his own inspiration. This spear was perfect. He would hurl it at David and pin him to the wall, ridding Saul of the man who was a threat to his kingship.

As Saul whirled around, he paused to take aim before heaving the weapon. The musician, more alert than the king anticipated, darted out of the way as the sharp point whizzed by him.

Saul stomped over and retrieved his spear. "I'm sorry. I forgot I'm at home instead of on the battlefield. Go ahead with your music."

David returned to the corner, but this time he kept his eye constantly on the king. It didn't seem logical that a man could mistake a dimly lit room for a sunny battlefield. He had seen the king depressed many times, but he had never seen this gleam of madness. He would take no chances. When Saul whirled around a second time, he moved before the spear left the king's hand.

Jonathan rushed over to hurry David out. "Father will be better tomorrow. He is weary from the campaign and isn't thinking straight."

"I'll pray for him." David headed to his living quarters.

Malki-Shua remained behind. He needed to know why his father tried to kill the slayer of Goliath.

∼

Unwilling to publicly admit his jealousy of David, and as much as Saul regretted his decision at Elah, he did not take away David's appointment as captain of the bodyguards. Instead, a week later he called David in and presented him with command of a battalion.

"The Tjekker are causing problems for the Manassehites near Megiddo. Take your troops and correct the situation." David seemed pleased with the appointment and bowed before him.

"Leave tomorrow." David nodded and hurried out to organize his men. Saul smiled. He hoped David would not come back alive.

Unfortunately for Saul, David's troops had quick and great success. Word of the triumph spread through the country and people loved the young commander all the more. Worse yet, when Saul went to dinner that evening, he found that Jonathan had seated the new commander next to himself. Now he had to look at David every day.

Saul recognized God's hand on David. His fear of the shepherd-turned-hero at times approached panic. When no one was around, he paced up and down the throne room, unsure what to do. When sitting on his throne, he drummed his fingers on the armrest.

The king faced a dilemma. Israel's great defeat of the Philistines proved the Israelite kingdom to be a powerful force. Surrounding nations became alarmed. To give David new enemies to conquer would present further opportunities for him to increase his status in the eyes of the people. To not assign David to eradicate problems would only invite more border scrimmages, the threat of invasion, even the loss of the kingdom—which must be avoided at all costs. In the end, before the days of rain, Saul sent David on another offensive.

As a precaution, the king gradually weeded out of his bodyguards soldiers from other tribes, appointing loyal Benjamites as replacements. He instructed Malki-Shua to be on the alert for signs of disloyalty.

When the winter rains began, the army became inactive, so Saul sent most of the troops home. David visited his family in Bethlehem, relieving Saul of the exasperating task of having to listen to talk about the war hero or to carry on a civil conversation with him at the dinner table.

The days of sun returned all too quickly for the wary king—and with them the army. Scouts reported new border conflicts. Saul dispatched David in one direction, Abner in another. The king received news of David's victory with ambivalence, and immediately sent him to another hot spot.

David came home from the second dry season of campaigns unscathed, and Saul settled on a new plan of action. He had promised his daughter in marriage to the man who defeated Goliath. He would present her to David, extracting from him, as the bride price, a promise of brave service and an obligation to fight Israel's battles. After the wedding he would order David to invade Philistia. The new commander would certainly be killed by the Philistines, whose superior horses, chariots, and weapons would prevail on the open coastal plain.

David was not surprised the king called him in and praised his excellent performance. He listened, astonished, however, when Saul presented the idea of his marriage to Merab. Although David had known of the reward offered back in Elah, he had never considered claiming this part of it. His father had already paid the brideprice for six sons; Jesse probably couldn't afford another just now. David feared to even ask what the amount for Merab would be.

"Who am I, and what reputation does my family or my father's clan have in Israel, that makes me deserving to be the king's son-in-law?" David asked, feeling totally unworthy of such an honor.

Although Saul had thrown a spear at him twice and at times seemed a bit testy with him, the king seemed genuinely disappointed that he refused the offer. David, however, did not change his mind. When he heard two months later that Saul had betrothed Merab to Adriel son of Barzillai from Meholah, he relaxed. He could concentrate on military action without worry of family obligations. After all, he was only nineteen.

Five months later, as the rainy season came to a close and the fields of barley ripened, David recalled his troops and left for southern Judah. Saul took on new interest in life, which Jonathan credited to the birth of Mephibosheth, Rizpah's second son. The king spent hours cuddling and talking to the infant. He even enjoyed holding Jonathan and Deborah's newest daughter, Jemimah. The prince felt thankful his father's condition had improved, since the musician was not around to help lift his spirits.

Smiling and cooing, Jemimah enjoyed her sisters' constant attention. Jonathan loved to spend evenings with his growing family, listening to the girls' chatter about the day's activities as they gathered on the sitting cushions for evening prayer. He enjoyed the camaraderie of dinner hour around the king's table with his military companions and Ish-Bosheth, discussing crop reports and swapping stories of bravery and dangerous encounters, the life of a soldier. But that hour held no comparison to being with his precious family of females. They were his—his own flesh and blood. Fatherhood was a privilege, a gift from God. The years of caring for his sisters were God's preparation for his own family of girls. God slipped that lesson in unnoticed. He smiled. When he was gone on military maneuvers, Jonathan missed their time together, so he cherished these moments he did have.

While Saul seemed more content than he had been in years, Jonathan soon found himself growing restless. He frequently paced up and down the fortress wall, at a loss to explain his feeling

of emptiness. He could not ask for a more fulfilling family relationship. It couldn't be that. Was it the lack of battlefield chal-
lenges? Did he miss the tiring long marches to confront the
enemy? or the celebratory cheers of townspeople they met as they
made their way home?

On a walk in the countryside one morning Jonathan realized
the cause—he missed David.

Over the past two years the commanders had had many exten-
sive conversations regarding not only military strategy, but also
deeper spiritual insights. It amazed Jonathan how similar their
thinking and concerns were. With David gone the past few weeks,
the prince had no one with whom to share his inmost thoughts
of God.

The young hero returned at the close of wheat harvest with news
of another victory. Jonathan hurried out to welcome him, anxious
to hear about his campaign. When the prince tried to discuss the
triumph with his father, however, he realized the king's despon-
dency had returned.

27

CUTTING THE COVENANT

Impressed with the spiritual perception of the nation's newest hero, Jonathan asked David one afternoon if he might visit Jesse's family in Bethlehem. The prince was curious to find out whether the father's devotion matched his son's, or if the young man had developed his insights on his own.

"Sure, we can go tomorrow if you want," the twenty-year-old replied.

"Will they mind me inviting myself?"

"Of course not," David said. "They'll be honored to have Israel's military hero as their guest."

Jonathan resisted the urge to smile. David still did not consider himself anything more than a man whom God happened to bless with success. The prince admired his humility all the more.

The brilliant sunrise heralded a new day as the two men followed the road that wound south from Gibeah past terraced vineyards and silver-green olive orchards. After walking four miles, they came to the Valley of Hinnom. East of the deep ravine, a mountain with sheer sides rose above them.

"Have you ever climbed this mountain?" Jonathan asked when they reached its base.

"No, have you?"

"No, but I've wanted to for a long time. If you aren't in a hurry, let's do it."

"Will the Jebusites care?" David asked.

"We're only two unarmed men. Why would they pick a fight with us? Harvest is over, so what could we destroy up there?"

They followed the steep incline up the north side, the only side accessible on foot. Jonathan led the way, the nimble shepherd closely behind. Gaining the height and stopping to catch their breath, they looked for familiar landmarks. The hilltop fortress of Gibeah could be seen to the north. The higher mountain west of Gibeah, from which one could see the Great Sea, was also easily identifiable.

"There's Nob." David pointed to the city of priests on a hill to the northeast. Seeing it brought back memories of the morning he'd presented Goliath's sword to the priest Ahimelech as a thank offering for God's deliverance.

The two moved on, wheat and barley stubble crunching softly beneath their feet. They walked the full length of the half-mile-long, flat-topped plateau.

"The wilderness is so desolate," Jonathan said, looking southeast toward the Wilderness of Judah. "So lifeless and harsh."

"It shows what constant lack of rain does for an area. The west mountains are fertile, the east barren. Like mankind. Some receive God and enjoy His blessings. Others don't obey Him, and their souls become parched and unfruitful."

"You sound like a prophet."

"I actually enjoy poetry more than prophecy." Without thinking, David began quoting one of his recently composed verses:

"You are great and You do wondrous things;
For You alone are God.
Teach me Your way, O Lord,
then I will know how to walk in Your truth.
Unite my heart, that I may reverence Your holy name."

"That's beautiful," Jonathan said in a hushed voice. "Who composed it?"

"I did." David blushed self-consciously. He cleared his throat nervously as he pointed to a walled town on a hilltop five miles to the south. "There's Bethlehem. In the valleys and on the hillsides surrounding it I've herded sheep for many years. There's not much else to do but compose poetry when you only have sheep for companions."

"Do you resent being the lastborn, the one left to herd sheep while your brothers went to the army or helped your father farm?"

"Why cry over your lot in life? If God gives you work to do, make it count for good. I might never have learned to play the kinnor so well or begun composing poetry if I had not been given the responsibility of caring for the sheep."

"Recite more of your poems for me." Jonathan sat down in the shade of a tree to rest.

"Wait until we get to the hills of Bethlehem. They are the best background for singing psalms of praise to God. While the sheep feed on the grass, I feed on the nearness of the Creator."

After a short rest, they walked to the east side of the ridge. Below them a deep valley divided the parallel hills.

"Jebus," Jonathan said. The walled town perched on the southern end of the opposite hill and spilled down the far side. "The Assyrians call it the Land of Urusalem. We call it the Land of Moriah."

Neither spoke as they recalled the well-known story that played such an important part in Israel's rich heritage. The Lord had commanded Abraham to take his son Isaac—the son of his old age, the son of promise—to the Land of Moriah and sacrifice him there. Without questioning God, Abraham obeyed, reaching Moriah the third day. After building an altar, binding his precious son, and laying him atop the firewood, he prepared to slay Isaac. At the last moment an angel of God had called Abraham by name. Showing him a ram caught by the horns in a nearby thicket, he told Abraham to offer it instead. "Now I know for sure that you fear God, because you have not refused to give Me your son, your only son," the Lord said.

Abraham had offered the ram and praised God for His provision.

Lifting his gaze toward the cloudless blue sky, David whispered Abraham's, and the Israelites,' affirmation of faith, "On the mountain of the Lord it will be supplied." He looked at the prince. "Someday the God of Israel, not the Jebusites' gods, will be worshipped on that mount."

Jonathan studied the serious face of his young friend. "Dislodging the Jebusites won't be easy." He eyed the fortress with the realism of a veteran army commander.

"The Jebusites have no more right to the city than the Israelites do."

"That is true. After the death of Joshua, the Israelites captured it from the Amorites. Only later did the Jebusites come and occupy it."

"It's a blot on the Land. Can God be pleased with a pagan shrine on the Mountain of the Lord?"

The narrow, oval-shaped city covered ten acres on the southern end of Mount Ophel. It was joined to the less protected northern end by a saddle of land. The steep sides of the mountain rose from the Kidron Valley on the east and the central valley on the west. The Valley of Hinnom, which skirted the western mount on which the men stood, circled, bent eastward, and joined the other two at a point below the V-shaped end of Mount Ophel.

"You can see the city better from the Kidron Valley," David

informed the prince. "That's the way we pass when we go to Nob for Feasts. The houses are built down the eastern hillside on terraces with supporting walls. Gihon Spring lies at the foot of the hill. Another spring, En-rogel, lies at the south end. You're right. With stone walls and a good water supply, it won't be easy to capture. It wouldn't be, that is, if it wasn't the Mountain of the Lord."

~

Jesse sighed as, with the back of his forearm, he brushed the sweat from his brow. He was getting too old to be stooping over tending vines. He pushed the pruning knife into the sheath attached to his girdle-belt and headed home for the afternoon. Passing through the town gate, he greeted craftsmen sitting in front of their shops, their hands in constant motion as they stitched, pounded, carved, or polished.

As Jesse climbed the hill, the smell of roasting meat floated down the narrow street to meet him. Someone must be entertaining visitors. He swallowed the saliva generated by the delicious aroma. Some host would be blessed tonight with a full stomach while Jesse ate lentils. He smiled at the thought of a happy reunion. With David away and the other sons and daughters married, his wife and Leah had few occasions to roast a lamb.

Coming through the gateway, Jesse grabbed the post to keep from falling as his frantic wife hurried out. She managed to hang on to her water pot as it slipped from her shoulder. Jesse helped steady her on her feet.

"We have visitors," she called as she rushed toward the town well.

Jesse swung the gate open again, this time with more caution. Across the courtyard two men rose to greet him. He recognized his youngest son. "The Lord be with you."

"The Lord bless you." After David embraced him, he turned to his visitor. "I'd like you to meet Jonathan, the king's son."

No wonder his wife looked so harried. The king's son! Why would he visit their humble home?

Jesse's sons had told him of David's great victory over Goliath and his new responsibilities with Saul. The farmer, however, had not considered him being on amiable terms with the king. He wondered if Jonathan knew the prophet Samuel had anointed his young friend for some special responsibility. Wisely, he kept quiet.

Abinadab, Shammah, Nethanel, Raddai, and Ozem arrived at sunset to share the feast with their father, two brothers, and the royal guest. The three older brothers were happy to see their army commander, and they reminisced about former battles. Before his sons departed for home, Jesse asked David to sing.

David excused himself to hunt in the storeroom for his grandfather's old kinnor. His search successful, for the next half-hour he sang one psalm after another. By the time the brothers left, Jonathan looked forward to hearing more the next morning.

The two guests were up at daybreak. David's mother packed a shoulder bag for them. The young shepherd tucked the kinnor under his arm as they set out to enjoy the early morning peace of the hills. Filling a water bag at the town well, David offered Jonathan a drink.

"There's no better water in the world than that of Bethlehem. No matter where I go, I always compare the water with ours. I've never found any that comes up to ours."

"There's nothing like home." The prince took a long drink. The water did taste a little different, but he couldn't say it was better than Gibeah's.

Walking across the valley, the men found a recessed spot eroded into the southern side of a hill and sat down in the shade, out of sight of the town. Flocks of sheep grazed in the distance, searching the grass for patches not yet brown from the summer heat and lack of rain.

The two sat in silence for a time, enjoying the tranquility. An eagle circled overhead, scouting the countryside for a meal. The bleating of a lamb echoed up from the pasture. Then the haunting notes of a shepherd's flute wafted across the plain.

"I see why shepherding is so conducive to composing poetry," Jonathan said. "Out here you are away from everyone else, and close to God."

"You still must be alert though. A shepherd carries great responsibility. Wolves, bears, and lions like nothing more than a sheep for breakfast." David looked at the sky. "Even that eagle can snatch a lamb if the shepherd is lazy or unobservant. This is where I honed my skills with my sling, never dreaming God would use it to rescue Israel from her enemies."

"If we are faithful to do what God gives us to do, He will use us for greater service," Jonathan said. "I will always remember the prophet Samuel telling my brothers and me of the night God called him when he was a boy living at the Tabernacle. Look how God used him to bless Israel."

David's heart skipped a beat at the mention of Samuel. He had never been sure what the prophet had anointed him to do. Anointings were usually reserved for high priests and kings. He came from neither a priestly nor a royal family, but he felt reluctant to tell his hero of the incident.

David studied the back of his hand, avoiding Jonathan's eyes. "Samuel is a mighty man of God," he said. "Israel needs more men like him."

"You may be one of them. Your poetry will bless many. May I hear more of what you've composed?"

"First, you must understand that my poetry doesn't come from my head." David picked up the kinnor and began to strum. "The God who rescued me from the paw of the lion and the paw of the bear, the God who delivered Goliath into my hands is the God who fills my heart with songs of praise to Him. I merely give them expression."

David sang his psalms, one after another, as the prince leaned back against the hillside and closed his eyes. An hour later David stopped.

"The sun is getting hot. Let's move to the shade for some breakfast."

Later, putting away the leftover raisins and nuts, David offered Jonathan a drink. Then he lifted the water bag and let the cool liquid trickle down his throat. "Bethlehem water," he said, awe in his voice. "The best in the Land."

"How about a few more psalms?"

"A few, then I'll close with one I recently composed. It's already become my favorite."

Jonathan marveled at David's good voice and, even more, the depth of his inspiration. He was unprepared for the promised favorite when David began quietly singing:

"The Lord is my shepherd, I shall never be in want.
He makes me lie down in lush pastures, He leads me
beside peaceful waters, He restores my inner being.
He leads me in pathways of righteousness
for His name's sake.
Even while walking through
the valley of the shadow of death,
I will fear no evil, because You accompany me;
Your rod and Your staff bring me comfort.
You spread a table for me in the presence of my enemies.
You anoint my head with healing oil;
my cup of blessing overflows.
Surely goodness and mercy will follow
me all the days I live,
and I will dwell in the Lord's house forever."

As the last note died away, tears trickled down Jonathan's cheeks, catching in his beard. "Beautiful," he whispered. "Just beautiful. David, I didn't think anyone could know God like Samuel does. I'm mistaken."

"We all can know God that way. All we have to do is follow our Shepherd."

"Please teach me this psalm." Jonathan swiped at his wet cheeks. "I know I'll need it in the days ahead."

While David sang and Jonathan listened, a feeling the prince had never experienced filled his heart. Although sixteen years younger than he, David was a man with whom he could truly identify. David also had walked alone onto a battlefield, facing overwhelming odds. He had experienced totally relying on God for victory. He had willingly offered his own life for the glory of God and deliverance of Israel. Furthermore, David's deep faith in God carried over into his daily life, affecting his values, his decisions, and his plans for the future.

Jonathan loved Deborah. But stronger than even the marital relationship and sexual passion existed a deep need to expose, not one's body, but one's very soul to another, knowing that person would understand completely and accept you for who you are. Only God could know you fully, but God had brought the two of them together because of their kindred spirits. Suddenly Jonathan wanted to become this man's Friend.

"David, forgive me if it is asking too much, but would you cut a covenant with me?"

The young war hero's lips parted, and he stared at Jonathan. "Oh, sir, I was born to a farmer. What would I have to offer a prince in exchange for his kindness?"

Jonathan smiled. "You forget I was also born a farmer's son. I was four years old when Samuel anointed Father as king. All I am asking is a pledge of loyalty and mutual protection. Israel is never truly at peace. We are surrounded by enemy nations that worship idols. Even within families there can be tension and division."

"How well I know."

By the tone of his voice, Jonathan knew David spoke from personal experience. "You don't have to decide today. But I would be very grateful to have you as my blood brother." Jonathan grew silent. How could he explain his inner feelings?

"It would be a great honor to be your blood brother. I'm not sure I'm worthy. I hope my poetry hasn't stirred your emotions and caused you to suggest something you might later regret."

"Your poetry hasn't caused me to make this decision." Jonathan recalled the feeling of emptiness he experienced over the past two months. "It has only confirmed what I already believed. God led us together, David. He knew we needed each other. Whatever the future holds, we will always have Him and each other."

David's face grew solemn. He still seemed overwhelmed by the invitation. "When did you want to cut a covenant?"

"Would next week be all right? When we get back to Gibeah I will make the arrangements."

"Could we . . . just keep it between ourselves? I wouldn't want others in the army to feel I received special favors from the king's son."

"I'll have Joel and Lamech help us. They're my most trusted captains. Otherwise, it will be our secret."

Jonathan and David returned to the fortress in time to join the others at the king's table that evening. Malki-Shua had missed them at the meal the day before and expressed surprise when Joel informed him the two had gone to Bethlehem. He now eyed them across the table, his interest piqued by the new level of friendship he observed. He frowned at Jonathan when they arose to leave.

~

The following week Jonathan, David, and two armor-bearers

tramped through the wooded area in the hills west of Gibeah all morning, but they didn't catch a glimpse of a single deer. The hunters managed to bag three quails and a rock partridge before heading home.

As they reached the valley below the fortress, Jonathan paused to send the two armor-bearers on with the birds, ordering Abel to give them to Jahra to cook for supper. "We'll come later. We will keep the weapons with us."

Abel and Elam unstrapped the sheathed swords and handed them to Jonathan and David.

The prince steered David south of town toward a big rock outcropping, which stood across the field beside a spreading terebinth tree. "That's the boundary marker of Grandfather Kish's field. We call it Ezel. As a boy, I loved to play there."

"I had my pastures; you had your rocks. We both have good memories of our childhood."

"Joel and Lamech are waiting for us there."

They walked on in silence, no further explanation necessary. As they reached the formation, no one appeared in sight. Were the army captains late? Then David spotted a campfire on the south side, beyond the formation. Jonathan gave a bird call and the two men stepped from a cleavage in the rocks.

"Do you have everything?" the prince said to his former armor-bearer.

Joel retreated into the hollow and returned with a lamb. After Lamech added wood to the fire, the four gathered around the little animal. Joel held it while Jonathan slit its throat, then he held it up to allow the blood to drain according to the regulations of the Law. A few minutes later Joel laid the carcass on the ground. The two men split it down the middle and positioned the halves three feet apart. Jonathan stood up and turned to his friend, his face solemn.

"Today I cut a covenant with you, David. The God of Israel is my witness that I pledge to love, loyally defend, and protect your life and the lives of your descendants. May I be cut in pieces as this lamb is cut in two if I ever break this covenant." Jonathan walked between the two halves as he spoke. "From now on I am your blood brother, closer to you than to the sons of my father. Your concerns are also mine and I will faithfully serve you." He blinked back tears. "Today Jonathan becomes the Friend of David, with all the obligations of true friendship. May God curse me if I ever break this covenant I make with you." He stepped over to touch the rock formation. "This stone is our witness stone that we are committed to each other for life."

David swallowed the lump in his throat as he looked deep into Jonathan's eyes and made the same pledge to the prince. After walking between the two halves, he embraced his new Friend.

Jonathan wiped the knife clean on the side of his tunic. Holding the blade to his left wrist, he made a thin one-inch incision that drew blood. He extended the handle to David, who then used the blade to cut his wrist. Jonathan raised his hand as red drops of blood trickled down his forearm. David brought his hand up to strike the prince's. Clasping hands, the blood from their wrists mixed together. As the cutting of the Covenant of Circumcision made a male a true Israelite, the cutting of this covenant made them blood brothers forever.

After the vows, Lamech cut hunks of meat from the lamb and placed them over the fire to roast while the two men sat down to wait. Joel brought out a basket, from which protruded rounds of bread. Removing a small jug, he poured red wine into a cup. David knew if they were pagans, they would drip their blood into the wine then drink each other's blood to seal the covenant. As God's Chosen People, who carefully avoided ingesting blood, they merely drank the wine.

When the meat was ready, the men partook of the sacrificial meal, a most ancient part of covenant making. As Jonathan lifted the bread from the basket, he broke a round and handed half of it to David. "This bread represents life and strength, which we now share."

At the close of the meal, Jonathan took off his robe and tunic and handed them to David. "These clothes represent me. As you wear them you partake of my life."

David removed his clothes and exchanged them with Jonathan, feeling a little lost in the larger garment after he pulled it over his head. Jonathan looked even more strange in David's shorter tunic and robe.

The prince picked up his sword, bow, and belt and handed them to his new friend. "These represent my strength. From now on my strength is yours. I will defend you and your descendants with my last breath."

David handed Jonathan his weapons and made a similar promise. The two embraced again. Woven together like threads on a loom. He was Friend of the king's son, forever.

MICHAL

Leaning through a gap in the fortress wall, Jonathan watched David and his men march up the valley toward Bethel. Messengers from Dan had arrived the day before with news that the Zobahites were harassing their villages near the Jordan River again.

"I wish you would send me on a mission again, Father," Jonathan said to the king, who stood beside him in the shade of the closest projection. "I really miss the action."

"I know you do, son, but I need you here right now. You can go later."

What did he do besides try to cheer up his father? Jonathan reminded himself of David's description of Joseph—a man willing to wait—and prayed for patience.

"What is that on your wrist?" Saul pulled Jonathan's left elbow back and turning the wrist over to inspect the red wound.

Jonathan's heart skipped a beat. "Just a cut," he said as nonchalantly as possible.

"Did you get it the day you went hunting?"

"Yes."

"Jonathan, you must be more careful. If that had gone any

deeper, you would have been in serious trouble. I don't know what I would do if anything happened to you."

"I'll be more careful."

Jonathan had promised David their covenant would be a secret, and he prayed his father would not ask further questions. More and more, Jonathan noticed the relief in the king's eyes each time David left on an expedition. Was Father anxious to get David out of the fortress? Or perhaps out of his life? He could not understand his father's feeling against the heroic commander. Based on all the clues, Jonathan knew never to mention the covenant.

Saul released the arm. "Please be more cautious."

David stayed in the region of Mount Hermon for three months to insure the Zobahites did not push back into the territory of Dan. By the time he returned, the royal family had begun making preparations for Merab's wedding, to be held in Meholah before the rains began.

Jonathan rejoiced to have David back. They could be separated for months, but when they got together again the friendship picked up like he had never left.

One noon as Saul and Jonathan finished their lunch of bread and fruit, Saul leaned back from the table. "David can't say he didn't have a chance to become my son-in-law," he told his firstborn.

"Father," Jonathan said hesitantly, "I've been meaning to talk to you about something."

Saul looked up. "About Merab?"

"About Michal."

Saul leaned forward. "Is something wrong?"

"No. At least I wouldn't call it wrong." Jonathan pushed the breadbasket aside. "Father, Michal is in love with David."

As Saul's eyes narrowed, Jonathan regretted revealing his little sister's secret. Then Saul's face broke into a big smile.

"Not many men get a second chance to join the royal family. Do you think David would take it?"

Jonathan was perplexed. At first his father seemed angry, now the man seemed pleased. What changed his mind so rapidly? "You can ask him," the prince replied as he picked up the last fig and popped it into his mouth.

Saul got up and returned to the throne room to think. This could be the opportunity for which he had been looking. Michal's submissive and trusting attitude could be used to enlist her help against David. Slapping his thigh, he laughed for the first time in weeks. "Just the thing," he declared to the empty room as he got up and hurried out to send a messenger for David.

Saul's interview with the young commander went much like the previous one concerning Merab, but the king noticed a spark of interest in David's eyes that had not been there at mention of the older daughter.

"Think about it and let me know what you decide. I don't want to get Michal's hopes up if you aren't interested."

After David left, the king launched a surreptitious campaign to influence him. He called Gatam and Pagiel in. "Speak to David privately. Tell him, 'The king is very happy with you, and his servants all like you. Please become his son-in-law.'"

A few days later Gatam informed Saul of his conversation with David. "Don't you think it's a serious matter to become the king's son-in-law?" David had told the servants who came to persuade him. "I'm only a poor nobody."

Encouraged, the monarch had his response prepared. "Tell David, 'The king doesn't ask a lot of money for the price for the bride. A hundred Philistine foreskins is enough. Revenge on his enemies is sufficient.' " There, he had said it. He congratulated himself.

Chasing the enemy from your territory was one thing; actually killing a hundred of the well-armed warriors was another matter. Saul could have asked for right hands. Most armies recorded their slain foe by collecting right hands and counting them. Collecting foreskins, however, posed a more gruesome challenge. Besides, other nations practiced circumcision. The Philistines did not. Saul wanted to guarantee that the cunning David did not cheat.

"Tell him to have them here by the time the early rains begin if he wants Michal," the king said before sending the men back to the young warrior.

With Jonathan now his blood brother, David felt more at ease with the royal family. The few times he had recently seen Michal, he noticed her blush and avert her eyes. Saul was probably right that she had fallen in love with him. Still, it was not an easy decision. His own sudden awareness of feelings for the princess, however, convinced him. When David heard the bride price, he took heart. Saul didn't demand money after all. Accepting the challenge, he mobilized his men and set out for Philistia, knowing he had only a few weeks to complete the assignment.

Saul waited anxiously for word David had been slain in battle and his troops routed. Before the report arrived, David returned, complete with not one hundred, but two hundred Philistine foreskins. Saul hid his bitter disappointment as he mouthed his congratulations and welcomed the man who would become his son-in-law.

After Merab's wedding Saul held a betrothal celebration for Michal and David. The year of engagement that followed seemed endless to the despondent king. The whole plan had gone awry.

Mere mention of David's name brought a sparkle to Michal's eyes. As Jonathan said, she was in love.

Since betrothed men were exempt from military service, the hope of David being killed in battle had been removed. Worse yet, the commander, unwilling to remain idle, took renewed responsibility for his original appointment, captain of Saul's bodyguards.

How could he have been so stupid as to fall in this trap? Saul fumed, angry at himself, and at Jonathan for bringing up the matter.

With David sidelined, Saul sent Abner and Malki-Shua several times to deal with border problems. He even let Jonathan go once.

News that Merab had delivered a baby boy prompted quick preparations for the journey to celebrate the circumcision with Adriel and Barzillai's family. Leaving Abner in charge of the fortress and army, Saul, Jonathan, Malki-Shua, and Ish-Bosheth set off for Meholah. The four rarely traveled together so they enjoyed the leisurely pace and free-flowing conversations as they covered the miles. The trip erased thoughts of David from Saul's mind. Only as they started home a few days later did Ish-Bosheth's comment about Michal's upcoming wedding bring back Saul's dark thoughts; depression threatening to overwhelm him once more.

Michal's wedding turned into a grand occasion. The royal family and army officers formed a long caravan as they made their way to Bethlehem. Saul forced himself to smile as he joined the festivities. Jesse's renewed expression of thanks for the exemption from taxes provided one more reminder of David's triumph over Saul. When the week ended, he heaved a sigh of relief as he caught sight of the royal fortress in the distance.

Following the wedding, David rented a one-room house down

in the town of Gibeah and moved his bride to it. One benefit—
David joined in fewer meals at the king's table.

Because of the newlywed exemption from battle, David spent a
second year at home. The more God blessed David and the more
Saul witnessed the love the couple shared, the more frustrated and
resentful the king became. What hope was there for David's death
when he wasn't even on the battlefield? The question plagued Saul,
and he pounded the armrest of the throne.

Thinking on the situation for hours at a time, the king became
obsessed with a plan to execute David. After plotting for several
days, he sent for Jonathan, Malki-Shua, and the palace servants.

The prince came through the back door of the room to see his
father seated on his throne, his fingers drumming the armrest.
"You called for me?"

"Yes. Wait for Malki-Shua and the others to come." When the
group assembled, Saul announced, "I no longer trust David. I want
you to kill him when you get a chance, out of public sight of
course. Make it look like an accident." No one spoke. "That is all.
You may go. Be sure to carry out the order as soon as possible."
Saul felt more relaxed after giving the order.

Jonathan left with the others. It would do no good to protest.
Malki-Shua remained behind.

When the king went to Rizpah's room after lunch to take a nap,
Jonathan hurried out the fortress gate and down to David's house.
Closing the door behind him and locking it, he turned to his
covenant friend.

"Father is planning to kill you. Be especially careful
tomorrow morning. Go hide at Ezel. I'll take Father out to the
field and speak to him about you, then I'll let you know what I
find out." Checking to make sure no one was in the street,

Jonathan slipped out the door and back to the palace before his father awoke.

The following morning dawned bright and sunny. In his father's presence, Jonathan thanked the Lord for the ideal rainy season. "Would you like to go down and see Ish-Bosheth's new crop of wheat and barley? I've never seen one so good."

Appealing to the farmer in Saul had been a wonderful idea, and Jonathan felt rewarded when his father accepted the invitation.

Saul seemed enthused to see the healthy green plants flourishing in the sunshine, and the two men walked for several minutes along the edge of the field. As they came to the oak tree, Jonathan said, "Remember the day I struggled to learn archery? That target was determined to avoid my arrows." He laughed. "I'll always be thankful for your patience."

Saul smiled. "The House of Kish aren't quitters."

"You've taught me that very well through the years."

Judging his father to be in a good mood, a few minutes later Jonathan brought up the subject of David. "I know you dislike David and want him killed, but perhaps you misjudge him, Father. The man hasn't done anything wrong. In fact, he has saved your kingdom more than once." He stooped and pulled a weed from among the plants. "David took his life into his hand when he fought Goliath. You were the first to rejoice in the victory the Lord gave that day. Why do you want to do wrong to an innocent man like David, killing him for no reason?"

Saul slowly exhaled. "I suppose you are right. I do sometimes get carried away. As surely as the Lord lives, I won't kill David."

Jonathan smiled inwardly, the heavy weight lifting from his spirit. He assured his father that he would live to appreciate his wise decision. As the men walked on, stopping occasionally to examine the green plants, the king yawned frequently. His father must have had a restless night. Maybe he regretted his order.

"I think I've gone far enough," the king finally said. "Go on ahead. I'll return home and see how Armoni is. He had a restless night and we got little sleep. He may be getting the fever."

Jonathan walked on toward the stone formation, pausing at intervals to inspect the wheat and barley. As he approached the rock, he gave a bird call and waited for his friend to appear. David rejoiced to hear of Saul's change of heart and the two men returned to the fortress, where Saul welcomed his son-in-law and invited him to join them for lunch.

The men had an enjoyable conversation as they ate alone at the king's table. Once Jonathan saw his father looking at the scar on David wrist. Catching David's eye, the prince surreptitiously touched his own scar. David turned his wrist over and kept it hidden the rest of the meal. After lunch Jonathan ushered his brother-in-law to the gate. David smiled, anxious to get home and tell Michal the good news of her father's improved state of mind. Jonathan called a blessing as he watched him go.

～

Near the end of the latter rains, the Philistines struck like lightning.

Figuring that David had lost his touch after two years absence from the battlefield, Saul ordered him to the Shephelah to deal with the incursion. The Israelite forces hit back so hard the Philistines scattered before them. Israel gained a great victory and David returned home to national acclaim.

"David! David!" the people of Gibeah chanted as they ran to the valley road to welcome home the troops. From behind a fortress wall projection Saul seethed as he heard the infuriating chant. Why couldn't David have died? He watched the commander lead his men up to report on their latest campaign. The king hurried down the stairs, but he refused to go greet the troops. Secluding himself in the throne room instead, he feigned illness.

Saul's jumbled thoughts flitted from the day Samuel anointed him at Ramathaim, to the morning at Mizpah when the prophet declared him to be God's choice for Israel's king, to the renewal of the kingdom at Gilgal. He recalled his apprehension as he hid among the luggage at Mizpah. He hadn't wanted to be king in the first place. But as a dutiful Israelite he had accepted God's will. First Samuel wanted to take the kingdom away from him. Now David wanted to steal it. If he, Saul, was God's choice for Israel, where was God now?

That afternoon Jonathan and David slipped into the dimly lit room. David began strumming the kinnor as Jonathan prayed for his father's depression to lift.

When Saul seemed pleased as news of David's victory first reached Gibeah, Jonathan had taken it as a positive sign. By the time the troops arrived home, his attitude had changed. It was five years since the day the king threw his spear twice at David. Now, as the men listened to the soft melodies, neither on alert, they presumed that the music soothed the troubled king.

Suddenly Saul twisted out of his chair, his spear in hand, and lunged toward David. The twenty-three-year-old, much more agile than the sixty-five-year-old king, ducked as Saul's spear struck the wall instead. Jonathan yelled as he grabbed his father, both to restrain him and to steady him on his feet. David dashed out the door to safety.

The sun descended lower over the western hills as Michal climbed the hill with her jug of spring water. She had just set it down inside the doorway when David ran in, panting for breath.

"What's wrong?" She had never seen her husband so frightened. When he described the incident with her father, Michal trembled in his arms. "David, if you don't run for your life, you'll be dead tomorrow. I know Father. This is no mere slip of memory, like he claimed the other time."

David held her close for a moment. "If I leave now someone is bound to see me go. Saul will send spies to watch for me."

Michal stepped back and surveyed the room. "Wait here," she called as she hurried out the door.

She returned in a few minutes, carrying an object covered with a blanket. When she unwrapped an ugly image of Baal, David nearly exploded.

"Where did you get that pagan idol?"

Putting her finger to his lips to silence him, she couldn't hide the mischief in her eyes. "Why not fight the ungodly with their own weapons."

Michal carried the image to the upper level and laid it on David's bed, then spread the blanket over it. Rummaging in a basket, she pulled out a handful of black goat hair that she had not gotten around to spinning. She arranged it around the head and stepped back to admire her handiwork.

"A perfect disguise. Now, pull the wooden chest over to the window." She opened the chest and pulled out a rope. "Tie it around the chest. I'll sit on it as a weight, and you can climb out and let yourself down by the rope. I'll pull it in and push the chest back later."

The activity helped take their minds off the terrible threat. When they finished preparations, David came up behind his wife, put his arms around her, and leaned down to kiss her cheek.

"I love you, Michal," he whispered in her ear. "Thank you for protecting my life."

She turned and buried her face against his shoulder. "Oh, David, I love you too. When will I see you again?"

"Only God knows." He tightened his embrace. "We must trust Him."

When darkness settled over Gibeah, David made his escape, squeezing himself through the small window in the back wall and letting himself down by the rope. After he had gone, Michal quickly moved the chest back into the corner and hid the rope. Lying down, she wept in the semi-darkness, the glow of the olive oil lamp her sole comfort. They had only been married a year and a half, and she was still not pregnant. Now David was gone. As the night dragged on, she tensed at every little noise in the street. At times she covered her mouth to keep from screaming. Finally, exhausted, she fell asleep.

The patch of sky in the window had turned blue-gray when a loud knock startled Michal awake. She ran down the short set of steps and cautiously opened the door, expecting to see soldiers. Instead, Gatam stood outside, holding a torch that illuminated his wrinkled face. Behind him in the shadows stood three men.

"Is something wrong?" She tried to keep her voice level.

"Your father has sent me with a message for your husband. The king needs to send David on an urgent mission."

"I'm sorry, he's sick." She noticed Gatam peer over her shoulder and prayed her disguise looked authentic in the shadows of the upper level.

"I'll tell the king. I hope your husband gets to feeling better."

Michal shut the door and returned to bed, fearing her hunch—more men would arrive shortly. Not surprised, a half hour later she heard a louder knock. The dreaded moment of truth had arrived. Cracking the door, she saw Malcam, one of her father's bodyguards, standing before her.

"Your father needs David's advice. He instructed us to bring him on his bed."

Michal swung the door open, and several men walked in. Malcam climbed the stairs first. Michal heard him curse as he discovered the fake body. Stomping down the steps, he grabbed her arm.

"What have you done?" he demanded, his breathing quick and

hard. "The king ordered us to bring your husband. Come with me. You have some explaining to do."

Michal meekly followed the men up the hill. Women on their way to the spring stopped to stare at the strange procession, but Michal held her head high and walked on.

Malki-Shua waited in the throne room with Saul, whose sword laid across the armrests. Michal looked at the iron weapon and shuddered. But for her warning, her husband would already be dead. Saul's face turned red with rage when the bodyguard explained what he found in David's bed.

"I needed David," the king hissed through clenched teeth. "Why did you deceive me like this and let my enemy escape?"

"David feared for his life. He demanded me to let him go or he would kill me." She blushed slightly at her lie.

Saul seemed to wilt before their eyes. He stared past her for a minute. "All right, move back to the palace. A man who deserts his wife is not worthy of her."

Michal hadn't expected that order, but what choice did she have? David probably would not be back as long as her father remained alive. Returning home later that morning, she packed her personal belongings. Servants came and cleared out the little house. After they had gone, she sat down on the lowest stair step and cried.

During the afternoon Jonathan found his little sister in the palace kitchen.

"Why are you here?" She told him David had run away.

"Be brave," he whispered. "God is in control of David's life."

Lying in bed in her old room that night, Michal prayed for the man she loved, and her father hated. She was only twenty and already a "widow." She shivered in the dim lamplight. She decided to ask Deborah to let Hannah sleep in her room from now on. She couldn't stand being alone at night.

~

The next morning Malki-Shua found Jonathan in the courtyard talking to Joel. "Do you have a few minutes? I need to ask you a question."

"Sure." Jonathan excused himself. "Is it private?"

"Yes." Malki-Shua's grim face evoked a feeling of dread in Jonathan.

"Let's go to the southwest tower. I find it a quiet place."

Jonathan had known he would eventually have to face questions about David. The differences between him and his father were growing more obvious. Jonathan never knew for sure whose side Malki-Shua took. As they climbed the steps, Jonathan sensed the coming conversation would not end well.

They paused at a gap in the fortress wall. "Why do you think Father hates David?" Malki-Shua said, not looking at his brother.

"He sees David as a rival."

"You don't?"

"Of course not." Jonathan cleared his throat. "A rival has to want what you have."

Malki-Shua turned to face Jonathan, his gaze penetrating. "Why do you want David for a close friend? You are almost old enough to be his father."

"He's Merab's age."

Malki-Shua would never understand the deep relationship Jonathan had with David; trying to explain would be useless. "You were there at Elah to witness Father celebrating Goliath's defeat," Jonathan said. "David has done nothing but win victory after victory for Father ever since."

"You don't see that as him preparing the kingdom for himself?"

"No, I see that as a loyal subject doing what God has given him to do. David trusts God with the future and doesn't try to take matters into his own hands."

"Jonathan, you are hopelessly deluded." Malki-Shua shook his head. "David may be a handsome harpist, but he is a cunning manipulator. Don't be beguiled by his appeal for friendship. He knows your soft heart. If he is so spiritual, how can he be against God's anointed? He uses all that talk about God to work you like a lump of clay, making you pliant so he can steal your kingdom."

Jonathan swallowed hard, praying for wisdom as he tried to compose a calm reply. He hadn't realized how thoroughly his father had poisoned his brother's thinking. "Hatred is a fire that consumes anyone who embraces it."

"The least you could do is appreciate Father's efforts to preserve the kingdom for you," Malki-Shua said, his voice sharp and accusing.

"It is the Kingdom of Israel, not the Kingdom of Saul or Jonathan."

Malki-Shua gave a snort of disgust. "Perfect example of what I mean."

"I pray someday you will see otherwise."

"That would take a century. I don't think I will live that long." Malki-Shua spat through the gap. "Don't say I didn't warn you." He turned and stalked off.

Jonathan drew his index finger back and forth across his eyebrow. From now on, discussing David when he was not present at the King's table must be avoided. He turned to watch Malki-Shua disappear down the stairs.

Jonathan headed for the tower corner. He sat down in his favorite place of prayer and lifted his eyes to heaven. "Lord God, You parted the Red Sea for Moses in one night. You can surely open the heart and mind of Malki-Shua in less time than a century."

2 9

ESCAPE

David lowered himself down the rope until his feet touched the ground. For a moment he held the rough cord, reluctant to let go of the last tie with his beloved Michal. Then he recalled the urgency of the night and released it.

Creeping up the dark narrow alley, feeling his way along walls, David paused occasionally to listen for footsteps. A lizard ran across the bricks, brushing his fingers and causing him to jump. He avoided the closed houses and shuttered shops of the main street, hoping to elude the night watchman. Pausing to inhale deeply and listening again, he slipped between two houses on the back side of town, out of sight of the fortress gate.

David made his way down the hillside to the road north. The moon came up and he thanked God for the light. After crossing the open valley that surrounded the hilltop town of Gibeon, he entered the far hills. With the imminent threat of danger behind him, he slowed his pace.

David's thoughts swirled in confusion. Saul was the strangest man he had ever met. While playing his kinnor to ease the king's bouts of depression, he had often studied Saul's expressionless face. He had felt sympathy for Israel's first monarch. The responsibility that weighed heavily on the man's broad shoulders seemed to weigh even more heavily on his mind. As David played, he had prayed for Saul.

The challenge of the pagan Goliath in the Valley of Elah had given David an opportunity not only to serve God, but also his king. After the victory, the ecstatic Saul had offered him more rewards and responsibilities than he could have dreamed of. He had done his best to be a good commander.

Saul had seemed disappointed when he had turned down the chance to marry Merab. However, it didn't take a seer's ability to recognize the thinly disguised hand of the king behind Gatam and Pagiel's attempt to promote a marriage to Michal. Accepting that offer had been easy. David loved Michal.

Saul had sent him off on many dangerous assignments. He relished the challenge and believed the king trusted him. Now he realized he had been wrong. What had changed? Or had Saul always viewed him as a threat? Why was the king suddenly bent on destroying him?

Growing weariness forced David to slow down. When he saw the dark opening of a cave in a hillside ahead, he cautiously approached it. He listened for sounds within, then called a greeting. Still nothing. Deciding it was unoccupied, he slipped inside, pulled his cloak around him, and fell asleep.

The bawling of a hungry calf in a nearby village awakened him at dawn. Leaving the cave, he started on. Without a water bag, his mouth felt as dry as wheat chaff. He scanned the hillsides he passed for a patch of green that might indicate a spring. His search led to a small stream of water that trickled from the foot of a bleak hill, and he quickly slaked his thirst.

David had never been to Ramathaim before, but the only place of escape he could think of was Samuel's home. Asking directions from shepherd boys, he arrived at the twin peaks in the afternoon. At first the elderly prophet did not recognize David, whom he had not seen since anointing him in Bethlehem nine years earlier. He listened to the sad story of Saul's depression and jealous hatred, showing no surprise.

"I don't want to put you in danger," David ended apologetically, "but I couldn't think where else to go."

"You are welcome here." The old man took David's right hand between his. "We will ask God's guidance."

David's fear drained away as he listened to the righteous man speak with his God. No wonder Jonathan admired Samuel so much.

"We will go up to Naioth," the prophet said when he concluded the prayer. "Saul visited the school of the prophets the afternoon before I anointed him king. He will respect the place."

On their way through town, David came face to face with the army captain Kileab, home for his father's funeral. Afraid that avoiding the officer might arouse suspicion, the king's son-in-law greeted him cordially and began talking. Samuel, sensing danger, cut the conversation short, but David feared the damage had been done.

Neither man was surprised two weeks later when they spied soldiers marching along the path from the town entrance to the school. Samuel and the prophets had just participated in the evening worship and sacrifice. As the unit of Saul's bodyguard approached, the prophets broke into Spirit-anointed praise to God. David hurried into the school building, leaving the door ajar to watch as he prayed for his safety. Gad, one of the student prophets who had befriended David, joined him. When Saul's soldiers reached the altar, they were struck with the joy of the service and joined in proclaiming the goodness of God. Taking it as a sign from the Lord, David sneaked down the opposite hillside to the valley below. He spent the night behind the nearest hill and returned after the soldiers had departed.

By the time the soldiers remembered their mission, David had disappeared. They returned to Gibeah empty handed. Saul, outraged at the soldiers' explanation of their unfruitful mission, sent a second unit. They also were caught up in the spirit of the worship service and returned without David. After it happened a third time, Saul determined to go himself. He had not told Jonathan he had sent out search parties, but he now informed his son he wanted to visit the aging prophet to seek his counsel and blessing. Ignorant of the true purpose of the journey, Jonathan encouraged him to make the trip.

As the king approached Naioth, the Spirit of the Lord came on him and he also began proclaiming the greatness of God. When he arrived at the school, he threw off his royal robes and danced about the altar in a state of joy and excitement until he collapsed from exhaustion. Slumping to the ground, he drifted off to sleep, not awakening until the next morning.

Seeing Saul and his retinue coming up the hill, David fled down the other side, this time not stopping in the valley. He decided to take a long route back to Gibeah, where he hoped to find Jonathan. The second night he crept into town and knocked on Joel's door. The captain exclaimed in surprise upon seeing the fugitive, but quickly took David to his upper room to hide.

The sound of a door opening the next morning woke David. He looked around, trying to figure out his whereabouts. Then he remembered the harrowing escape. Joel must be going to the fortress to inform Jonathan. The sun had risen long before, he realized, and he thanked the Lord he had been able to sleep through the night. He dressed, then sat down to wait. If only he could see Michal.

Lost in thought, David jumped when he heard a knock on the door. He opened it a crack. The crown prince squeezed through and shut it behind him. The two men embraced in greeting, neither knowing what to say. David spoke first. "Jonathan, what have I done? What crime have I committed?"

The prince looked confused. David paced up and down the small room like a caged animal. "Tell me how I've wronged your father to make him want to kill me."

"No!" Jonathan objected. "You aren't going to be killed. You know Father's temper occasionally flares up, then he's all right for a while. He got back late yesterday afternoon from visiting Samuel. I mentioned your name at supper, and he never said a word against you." David stopped pacing. Jonathan stepped over and placed his hand on his shoulder. "Father doesn't do anything unless he first consults me. Why would he hide such a plan from me? I'm sure he doesn't intend to kill you."

David wondered how well Jonathan really knew his father, but he didn't say so, not wanting to hurt his feelings. "Your father knows you have befriended me. Why would he inform you of a plan that would bring you grief? As surely as the Lord lives, I'm one step away from death."

Jonathan seemed to detect the despair in David's voice. "What do you want me to do about it?"

David turned to his blood brother. "Tomorrow is the New Moon festival. If the king knows I'm in town, he will expect me to come to the feast. I'll go into hiding until the following evening. If Saul misses me, tell him I asked permission to go to Bethlehem to an annual sacrifice for my whole clan. If he doesn't object, I'll know I'm safe. If he loses his temper, you'll know he's determined to kill me." He took a deep breath. "As far as you are concerned, please show kindness to me, your servant. Remember, you cut a covenant with me in the sight of the Lord. If I'm guilty of some crime, kill me yourself. Don't hand me over to your father."

Jonathan saw the haunted look in David's eyes, a look he had never seen before. "Absolutely not!" he protested. "I would never harm you, and if I had the slightest hint Father would, I would immediately tell you."

Saying nothing for a moment, David finally asked, "If Saul objects violently to my absence, how will I find out?"

Jonathan contemplated the question. "Come."

He walked out the door, and David followed. The movement seemed to ease the tension. By the time the two arrived in the valley, the prince had formulated his plan. Pausing a moment, he seemed to see into the future and the end of his father's kingdom. Grasping David's arm, his hand trembled.

"May the Lord be with you as he's been with Father. But show me the same unfailing kindness that the Lord does as long as I live, so I won't be killed. Please never cut off your kindness from my family not even when the Lord has cut off every one of David's enemies from the earth."

He sounded like David now, pleading for mercy. Would their positions someday be reversed?

The two men solemnly renewed the terms of their covenant, then embraced as they wept for the uncertain future.

"When Father misses you at the New Moon celebration, I'll give him your excuse and evaluate his response. Go hide at Ezel, like you did before. I'll send Joel with food and water for you." Jonathan glanced up at the fortress.

"I'll come out to the field at least by the day after tomorrow for target practice," Jonathan continued. "I'll shoot three arrows to the side of the stone. Then I'll send my armor-bearer after them. If I tell him the arrows are on this side of him, you will know everything is well. If I tell him the arrows are beyond him, you'll know you must escape. Just remember, the Lord was our witness when we cut the covenant."

Jonathan felt his feet were weighted with stones as he made his way up the hill. Conflicting loyalties tore at his spirit. He stopped by Joel's to request delivery of provisions for David. When Jonathan got home, he told his father he had seen David.

"Will he be up today?"

"He didn't say, but with the New Moon celebration tomorrow, he should be here for the feast."

The following morning the people assembled for the special sacrifice, which Ahimelech came to offer. David did not attend. When the men assembled in the evening for the feast, Jonathan waited for his father's reaction, but the king said nothing about his absent son-in-law. The prince relaxed and enjoyed the meal.

When David did not appear for supper the second day, Saul inquired why. "If he was ceremonially unclean yesterday, surely the specified period for cleansing is over by now."

Jonathan relayed David's message about going to Bethlehem, then paused for the response. Saul glared across the table at his firstborn.

"You son of an obstinate and rebellious woman!" he snarled.

Jonathan sat shocked at the vulgar expletive. His face reddened with embarrassment and anger. That sounded like something that would come out of Doeg's mouth. The men assembled at the table stared at the king in disbelief. Malki-Shua looked down, his face expressionless.

"Don't think I don't know you've taken the side of Jesse's son to your own humiliation and to the humiliation of the mother who bore you," Saul continued, his voice rising. "As long as that David lives on this earth, neither you nor your kingdom will ever be established. Go bring him to me. He must die!"

For the first time, Jonathan comprehended how deeply his

father hated the popular commander. The ugly boil of jealousy and hatred that had been festering for five years had finally burst.

The prince forced himself to stay calm. "Why should David be killed? What has he done wrong?"

Seated at the end of the table next to the wall, the king yanked his spear from its stand and pointed it at his son. Jonathan momentarily froze as he saw an evil gleam of insanity flash from the king's eyes. His heart pounded wildly as he tried to break free from the paralysis. The instant seemed an eternity and, horrified, he saw the point of the spear move closer. Suddenly a power not his own pushed him, and he ducked as the weapon came hurtling across the table. Someone let out a scream.

Jumping up, Jonathan stormed out of the room, totally humiliated by the man who gave him life. If Father would kill him, his firstborn, in a fit of blind rage, he would kill anyone to preserve his kingdom. Jonathan ran out the door, his cheeks still burning. Taking the stairs two at a time, he rushed to the fortress rooftop to avoid meeting anyone who might question his early departure from the meal. Gasping deep gulps of cool evening air, he collapsed against the wall, his legs as weak as wet flax.

An hour later Jonathan eased himself over to a gap, where he stood looking at the black landscape. Somewhere in the darkness David hid, waiting to be told the terrible truth he no doubt already knew. Tomorrow they would meet at Ezel. Jonathan would send away the only man who understood his heart, probably to see him no more. Why did it have to end this way? He leaned against a projection, too deeply hurt for tears.

Having gone without supper, Jonathan's stomach rumbled with hunger as he slipped out of his room early the next morning. Churning thoughts had kept him awake half the night. He felt exhausted. But the urgency of his task propelled him on.

Making his way downstairs, he recalled as a boy once creeping into the kitchen and taking a bite from a cake of pressed dates. Jahra had later scolded him, and for years Jonathan wondered how the servant knew it was he. Oh, for the carefree days of childhood. In the kitchen he picked up a round of bread and scooped up a handful of raisins before starting for the fortress armory to collect a bow and quiver of arrows.

Jonathan greeted the gatekeeper, who let him out. Heading to the edge of town, he knocked on Joel's door and asked for help. The captain, glad to assist his friend, called his nephew Aaron to accompany the prince.

The two made their way to the field as the sun rose over the horizon. Jonathan shot at various objects as they worked their way across the dry brown stubble, Aaron retrieving the arrows after each round.

"I need to do this more often," the prince said after he deliberately missed several targets. "I'm really out of practice." As they neared the rock formation, Jonathan shot an arrow beyond the youth. When Aaron reached the place the arrow landed, the prince called to him, "Isn't it farther than that? Be quick. Don't waste time."

Aaron stooped, picked the arrow up, and ran back to Jonathan.

The prince yawned. "I think I'll quit for today. I'm really a poor shot anymore." The teenager did not reply. "Take these back home." Jonathan handed him the bow and quiver. "Your uncle can bring them to me later. I think I'll enjoy a little fresh air before returning."

When Aaron reached far enough down the field, Jonathan walked around the stone formation and gave his usual bird call. David came out of the cleft in the rock. From the prearranged signal, David already knew the terrible verdict. He bowed down before Jonathan three times, the sign of honor to royalty. The two embraced, their tears of sorrow mingling as they kissed each other's cheek in customary greeting,

"Go in peace," Jonathan said, "We've sworn friendship with

each other in the name of the Lord, promising, 'The Lord is witness between us, and between your descendants and my descendants forever.' "

Jonathan retrieved the empty provisions sack and the waterbag from the hiding place and held them out to David. After untying his girdle-belt, Jonathan pulled out his money bag and pressed it into the hand of his covenant brother. David gave him one last embrace and, wordlessly, turned to go.

Watching him, Jonathan struggled with a rising feeling of hatred for his father, a man who refused to obey God completely and sought to destroy anyone who, in his warped mind, he viewed as a threat to his kingdom.

"Help me, O Lord, to not become like Father," the prince desperately prayed. "Keep David safe from the evils that threaten him. Whatever happens to the kingdom, help me wait for You to act."

Jonathan lowered himself to an outcropping of cool stone and waited in the morning stillness as the Lord washed the hatred and disappointment from his heart. Renewed in spirit, he started back to the fortress. Words he had memorized long ago came to him. His heart welled up with thanks as he quoted:

"He makes me lie down in lush pastures,
He leads me beside peaceful waters,
He restores my inner being."

David listened to Jonathan restate their covenant pledge, but overcome with emotion, said nothing. He was surprised when Jonathan pressed the money bag into his hand. Partaking of the covenant meal, the prince had said, "This bread represents life and strength, which we now share." David felt the pieces of silver through the cloth. This was proof of that sharing. He tucked the bag into the fold of his girdle-belt. Tearing himself away, he turned and began his long journey away from Gibeah, wondering if he would live to see it, or Jonathan, again.

David covered the three miles to Nob in less than an hour. He found Ahimelech preparing for the morning sacrifice as he entered the Tabernacle enclosure. The priest looked up and, seeing the army commander, hurried over. He probably expected another request to bless the troops as they set out for battle.

When the priest saw no one with the commander, he looked about, puzzled. "Where is your battalion?"

David rubbed his right cheek, then pulled at his ear. Regretting his nervous movements, he lowered his arm.

"Is something wrong?"

"The king is sending me on a secret mission," the commander replied in a low voice. "I can't divulge the instructions. I ordered the men to meet me at a certain location." His eyes scanned the Tabernacle. "What do you have on hand to eat? I had to rush off before Pilha pulled his first loaves of bread from the oven. If you have any, give me five loaves, or whatever you can spare."

"I don't have any ordinary bread here, just consecrated bread. I guess I could give it to you if the men have kept themselves from women."

"They have, as usual when we are on maneuvers. The men's bodies are holy even when we are on missions not considered holy."

Going into the Holy Place, the priest returned with consecrated bread that had been replaced with fresh bread. He handed it to David.

"Thank you so much." David wheeled to go, then turned back. "I hate to be a beggar, but I left in such a hurry I forgot to go up to the armory to pick up my sword. Do you have a weapon I could borrow?"

"The only thing here is the sword of Goliath that you brought to me after the battle in the Valley of Elah. We keep it wrapped in a linen cloth behind the ephod. Take it if you want, I have nothing else to offer you."

"There is nothing like that sword," David answered with a trace of awe. "I'll take it." Behind him, he heard movement and the bleating of a lamb. Others were coming for worship. He must hurry. As the priest started back into the Tabernacle, he added, "Also, pray for our success."

The priest returned a few minutes later with the sheathed weapon and belt. "God's presence will be with you on your journey," he assured the commander, smiling as he handed him the sword.

David thanked Ahimelech, feeling slightly uncomfortable because he had lied to the man of God. The lamb bleated again. A priest smiled as he walked past David to the other worshiper.

"I've brought a sacrifice from the king," a voice said.

Turning, David nearly dropped the bread and sword. Doeg, Saul's chief shepherd, stood a few feet behind him, the lamb in his arms. David hurried past the Edomite without offering a greeting. Next to Saul, Doeg was the last person in the world he wanted to encounter.

3 0

SAUL'S REVENGE

Unsure where to go to escape Saul's wrath, David wandered in the familiar hills around his beloved Bethlehem, afraid to go home. Then he felt drawn to the Valley of Elah.

The next morning, he climbed the hill to Israel's old bivouac site. Ashes of the campfires were long gone, but several stones that had supported cooking pots remained in place. He sat down on one, facing the plain. His gaze traveled along the ravine, singling out his special terebinth tree. His pulse quickened. God was still in control of his life. Encouraged, he pulled the sword from its sheath and ran his hand down the shaft. He still must find a refuge from Saul. A hawk flew over, heading west. He watched it disappear beyond Azekah.

Gath. Saul would never attack a walled Philistine city.

The idea seemed unthinkable. David studied the weapon, his mind in a quandary. How long would it take Saul to figure out he had escaped and come after him? Where else could he go? No other plan came to mind, so he started down to the plain.

By early afternoon David saw in the distance the gap in the hills. The city looked like a speck above the entrance to the coastal plain. If they saw Goliath's sword, would they allow him in? Removing his cloak, he wrapped the weapon to disguise it.

"I've escaped from Saul, King of Israel," David told the watchman at the gate. "I beg asylum with the lord of Gath."

"An enemy of Saul is a friend of Achish." The watchmen stepped aside and let him pass.

David slept in the open marketplace, afraid to chance the crowded open rooms of the inn. A week later, as he stopped at the baker's, he heard a voice behind him.

"Isn't that the man who killed Goliath? Look at the sword he's carrying."

David ignored the man as he selected six rounds of bread and paid the baker. Hurrying down a side street a minute later, he looked up at the sky. "I'm in trouble, Lord. What shall I do?"

Keeping to the streets farthest from the market, when the sun set David found a place to sleep behind a small house. He pulled his cloak around him and, placing his sword between him and the wall, fell asleep. At midnight the full moon illuminated the spot, awakening David. Crawling into the shadow of another house, an idea came to him.

"Thank you, Lord, for answering my prayer."

The next morning, after eating part of the second round of bread, David headed for the marketplace, chuckling at his appearance. Michal would be horrified. He looked down at his wrinkled tunic and crumpled a remaining smooth spot with his hand. His cloak hung off one shoulder. He hadn't put on his headdress, mussing his hair instead.

Merchants were opening their shops when David entered the square. They stopped to stare. Drawing his sword, David began combat with an invisible challenger, grunting with each thrust. After several minutes, he declared himself the winner and lowered the sword.

Housewives with market baskets paused while purchasing vegetables to point and whisper.

"He's insane. Drooling all over his beard."

"Possessed by a spirit."

A group of boys soon followed David, snickering as he carved on the town gates with the point of his sword. Sudden silence caused David to pause.

"Achish," one of them said. The thud of running feet followed the scattering crowd.

David turned to see the lord of Gath, accompanied by a retinue of men. Achish paused to study the unkempt man.

"You're right, it is Goliath's slayer. Look at the mighty hero." He laughed with contempt. "They sing that David has slain his tens of thousands. Ha! He contained Israel's enemy, but can't even contain his own spit." Achish turned to his assistant. "Don't we have enough madmen in the city without importing Hebrew lunatics?"

David smiled the weirdest smile he could conjure up. With a shrill laugh, he sauntered out the gates, muttering as he went.

Once again, he had escaped danger.

Making his way up the Valley of Elah, David paused across the ravine from the memorable terebinth tree. God had given him one miracle on this plain. Now he needed another. He prayed for God's guidance, then turned south and followed the *wadi* Sur below Socoh. Three miles beyond lay the town of Adullam, surrounded by hills honeycombed with caves.

Choosing a concealed cave as his home, David deposited his sword inside and went to look for a band of shepherds. After listening for some time, he heard a flute in the distance. In the adjoining hills, he found three youths caring for a large flock. They exchanged greetings and visited for a few minutes.

David offered one teenager a small piece of silver if he would deliver a message, promising another if he brought proof that he had fulfilled the errand. When the teenager agreed, David sent him to Bethlehem to call his family. "And tell them to bring Grandfather's kinnor with them."

The third afternoon, David stood on the hillside at sunset. A small caravan came through the valley, and he ran to greet his kin. David paid the messenger boy and thanked him for his help. When they reached the cave's mouth, David explained his presence there. His story of Saul's jealous rage left his parents and the families of his six brothers and two sisters shaken.

"Soldiers were in Bethlehem yesterday, inquiring about you," Jesse said. "How little did we know their true mission. Then the messenger boy appeared. We have escaped the king's vengeance in the nick of time."

Over the next few weeks more men arrived from Judah to join his band. Soon it grew to four hundred. David knew God had answered his prayer beside the stream at Elah when one day the prophet Gad arrived from Ramathaim, saying Samuel had sent him to be David's spiritual advisor.

～

Saul awoke from the nightmare in a cold sweat, his tunic saturated. In his dream Jonathan lay dead on a battlefield and David led an army against the king. Saul sat up. Today he would get his hands on that scoundrel, or else. After changing his tunic, Saul hurried down the stairs to instruct a bodyguard to go call Zimran.

The captain looked half-asleep as he stood before the throne. "Go to Bethlehem and bring David immediately."

"At your orders, O King."

The captain and his company started south as the sun came up. The men were back in Gibeah by late afternoon—without David. People in Bethlehem, including Jesse, had not seen him for some time. The king grew furious when he realized David had once again escaped.

In spite of Jonathan's attempt at reconciliation, Saul refused to talk to him. As the week passed, the king accepted the fact David had escaped. Gradually his mood improved.

A few days later he rejoined his men for supper in the palace dining room. When the subject of weaponry came up, everyone had a comment or story to tell.

Jonathan, sitting diagonally across the table from his father, began describing an old bow he had recently seen. Concentrating on the account, Saul leaned forward as Jonathan spread his arms wide apart to demonstrate the great distance one could pull the string from the grip of the bow.

With the lamplight shining across Saul's shoulder, he looked up in time to see the narrow scar across his son's left wrist. Pausing with his next bite halfway to his mouth, the king looked up at the ceiling for a moment, trying to draw from his memory some elusive fact.

"Is something wrong?" Malki-Shua asked. He looked up at the spot at which his father seemed to be staring.

"Huh? Oh, no." Saul shook his head. "Nothing's wrong. I was just thinking."

The conversation resumed, but Saul did not join in. He suddenly remembered. David! He had seen an identical scar on David's left wrist one day at lunch. He couldn't believe it. A covenant? Surely not Jonathan and David. He started to reach for his spear, but he recalled the last time he let his temper get the best of him. If he fulfilled the first part of his nightmare, the second part was sure to happen too. He glowered at Jonathan, then got up and left.

The next morning Jonathan prepared to take his soldiers for drill when Malki-Shua came to inform him of a council meeting. Putting his bow back, he headed for the tamarisk tree in front of the fortress. In hot weather Saul preferred to hold court in the shade.

Jonathan stood waiting with the bodyguards, army captains, and commanders, curious about the impromptu meeting. Usually, his father consulted him beforehand. An armor-bearer planted the butt of the king's spear into the ground, and Saul called the council to order.

Out of the corner of his eye, Jonathan noticed Doeg coming up the hill. He probably had a question concerning the royal flock. He would have to wait until the meeting adjourned. Doeg took his place behind the group. Jonathan turned his attention to his father.

Saul did not say anything at first. The men grew quiet as the king's eyes roved back and forth, surveying the three dozen men. What was wrong? Jonathan saw his father's jaw jutted out and his narrowed eyes. Saul was not in a good mood.

The king's searching gaze came to rest on Joel. He called the captain forward. "Joel, are you aware my son Jonathan made a covenant with David the son of Jesse?"

Standing behind Abner, Jonathan gasped. So that was what Father realized last night at supper. Jonathan should have known his father would eventually learn the truth.

"Yes, O king," he heard Joel reply.

The king again scanned the audience. "Lamech," he called, singling out a second captain. Lamech already knew the question and was forced to give the same reply. As Saul rose from his chair, his expression turned from one of confrontation to fury.

"Listen, you Benjamites!" he shouted, shaking his finger at the group.

It was uncanny that Father would question only Joel and Lamech, the two who witnessed Jonathan and David's covenant ceremony. Perhaps because they were not Benjamites. Jonathan also remembered Joel had served as his first armor-bearer.

Saul stepped closer to the group and launched into a tirade. "Will the son of Jesse give all of you fields of your own and vineyards to harvest? Will he appoint all of you commanders of thousands or of hundreds? Is that the reason you have all formed a conspiracy against me?" Traces of foam formed at the corners of Saul's mouth. "No one tells me when my own son cuts a covenant with the son of Jesse. None of you is concerned enough about me to report that my son has inflamed my servant to plan to ambush me, like he is doing today."

No one spoke. The king slumped back into the throne. Jonathan used all the restraint he could muster to keep from denouncing Saul's false accusation. His paranoid father no longer trusted him. Would the spear meant for David yet kill him?

"Pardon me, my lord," Jonathan heard someone call from the back of the group. The nervous men stepped aside to clear a path for the speaker, and Jonathan saw Doeg come forward. What was he up to?

Reaching the throne, the chief shepherd bowed before the monarch. "Oh king, I think you are accusing the wrong men of conspiracy. When I went to Nob the other day, I saw the son of Jesse come to Ahimelech the priest. Ahimelech inquired of the Lord for him. He also gave him bread and the sword of Goliath the Philistine."

A sadistic flash came from Saul's eyes. He smiled faintly before turning to order a messenger to Nob to immediately bring Ahimelech and his whole father's family.

"You may relax until you hear the trumpet calling you to reconvene," he told the officers, then headed into the fortress.

Jonathan hurried to catch him. "Father, please don't punish the priests," he begged, trying to hide his horror at the idea. "If you must punish anyone, punish me."

"Humph," Saul snorted. "And fulfill the prophecy of Samuel?

Never! David would like nothing better than to know you are dead and the kingdom is his."

Jonathan's mouth dropped open. "Surely you aren't going to kill the Lord's anointed."

"I am the Lord's anointed," Saul shouted. "I will do what I have to do to preserve my kingdom. Do you understand?"

Jonathan said no more, afraid if he continued his father might also seek revenge on Joel and Lamech. Tears blurred the prince's vision as he climbed the staircase to the fortress roof and watched for the priests to appear across the valley. He could only hope that over the next hour or two his father's anger would cool. As he stood sentinel near a gap, he prayed desperately for the situation. Eventually, he saw them coming. When the trumpet sounded, he hurried down to the tamarisk tree.

Ahimelech and the other priests were standing in a group to the right of the throne, near the altar. Jonathan slipped behind Malki-Shua to hide, unable to look the unsuspecting priest in the eye. When the officers had gathered, Saul called Ahimelech forward.

"Listen, son of Ahitub."

"Yes, O king."

Saul's penetrating stare bore through the priest as he began his accusation. "Why have you conspired against me, along with the son of Jesse? You furnished him bread and a sword and inquired of God for him. Now he has rebelled against me and lies in ambush for me."

At first Ahimelech frowned in confusion, but by the time Saul finished his question, his face had turned as white as sheep's wool. He swallowed nervously. "Who of all your servants is more loyal than David? He is the king's son-in-law, captain of your body-guards, and highly respected in your palace," Ahimelech said. "Was that the first time I inquired of God for him? Of course, it wasn't!

Please, O King, don't accuse your servant or any of his father's family of disloyalty," he begged, "for your servant doesn't know one thing about this whole matter."

Jonathan knew his father would not be swayed by the explanation. He had decided the verdict before the priests arrived.

"You will all die today, Ahimelech," the king announced, his voice hard and cold. "Bodyguards." Six men stepped closer to the throne. "Kill these priests of the Lord for siding with David. They knew he was escaping from me, yet they did not report it." Saul watched the priests' alarmed reaction.

The silence grew palpable. None of the guards moved. Saul whirled around to discover the cause of the delay. All the guards were looking at the ground.

"I said, kill them," he shouted. Still, no one drew his weapon. "All right, don't, you cowards." He spat out the words, then signaled to the Edomite. "Doeg, you alone are my loyal servant. Strike the priests down."

Doeg had been disappointed when he arrived too late to consult the king before his meeting. All he could do was wait—a waste of his valuable time. When the subject of Saul's wrath became apparent, however, Doeg's impatience turned to delight. He had never cared for Jonathan. Even less for David. The morning he saw David at Nob, he had sensed the commander's distaste for him. Implicating the priests provided an opportunity not only to get back at Jonathan and David, but also the god of Israel. Now he had the privilege of destroying the priests and showing loyalty to the king at the same time. Since the cowardly bodyguards had refused to obey, this should be worth a big reward.

Doeg hurried forward and pulled out one of the bodyguard's sword. He smiled at Ahimelech as he began. The chief priest's body dropped before the king. The others stood, mute and motionless. Doeg continued through the group, stabbing, slashing, decapitating, or dismembering until he had finished the eighty-five priests. Baal had won a great victory today. He handed the dripping sword back to the bodyguard. Doeg now knew his god was more powerful than the unseen god of these proud Israelites. Even their king was fighting for Baal.

Watching the gruesome fulfillment of his order, Saul recalled Samuel slaying Agag at Gilgal. The prophet said he didn't carry out the ban against the Amalekites, the enemies of Israel. Samuel said God had torn the kingdom from him. An idea struck Saul, and his lip curling in scorn. Well, he would show Samuel he knew how to carry out a ban—a ban against his real enemies.

When Doeg had finished the grisly assignment, the king said, "Now, go destroy Nob. Every man, woman, child, infant, and all the livestock."

Without hesitation, Doeg commanded the bodyguards to bring their weapons and headed for the edge of town. There he enlisted the help of off-duty shepherds, many of whom were also captives of war. Commandeering the bodyguards' swords, they started for Nob.

Jonathan and the other officers watched in horror as Doeg, one by one, killed the priests. Sacrificial lambs. Dying for the sin and self-ishness of Father. Jonathan buried his face in his hands and wept. As inconspicuously as possible, Joel and Lamech tried to comfort him. He felt faint as Lamech tried to steady him.

A sense of revulsion gripped Jonathan's stomach; he pushed his way to the edge of the group and vomited. He had witnessed chilling scenes of battle many times as Israel's enemies paid the price for their deadly invasions, but he had never before witnessed fratricide. These were fellow Israelites, the priests of God! Looking up, he saw the inert bodies lying in heaps where they fell.

Sunlight played through the branches of the tamarisk tree, painting the pools of blood a grotesque mosaic. He closed his eyes to avoid the repulsive scene.

"Bury these men who brought about their own deaths," he heard Saul order his officers. "Leave no one here by sunset."

The Law. How ironic! Father insisted on keeping the Law of God regarding burial even after slaughtering the men of God.

The sun passed behind a cloud, casting a shadow over the hill-top. The prince shuddered as he felt the forces of evil around him. In the Garden of Eden, the viper had been cunning and gracious. Today the viper showed his true self—vicious and deadly. All the bulls in Israel could not atone for Father's sin. Anyway, no priest remained to sacrifice them—for Father or for anyone.

"Oh, God," Jonathan's heart cried out, "it was better that I died than they. Now I know why Father has experienced so many bouts of depression since our war with the Amalekites. He did not obey Your command. Your Spirit has departed from Father. His kingdom is finished." He groaned. "How can I endure until the day of his death?"

"Wait on the Lord," a Voice whispered to his heart. "God will strengthen you each day if you trust Him and obey."

Jonathan did not assist in the burial. Instead, he walked toward the fortress. Malki-Shua saw him coming and averted his gaze. Jonathan hoped his brother did not see the massacre as justified.

The captains hurried down to the barracks to recruit soldiers for the burial. Joel stopped by his house and announced the news to his nephew Aaron. He sent Aaron on a swift errand to warn the people of Nob of what happened. Next Joel went to Pharez' house to report the tragedy.

Joel did not return to the fortress. Since giving his truthful answer to the king, he was sure his life in the army had ended—

maybe his actual life. After locking the door to his house, he gathered his family in his embrace, and they cried together.

Whispers of the atrocity spread over the town like a smothering blanket. Sounds of life abruptly ceased. Shop keepers closed their doors and wordlessly scurried down the street to their families. Farmers unhitched their animals at the pen and took the closest street home. Children abandoned play to run to the safety of their mothers' arms. Suppressing normal death wails for fear of the king's wrath, people gathered behind closed doors and quietly wept.

Leaving his shop, Gera caught up with Pilha as he hobbled through the marketplace, leaning on his walking stick. Gera slowed his steps to match the old baker's pace. As they approached the barracks street, Pilha turned to him. "When the delegation went to Ramathaim to ask for a king many years ago," he said in a subdued voice, "Samuel warned them about all a king would do to us." He paused and shook his head. "Even he could never have imagined this."

Soldiers carried the priests' bodies down the hill from the fortress to the cave-tombs of the various town families, where they stacked them inside and rolled the stones back over the openings to prevent wild animals and dogs from entering.

When Pharez saw Doeg's men returning from Nob, he enlisted townsmen to collect tools and go bury the priests' families. He hoped there were cave-tombs, and they wouldn't have to dig graves.

Watching from his housetop that afternoon, Joel breathed a sigh of relief as he observed Pharez' procession head down the road. No Israelite body should be left overnight for scavengers to desecrate.

～

Leaving the gruesome scene of death, half-blinded by tears Jonathan stumbled up to the fortress rooftop. He slumped in a corner of his favorite tower, dazed. His father completely baffled him. After all their marches together to battlefields, all the blessings and sacrifices Ahimeleck offered for Israel's army and the king, how could his father so callously slaughter the priests like a herd of cattle?

"God, keep David from Father's wicked wrath," Jonathan prayed. "David is now the Lord's anointed. Help Saul's family as we bear the punishment for the sins of our father. And, God, spare Israel from the pagan nations who right now seem more righteous than Your own people." He sniffed loudly and swiped at his tears.

Gibeah grew eerily silent; quieter than any Sabbath Jonathan could remember. Hours passed; he did not move.

Voices from the courtyard below caught Jonathan's attention. He heard the beam on the fortress gate drop in place, barring the entrance for the night. He looked around, as if wakening from a horrible nightmare. Then he remembered the afternoon tragedy.

Jonathan lifted his eyes to heaven. "God of Israel, help us. Shiloh is no more. The Philistines destroyed it. They killed Hophni and Phinehas and caused Eli's death. Tonight, Lord, Nob is no more. Father has wiped it from the face of the earth." One glimmer of hope came to his mind. The Ark of the Covenant remained in Kiriath-jearim. The word covenant reminded him again of David. "Whatever happens, keep me faithful to my covenant vow," he continued. "You promised Joshua You would be with him as You were with Moses. Please be with me as You are with David."

The moon rose, full and brilliant. The evening breeze sent a chill through Jonathan. He got up, his legs stiff from the long vigil, and limped over to the nearest parapet gap. In the moonlight he saw a column of men coming up the road, tools over their shoulders. From Nob, no doubt. He choked back a sob.

Jonathan went down to his room, praying he would not have to face anyone. The girls were already asleep, but Deborah sat waiting for him, her eyes red from weeping.

She stood up and, without a word, wrapped her arms around her grieving husband. Jonathan's tears dampened the shoulder of her tunic as he tried to muffle his sobs. He took off his cloak. Deborah eased him to their mat, laid down beside him, and pulled up the blanket. He held her tightly in his arms as her caring presence comforted his shattered heart. God felt a world away. For the first time in their marriage, he couldn't bring himself to offer an evening prayer.

Jonathan felt relieved when he heard Deborah begin in a broken voice, "Lord God of Israel, only You know why. We can't understand. Forgive Father for this awful deed, and do not hold us guilty . . . . You know our hearts. Fill my Beloved with Your strength and peace. May our daughters grow up to be like him."

Emotionally exhausted, in a few minutes Jonathan drifted off to sleep.

THE MANHUNT

Abiathar stopped to catch his breath. The king was calling all the priests. What honor did Saul plan to give them? He wiped the back of his forearm across his sweaty forehead. He wished his father and the others had waited for him. Abiathar hated leaving the flock with Zerahiah. His cousin was too young to be left alone with the sheep. What if a wild animal came along? He couldn't miss the important meeting, however. The messenger said all priests must come.

Taking another deep breath, he jogged on. The other priests were nowhere in sight. He was really going to be late. Coming around the side of a hill, he saw a figure running up the road toward him. He supposed his father was sending someone to check on him. It wasn't his fault the flock was so far away.

As the runner came closer, Abiathar saw it was a young man. The breathless youth came to a stop in front of him and asked, "Are you a priest?"

"Yes, the youngest son of Ahimelech."

"I am Aaron, nephew of Joel, a captain of Saul's army." The runner's chest heaved up and down. "King Saul just had Doeg kill all your family. Now he's coming to destroy Nob. Run for your life."

At first Abiathar thought the heat had gotten to Aaron. Or maybe he liked playing tricks on people. Not about to miss the king's meeting, Abiathar started on. The young man grabbed his arm and jerked him around.

"Don't you understand? Flee for your life."

Abiathar saw a group of men in the distance.

"Run," Aaron cried. "And warn the others." Releasing the priest's arm, he took off toward a grove of trees on a western hill.

Fear gripped Abiathar as he rushed back to Nob. Already tired from jogging toward Gibeah, his legs felt heavy and weak. When he reached the foot of the hill, he turned to see a leader and his men close behind.

"Run for your lives," Abiathar warned as he dashed through the village. People turned to stare at him. "They are coming to kill you."

Abiathar hurried directly to the Tabernacle and grabbed the linen ephod that held the Urim and Thummim. He started to take more but screams of the dying filled the air. Darting out of the Tabernacle, he ran east toward the Wilderness of Judah, barely escaping with his life.

A week later Abiathar reached David's hideout. The commander listened, dumbfounded, to the horrific news and wept for the men who died because of his brief stop in Nob.

"I knew when I saw Doeg that morning there would be trouble," David said to Abiathar. "No one is left in your family, and I'm to blame. Stay with me. The man seeking your life is seeking mine too. I'll protect you."

Concerned for the safety of his elderly parents, the women, and children, David took his group to Moab, where he asked for protection. When the king learned that Jesse was the grandson of Ruth, a Moabitess, he agreed to the request.

With his parents and family cared for, David and his men moved to the stronghold, *metsudah*. When Gad told them to go to Judah, they left, hiding in the forest of Hareth. Hunters, however, recognized the war hero and word got back to King Saul.

Having vented his wrath on the priests, Saul sank into a deeper state of depression. If he had any remorse for his deed, Jonathan couldn't tell it, but neither did he seem happy. Within a few weeks, however, the king recovered his will to fight and called for immediate pursuit of David. Jonathan prayed for a miracle and God answered his plea. The heat became unbearable as the summer drew to a close. The *sharav* came early, the dry east wind blowing unmercifully as it filled the air with a dusty haze. Temperatures rose to oppressive levels and even Saul's venomous spirit seemed to evaporate.

Jonathan stood on the fortress wall one afternoon and watched clouds form in the west, a welcome sight. Clouds signified the promise of rain, the halting of troop movement, the guarantee of safety for David. Jonathan could relax his guard for a few months.

As the days grew shorter and more clouds appeared, other clouds gathered over Israel. After completing grape and olive harvests, people were at a loss. No sanctuary remained to draw them to the annual Feast of Tabernacles, no priests to accept their offerings to God. The king they had chosen had destroyed it all.

Winter arrived, and David and his men moved into caves that pocked the wilderness hills. The rain fell less in that area than in the central mountains, so they kept warm and dry. The end of the rains pleased David, although the latter rains would no doubt herald Saul's renewed pursuit. Before he heard of the king's movement, however, he received word that Philistine marauders were raiding Keilah, looting new grain from the threshing floor.

A seasoned commander who had spent the past six years fighting Israel's enemies, David saw no reason to quit. Being well acquainted with the area, David ordered his men to prepare to attack. His soldiers raised their eyebrows at his daring command.

"If we are afraid while hiding in home territory, how much more so moving against the powerful Philistines?" they asked.

David had never let fear stop him. He believed God fought for His People. Using the Urim and Thummim Abiathar brought from Nob, he inquired of the Lord. When David knew God approved of his plan, he set out for Keilah.

Located four miles south of Adullam, the town crowned a hill that guarded the ascent through the central mountain range to Hebron, eight miles to the southeast. As David's men approached the town, they could see the fields on which the people depended for their livelihood and the abandoned threshing floors. The nearby Philistine camp hummed with life. Soldiers cared for the cattle and sheep they had captured. Others filled sacks with stolen grain while the people of Keilah watched helplessly from the town wall.

David's band struck unexpectedly, dealing heavy losses to the Philistines. They rescued the livestock and grain and returned them to the people of Keilah, then took up residence in the town, waiting to see if the Philistine army would retaliate.

One afternoon David browsed through the marketplace, contemplating buying a cake of dates. Someone placed a hand on his shoulder, and he turned around to see Joel.

"What are you doing here? Is Jonathan with you?"

"Come."

David followed Joel out the town gate and along the path to the olive grove. There, the former captain related the story of the slaughter of the priests. "Afterward, Saul discharged Lamech and me from the army, declaring us disloyal. Lamech returned to Dan, but I remained in Gibeah. You and Jonathan both need me."

"Thanks for your thoughtfulness," David said, his eyes warm with appreciation. "Would you like to join my group? I need good soldiers."

"I would be more valuable to you in Gibeah." Joel stepped closer and lowered his voice. "When Saul learned of your whereabouts, he praised God for handing his enemy over to him. He gloated, 'David walked into a prison when he entered a town with gates and bars.' He has mobilized the army and at this moment is on his way to lay siege of Keilah."

"Jonathan sent you?"

Joel nodded. "Sorry I can't stay around to help you. I must get back before anyone misses me." He made a swipe across his neck with his index finger. "Doeg is like a bear that has gotten its first taste of blood."

David walked back to town alone. How strong were these walls and gate? He reached out to thump one of the heavy wooden doors. Reentering the busy marketplace, another question surfaced. How loyal were these people to him? to Saul? He set out to find Abiathar.

Inquiring again of the Lord, David learned of the fickleness of those he had rescued. God replied through the Urim and Thummim that the people of Keilah would surrender him to Saul. Late that afternoon David took his men, now numbering six hundred, and left.

David's band began roving from place to place, keeping one step ahead of the king. Saul, upon learning of David's escape from Keilah, called off the siege and returned to Gibeah. The relieved David, however, did not relax his guard. Saul had scouts searching for him.

One day at camp David slowly turned a complete circle, his gaze sweeping the distant horizon. By now he had become as familiar with the area south of Hebron as with the mountain range surrounding his beloved hometown. Here, however, the undulating hills leveled off in a plateau nine miles long and three miles wide. The towns of Ziph, Carmel, and Maon, which sat among its fertile fields, reminded him of Bethlehem; the fields reminded him of Jesse's fields.

Jagged ends of barley stubble poked through the openings of David's sandal, stabbing at his foot. He lifted it to trample a spot smooth. As he had watched the threshers a few weeks before, he had wondered who might be harvesting his father's fields in Bethlehem. The sadness lingered. Driven from the inheritance of their forefathers. The Land was Israel's proof of God's favor. An Israelite separated from his ancestral land was a man separated from his identity.

David turned east. Between the plateau towns and the Dead Sea lay seventeen miles of wilderness. Its soil was no different than that of the central mountain range, but the mountains drained the moisture from the clouds, depriving the area beyond the watershed of needed rainfall. People spoke of the wilderness as two distinct regions. The *midbar*, or grazing land, received sufficient rainfall to sustain rich pastures, if not crops. The *yeshimon* did not. Often called a desert, the vast mountainous Yeshimon of Judah began north of Jericho and stretched south for over fifty rugged miles. David had already explored its fringes, wondering how soon he would be forced into its stark shelter.

Sections of the *midbar* were named for their neighboring towns, and David soon led his men to the Wilderness of Ziph.

The door opened. Jonathan looked up to see Abner enter. Saul had not responded to his son's presence that morning; neither did he respond to the new arrival. The commander walked briskly to the throne, where Saul sat slumped with his head in his hands.

"O king, I have good news. David is in Horesh in the Wilderness of Ziph," Abner said. Jonathan cringed when he saw his father stir.

"Are you sure? I don't want to pursue another false alarm."

"A messenger arrived a few minutes ago."

"Great, call the troops." Saul stood up with more energy than Jonathan had seen in weeks. "We will leave within the hour."

From the fortress wall, Jonathan stood quietly praying as he watched the army depart for southern Judah. Would his father's insane searches never end? His index finger traced the scar on his left wrist. Not until David was dead, he supposed.

By the time the last soldier disappeared behind a hill, Jonathan knew what he must do. Whirling around, he ran down the staircase to find Deborah. He whispered his plan to her, then headed down to Joel's house in town. They must plan carefully. Malki-Shua, thankfully, had gone with his father.

When the sky darkened, the prince and former captain, dressed as peasant shepherds and armed with only slings and staffs, slipped out of Gibeah and hurried south. They slept in an empty field and were up at dawn. Soon they saw the king's troops in the distance. Keeping behind Saul's men, when the soldiers stopped for the night, the two slipped passed under cover of darkness. They were well ahead of the army when day broke.

Along the way, Jonathan tried to inquire about David's location. Few people seemed willing to offer information. He wasn't sure whether they didn't know or were afraid of being disloyal to the king. Unwilling to press his case for fear of being recognized, he would drop the matter and move on. That afternoon he moaned as he and Joel watched Saul's men leave Hebron before sunset.

Camped in an inn that night, Jonathan prayed for God to show him the way before it was too late. He and Joel were on the road at dawn, alert for any sign of the troops ahead.

A mile down the road they came upon a traveler who had stopped to repair a broken sandal strap. The man stood to greet them, and the prince said, "I hear that King Saul passed this way yesterday." Studying the man's face for any clue to his loyalties, Jonathan was rewarded for his effort when he saw a flicker of fear cloud the man's eyes. The traveler quickly looked down.

"What is your name?"

"Gad son of Reuben."

"Aren't you one of the prophets who sometimes accompanied Samuel?" Joel asked.

The man nodded. Sensing they had found an ally, Jonathan revealed their identity and begged Gad to lead them to David before his father reached him. The prophet smiled with relief to hear his fellow travelers were on a rescue mission. The three hastened on.

Drops of olive oil beaded across the leather shield cover, and David quickly rubbed them into the surface before they could cascade into the dirt. The woolen cloth moved in a circular motion, the pressure firm. As a commander, he insisted his men keep their shields polished—especially in such arid territory. A brittle shield cover would easily crack when struck by a sword, even by an arrow. A dull one brought shame to any soldier.

David smiled with satisfaction as the gold of sunset touched the glossy finish, bringing out the rich, dark tones. He raised his eyes appreciatively to the sky, but his gaze stopped on the path leading up to camp.

Three men approached from the north. David stood to get a closer look. He recognized the gait of Gad, but not the two shepherds with him. He focused on the man in the middle. Something looked familiar about his stride. But who? Laying down the shield, he racked his mind for a clue. Jonathan! The other must be Joel. David ran to greet his precious friends. Even as they embraced, overjoyed to see each other, he knew the reunion was bittersweet.

Men dropped what they were doing and crowded around Jonathan and Joel. Their news of Saul's renewed search had a sobering effect, dampening supper conversations. Most in the camp retired early. After the others had gone to sleep, the blood brothers sat under the stars, talking.

As their visit drew to a close, David said, "God certainly works in strange ways, doesn't He? You always wanted to be a soldier and defeat the Philistines to save His Chosen People. I contentedly played the kinnor for my sheep. God brought us together."

Jonathan tossed a twig into the campfire. "I give you warnings, and you give me poems of praise to God." He took a deep breath. "But I guess both can be lifesaving—protection and psalms."

David cleared his throat. "I'm working on a new one now," he said. "I change words around a lot until it sounds exactly right. Sometime that takes a very long time. It will go something like this:

> "Trust in the Lord and do what is right.
> Delight your heart in the Lord and He will
> give you the desires He wants your heart to have.
> Commit your life to the Lord and trust in Him.
> Be still before the Lord and rest patiently in Him.
> Do not fret when evil people triumph; they will be cut off.
> But those who hope in the Lord
> will receive His inheritance."

Neither spoke immediately. "Another psalm of eternal truth," Jonathan said. "I wish Father had your understanding. He makes your life so difficult." He removed his headdress and combed his fingers through his dark wavy hair. "Do you remember the words

MARK OF THE COVENANT

you spoke to me in the Valley of Elah about being faithful, like Joseph in Egypt. They have been a great inspiration to me."

David nodded.

Jonathan replaced his headdress. "Tonight, I would like to give you words of encouragement—not ones I composed but those God gave to Joshua after the death of Moses. I could never have imagined when my teacher Ethan made me memorize them years ago how helpful they would be to me now. They are from Joshua's scroll and go something like this:

> 'Be strong and of a good courage, because you will lead these people to inherit the land I promised to their forefathers. Courageously obey all the law my servant Moses commanded you. Do not deviate from it, neither to the right nor to the left, so you will prosper wherever you go. Remember this Book of the Law; meditate on it day and night. Carefully do everything written in it. Then you will prosper and be successful . . . . Do not be fearful or discouraged, for the Lord your God is with you wherever you go.' "

Jonathan brushed at a tear that rolled down his cheek. "Don't be afraid. God will not allow Father to harm you. You will be the next king of Israel, and I'll be second to you. Even Father knows this." Looking up at the dark sky, he prayed for David's safety and his future, then they renewed their covenant. Reluctantly, the two went to sleep.

The first pink traces of dawn lightened the sky above the Wilderness of Judah the following morning when the friends said goodbye one more time. Would it be the last?

Jonathan and Joel slipped out of camp.

Thanks to the warning, David eluded his pursuers, and Saul eventually called off the search. David continued staying in the area of Horesh, moving to the hill of Hachilah, a ridge six miles east of Ziph. The area was a desolate region of steep chalky lime-stone hills dissected by winter torrents and intersected by valleys, a pathless wilderness dotted with thistles and broom bushes but devoid of all but an occasional tree. The town-free area offered an ideal place of refuge.

~

Gedor stood in the cave opening, his eyes roving back and forth as he surveyed the countryside. Another day of fruitless searching probably. How could the ram have strayed so far? He picked up his waterbag and stepped into the morning light. "Coming?" he called over his shoulder.

"As soon as I get my sandals on," Hosea replied.

Gedor knew his son hadn't slept well in their make-shift quarters, but they couldn't waste the hours of sunlight. Every additional day decreased their chances of finding the ram alive. Gedor started up the hillside above the cave. Perhaps they could spot the sheep from there.

As the two stood looking around, they heard voices. Gedor stepped to a nearby broom bush and squatted behind it. Hosea followed. The blooms were long gone from the bush. Gedor could only hope the small sparse leaves and the long branches formed enough cover to disguise their presence. Their brown tunics and cloaks helped. The voices came closer. The men did not move.

A few minutes later, they heard someone say, "Here's a cave. Let's get some sleep."

Gedor turned to his son and mouthed the word, "David." When they could no longer hear talking, the father and son stole down the back side of the mountain and rushed home. The ram would have to wait.

Years before Gedor had proudly served in King Saul's original standing army. The other villagers had been just as excited that the skills of one of their own attracted the king's notice. Gedor was nearly as proud when his youngest brother, Ishbak, had been recruited the previous year. Everyone in the region around Ziph identified the house of Magdiel as completely loyal to their king.

They had reason to be. For the past ten years the people of the area had enjoyed peace. Occasionally marauding bands stole sheep, but the people were free from Edomite and Amalekite attacks that once disrupted life. They had Saul's army to thank for their prosperity—and a monument at nearby Carmel to remind them of it.

Gedor had been surprised when a scouting party stopped by his house the past week, inquiring if he had seen David. It was the first he knew the hero of Elah had become a rebel. He regretted not being able to help the men, but he promised to keep an eye out for the warrior. Now they had located the villain.

Early the next morning Gedor and three other men from the village started for Gibeah. When they stood before the king the following afternoon and delivered the good news, Gedor saw the look of relief in the king's eyes.

"I appreciate your loyalty," Saul told them. "At times I feel like no one else cares about my quest to stamp out the traitor." He paused, then leaned forward on his throne. "God bless you for your concern. Go back and make further observations. Find out where David usually goes, who has seen him. They tell me he is very crafty, using many hiding places. Then come back to me with specific details. I will go with you. If he's in the area, I'll track him down whatever clan of Judah he happens to be with."

Gedor and his friends went home. A few weeks later they located David again. Sending word for Saul to come, they began pursuing him themselves, at times losing sight of him, then locating him again. When the king arrived, men of Ziph led him to the Wilderness of Maon.

Between the ridge Hachilah and the region of Maon lay a gorge called *Sela ham-Mahlekoth*, the Cliff of Division. The deep, narrow chasm was impassible except by detouring for many miles. When Saul arrived, David and his men were moving down one side of the gorge. Gedor and his men were on the opposite side. Catching sight of his enemy across the treacherous divide, Saul smelled victory.

He mustn't be impetuous. This called for careful planning. The troops could shoot at them, but David was as good with the shield as with the bow. They mustn't waste their arrows.

"Let's split forces," Saul said to Malki-Shua. Sending Malki-Shua with some men back to guard the end of the gorge in case David returned, he hurried with the rest toward the other end, hoping to trap his prey. When the sun began to set, Saul fought off the threat of depression. If only he had power like Joshua at Gibeon, he'd tell the sun to stand still. He lifted his eyes to heaven. "Tomorrow, God, please give the enemy into my hands."

Saul didn't sleep well and sighed with relief when the stars began to fade. Being the first up, he quickly roused his troops. It didn't take long to spot David's men on the far side, and the race was on. Saul's men made good progress and were soon directly across from David. At this rate they would beat him to the end of the gorge. Saul smiled.

Standing aside, Saul sent his fastest men on ahead. As he stepped forward to join the remainder, someone touched his arm. He turned to see one of his captains with Reu, one of the royal armor-bearers back in Gibeah, beside him.

"Oh, king, a courier just arrived from Jonathan," the captain said.

When the king heard Reu's message, he scowled in dismay. The Philistines had launched an invasion of Judah. The prince and Abner were rallying the troops that remained in Gibeah and heading for the Shephelah.

Saul acknowledged only one true personal enemy, but even he

knew he could lose his kingdom to the Philistines as well as to David. His temper flared. Even the Philistines seem to side with David, Saul groused to himself, looking across the gorge at David's fleeing band. He considered continuing the pursuit, but the seriousness of Jonathan's message persuaded him to abandon it.

"So close, yet the traitor escapes," Malki-Shua said when his father rejoined him.

The king and his men arrived in the Judean foothills the day after Jonathan did. Over the next several weeks, the army managed to repel the Philistines. When the fighting ended, Jonathan encouraged his father to return to Gibeah to celebrate his newest victory.

David temporarily forgotten, the king headed home, basking in the women's jubilant chants of praise as the triumphant army passed through town after town.

32

A FAMILY SURPRISE

Walking up the hill to Gibeah, Jonathan looked at the stone fortress silhouetted in the pink-orange sunset blazing across the western sky. Safely home. He smiled. One more war over. And the days of rain would soon arrive, preventing Father from renewing his manhunt for David.

Jonathan's wife and daughters ran out to welcome his arrival as everyone in the palace turned out to rejoice over Saul's victory. Deborah's surprise made the crown prince happiest of all.

After listening to their father's story of battle, the girls hurried off to their Aunt Michal's room, where they all now slept. Deborah refilled the lamp with olive oil and placed it in the niche in the wall for the night. The couple lay down on their sleeping mat, and Jonathan reached out to draw his wife close. They lay in each other's arms a few moments, words unnecessary.

"Jonathan," Deborah whispered, "I have news for you. I am expecting another baby." He took a deep breath and his arms tightened around her. "About the time of the latter rains," she added.

With her miscarriage two years before and no subsequent pregnancies, Jonathan had given up on her delivering another baby. Secretly he grieved. Every man needed a son. Sons inherited property and carried on the family trade. For a king, however, having a son was paramount, though Jonathan knew now that he would never be king. God's blessing on David and his own father's wrong choices had erased that hope. Still, he longed for a son.

He leaned back and looked lovingly into Deborah's brown eyes. Seeing the beam of joy, he hid his secret desire as he pulled her closer. Hannah, Rebekah, and Jemimah would be great nursemaids to their new sister. They all loved babies. Then he chided himself for already determining it to be a girl.

"God, if it would please you, I would like a son to love and train in the ways of the Lord," he prayed silently. "I would teach him, as Ethan did me, to obey Your Law and help him memorize it. Whatever the baby is, please keep Deborah safe and healthy. I've lost David; I couldn't bear to lose her too." Worn out from the long trip, he drifted off to sleep with dreams of a son floating through his mind.

The hours of daylight gradually shortened with the approach of Fall. Jonathan continued to commit his desire to the Lord. With a renewed focus on parenthood, he soon realized others needed his fatherly help.

Abinadab, nearly fifteen, had not yet been given archery training. The crown prince smiled as he recalled Grandfather Kish thirty years before teaching him to use the sling. Saul showed no interest in instructing his fourth son in the use of the bow and arrow. Now that the king relied on sword and spear, Jonathan figured he had lost his skill. Jonathan asked permission to give his half-brother lessons, and Saul agreed.

From comments Abinadab made, Jonathan knew his brother felt the neglect of his gloomy, embittered father. Abinadab thrived on the attention, and Jonathan inwardly rejoiced that he had taken the initiative to train him. The young prince proved a good shot, and his brother's enthusiastic encouragement motivated Abinadab to do his best.

Jonathan also turned his attention to Armoni, now eight, and Mephibosheth, five. He knew Rizpah had no choice in his father making her his concubine. Women had so little voice in decisions. Her sons would need training, both military and spiritual, and he vowed to help.

As the winter rains tapered off, Jonathan noticed his father's restlessness return. More than once, Jonathan entered the throne room to hear Saul's fingers drumming the arm of the throne. Without asking, he knew the king's mind had formulated plans for another search for David. The prince tried to intercept his father as he paced around the fortress wall or distract him as he inspected the armory daily. Saul, however, could not easily be deterred. All Jonathan could do was pray.

One night Deborah's loud moan roused Jonathan from deep slumber, and he knew her time had come. He lit a second lamp and hurried with it down to the kitchen, where the town midwife had been sleeping for the past two nights. He awakened her with the word, "Come." Abihail quickly followed him up the staircase, and he walked over to knock on Huldah's door.

With the women in charge, Jonathan returned to the kitchen to wait. Abinadab came down to join him and, between lapses of silence, the two discussed matters of the kingdom.

A few hours later the sound of movement in the courtyard stirred Jonathan from his drowsiness. When he opened the door and peered outside, the bracing morning air hit him in the face. Behind him, he heard Abinadab say, "Mother." Turning, Jonathan saw his stepmother hurry across the room, a big smile on her face.

"It's a boy, Jonathan, a boy." She rushed over to hug the forty-one-year-old. Dancing around the room, deftly skirting the cooking pit, she thanked God for the safe delivery.

For a few seconds Jonathan did not move, too dazed to react. After months of praying for a son—but expecting another girl, he did not comprehend the amazing news. A son?

"A son?" he asked. "Are you sure?"

"I'm certain."

"Praise be to the God of Israel." Jonathan waved his hands toward the ceiling. "Today I am father of a son."

He grabbed Abinadab and embraced him, then hurried out the door and up the staircase. A son! The girls would be surprised.

Jonathan felt his hands tremble slightly as he waited for Abihail to answer his light knock. Finally, she swung the door open, and he stepped in. The flames of the three saucer lamps illuminated every corner of the room. He'd never seen the bedroom so well lit.

Jonathan's eyes went immediately to the mat where Deborah lay. She smiled up at him, and he knelt beside her. He knew by the sparkle in her eyes she was as pleased as he.

"You've made me so happy," he said in a low voice. "Thank you so much."

It would be improper to display affection in front of the midwife. After Deborah had a chance to rest and they were alone, he would hold her close and try to convey his deep gratitude more adequately.

Deborah pushed the blanket down. "Your son."

The usual strips of swaddling cloth bound the baby's body. Only his face showed, his little nose round like a soft young grape. Their son didn't look any different than Hannah or the others had at birth, but a totally different surge of emotion engulfed the prince.

"My son," he whispered. The baby blinked his eyes. "Heir to Jonathan. A warrior for Israel. God be praised for His wonderful miracle." He lifted the infant and planted a kiss on his exposed cheek.

"God knew you needed someone to help fill the void left by David's departure," Deborah said in a low voice.

Their eyes met and Jonathan realized how much Deborah really understood him. "The Lord is my shepherd, I shall never be in want," he quoted. "A caring wife and a son to carry on my lineage. What more could I ask?" He kissed the baby again and as he laid him back down on the mat, noticed how tired Deborah looked. "Rest now. The Lord be with you and reward you as a great mother in Israel."

He squeezed her hand as Abihail came over to the mat. Rising, he left the room.

Up on the southeast corner of the fortress wall, as Jonathan watched the sun rise above the hills in brilliant splendor, he felt his heart would burst with praise. God had given him a special, unexpected gift today. He wasn't sure he was worthy.

"Help me be a faithful father who trains his son in Your ways," he prayed. "Help me be a Samuel and an Ethan to my boy."

Thinking again of the girls, he hurried down to wake them. Taking the steps two at a time, he could envision Jemimah's squeal of delight, Rebekah's dance of joy, and the gleam of protective love in Hannah's eyes as they saw their little brother for the first time. "Thank You, God, for my wonderful family," he prayed as he lifted his hand to rap on Michal's door.

Even Saul grew excited for his firstborn's joy. He sent messengers to Bethel. Gamaliel and several of his family arrived the third day to celebrate with Deborah. On the eighth day, as the men of the two families met in the throne room for the ritual of circumcision, Jonathan resolved to reach out to his father with a gesture of reconciliation. He had noticed when Saul sat brooding over David, an unexpected appearance of young Mephibosheth seemed to momentarily brighten his father's troubled mind. Jonathan decided to name his son for his little half-brother. Perhaps this child too would be a bright spot in the gloomy palace.

Jonathan asked Abner to serve as *mohel* for the ceremony. As the army commander lifted the sharp knife and skillfully performed the circumcision, the baby let out a wail that could be heard out in the courtyard. Jonathan felt the pain of his son's incision, but also the pride of welcoming the newest male in the House of Saul. One day he too would be part of the Congregation of Israel, partaking of her blessings, fighting in her defense.

Jonathan blinked back tears of gratitude and joy as he held out his arms to receive his son. From today forward Mephibosheth would bear the mark of Israel's Covenant with God. The Lord had blessed him beyond measure. Jonathan held the baby close, patting him to hush his whimpering. Then Jonathan recalled another covenant, one as meaningful and permanent, one that guaranteed Mephibosheth protection and privileges as important as circumcision. If God could give him a son when it seemed impossible, He could keep David safe in the wilderness.

A few weeks later, Jonathan awoke to the sound of voices in the courtyard below. Thinking news of a Philistine invasion had arrived during the night, he shoved back his blanket and jumped up from his mat. He slipped into his sandals, then donned his cloak as he hurried out the door. Pausing at the bottom of the stairs, he pushed the door open in time to see armor-bearers assembled near the front gate in the predawn grayness.

An invasion would have prompted Father to call him first. A knot formed in the pit of his stomach. Another manhunt for David. The door to the throne room opened. The king stepped out, followed by Abner and Doeg. Jonathan pulled the door closed, leaving a slit to watch. Without looking back, the men moved across the courtyard to the gate. The prince tiptoed back up to his room.

Jonathan didn't realize his hasty departure had awakened Deborah until he turned from closing the door. Her eyes met his and the warmth of her understanding lifted his drooping shoulders.

"I guess I wasn't needed after all."

"David?"

He nodded, then tossed his cloak into the corner and dropped to the mat. Sitting up, Deborah reached out to take his hand. They sat for several moments without speaking, then Mephibosheth stirred.

Jonathan picked up his son and kissed him. "God, help me be a father my son can be proud of," he prayed aloud.

Later that morning Jonathan left the fortress alone. Bypassing the noisy town, he walked down to the valley and across the empty barley fields, coming at last to Ezel. Dejected, he sat down on the rock formation, scene of so many pleasant and unpleasant memories. He recalled the morning he and David had parted there. After communing with God, the Lord had restored his soul.

Looking up at the clear blue sky, he prayed again for his father, for David's safety, and for his own attitude. He asked the Lord to fill his heart with love for the one man he should love the most, yet he respected least. Why couldn't his father have been a man of God like Samuel?

Not wanting to face questions just yet from his brothers or townsmen, Jonathan decided to extend his walk. Continuing south, he paused to watch a huge flock of white storks fly over, winging their way north in their annual migration to the warm climate of lands he would never know. He wandered aimlessly, crossing hillsides and valleys until he reached the destroyed village of Nob.

A shudder passed through Jonathan as he walked past empty houses that lined the narrow dirt streets. Doors sagged on their hinges, revealing littered rooms and blood-stained floors. House furnishings and personal possessions lay covered in dirt and spots of mold, untouched from that fateful day.

Ends of twigs and dry grass stuck out from a bird's nest built in a hole left by a dislodged brick. Lizards darted in and out of cracks and crevices. A pale brown gecko sunned itself in the morning sunshine, clinging to a brick with its broad fan-like toes.

Coming around a corner, Jonathan startled a stray goat that nibbled at a bush growing beside a foundation. After it ran away, the prince climbed the stairs, sidestepping crumbling areas of the treads. Grass grew from the neglected packed-clay rooftop. The northwest corner had caved in from the force of the past rainy season's storms.

Shielding his eyes against the bright sunlight, Jonathan's gaze swept over the ruined town. Out on the hillside a heap of whitened bones reminded him Doeg had slaughtered the livestock, as well as people.

Descending the steps, Jonathan walked out to the abandoned Tabernacle. The wind and rain had whipped its curtains, now faded and frayed, and had knocked down several of the posts. The Holy Place stood exposed to view; a once-sacred utensil lay on the floor, caked with dried mud.

Tears coursed down Jonathan's cheeks as he thought of Ahimelech and his family. If for no other reason than Nob, David deserved to escape Saul's wrath. God had told Moses and the Children of Israel to destroy the pagan religions in their new homeland. Words Jonathan had memorized thirty years before in Ethan's class came to him.

"Destroy the pagan altars, shatter their sacred stones, chop down their Asherah poles and burn their idols. You are a holy people unto the Lord your God. The Lord has chosen you out of all the peoples on earth to be his special possession."

"A holy people to the Lord," he repeated. "His special possession." Leaning against a corner post, Jonathan moaned. Israel was to destroy heathenism but his father, instead, had destroyed God's servants. Jonathan bowed his head and covered his eyes with his right hand. "God, help me to be a holy man even in my unholy circumstances," he prayed, his voice choking.

As Jonathan waited in the presence of the Lord, the sunshine grew warmer. So did his heart. God's priests may be dead, but God was eternal. He walked out of the ruins and started home. Reviewing the words of Moses again in his mind, a later part of the passage came to him. He quoted it aloud as he descended the hill.

"Know that the Lord your God is God; he is the true and steadfast God. He keeps his covenant of love and mercy to those who love him and keep his commands to a thousand generations."

Jonathan's right index finger traced the scar across his left wrist. Covenant of love. That is what he had with David, and with the Lord. God was a faithful God. With His help, Jonathan determined anew, he too would be forever faithful.

He quickened his pace, anxious to get home and share God's promise with his family.

The rugged, rock-strewn hills of the Wilderness of Judah stretched out before David and his men. *Yeshimon,* it was called—desolation. This area of the wilderness had no real passes, only gorges torn by winter downpours that were too narrow and crooked for proper roads. But people forced to cross the six to eight hours of bleak terrain had found the best ways to their destinations. David followed the wide path that led from Hebron southeast to the Dead Sea.

The men had walked since before dawn across the dusty, waterless wasteland—the last few hours with hardly a bush to break the monotony. Shortly after noon they came to the edge of a precipice. Four hundred feet below, a river of refreshing water burst from a rock platform and plunged three hundred feet to a broad, mile-long fertile plain on the western shore of the Dead Sea. En-gedi, Fountain of the Wild Goat, was the second most famous oasis of the Jordan River area, outranked only by the more accessible Jericho, eighteen miles to the north.

The smell of sulfur from the stagnant sea assailed the men as they descended the steep stair-like path down the cliff. Before them gardens of leeks, melons, lentils, and greens lay amid patches of wheat and barley stubble. Vineyards bearing luscious grapes and silvery-gray olive groves rose along the slopes. Graceful fronds of date palm trees lazily swayed in the afternoon sunshine.

After living in the wilderness so long, David's men enjoyed the luxury of the town. As the days of rain approached, they purchased supplies and headed back into the hills, Crags of the Wild Goats, to find shelter in the numerous caves. They found some of the entrances inaccessible.

Months later, with the end of the latter rains, David began moving frequently. News of his whereabouts had reached Saul, he learned, and he could take no chances.

Since leaving Gibeah, David had often examined his heart for reasons why Saul hated him. Perhaps in his youthful exuberance he had offended the king. Often, he prayed, "Search me, Oh God, and expose any wicked way in me." Instead of the longed-for revelation, however, a deep peace settled over him and he sensed God's approval. He could endure life as a fugitive if he had God's acceptance.

David and his men traveled farther west. One day they came to an area used to pasture flocks. There were empty sheep pens there, and a cave used by shepherds for shelter. David decided to stay a few days. He was enjoying a peaceful rest one afternoon when a scout rushed in to alert the band of followers. Saul and his army were rapidly closing in on them.

David pushed his men deep into the cave and ordered complete silence, then began praying. A half-hour later they heard voices outside as Saul's troops gathered near the sheep pens. The patch of sunlight that marked the cave entrance darkened. Someone had come inside.

No one moved as they waited. David made out the tall form of his father-in-law, silhouetted against the light. He held his breath, afraid the sound might carry to the king.

Several of the royal bodyguards came to stand as sentries at the cave entrance. Having decided to use the privacy of the cave to relieve himself, the king slowly took off his armor and handed it to the soldiers. He then moved farther into the darkness and removed his robe. Laying it on the ground in the middle of the cave, he turned to face the entrance as he squatted on the ground.

One of David's men crept up beside his leader and touched his arm. "This is the very day the Lord predicted when he promised, 'I will deliver your enemy into your hands for you to deal with as you desire,' " the soldier whispered in his ear. David removed his sandals and sneaked forward, his movement masked by the sound of laughing and talking coming from the bodyguards who waited several feet away.

Using his hunting knife, David cut a corner from Saul's robe. He slipped back into the inner recesses of the cave, carrying his prize with him. As David turned with satisfaction to watch Saul don the robe again, a weight of guilt hit him like a boulder in a rockslide. He had disfigured the royal robes of Saul, God's anointed king of Israel, his conscience accused. As he watched Saul leave the cave the sense of God's approval exited with him.

Behind him, David's men waited for their signal to move, weapons drawn. David bowed his head.

"I did wrong," he said, his voice low and apologetic. "I shouldn't have done such a thing to my master, the Lord's anointed. I can't lift my hand against him, for he is the Lord's anointed. I cannot attack the king—and neither will you."

David heard whispers of complaint as he finished speaking, but he did not change his mind. A few minutes later he started out of the cave, his men close behind. When they stepped into the daylight, Saul had already reached the sheep pens, where his troops were waiting for him. He stood talking to Doeg and Abner. David didn't see Malki-Shua with them.

"My lord the king," David called to the monarch. Saul turned around to see his son-in-law bowed down, his face to the ground. "Why do you listen to those who say, 'David is determined to harm you?' Today you've seen for yourself how the Lord delivered you into my hands in the cave. Some tried to persuade me to kill you, but I spared your life. I said, 'I can't lift my hand against him, for he is the Lord's anointed.'"

David waved the jagged piece of cloth in the air. "My father, see this piece of your robe I'm holding! I did cut off the corner of your robe but didn't kill you. Please understand that I'm not guilty of wrongdoing or mutiny. I have not done wrong to you, but you are hunting me down to kill me." He took two steps toward the king. "May the Lord judge between us. And may the Lord pay you for the wrongs you've done to me, but my hand will not harm you. Remember the old saying, 'From evildoers come evil deeds,' so I will not harm you."

David walked closer. "Who has the king of Israel come out against? Whom are you chasing? Some dead dog? Some flea?" David had never been able to understand why the king would expend such time and effort to destroy him, the lastborn of an ordinary family, a man with no royal ambitions. "May the Lord judge which of us is right. May he consider my cause and vindicate me by delivering me from your grasp."

"Is that you, David, my son?" the king asked, beginning to weep. "You're more righteous than I, for you have rewarded me with good when I rewarded you with evil." He stepped forward. "When a man finds his enemy, he doesn't let him escape, but you didn't harm me. May God reward you well for your kindness today. I know you will surely become king and will establish the kingdom of Israel. Now pledge to me by the Lord that you won't eliminate my descendants or wipe out my name from my father's clan."

"I swear to you that I will not," David said. "Return to Gibeah in peace and may God be with you."

Saul ordered his men to abandon the chase. David sent one of his men to hand back the severed piece of robe, then stood with his band of men, watching the soldiers go. With all his heart he wished he could inquire about Jonathan, but he knew he couldn't take the risk. The covenant between them ignited Saul's fire of hatred. David must content himself, instead, with knowing he had bought a few months of peace—but with Saul even that seemed unsure.

David turned to his men, "Let's get back to our hiding place. The people of Keilah taught us that appreciation can be very short-lived."

33

A COMPOSITE BOW

Jonathan shook his head with a jerk, realizing Abner's nudge had interrupted his daydreaming. Looking up from the mended hem of his father's robe, he recognized the clear warning that flashed from Abner's eyes. It was more than an accidental tear, Jonathan surmised as he returned his attention to the king's speech. The warm breeze that stirred the tamarisk leaves overhead did little to assist the military leaders' concentration.

Jonathan sighed, as glad as the others when the meeting ended. Calling Abner aside as they walked toward the fortress, the prince asked what caused the tear. Abner hesitated before launching into the story of the encounter near En-gedi. By the time the commander finished, Jonathan understood his reluctance. Abner's first loyalty remained to the king, and he knew of Jonathan's covenant friendship with David.

"Sounds just like David," the prince said. "I hope this cures Father's incessant compulsion to destroy his most loyal subject. What other Israelite would spare anyone's life if he knew the choice to be either him or them?"

"The king has been rather quiet since returning home. Only time will tell whether his promise holds," Abner responded.

~

Over the next few weeks Saul's mood did improve. He took more interest in his family and even went to watch Abinadab's bow practice. One morning as Saul and his firstborn stood on the fortress wall, the king told the story of David's kindness in sparing his life.

"I guess I've been rather foolish," Saul admitted. "Next time I start to do wrong, please remind me of this mistake."

"Israel is a great nation—God's Chosen People. We need your wisdom and leadership to ensure the safety of all."

"I'll try to do better." The king looked through a gap to the brown fields in the valley below town. "God bless David."

Jonathan stood in front of the fortress the following morning watching a platoon of soldiers practice a drill. Reu approached him.

The armor-bearer looked around in all directions. "Aaron came earlier," he said in a low voice. "Joel would like to see you today."

Thanking the young man, the prince continued supervising the drill, but his mind kept returning to the invitation. With Saul's antipathy toward the former captain, Jonathan saw little of him. The prince still deeply appreciated his first armor-bearer. Remaining in Gibeah must be difficult for the man from Dothan. Jonathan knew Joel had based his decision on his devotion to David and to him. Joel and his orphaned nephew had helped save David's life more than once. Secretly, Jonathan hoped Joel would ask for one of his daughters as a bride for Aaron.

Following lunch, the king retired to his bedroom for a nap. Jonathan made his way down to Joel's house, where the man warmly welcomed him. The ex-captain introduced him to a shaggy-looking visitor, and they exchanged greetings.

"I bring you a gift," Sakia said, his clothes permeated by the smell of field and flock. Untying the top of a well-worn grain sack, he pulled out a pair of animal horns. "The horns of a wild goat make the best composite bow," he said, handing one to the prince.

Jonathan stood momentarily speechless. The wild goat, or Nubian ibex, lived in the wilderness hills of eastern Judah.

David!

Jonathan reached out to receive the valuable gift from his blood brother. The ridged horns were thick at the base with knotted fronts—obviously from a male goat. The prince ran his fingers up the sweeping backward curve of the smooth underside. So graceful and majestic! Laying his elbow against the base, he extended his arm up the length, then repeated the process with inches to spare. Over three feet long. Perfect.

In spite of Saul's seeming change of heart, David remained in hiding. Yet even while considering himself a hunted man, he remembered his covenant friend's long-held dream of making his own composite bow. Knowing the wild goat's ability to nimbly climb the sheer face of a cliff or gorge to escape danger, Jonathan realized the effort it took David to obtain the horns.

"Tell your master I am deeply grateful to him," Jonathan said. "Tell him we are well, and the palace is peaceful at present. If God wills, someday we will meet again. In the meantime, tell him to keep encouraged in the Lord." The prince withdrew a money bag from the folds of his wide girdle-belt and extracted a small piece of silver. "For food for your trip home," he said, handing the shepherd the metal. Retying the mouth of the bag, he extended it also to the shepherd. "For David and his men."

Sakia bowed in thanks. The prince prayed a blessing on the messenger and his return journey, then left for the palace empty-handed.

That evening Reu slipped down to Joel's and brought up the

bag of horns. Jonathan hid the gift in a chest in his bedroom, having already decided to seek Abner's help in crafting the best composite bow in Israel.

Abner rejoiced a week later to hear that his cousin's son had finally decided to make the powerful weapon. As they talked, the army commander removed his own bow from its storage case and showed Jonathan the various parts. The prince listened attentively as Abner named the best types of wood to use for the body of the bow. Next, he talked about the pieces of horn. Jonathan nodded but did not inform him of the special horns hidden in his bedroom. The tendons of wild bulls were best for the bindings, Abner said, but without them Jonathan could use those from an ordinary bull.

Accompanied by his favorite armor-bearers, Reu and Asshur, Jonathan set out the next morning for the woods west of Gibeah. The men chopped stout branches from three different trees and dragged them home. Jonathan spent the next few days lopping off the twigs and side branches, then peeling off the bark. When he finished, he stored the poles in a corner of his bedroom for several months to dry. He gave the girls orders not to touch them.

The rainy season began. Ish-Bosheth's fields sprouted a fuzz of green as seeds responded to the welcome moisture. The king inquired frequently about the progress of the crops, and Jonathan praised God for his father's contentment with domestic issues. When the almond trees burst into bloom three months later, heralding the new growing season, Jonathan watched Saul for the usual signs of morbid restlessness. The king's peace continued, and the prince's hopes rose as he turned his attention to making his new double-span composite bow.

After carving the wood, Jonathan experimented with the pieces until he had the combination that would give the best tension to the arms and grip. Next, he carefully cut two long strips from the inner curve of the goat horns to add to the belly. Reu brought tendons and sinew from a bull to the palace, and Jonathan began binding and gluing all the parts together. When he finished, he held the body out to admire the sleek weapon. The tips of the arms bent outward.

After the bow had dried, Jonathan braced the wood against his knee and strained as he pulled one arm down to attach the string. After he attached the second end, the tips still curved back away from the arms—the mark of a composite bow.

Calling in a carpenter, Jonathan supervised the making of a special carrying case. He did not want the weather to ruin his new weapon before he had a chance to use it. With the return of sunny days and with Abner as his teacher, the prince began archery practice in earnest. He did not realize how much muscle power the bow would require; he spent hours each day gradually increasing his strength.

One morning Abner watched the arrows whiz through the air. "You are one amazing archer, Jonathan. I envy your talent."

"And hard work. If I had a piece of silver for every hour that I've spent practicing, I'd be a rich man."

"You will never regret your effort," Abner said as they started back to the fortress.

Several evenings later, Jonathan watched one-year-old Mephibosheth attempt his first steps. Occasional wails signaled failures, but he soon got up and tried again. The girls adored their little brother, and, with his ready smile, he never lacked attention. As the weeks passed, he became even more active.

Returning from bow practice one noon, Jonathan came through the fortress gate to see women on the palace roof, the tops of their heads showing above the parapet. The palace wives loved to sit in a circle on sunny days, chatting and laughing as they stitched their latest sewing projects. Keeping up with the clothing needs of their growing families had to be squeezed in between daily household chores, caring for grape and olive harvests, and spinning and weaving cloth after sheep shearing. They relished the more relaxed atmosphere of sewing.

Taking the steps to the second floor, Jonathan heard the shouts and giggling of children's voices coming from Michal's room. He reached the floor in time to see Mephibosheth crawling at full speed down the hallway toward the stairs to the rooftop. Jonathan caught up with him on the third step. Scooping him up, Jonathan carried him on to the roof.

"We need to hire a nursemaid for this boy," Jonathan said. "I just found him on the stairs."

"That child!" Deborah put down her sewing. "Hannah and Ahinoam are supposed to be watching the younger ones."

"He obviously escaped."

She stood to retrieve her son.

"I think I'll see if Gera's sister would like a job. Since her husband died and her children are older, she might be available."

Helah readily agreed, grateful for a steady income. She proved to be an attentive nursemaid; the whole family could relax their vigilance.

After a late cold snap, news reached Gibeah the frail prophet Samuel suffered a serious illness. From palace rumors and personal observation of his father's occasional outbursts, Jonathan knew over the years Saul had had serious confrontations with the prophet. How would his father take news of the aged Samuel's death?

After wheat harvest, word came the great spiritual patriarch had died. Saul issued a national call for mourning and set out for Ramathaim with his sons and army. People from all over Israel poured into the town to express their grief and remember Samuel's righteous life and leadership.

Publicly, Saul displayed the correct signs of sorrow. Inwardly, however, he felt relief that Samuel had died before any of his dire predictions occurred. Perhaps the prophet was wrong after all, Saul thought with a glimmer of hope. He was still king, and his kingdom was strong.

Sitting with his army officers in the school of the prophets, Saul recalled the afternoon Samuel had honored him at the feast and the following morning anointed him king. The prophet had made many visits to Gibeah in the early years of Saul's reign. The king reminisced about them until he came to the afternoon Samuel warned him not to make the same mistake that he, Samuel, had made regarding his sons. Saul was proud of his sons. He smiled. They had followed in his ways and all Israel trusted them. His leadership would never be rejected because of his sons. Still, he would miss Samuel. Even when he came down hard on him, the prophet delivered the truth from God.

One morning Jonathan engaged Samuel's son Joel in conversation. After the debacle in Beersheba, he and his brother Abijah had returned to Ramathaim.

"With Saul as king, we no longer had work to do," Joel said. "My biggest regret in life is what a disappointment we had been to Father. The whole nation knew of our sin." He shook his head. "With our reputations destroyed, we were too embarrassed to leave town. After a few years we began to seriously listen to Father's messages and lessons at the school of the prophets. God convicted us and, praise be to Jehovah, He forgave us. Now we are leading the school."

Tears filled Jonathan's eyes as he listened to Joel's testimony. If only his father was as repentant.

Jonathan looked up to see a man headed their way. He appeared to be younger than Ish-Bosheth. Joel introduced his son Heman. With a slim face and prominent ears, their resemblance was striking. Their hair was shorter, like others and unlike Samuel. The prophet had fulfilled the life-long Nazarite vow made by his mother before he was born.

"Heman brings joy to our school with his music," Joel said. "Father prophesied he has a calling from God, a special gift which the Lord will use to bless Israel."

"If anyone heard a call from God, it was the boy Samuel," Jonathan said. He paused to recall the story he heard that long ago afternoon in the courtyard. Neither of the others spoke. They too, no doubt, had wonderful memories.

"May God's favor be upon you, Heman." Jonathan placed his hand on the man's shoulder. "When I was young and inexperienced, your grandfather encouraged me so many times. When he sent Ethan to be our teacher, he changed our lives."

The thirty days of mourning ended. By the time Saul and his men arrived back in Gibeah, the cooler part of the dry season was over. Saul seemed subdued and Jonathan saw no hint of his father's obsession to pursue David. He thanked the Lord, then prayed, "Please, God, help Father remember his promise to David." Nagging doubts nibbled at the edges of his mind and he added, "At least for this year."

Samuel's death left an emptiness in Jonathan's life. He had rarely seen the prophet in the past few years, but he knew the man of God prayed for him daily. That knowledge had served as a source of strength as he coped with his father's unpredictable behavior.

Thinking of Samuel's spiritual influence over Israel, the prince realized he had the same obligation to his people, beginning with his own family. Mephibosheth seemed to grow taller each week and Jonathan tried to spend time daily with his son. Sometimes he carried the boy on his shoulders to the top of the fortress, where he told him of Israel's God as they walked along the rooftop.

"Someday I'll tell you all the stories Grandfather Kish told me," he promised as he pried the toddler's fingers from a fistful of his beard.

~

The cessation of Saul's manhunt held. As the second year approached, David relaxed his guard and returned to his old quarters at Hachilah. News of the death of Samuel brought deep sadness. Samuel had anointed David for God's special service; he did not live to see his prophecy fulfilled. But Samuel did not need to see it completed. One who spoke for God leaves the results with Him. His responsibility was only to deliver the message. Faith saw beyond the present situation. David praised God for this assurance.

David prayed for Jonathan, who he knew grieved for the loss to Israel. Samuel had offered great encouragement to the young prince before his daring attack on the Philistines at Michmash. What Israel needed was not a new king, but more Samuels, David concluded as he stood at the mouth of his cave home.

Spotting a figure in the distance, David hurried down the hillside. Gad's arrival from the funeral might bring a message from his covenant friend.

Gad smiled broadly as he brought greetings from Jonathan and told of Saul's change of heart. He reported on the funeral and the godly memories shared by the thousands who attended.

"You should meet Samuel's grandson Heman," Gad said. "He reminded me of you—great singing voice and blessed by God in leading worship. He has only gotten better in the years since I left to join you."

With the good news of Saul's kinder attitude, David's men passed the dry season moving about openly in the Wilderness of Maon. They frequently attached themselves to shepherds of large flocks, offering them protection from wild animals and marauding bands of desert thieves.

When the rainy season arrived, the men returned to the caves. David often prayed about what he should do next. The example of Joseph waiting for God to act encouraged him when he grew frustrated and impatient. One morning after completion of barley harvest, a young man appeared at the door of David's cave, accompanied by one of David's scouts.

"I am Aaron, nephew of Joel. Uncle and Jonathan have sent me with word that Saul has renewed his hunt for you. Doeg has encouraged him to try again."

David sent scouts to Hebron, who confirmed the warning.

Saul's army, three thousand strong, had descended on the Wilderness of Ziph, where they were camped beside the road that crossed the long hill of Hachilah. David moved farther into the wilderness. Saul soon followed. When David learned of the king's latest campsite, he sent scouts to validate the information.

Climbing an adjacent hill, from behind a large rock he viewed the huge army spread out along the hillside. Near a twisted, gnarled acacia tree, Saul, Abner, Malki-Shua, and Doeg stood talking. The king had planted his spear beneath the tree.

David sneaked down the back side of the hill. Ahimelech the Hittite and Abishai, son of David's older sister Zeruiah, were waiting for him.

"Tonight, I'm going into the camp to Saul," David informed them. "Who will go with me?"

"I will," Abishai said without hesitation.

The three returned to the hideout. As the sun faded from the sky, the two brave men set out for the army camp. Positioning themselves across the ravine from the acacia, they waited until the soldiers settled down. The stars came out to provide light, and the two crept across the narrow valley. During the third watch of the night, they started up the hillside.

Cautiously moving past dozing pack animals, they picked their way between slumbering soldiers. Under the acacia, Saul lay in a deep sleep, Abner and Malki-Shua on either side.

A loud snore punctuated the stillness, causing the two men to tense. Abishai took advantage of the next snore to whisper in David's ear. "God has surely delivered your enemy into your hands. Let me pin him to the ground with the spear. It won't take a second attempt."

David placed a restraining hand on his nephew's arm and shook his head. "No, don't destroy him! Who can lay a hand on the Lord's anointed without being judged guilty?" He removed his hand. "As surely as the Lord lives, the Lord himself will strike him; either by natural death or in battle. But the Lord forbid that I should lay a hand on His anointed. Now go get the spear and water jug that are standing near his head, then let's get out of here."

Without a sound, Abishai crept forward. He pulled the end of the spear from the ground and picked up the water jug. Handing the weapon to his uncle, they started down the hill. A sporadic break in a soldier's steady rhythm of breathing and the occasional snore kept them alert, but David knew God was preventing any of the men from awakening. Crossing the ravine, they climbed to the top of the opposite hill. The muted light of the moon outlined the slumbering encampment.

David cupped his hands around his mouth and shouted, "Abner. Abner, head of Saul's army. Aren't you going to answer?"

The commander arose from his place next to Saul. "Who's calling the king?" he called in a groggy voice.

"You are a real man," David taunted. "There is none like you in Israel. Why didn't you guard the king from harm? Someone could have killed your lord the king. You have done wrong and deserve to die for your negligence in not protecting the Lord's anointed." He paused a moment. "Look around. Where are the king's spear and water jug that you placed near his head?"

Saul, awake by then, called out, "Is that you, David, my son?"

"Yes, it is, O king. Why is my lord hunting down his servant? What have I done wrong, and what is my crime? Now please, my lord the king, listen to the words of his servant," he appealed to reason. "If the Lord has stirred you up against me, then may He accept an offering. But if men have done it, cursed be they before the Lord! Men have driven me from my share in the Lord's inheritance, from my tribe of Judah and the altar of Jehovah, and have said, 'Go, serve other gods.' Please don't make me die far from the Land and the presence of the Lord of Israel," David begged. "The king has come out to look for a flea—like hunting a partridge in the mountains."

Abner's search produced no spear or water jug.

The spear the king had hurled at David three times could minutes ago have been thrust through Saul's heart, ending his ceaseless manhunts, ending his life.

"I've sinned in hunting you," Saul called back. "Come home, David, my son. Today you have valued my life; I promise I will not try to harm you again. I have acted foolishly and made a great mistake."

"I have the king's spear," David answered, holding it aloft. "Let one of your young men come get it. The Lord rewards everyone for his uprightness and faithfulness. The Lord delivered you into my hands tonight, but I would never touch the Lord's anointed. Just as I valued your life today, so may the Lord value my life and deliver me from all trouble."

"Bless you, my son David. I know you will do great things and triumph in the end."

The young man reached David, and Abishai handed the two items to him. "Goodbye, my lord the king," David whispered as he slipped away in the moonlight.

When dawn came, Saul organized his troops and started home. This was the second opportunity David had had to kill him and refused. David wasn't an enemy. Jonathan has tried to tell his father that many times, but he wouldn't listen.

~

As the weeks passed, Jonathan praised God that David had escaped again. One evening both Saul and Malki-Shua were missing at the king's table. Leaving the group, instead of going to his room Jonathan headed to the tower. He felt the urge to pray. Seated in the corner, he closed his eyes and communed with his God.

After several minutes, Jonathan felt a presence nearby, then he heard a sniffle. He opened his eyes to see Malki-Shua seated beside him, an arms-length away.

"I owe you an apology, brother," Malki-Shua said, wiping tears with the back of his hand. "I let loyalty to Father blind me to the truth. I know my cutting words and harsh attitude hurt you. Forgive me."

"You are forgiven." Jonathan reached out to give his brother's arm a quick squeeze.

"Watching Father order the priests slaughtered, I finally admitted to myself that his hatred of David had become an irrational obsession. I knew Ahimelech. He was not disloyal to Father. I bear guilt for their deaths. I should have spoken up."

"Nothing would have stopped Father that day. He refused to see that his enemy is not David, but himself."

"That night on the hillside in the Wilderness of Ziph David could have plunged Father's spear into him—even into me—and crept away. No one would even have known who did it."

Malki-Shua stroked his chin. "David never has tried to steal the Kingdom. By Father's own sin he has forfeited it. He knows David will become king of Israel."

"May God bless and protect David. He deserves the kingdom more than the House of Saul."

They sat in comfortable silence, united in spirit.

The sound of a child's squeal echoed up from the palace below. "I guess I'd better get down to the family," Jonathan said. "They're waiting for evening prayers."

"You need to teach me how to do those."

They rose and Jonathan gave his brother a firm hug. He lifted a prayer of thanksgiving to God. In the days ahead they would surely need each other.

"Oh," Malki-Shua said, giving his brother a wry smile as they walked to the stairs. "And it didn't take a century, after all."

34

ATTACK ON THE GIBEONITES

While Saul's family often tiptoed round him, they had decided long ago that they would not be held captive to his erratic dark moods. When Ahinoam turned fifteen, Malki-Shua and Sarah had betrothed her to Abner's youngest son. Seeing the glow in Hannah's eyes, Jonathan realized the time had come to think about a husband for his firstborn.

When the heat of the dry season eased, Jonathan took Deborah and the children to Bethel to visit her family. Some had not seen Mephibosheth since he began walking. The girls had also grown during the past year.

As they traveled north, accompanied by four bodyguards, Jonathan recalled his own trepidation seventeen years before as he walked up the road to meet his prospective bride. Every day he thanked God for Deborah. The family of Gamaliel was righteous and of excellent character.

Jonathan prayed that Hannah would find a good husband among her mother's relatives. As his father-in-law hosted a big family feast soon after their arrival, Jonathan caught himself eyeing the young men for future prospects.

The next week Jonathan was happy to see Hannah helping with the meals. Palace cooks prepared food for the king's table and planned extra for the royal family. The palace wives helped with some kitchen duties but were not responsible for the dinners. They did do more, however, when many cooks accompanied the army to the battlefield.

Jonathan watched Hannah one afternoon. They would have to change things when they got home. There probably wouldn't be hired cooks for a new bride in Bethel.

The family left for home a month later, Jonathan's heart full of gratitude to the Lord. Meshullam son of Obadiah, Gamaliel's brother, had approached him about a betrothal between his son Elisha and Jonathan's Hannah. Gamaliel assured the prince that the young man was the best in town, one he himself had thought of the moment he saw the maturing Hannah. With arrangements made for a betrothal celebration two months later, the happy family headed home.

One cloud darkened the sunny picture. Hannah would be leaving home forever. Life moved on. Jonathan was already forty-four. What did the years hold for him and his loved ones? With Saul's unhealthy state of mind and spirit, Jonathan could not be sure. The words of Joshua's farewell address came to mind. As the travelers passed the turn-off to Michmash, he quoted the passage to his family as best he could remember:

"Now fear the Lord and serve him faithfully. Get rid of the gods your forefathers worshiped on the other side of the River and in Egypt and serve the Lord. But if serving the Lord seems unacceptable to you, then choose today whom you will serve—the gods your forefathers served beyond the River or the gods of the Amorites, who lived in this land. As for me and my household, we choose to serve the Lord."

"Thank you for choosing the Lord, Father" Hannah said, "And for choosing Elisha. I know God will make him a man of God like you."

Preparations for Hannah's betrothal ceremony enlivened the palace as winter approached. Also, Sarah and Huldah began sewing garments for Ahinoam's wedding, scheduled for the month of Adar, at the close of the latter rains.

Relatives from Bethel and Mizpah arrived to join Hannah's betrothal celebration. Jonathan was proud of his daughter and thankful for the prospective groom. God had been good to him; his heart overflowed with gratitude.

The following week the rains set in. When claps of thunder and flashes of lightening announced a coming downpour, Saul would retreat to his throne room and sit alone in the gathering gloom, the silent bodyguard behind him keeping watch. The family did not disturb him.

On sunnier days Saul resumed his pacing around the fortress wall. Jonathan knew instinctively his father had reneged on his promise to David. He dreaded the coming dry season.

Then word spread that Israel's army hero had fled to Philistia.

Saul was stunned. An Israelite commander taking refuge among the enemy? Shock gave way to fury as he realized David had eluded his grasp. As much as he wanted his son-in-law dead, even he would not invade the coastal plain to face the Philistines' swift chariots and powerful army.

"Son-in-law!" He spat out the word. His lip curled in disgust.

Saul had consented to Michal's marriage, hoping she would aid him in destroying the popular youth. Over the months after

David's flight from Gibeah, the king caught glimpses of her long face and red eyes and decided she had probably been more of a volunteer in assisting her husband's successful escape than she admitted.

"Son-in-law," Saul repeated, with contempt.

Now David was beyond his reach—or was he? He paused in his pacing to look south toward Bethlehem, hometown of the fugitive. A smile replaced his scowl as an idea formed in his mind. Maybe he could reach David after all. He would touch him in the one spot that, next to his life, mattered most. Hurrying down the staircase, he sent a messenger to call Abner.

As Jonathan observed his father's more relaxed disposition during the following weeks, he praised God his prayers for David's safety had been answered. Saul had remembered his promise and decided to honor it. Still, something didn't quite seem right. Was the king glad David had escaped to Philistia? Perhaps having him out of the country was enough.

One evening Michal knocked on their bedroom door after Hannah, Rebekah, and Jemimah had gone to bed in her room. "You will need to make other arrangements for the girls at night," she said, her eyes misting over.

"Are you leaving?" Deborah asked.

"Father is marrying me to Paltiel son of Laish from Gallim." She stared down at the floor.

"But you are a married woman," Jonathan protested, his temper flaring.

"Not in Father's eyes," she said, shaking her head. Jonathan saw her chin tremble as she sought to control her agitation. "He says David has joined the uncircumcised heathen and is fighting for Israel's enemy. He is no longer worthy to be the king's son-in-law."

"It's his fault. He drove David away." The prince's voice rose. "Why must Father use you to fight his battles?" He paused, thinking. Finally, he exhaled. "He knows David will become king and you will be queen. He can't stand to think any of his grandchildren will be part of another kingdom. If he can't keep it, no one else should have it either."

"Do you want to remarry?" Deborah asked, focusing on the more personal side of the matter.

Michal shrugged. "What choice do I have? For over five years I've been a childless 'widow.' Anyway, what Father says is law."

"His law," Jonathan shot back, "but certainly not God's. How can he force you to commit adultery?"

When Michal burst into tears, Jonathan regretted the insinuation. Deborah put her arms around her distraught sister-in-law, and Jonathan walked over to embrace them both.

"Oh, dear Lord," he groaned, "why must Father hate a man who loves You with all his heart?"

"Because the king doesn't," a Voice inside his soul replied, the answer painfully true. Saul's commitment to God conveniently began outside the border of his own selfish ambition. "Please, God, don't let him take Michal from us," Jonathan prayed silently. David would be crushed to hear the news. The words had barely formed in his mind when a sinking feeling overwhelmed him. He bit his lower lip. So that was why Father was so happy. He had finally found a way to defeat his enemy. Why didn't Jonathan ever learn? Father was only cheerful when he was up to no good.

The next morning Jonathan approached Saul in the throne room and asked why he was giving Michal to another man.

"David has removed himself from the Congregation of Israel. He has joined himself to worshipers of Dagon and Baal."

"With his own countrymen trying to kill him, where else is he supposed to go? I dare say you would do the same thing."

"You are hopelessly deceived, my son. Nothing will ever convince you of the danger of David, will it?"

"No." Turning, Jonathan strode angrily out of the room.

~

The crops grew taller, the rain clouds disappeared from the sky, and the days became warm. Ahinoam's wedding turned into a big event. Even Saul joined the festivities. Abner couldn't stop smiling, thrilled to see his son become part of the royal family.

With the wedding over, the king held Michal's betrothal ceremony. He scheduled her marriage to Paltiel for the following spring. The satisfaction of inflicting punishment on David didn't last long, however.

Saul's bouts of depression lengthened. On the rare evenings when he had enough appetite to eat, he joined the men in the dining room. Seated across from his firstborn, his eyes were drawn to the scar on Jonathan's left wrist like the tongue to a loose tooth. He came to despise the word covenant.

Awaking long before daybreak, Saul spent many early mornings pacing on the fortress wall. One dawn he stood on the northwest tower looking toward Gibeon, three miles away. The town had been assigned to the Levites by Joshua during the Land apportionment to the Children of Israel. Levites had been given cities throughout the tribes, rather than a specific territory.

As the sun rose behind Saul, a long-forgotten scene surfaced from his memory, a scene from the courtyard of the old house down in the town. He had listened as Father Kish told little Jonathan the story of the Gibeonites' deception of Joshua during the conquest of Canaan. The local Hivite tribe had tricked the Israelite leaders into believing they were from a far distance, and the two made a covenant, promising mutual protection. Later the truth came out. "Let that be a lesson," Saul could hear himself warning the six-year-old as the glow of firelight illuminated his small face. "Never make a covenant with the enemy."

"But Jonathan did!" the king exclaimed aloud, breaking the morning stillness. "David is more dangerous than those sneaky Gibeonites who today live among us in safety, never once punished for their treachery." Taking one last look to the northwest, he nodded slowly, then turned toward the stairs.

Jonathan entered the courtyard mid-morning in time to see Abner mobilizing the army. "Are the Philistines attacking in the Shephelah?" Jonathan said. Malki-Shua stepped closer to listen.

"I don't know."

Jonathan frowned. "So where are you headed?"

"On a secret mission for the king."

Saul came over and the two men walked out the gate, followed by royal bodyguards and armor-bearers. When the battalion of soldiers moved down the hillside, Jonathan went up to the fortress wall to watch them march north. After they were out of sight, he returned to the courtyard.

Staying home—a constant reminder of being shut out from his father's confidence—weighed heavily on Jonathan so, finding Abinadab, he suggested they go shoot arrows. Malki-Shua's son Kish tagged along to watch.

As the afternoon progressed, Jonathan prayed that God would protect Israel's army and grant them victory. The sun began to set as he and his brothers gathered in the dining room for supper. Hearing voices in the courtyard, the men hurried to the door in time to see the returning soldiers pour through the fortress gateway. The princes went to welcome them.

Jonathan looked for Asshur and Jadon, his two reliable sources for information. A gut-wrenching account spilled from the grim-faced young men.

The army had marched to the plain surrounding the free-standing hill of Gibeon. Saul had called a halt and delivered his military order. "Attack the Gibeonites. Kill any who are descendants of the original pagan tribe." Noticing the horrified look of the soldiers, Saul explained, "We can no longer accept the heathen living among us as equals. Israel must be separate and pure. The kingdom will never be strong if we tolerate the enemy within."

Asshur told how the soldiers looked out across the plain, where unsuspecting men and laden donkeys moved across the ripe wheat fields. Sickles flashed in the sunlight. Voices called back and forth as workers talked and laughed together. At the threshing floor, teams of oxen made their endless circuits over the stone surface while, nearby, women sifted the winnowed grain. A perfect picture of peace. A peace about to be shattered.

The soldiers had engaged in many battles against their enemies. They had pursued David's band of armed dissidents. But they had never assaulted unarmed civilians in their home territory.

"Attack or be attacked," Saul shouted as he started for the nearest harvesters. The perplexed soldiers followed, capturing the workers and questioning them about their lineage. Others invaded the town, doing the same.

By mid-afternoon Amariah, Saul's current armor-bearer, blew the trumpet. The soldiers gathered on the plain for their homeward march. Some had never heard of Joshua's covenant with the Gibeonites, but even they questioned the unreasonable attack on their peaceful neighbors. More and more, Saul was becoming a very unstable leader.

When Asshur concluded his report, Jonathan followed his father into the throne room. "What have you done?" Jonathan demanded, his face flushed. "You know Israel made a covenant with the Gibeonites."

Saul spun around to face his firstborn. "Tell me about covenants, since you are such an expert in making them."

Jonathan's jaw dropped and his shoulders sagged. Surely his father would not take revenge on the defenseless Gibeonites because of his own covenant with David. A stab from Saul's spear could not have hurt more.

"Father, a curse is on the House of Saul and on Israel for

breaking a covenant made before the Lord." Jonathan struggled to control his anger.

Saul took a step toward his son, stopping inches from him. "Samuel is dead. Stop trying to take his place." He sneered, shaking his finger in warning. "When I need a prophet, I'll find one on my own. Now get out."

Jonathan turned and fled from the room, thankful his father had no weapon in his hand. Bounding up the fortress staircase to the rooftop, he sank to the floor in a corner of the southwest tower, his private sanctuary in time of crisis.

If there had been any uncertainty why God had rejected Saul's kingship, this unprovoked slaughter removed any shred of doubt.

Grape and olive harvests helped take Jonathan's mind off the tragic attack on the Gibeonites. Occasionally Jonathan invited Malki-Shua and Ish-Bosheth to join him for prayer up in the fortress tower evenings after supper and their bond of kinship grew strong. Jonathan prayed for peace and the ability to forgive his father. He vowed to not let his attitude towards his father cloud the preparations for Hannah's wedding.

They celebrated the wedding in Bethel just before the early rains. Jonathan's family and many members of Saul's household made the trip to attend the ceremony and festivities. The king stayed home, his state of mind degenerating further with each passing month.

Bedding down with his family in Gamaliel's upper room, Jonathan lay awake long after the others had gone to sleep. Tonight, for the first time, he realized he had joined the older generation. He glanced over at Deborah, her face soft and beautiful in the lamplight. Soon she would be a grandmother. It hardly seemed possible. One by one, Jonathan prayed for his wife and children. Last of all, he asked God to protect and lead David.

Would he ever be able to share a family celebration with his covenant friend?

The days of preparation were busy as the women scurried around cooking, washing clothes, making last-minute adjustments to Hannah's gown, and gathering and borrowing jewelry to bedeck the bride. Rebekah and Jemimah joined their cousins in picking what foliage they could find near the village spring, then they carefully wove Hannah's bridal crown.

The big evening finally arrived. Jonathan waited with the other men out in the courtyard while the women congregated in Gamaliel and Eve's bedroom to dress the bride. The murmur of voices inside was punctuated at times with a squeal of delight—probably from Jemimah.

The prince could envision Deborah and her sisters dressing the bride in her new white woolen tunic and gown, the young girls standing behind them, watching closely. Rebekah's eyes would be sparkling. It wouldn't be long before she was a bride too. Where did the years go? Sarah, who loved to comb the girls' hair, probably would claim the privilege of preparing her niece's dark hair and positioning it on her shoulders. Grandmother Eve would dab a few drops of her precious perfume on Hannah's neck and arms. Deborah would add the jewels, then place the leafy crown on her daughter's head. When everything was ready, Eve would fasten the veil over the bride's face.

"Everything is prepared."

The call came sooner than Jonathan had anticipated. The men stepped into the room to pray a blessing on Hannah as she began a new life. Gamaliel's voice had hardly ceased when Jonathan heard the noisy procession coming up the street. The groom and his friends had arrived.

A sudden urge to turn back time gripped Jonathan. He wasn't ready to give his firstborn away. The glow in Hannah's eyes halted his mental protest, however. Smiling down at her, he asked, "Are you ready?"

She nodded, and he took her hand as they moved toward the door.

The sound of flutes, the strum of kinnors, and the metallic jingle of tambourines nearly drowned out the cheers of the crowd of friends and family who filled the street in front of the house. Gamaliel opened the gate, and the light of burning torches and saucer lamps bathed the celebrants in a yellow glow.

Elisha, dressed in a fine new indigo tunic and cloak, stood surrounded by his cousins and boyhood friends. His brother Eber helped Hannah onto a litter. The men hoisted her for the noisy ride through the streets to the home of Elisha's father. Rebekah, Jemimah, and the cousins took their places behind the litter, followed by Jonathan and his family.

The wedding *huppah* sat in the middle of Meshullam's court-yard. Green foliage decorated the sides of its roof. Friends escorted the couple to the two chairs that awaited them under the canopy. Neighbors and family members found seats on mats. When the celebration got underway, Jonathan took his turn pronouncing the blessing on the young couple.

"Our sister, may you be the mother
of thousands upon thousands;
may your children possess
the gates of their enemies."

The people joined in quoting the ancient benediction. The festivities brought back vivid memories to Jonathan of his own wedding seventeen years before.

At the end of the week-long celebration the people from Gibeah started home. Planting would soon begin, and work awaited them.

The winter months brought the usual rounds of depression to the king. He did manage to rouse himself to attend Michal's wedding, but from his expressionless face Jonathan knew the original thrill had disappeared long ago.

It was the most difficult celebration the prince had ever attended, but for the sake of his little sister he tried to smile as he joined in the festivities. Standing on the sideline, he thanked God for creating him a man, with the right to make decisions regarding his life.

Back home, as the days passed, little Mephibosheth became the joy of Jonathan's life. He spent hours telling his son stories of God's help to Israel's patriarchs and leaders—Abraham, Jacob, Moses, Joshua, Gideon, and, of course, Joseph, the man who waited for God to act.

Jonathan longed to tell him of his heroic uncle David, no longer a member of the family. But Jonathan feared the boy might slip and mention something in front of his grandfather, provoking an unpredictable outburst and possibly turning the king against his grandson.

One afternoon Jonathan ushered Mephibosheth down the hill and across the fields to Ezel. Sitting on one of the lower rocks, he told the five-year-old how he had loved to play on the stone formation with his young friends.

"It was our secret hideout," he whispered, showing him the hollowed-out spot on the south. Someday he would tell his son that he and David made a covenant there. "This is a special place to me," he added, "one I will always remember."

Sensing his father's spirit, Mephibosheth placed his small hand in Jonathan's and silently surveyed the large rock. "God created it just for you, didn't He?"

"God has done so much for me. This is just one symbol of His love." Jonathan picked the boy up and hugged him tightly. Swallowing the lump in his throat, he said, "You are another."

35

THE WITCH OF ENDOR

Deprived of his prey, the king felt like a lost sheep wandering aimlessly in a barren wilderness, without friend or purpose. Why did David run off to Philistia? All Saul cared about was the kingdom. David proved to be the biggest threat to his sovereignty. Now he was gone. What other goal was there to pursue?

Leaning down from the throne, Saul stooped to adjust his sandal strap. In the process, his hand brushed against the mend in the hem of his robe. He shook his hand, as if to rid it of unwanted water. "Why didn't I throw this thing away after Huldah made me the new one?' he said. "Do I have to be constantly reminded of that wicked scoundrel?" The bodyguard standing behind him remained silent.

A knock on the door interrupted his soliloquy. He ignored it. The knock persisted, but he did not move. Minutes later the door opened, and Abner walked in. He bowed before the monarch.

"O king, we have just received bad news. Scouts report that Achish and the other lords of the Philistines are moving up the coast."

Saul sighed wearily, not looking up. "Call the army to defend Israel," he replied, his voice flat.

"There is more. They have chariots with them. They are now on the Plain of Sharon. Scouts say a forward party has reached the pass. They are surely headed for the Plain of Jezreel."

Saul's head raised quickly. "Jezreel? Surely not."

"I'm afraid so. If we have any hope of withstanding them, we must issue a general call-up of all able-bodied men."

"But Jezreel is open country," Saul protested. "Their chariots will have free range."

"I didn't choose their destination, Your Honor," the commander said. Abner paused to wait for orders, but the king did not speak. "I'll go ahead and send out a call-up. Prepare for battle." Abner bowed and strode out of the room.

Saul slumped in his throne, and the words of Samuel echoed through his mind: "Because you have disdained the word of the Lord, he has rejected you as Israel's king." Saul stared at the floor, his mind a blank.

Jonathan found him there an hour later. "Father, the troops are ready to move."

"Go without me."

"The army will not march without their leader." The prince walked over to the throne. "You are not sending a battalion to quell a border raid. This is all-out war, Father." He paused. "Remember, the House of Kish aren't quitters. Now, get up." He grasped his father's elbow. "Let's go."

The king reluctantly got to his feet. Jonathan led him to the door and the two walked out into the courtyard. The bodyguard grabbed the king's spear from its holder and followed.

The women and children stood beside the palace wall, somber-faced and teary-eyed. The bodyguards were gathered near the fortress gate. The royal armor-bearers finished emptying the armory as they piled weapons, helmets, and armor into carts.

Malki-Shua, Abner, and Abinadab waited alone in the center of the courtyard.

The king eyed the only child Huldah had borne him. "You can't go, Abinadab."

"I'm twenty now, Father."

A frown creased Saul's brow. "Are you sure?"

"Yes," Abinadab said with a nod.

Confused, Saul hadn't noticed Abinadab maturing.

The five men walked to the gate and Amariah stepped in front of the king. The other bodyguards and armor-bearers followed them out. The front line of soldiers stood in companies with their captains near the tamarisk tree. The rest of the standing army spread out down the hill. To the side, loaded pack donkeys waited to bring up the rear. Saul felt relieved to see Doeg in charge of the animals. Israel needed all the men they could muster.

As the procession marched down the hillside, children ran out to watch. Women hurried from their houses to call out blessings on the passing men. Old men paused to pray.

By the time the troops left Gibeah, the sun stood overhead. When they reached Bethel, eight miles to the north, they set up camp in the valley below town. Jonathan wished he could go see Hannah and Elisha, but he knew it would be inappropriate to indulge in a selfish visit. None of the other men had been able to go home to tell their families goodbye. Exemption from military service during the first year of marriage prohibited Elisha from joining them. Jonathan looked up at the town. By this time next year perhaps Hannah would have presented him with his first grandchild.

At dawn the army broke camp. Jonathan insisted that his father ride a donkey. After covering the twenty-two miles to Shechem by evening, Saul was glad he had. Along the way, bands of men from the towns of Ephraim and Manasseh joined them. Scouts from

Jezreel met the king with a report the Philistines had set up camp at Shunem, west of the Hill of Moreh.

The next morning the Israelites pressed on to En-gannim, eighteen miles farther north. Men from the southern territories of Judah and Simeon and the tribes across the Jordan—Gad, Reuben, and Manasseh—caught up with them by nightfall.

As the troops marched through the valleys, Jonathan knew why the Philistines had decided to launch their assault on the northern plain. The Shephelah formed a natural barrier between coastal Philistia and the central mountain range of Israel. Valleys separated the mountains from the contested foothills. Gaining the latter did not assure victory over Israel. North of Philistia, the Tjekker held the Plain of Sharon. The foothills of Ephraim and Manasseh, however, were connected to the central mountains behind them by long, sloping ridges. Gaining them was a first step in conquering the Land.

Unlike the territories of Judah and Benjamin, these mountains had broader valleys and easier passes—more vulnerable to attack. Nearly two hundred years before, the Midianites chose the Valley of Jezreel to launch their assault on Israel. Only God's intervention on behalf of His People had given Gideon's army a victory.

Now the Philistines were joining forces with their distant relatives, the Tjekker and the Sea People living in Beth-shan, to invade Israel, dividing the northern tribes beyond the Plain of Jezreel from those of the southern mountains. The large open valley would allow chariots to move about unhindered. Those swift-moving firing platforms were perfect for providing quick help to hard-pressed battlefield hot spots.

Most painful of all, Jonathan realized Israel's lack of spiritual leadership, not geography, had encouraged the Philistine aggression. Saul's depression, his endless pursuit of his imaginary enemy —David, his slaughter of the priests of Nob and the Gibeonites, and Samuel's death had left him a dispirited man, engulfed in self-pity and saturated with hatred. Wrapped up in himself, he had lost concern for his people. The Philistines were quick to grasp this fact and take advantage of Israel's weakened condition.

Covering the last seven miles from En-gannim to Jezreel on the fourth day, the army passed through the southern branch of the Plain of Jezreel. The broad valley paralleled Mount Gilboa to the east. The mountain's unpretentious limestone peaks ranged over eight miles. It ran from north-northwest to south-southeast, where its eastern slopes fell off abruptly to the Jordan River area. The western slopes facing the army, Jonathan noticed, had gradual inclines.

The last leg of the journey took three hours, and the Israelites reached Jezreel by late morning. Men from the tribes of Zebulun, Issachar, Dan, Asher, and Naphtali were there to greet them. Jonathan recognized Lamech among the Danites and went over to give him a warm embrace.

The advance patrol had selected a camp site near the town of Jezreel. As the armor-bearers and bodyguards began unloading the pack animals and carts, Jonathan looked out over the long triangular Plain of Jezreel, which ran from the seaside Carmel Mountain Range on the west to the Jordan River on the east. Twenty-four miles inland the plain's elevation dropped, and it divided.

The prince's only trip to the area had been twenty years before on his way to fight the king of Zobah. Then, as today, the army had traveled from En-gannim up the southern branch of the plain. The northern fork ran between Mount Tabor and the Hill of Moreh. The middle branch, between Moreh and Gilboa, formed the Valley of Jezreel, which descended from Jezreel on the west to Beth-shan eleven miles to the east.

The rugged heights rose above the soldiers as they set up camp between Jezreel, which sat on a spur of Mount Gilboa, and the Well of Harod to the east. A spring gushed from under the cliffs in a rocky cave and formed the pool fifteen feet wide and two feet deep. The clear, cold water looked inviting. The deep streambed and the soft banks made a formidable ditch in front of the steep mountainside. Reeds and scrub lined the stream, making an ideal hideout for an ambush.

Jonathan walked along the watercourse, thinking of Gideon's men, who were once tested beside that very stream. "God help us to be as successful," he prayed.

After a brief rest upon arriving, Saul planted his spear outside his tent. Then he convened a war strategy session with his commanders and captains to discuss tomorrow's inevitable battle. When they dispersed an hour later, he went to his tent. After a few minutes, he called Abner and his armor-bearer Amariah to accompany him up Gilboa to study the Philistine position.

Climbing high enough to gain a good view, the king paused to catch his breath as he turned to look across the long plain to Mount Carmel, looming on the western horizon. His eyes swept along the distant brown wall of hills that marked the territory of Issachar to the north. Below the hills the River Kishon flowed through the plain, watering the red and black soil. Saul's gaze came at last to the Hill of Moreh. Below the western slope near Shunem, five miles away, the enormous Philistine army camp stretched out over the plain, the goats-hair tents blending into a sea of black.

Saul's heart sank; dizziness threatened to engulf him. Turning to Abner, he said, "Do you think they will send out a giant to challenge one of our men?"

"I don't think so."

"David could have helped us had he not turned traitor," Saul said. Abner did not respond. The king struggled to keep the panic from his voice. "What will we do?"

"Pray."

"That's useless." Saul wrung his hands. "God does not answer me. He has sent no dream, the Urim is lost, and no prophet steps forward to advise me. The only one who might help is Samuel."

"Samuel is dead."

"I know."

The three men stood for several minutes on the hillside, the brown grass beneath their feet and the hot sun overhead. Suddenly Saul had an inspiration. He turned to his cousin.

"Let's go. I think I may know how to get a message from the Lord, after all."

Amariah led the way down the hill to camp.

Back at the tent, Saul sent his armor-bearer to call Doeg, to whom he whispered a secret message. The Edomite hurried to Jezreel. Waiting, Saul felt a touch of the old enthusiasm for battle. He lay down to relax and was soon asleep.

Doeg returned later in the afternoon with Hanan, a resident of Jezreel, and they entered Saul's tent. Amariah stood at the tent flap guarding the royal shelter, within earshot of the low conversation. Saul finally called him in and explained his plan. The man from Jezreel knew a sorceress living in Endor. The three men would go there before sunset.

The four moved out, walking to the stream. Hidden by the reeds, Saul removed his royal robe and put on the well-worn tunic and cloak Doeg pulled from a grain sack. The king ordered Amariah to wait until complete darkness provided cover, then carry his robe back to the headquarters tent in the sack.

While the soldiers began gathering around the campfires for supper, the three headed along the stream. Once they reached beyond the eastern perimeter of the camp, they slipped away.

Endor lay across the Valley of Jezreel on the north side of the Hill of Moreh. Since the Philistines were camped on the western end of the mount, the men planned to skirt the eastern side, a journey of eight miles. Three hours later, they watched the sun sink beneath the horizon. They approached the village, silhouetted in the gathering darkness, just as the first star twinkled overhead.

Nearing the edge of Endor, Hanan left the king and chief shepherd under an oak tree and approached the closest house. Return-ing, he led the way past several buildings to a cave. In a shallow pit near the entrance, coals from a dying cooking fire glowed in the darkness. A set of millstones lay beside it, traces of ground barley dusting the large lower stone. Hanan cleared his throat and called a greeting.

A wisp of a woman appeared at the mouth of the cave with a saucer lamp in her hand. The light, flickering in the evening breeze, engraved the age-lines deeper in her face and revealed a strand of gray hair that had escaped her headscarf.

"What may I do for you?" she said to Doeg.

Saul was thankful she did not recognize any of them. He stepped in front of the Edomite. "Please consult a spirit for me and bring up the one I name."

The sorceress gasped and her hand flew to her chest in horri-fied reaction. She drew back. "Surely you know King Saul's decree. He has cut off the mediums and spiritists from the Land. Why do you want to set a trap for my life and bring about my death?"

"This is a secret," Saul assured her in a low voice. "As surely as the Lord lives, I promise you will not suffer for giving me assistance."

The sorceress hesitated as her piercing gaze shifted from one face to another. "All right, come in." She stepped aside and Saul and Doeg entered.

A curtain hung across the sparsely furnished cave, partitioning it into two rooms. The sorceress pointed to a pile of cushions. When the men were seated, she knelt before Saul. "Whom do you want me to bring up?"

"The prophet Samuel."

Her eyebrows raised, but she said nothing. She picked up a small clay cup and stepped outside. Returning with coals from the fire, she set it on a low table beside the wall. From behind the curtain, she retrieved a tiny jug. Kneeling before the table, she shook a small amount of powder into a saucer, then let a coal drop onto the incense. A cloud of scented smoke billowed up to fill the air, and she began mumbling a chant. Her voice rose as she continued the incantation. Suddenly she let out a spine-chilling shriek, causing the men to jump.

She whirled around to face the king, her eyes full of terror, her boney index finger pointed at him. "You have deceived me," she screeched. "You are King Saul."

He lifted his hand to reassure her. "I told you not to be afraid. What did you see?"

"I saw a spirit coming up from the ground."

"What does it look like?"

"It is an old man wearing a robe."

"Samuel," Saul whispered in relief. Rising from the couch, he bowed with his face to the cave floor.

"Why did you disturb me, bringing me back like this?" a voice asked the king.

"I am in great distress," Saul said. "The Philistines are warring against me. God has departed from me. He will not answer me, either by prophets or by dreams. So, I've called on you. Please tell me what I should do."

"Why do you seek advice from me, since the Lord has departed from you and become your enemy?" Samuel asked sternly. "The Lord has done what he prophesied through me. As you tore my cloak at Gilgal, the Lord has torn the kingdom out of your hands and given it to your neighbor—to David."

Saul groaned at the thought of his rival finally achieving kingship. He pounded the ground with his fist.

"Because you refused to carry out the Lord's fierce wrath against the Amalekites, the Lord has done this to you," the voice of Samuel continued. "Tomorrow the Lord will hand over both Israel and you to the Philistines. You and your sons will join me in death. The Lord will also deliver the army of Israel to the Philistines."

Doeg only heard Saul's part of the conversation. He saw Saul's body slump forward full length on the dirt floor and lie motionless. Had the message caused Saul's heart to fail? Dropping down beside the inert monarch, he lifted a limp hand. The king turned to his chief shepherd and, in the lamplight, Doeg saw the stark fear in Saul's eyes.

"Let me help you up."

"I don't have strength to move," the king muttered.

"You haven't eaten all day, have you?"

The king shook his head ever so slightly.

The sorceress, perceiving the spirit had departed, turned to the king. Overhearing the question, she knelt beside Saul. "Look, I've obeyed you, taking my life in my hands by doing what you asked. Now, please listen to your servant and let me fix you some food so you will have enough strength to get back to camp."

Saul refused, but at Doeg's insistence he finally consented. The woman hurried out to kill a fatted calf and make bread. Saul stretched out on the cushions and stared at the cave ceiling. Two hours later, the woman served the food.

Saul and his assistants thanked her for her help and, giving her a piece of silver, started back to Jezreel. Watching the king stumble along, the shepherd wished he had brought a donkey to carry his master back to camp. But that would have raised too many questions.

Whatever Samuel told Saul, Doeg knew it could not be good.

3 6

MOUNT GILBOA

Arriving at the Jezreel camp site at the end of their march, Saul set up his headquarters and took a short rest. Then he convened a war strategy session with his commanders and captains. Afterward, he returned to his tent.

Jonathan headed to the encampment. Making his way from company to company, he encouraged the soldiers to trust in God's help for the upcoming conflict. Without a priest to offer the sacrifice and pronounce the blessing, it was the least he could do. Coming across Joel and his nephew, Jonathan stopped to visit. Seeing his former armor-bearer renewed his courage as he recalled their first confrontation with the Philistines at Michmash.

The sun dropped toward the Carmel Mountain Range as he returned to the tents serving as camp headquarters. "Where is Father?" he asked Malki-Shua.

"I don't know." His brother looked quickly around the tents, then out over the crowd of milling soldiers. "I haven't seen him since the meeting this afternoon."

The cook brought food and, after waiting awhile, the two men decided to eat. Coming from the encampment a few minutes later,

Abinadab joined them. Jonathan could sense the apprehension in his little brother as he watched Abinadab pick at the bread, lentils, and meat.

"I remember my first battle," Jonathan said, hoping to ease the tension. By the time he finished retelling the encounter, Abinadab's somber face had a smile; the food bowls and bread-basket were empty.

Malki-Shua scooted back from the dishes. "If there are no more preparations to make, I think I'll go to bed."

"Before we turn in, why don't we pray for God's blessing and protection?" Jonathan said. Lifting his eyes to the heavens, he led in prayer, voicing his confidence in the Mighty God of Israel. The last streaks of twilight were fading from the western sky when the two brothers, weary from nearly four days of marching, made their way into the tent next to their father's.

Jonathan remained seated as night settled over the Plain of Jezreel. Where would he be tomorrow night when the sun set? His heart beat a little faster as he contemplated the uncertainty. Behind him the rugged northern shoulder of Mount Gilboa loomed protectively into the blue-black darkness. The subdued voices of the army camp seemed to pause a moment, and Jonathan caught the faint gurgle of water rushing from the nearby mountain spring. Around their tents trained Israelite soldiers and inexperienced village volunteers huddled in small groups discussing the enemy, comparing weapons, trying to hide their fear. The smell of cooked lentils and baked unleavened bread wafted through the camp, mingling with the haze of campfire smoke that hung over the valley.

Where was Father? The crown prince glanced around, still perplexed that King Saul hadn't appeared for supper. *So unlike him.* He reached his hand up to rub it back and forth across his eyebrow. Shifting his weight, he sought a more comfortable position on the clumps of grass. He knew he must talk to the king about any final instructions before he went to sleep.

The vast Philistine army spread out across the valley five miles away. Below the western slope of the Hill of Moreh their commanders were, no doubt, reviewing last-minute preparations for tomorrow's assault. Armed with iron swords and spears, protected by metal breastplates and shields, and equipped with swift horse-drawn chariots, they would sleep tonight with confidence.

The Philistines. Jonathan raised his eyes to the dark heavens. He thanked God this was not his first encounter with the powerful enemy. One by one, he recalled battles during the past twenty-six years in which the Lord Jehovah helped Israel face—and defeat—the coastal warriors. All he had ever wanted to do with his life was keep God's Chosen People free from the pagan Philistines. An evening breeze had come up, clearing away some of the smoke, and he took a deep breath. Was that desire perhaps a call from God, after all—like the boy Samuel's?

The unbidden idea startled, but intrigued, him. Snatches of an early childhood conversation teased at his thoughts. He closed his eyes as he tried to coax from his memory details of a long-ago day back in Gibeah. A day that had changed his family forever—the day his father went searching for the lost donkeys.

Over the next hour Jonathan relived the highlights of his life. While recalling the morning he took little Mephibosheth down to Ezel, Jonathan saw movement in front of Saul's tent out of the corner of his eye. He rose and hurried over to talk to his father. The man stepped into the starlight, and Jonathan recognized Amariah, instead. Disappointed, he greeted the armor-bearer.

"Has the king returned?"

"Not to my knowledge."

"Do you know where he is?"

"Do you need him for something?" Amariah lifted the tent flap and peered inside. "He doesn't seem to be here."

"You have no idea where he went?" The prince tried to

suppress his annoyance. "The Philistines are sure to attack tomorrow. I want to discuss any final changes in our battle strategy."

"Why don't you have a seat and wait."

Jonathan sat down, cross-legged, in front of the king's tent. Amariah joined him. "Why aren't you with Father?" Jonathan said.

"The king told me to wait for him at his tent."

"What time was that?"

"Just before sunset."

"I didn't see him among the troops," Jonathan said slowly. "I can't understand him disappearing the night before battle. The one thing he taught me was to get adequate sleep before a tough flight. He's too old for combat, anyway. He needs his rest."

"That's what he is hoping to find."

"What do you mean?"

Amariah did not respond, and Jonathan realized he had divulged more than he intended. He could hear Amariah nervously scraping his sandal back and forth across the ground. "So, you do know where Father is," Jonathan said, his voice low and accusing.

"Yes." The armor-bearer did not turn toward him.

"Has he left camp?" Jonathan couldn't believe his father would do that—tonight, of all nights.

"Yes," Amariah said, the monosyllable barely a whisper.

Jonathan moved closer. "Father went somewhere looking for rest?" In the starlight he could see Amariah nod. "Where?" he demanded, exasperated as the uncommunicative soldier.

"Not sleep," Amariah reluctantly replied. "But rest in here." He placed his hand over his heart. "Since Samuel's death, the king says he has no one to advise him. God does not answer him anymore."

"So where did he go to find guidance tonight?" Since the slaughter of Ahimelech and his family, there were no priests serving at a sanctuary.

"To Endor."

"Endor? There's a prophet living there?"

Amariah paused so long Jonathan thought he was not going to answer. "A witch," he finally said.

"A witch!" The words exploded from the prince as a loud hiss. "I thought Father eradicated witches from the Land thirty years ago. Why does he want to consult a sorceress?" He moaned. "God will never give us victory if we rely on the forces of evil."

"He doesn't want to consult the forces of evil," the armor-bearer replied, defending his master. "Samuel was the one man who wasn't afraid to speak for God. The king plans to ask the witch to bring up Samuel from the dead."

Jonathan gasped, then he sat in dazed silence, unable to move. "I . . . I can't believe Father would do such a wicked thing," he finally said, more to himself than to Amariah. "He knows what the Law of Moses says about consulting the dead. How could he betray the army of the One True God like this?"

"He is desperate. In all the years I've served the king, I've never seen terror in his eyes before. As we stood on the heights of Gilboa, looking out over the huge Philistine camp at Shunem, he trembled with fear. When we came down, he sent someone looking for a witch. The messenger returned before sunset with a man from Jezreel who knew of a sorceress at Endor."

"Father fears the army of the Philistines more than the wrath of God," Jonathan observed, his voice flat with dejection. "How will a witch agree to help the king, when she knows it is illegal for her to exist in Israel? Father is the one who drove them from the Land."

"Saul disguised himself in peasant clothes and carried no weapons. He went without a retinue, accompanied only by two men."

"One of them Doeg, no doubt."

Amariah nodded. Jonathan rued the day he first laid eyes on the Edomite. Neither spoke for a moment. Jonathan sniffed, not caring if the armor-bearer knew he was crying.

"The king only wanted to request God's help," Amariah said,

trying to emphasize Saul's anguish. "He only wants to save the kingdom."

Jonathan exhaled slowly, then stood and walked back to his tent. It's too late for that, he thought as he sat down to sort out his troubled thoughts in solitude.

The camp grew quiet as the apprehensive soldiers bedded down under the open sky, their weapons within reach.

Jonathan's thoughts turned to Deborah and the children. He praised God he had time to gather them together to pray before his departure. One by one he lifted them to the Lord in prayer. "God, keep them in Your care until I return home," he prayed in closing. A lump caught in his throat. "If I return home." He had never been seriously injured in battle, but he did not take life for granted. He had never lost a battle, but he did not take victory for granted. "Lord, my life is in Your hands."

And Father's. His mind resisted that unwelcome idea.

Still, Jonathan recalled the night twenty-six years ago when he lay beneath the stars near Aijalon. An hour before, Saul had wanted to kill him for breaking a vow he knew nothing about. For the first time Jonathan had doubted his father. Tonight, the memory remained as vivid as the Philistine encampment across the valley near Shunem.

He recalled the day his father spared the life of the pagan ruler Agag in direct disobedience to God's command through the prophet Samuel. The king erected a monument to himself at Carmel in Judah to commemorate his victory over the Amalekites. In reality, the monument commemorated his pride and independence—a record of his disobedience etched on stone.

Jonathan trembled as he thought of the afternoon Saul threw a spear at Israel's young hero, David. At first, he believed his father was merely jealous of the innocent praise of the women during the victory celebration. Later he came to realize David symbolized God's rejection of Saul. The king's confidence in Jonathan was tainted by his fellowship with Goliath's slayer. Hatred and vindictiveness had insidiously alienated the king from those he needed most.

Tears came to the prince's eyes as he relived the awful day his father called Ahimelech and eighty-four other priests of Nob to the fortress and ordered Doeg to execute them for unwittingly assisting his enemy, David. Tough soldier that he was, he had turned aside to vomit, unable to endure the repulsive sight of holy blood that stained the hilltop. From that afternoon until now, he had never walked over that hallowed spot of ground near the tamarisk tree. Watching the priests' bodies being carried to the hillside tombs near Gibeah, he had thought it couldn't get worse. Tonight, he knew better.

Unable to control his deep anguish, Jonathan let the tears flow. Pride, jealousy, rage, and murder were terrible sins. Disobedience to God led to greater disobedience. But tonight, Father had sold his soul to evil. What hope was there for Israel's army? for the kingdom? for himself? He brushed the tears from his cheeks. "Why, God, why?" his heart cried out. "I tried so often to warn Father, but he would not listen."

Jonathan looked up. Through tear-filled eyes the sky looked black and cold, the stars a faint blur. He had never felt so completely alone in his life. In his grief he longed for just one person to whom he could pour out his feelings of hopelessness and grief, one person who would share his pain.

He wished he were a boy again, sitting before his teacher in the courtyard corner at the old house in Gibeah. So many times, throughout the past thirty years, the Law he had memorized and truths Ethan taught had been guiding lights in dark days. Tonight, Ethan would have listened and understood, but Ethan was back home in his village, his body wracked with pain, unable to walk.

Jonathan thought of the man who first taught him that God was personal and real—the boy who one night in the Tabernacle heard God call his name, the youth who became Israel's spiritual leader, the old prophet who embraced a young prince and told him

to be strong in the Lord as he faced the pagan Philistines. Tonight, Samuel would have encouraged him to trust God, but Samuel was dead.

Jonathan drew his knees up under his chin, hugging them to him as he buried his face against them. There was one living person whose comfort he ached for most, but years ago his father had driven David away, hunting him down like a rogue bull. Every day Jonathan missed his friend's caring love, his total understanding. "Blood brothers, loyal to the end," he whispered. His right thumb moved across the thin scar on his left wrist. If only they could have one moment together, he could face tomorrow's battle in peace.

In the stillness, Jonathan recalled the closeness of that spiritual fellowship. His heart grew quiet, and he sensed God's nearness.

Suddenly Jonathan knew he didn't need Ethan's advice or Samuel's encouragement—or even David's comforting presence. Long ago below a hillside outside Bethlehem a twenty-year-old shepherd had given him all he needed for tomorrow. Jonathan looked up at the sky again, where one brave star shone brightly among the others. His heart lifted as he softly quoted:

"The Lord is my shepherd, I shall never be in want.
He makes me lie down in lush pastures, He leads me
beside peaceful waters, He restores my inner being.
He leads me in pathways of righteousness for His name's sake.
Even while walking through the valley of the shadow of death,
I will fear no evil, because You accompany me;
Your rod and Your staff bring me comfort.
You spread a table for me in the presence of my enemies.
You anoint my head with healing oil;
my cup of blessing overflows.
Surely goodness and mercy will follow me all the days I live,
and I will dwell in the Lord's house forever."

"I will fear no evil." No evil. Not Philistines, not Father, not a witch at Endor. "You are with me." The words were a precious promise from the heart of God. Jonathan smiled as he rose and entered his tent to prepare for bed.

The next thing Jonathan knew, Malki-Shua knelt over him, shaking him awake. Morning had arrived.

The sound of the Philistine war cry echoed across the valley. Israelites scrambled up from their places of sleep, grabbing their weapons as they hurried out of camp. The three princes began dressing. Jonathan lifted the tent flap and called Reu to strap on his breastplate. Two other armor-bearers came to assist Malki-Shua and Abinadab.

Bringing his bronze helmet down over his head, Jonathan secured the leather strap as Reu tied the sword sheath to his own belt and inserted the weapon. The others had already left when Jonathan stooped to open the case of his double-span composite bow. As he lifted it out, he thanked God again for David's gift of wild goat horns and for the many hours of bow practice back in Gibeah. Reu handed him a quiver of twenty arrows, then slung another one over his own shoulder and picked up Jonathan's large rectangular shield. Exiting the tent, the two ran across the valley to join the assembled men, stepping over abandoned blankets and zigzagging around piles of cooking utensils as they went.

Saul and Abner climbed the hillside to oversee the battle while the commanders and captains formed their men into deep phalanxes. When the Philistines were about a mile away, the Israelites shouted their own war cry, closed ranks, and marched straight across the flat terrain. Jonathan led his men toward the on-coming Philistines. As the enemy drew closer, the Israelites formed their battle line and stood their ground. When the Philistines were less than a quarter of a mile away, Jonathan took aim with his bow. The first arrow found its mark.

"You got him," Reu said. "What a bow!"

Jonathan kept firing as the enemy drew closer. By then, the archers with shorter-range convex and compound bows began firing. Reu handed Jonathan the second quiver. He thanked God for the accuracy of his aim—forty arrows, forty dead Philistines. All too soon he exhausted his supply. There weren't enough arrows in Israel to stop this hoard. Jonathan placed the last one against the body of the bow and aimed.

Other archers soon ran out of ammunition. They fell back, letting the javelin throwers advance. Jonathan turned to Reu, who handed him his sword and shield. When the throwers had used all their javelins, the swordsmen and those carrying spears, maces, and battle-axes took front rank, engaging in hand-to-hand combat as they faced the powerful enemy. Reu grabbed a sword from a fallen enemy soldier and wielded it in front of the prince.

Jonathan fought bravely beside his men. The immense Philistine army with chariots and superior weapons, however, quickly overpowered Israel's dwindling forces. Jonathan ordered his men to push back closer and closer to the slopes of Gilboa. The sun rose higher in the sky, intensifying thirst and fatigue. There was no time to stop and rest, not even to quench their thirst.

Men were going down all around Jonathan. Up ahead he saw Lamech fighting valiantly, and he worked his way toward him. Suddenly the enemy's spear caught the ex-captain, flinging his body to the ground. Jonathan's heart bled for his former army captain and friend, but he dared not stop.

The stream from the Well of Harod proved a useless barricade as the Philistines swarmed down its soft banks and through the water. The Israelite soldiers fled up the steep northern flank of Gilboa, the Philistines in hot pursuit. Other Philistines rode down the southern fork of the plain in their chariots, then wheeled them up the more gradual incline of Gilboa's western side.

Hearing Reu's warning scream behind him, Jonathan turned to see a half-dozen Philistines advancing toward him. One dispatched the armor-bearer as the others moved in. Jonathan lunged at the closest one, felling him with a gash to his neck. He brought the second and third down also, deflecting blows with his shield and breastplate as he dodged their weapons.

"I will fear no evil, because You are with me," he quoted as the fourth man moved closer. Jonathan did not feel his sword make impact.

Another Philistine soldier, coming up Gilboa, saw his comrades engaged with the armored Israelite. Sensing only kings and princes of Israel wore the scarce metal helmets, the Philistine recognized the prized trophy. Circling behind the fray, he raised his javelin, pulled back his arm, and hurled it with all his might.

The sharp point penetrated Jonathan's left back, and he pitched forward. "I will dwell in the Lord's house forever," the prince said, then drew his last breath.

~

Vultures and hawks circled above the battlefield as Joel, the former army captain, scanned the landscape of devastation. If he could locate fellow Israelites, they could stand together in their desperate fight for survival. Alarm grew when he saw no one wearing a helmet. Were the king and all the princes down? He rushed up the hillside. Another quick glance revealed none of them. It was a rout. He'd better get out of there.

Joel ran farther up the hill, following others who fled the chaotic scene of defeat. Out of the corner of his eye he saw a glint of sunlight off metal. He deviated to the left. Was the king still alive? He stepped around the four corpses as he came closer to the sprawled body. It appeared too short for the tall monarch.

"Oh, Jonathan," Joel cried in recognition. "Oh, Jonathan." The spear in his hand shook as he choked back a wail. "The nation loved and respected you." His voice quivered. "Now you are gone."

The shaft of a javelin protruded from the side of the crown

prince's chest below his left shoulder. Dark red blood soaked his tunic. A pool of clotting blood spread in increasing diameter across the trampled dry grass next to the motionless body. There was nothing Joel could do.

Cries from the wounded and moans of the dying penetrated his dazed mind. He started to flee, then turned back. He'd better take Jonathan's sword. Tomorrow the Philistines would strip the dead. He didn't want the pagans to ever use the weapon of the godly prince against his own people.

Joel stooped to pick up the dropped sword that lay near Jonathan's right hand. He could see the prince had fought valiantly; streaks of enemy blood covered its iron shaft. As the former captain straightened up, his gaze shifted to the left. Jonathan's left arm lay outstretched, cradled in the rectangular shield that failed to protect him. His bronze helmet rested on his upper arm, strands of wavy black hair protruding from its rim. Fingers that once positioned deadly arrows spread out stiff and still beneath the shield's grip. The pale palm lay open to the sky, empty in surrender of life back to God who gave it.

Joel's eyes moved down from the hand, and a sob caught in his throat. The glaring sunlight beat down on the light brown skin of the muscular arm, now as lifeless as the grass beneath the shield. Joel leaned closer, his eyes drawn to the wrist. His thoughts flashed back to the afternoon at Ezel ten years before, back to the ceremony of commitment that symbolized Jonathan's entire life.

"Lord God, help me be like Jonathan," Joel prayed, "loyal and faithful to the end." His hand tightened around the hilt of the prince's sword as he looked one last time at the thin straight scar— the mark of the covenant.

AFTERWORD

Following Israel's disastrous defeat on Mount Gilboa, the army fled across the Jordan River to Mahanaim. The next day the triumphant Philistines combed the battlefield. Finding Saul and his three sons, they cut off the king's head to hang as a trophy in the temple of Dagon. They stripped off Saul's armor to exhibit in their temple of Ashtoreth. Then they fastened the four bodies to the city wall of Beth-shan. Still remembering after four decades how Saul had rallied his forces to deliver them from the Ammonites, the grateful men of Jabesh Gilead made a daring night raid to Beth-shan to rescue the bodies from such humiliating display.

Many Israelites deserted their towns and villages, which the Philistines soon occupied. Abner, the army commander, brought Ish-Bosheth, the forty-year-old son of Saul, to the new capital and installed him as king. The tribe of Judah chose to follow David, then thirty years old, as their king with Hebron as their capital.

David mourned the death of Saul and his sons.

The length of Ish-Bosheth's reign is uncertain. 2 Samuel 2:10 speaks of two years. A duel was fought between the two sides (perhaps at the end of the two years), with David's men suffering the fewest losses. The war between the two factions lasted "a long time." David grew stronger and stronger, Saul's side weaker and weaker (2 Samuel 3:1). During this time Abner enhanced his own position. When Ish-Bosheth accused him of having an affair with Rizpah, Saul's concubine, the insulted army commander deserted to David's side. As part of a peace-pact with Abner, David demanded the return of his wife, Michal, which Ish-Bosheth fulfilled.

Abner was later killed by David's nephew and army commander, Joab, in revenge for a brother's death during the duel. Alarmed, Ish-Bosheth's courage evaporated. Shortly thereafter two of his assistants assassinated him while he slept, thinking it would please David. Instead, David had them executed for the cold-blooded murder of the napping king.

After David reigned for seven years and six months in Hebron, all Israel made him their king. He drove the Jebusites from Mount Moriah and made Jerusalem the capital of Israel (2 Samuel 5:6-10). Later, when a three-year famine ravished the Land, David inquired from the Lord for the reason. God revealed it was punishment for Saul breaking Israel's covenant with the Gibeonites by slaughtering them. According to the system of justice of the Law, seven male descendants of Saul were executed for the king's crime— Armoni and Mephibosheth, sons of Rizpah, and five sons of Merab. The drought ended. Afterward, David had the bones of Saul and Jonathan and the bodies of the seven buried in the family cave-tomb at Zelah. (2 Samuel 21:1-14)

David set up the Tabernacle in Jerusalem and brought the Ark of the Covenant from Kiriath-jearim. He established the priesthood under Abiathar, renewed the sacrifices, and organized worship. Among the Tabernacle officials, 1 Chronicles 6: 33 mentions Heman, son of Joel and grandson of Samuel, as the musician and his associate Asaph, who served at his right hand (v. 39). 2

Chronicles 29:14 mentions Heman's descendants serving under King Hezekiah three hundred years later.

During the flight of Saul's family from Gibeah after the defeat on Mount Gilboa, the nursemaid had dropped Jonathan's five-year-old son, leaving him crippled. David always remembered his blood-brother. In recalling his covenant with Jonathan years later, David inquired if there were any survivors of the House of Saul. The servant Ziba informed him about Mephibosheth, who was living with a family in Lo Debar. David sent for the prince, honored him with royal privileges, gave him a permanent seat at the king's table, and restored his inheritance of Saul's property.

David reigned thirty-three years over the united Israel. He subjugated the Philistines and expanded the nation's borders. He was succeeded by his son Solomon. Another son, Adonijah, tried to make himself king, soliciting the support of Abiathar the priest. Because of his disloyalty, Solomon removed Abiathar from the priesthood, thus fulfilling the prophecy spoken at Shiloh about the House of Eli (2 Samuel 2:35-36, 1 Kings 2:27).

ABOUT THE AUTHOR

Eleanor Hunsinger grew up in parsonages in rural Kansas. She studied theology and nursing in preparation to answer God's call. She served as a missionary nurse in Zambia for over twenty years, in charge of different small rural clinics and hospitals and in spiritual ministries. She enjoyed writing articles for the denomination's missions magazine.

She retired from missionary work to the Kansas City area, where she did home care nursing, was involved in church activities, and pursued her desire to write biblical fiction.

After retiring to Florida, she became very involved in church and retirement community activities. Her writing was put aside.

Then the Covid-19 pandemic hit in March of 2020. The Lockdown brought her ministries to a halt. However, God's perfect timing opened the door to revive her desire to write. She unearthed the manuscript of *Mark of the Covenant* and began rewriting. This novel is another fulfillment of her life's theme song, "Jesus Led Me All the Way."

Made in the USA
Columbia, SC
20 July 2021